Shad

Books by John William Corrington

Poetry
Where We Are
Mr Clean and Other Poems
The Anatomy of Love
Lines to the South

Fiction
And Wait for the Night
The Upper Hand
The Lonesome Traveller and Other Stories
The Bombardier
The Actes and Monuments
The Southern Reporter
Shad

Edited with Miller Williams
Southern Writing in the Sixties: Fiction
Southern Writing in the Sixties: Poetry

SHAD

John William Corrington

Copyright © John William Corrington 1984

All rights reserved. No part of this publication may be reproduced or transmitted, in any form or by any means, without permission.

ISBN 0 333 37179 8

First published in the United States of America 1984 by Congdon & Weed Inc., New York

This edition published in Great Britain 1984 by
Macmillan London Limited
London and Basingstoke

Associated companies in Auckland, Dallas, Delhi, Dublin, Hong Kong, Johannesburg, Lagos, Manzini, Melbourne, Nairobi, New York, Singapore, Tokyo, Washington and Zaria

Typeset by Rowland Phototypesetting Limited
Bury St Edmunds, Suffolk
Printed in Hong Kong

A. M. D. G.
and for
SAMUEL WARD LACHLE
Shad's most beloved son

A piece you miss is a piece you'll never get.
Ronnie Gallagher
Shreveport, 1953

Overture
28 February 1960

> ... for I am faring to visit the bounds of all-nurturing earth, and Okeanos, from whom the gods are sprung.
> *Iliad*, xiv, 201–2

It was raining, and it was going to rain. The windows of the room were awash, wave after wave slamming against the panes like something ancient and angry trying to get in. I had been studying Historical Geology all evening with the radio playing in the background. It was now past midnight, and the LSU campus station was doing famous overtures. *Rienzi, La Gazza Ladra, Don Giovanni*. But with the storm, the music kept breaking up. Some station in Mexico would override it with the ravings of a preacher proclaiming the Kingdom, the Punishment of Sinners, the Expulsion of the Great Beast, the Apotheosis of the Son of Man, Dissolution of the Material World, Subjugation of the Whore of Babylon, All Souls Gathered and Judged. Somebody in the room across the hall, deep in a game of bourrée, said if he lost another hand he was going to kill himself. Bullshit, somebody else said. You still got Mary Ellen's ass to bet. You cocksucker, the first voice replied hysterically, I'm going to marry Mary Ellen. Not if you kill yourself you ain't.

Even when the bourrée game and that lunatic preacher from Mexico gave way, I still couldn't hear the music. They kept putting on weather bulletins. A later winter front. Wind gusts up to seventy miles an hour. Tornadoes in East Texas. Small craft warnings from Galveston to Pensacola. High seas, violent thunderstorms associated with the front. The weather reports seemed to support the preacher. I caught a piece of *The Marriage of Figaro*, static, then the Reverend Bywater describing hell stone by stone as if he had done fieldwork down there.

All of this as I tried to study, to arrange in my mind the web of names and times and phenomena that supposedly described the fundament of this pendant world. The Cryptozoic Aeon. Precambrian, Devonian, Ordovician—a vast history without people. The Pennsylvanian has no William Penn, the Mississippian no Jeff Davis. Only silences or the resonant squawks of great saurians stomping, slashing, and farting their way through forests of ferns.

I opened a beer hidden in my footlocker for nights like this when the weather was too bad even for a nineteen-year-old chronic drunk to go out, and tossed the Historical Geology aside. Screw it. If God wanted me to be a geologist, He would have made me of stone, right? I picked up another book—one of *my* books—and opened it.

And he said that the origin of all things is the Illimitable —that into which all is dissolved again according to Necessity. For they pay penalty to one another for their injustice according to the ordinance of time.

I shook my head and stood up, staring out into the darkness broken by streaks of lightning. Every second or two, the great bulk of the LSU stadium across the way was illuminated. On the radio, the music broke up again, but this time it was replaced by some garbled announcer's voice taut and brimming with that pseudoexcitement which is supposed to keep us tuned.

—... destroyed ... lighting the sky, visible from the Louisiana coast ... casualties uncertain ... Omega Oil's ... Okeanos Number One ... multiwell platform ...

The words *Omega* and *Okeanos* twisted my head around as if, an ancient Greek, I had found myself at the awful shore of the river-ocean. I almost fell over reaching for the radio, trying to paw the fading signal back in. It was no use. The breathy announcer had vanished as quickly as he appeared. Even the music was gone. All I could tune in was the Reverend Bywater, who had moved on from hell and was proclaiming this night, this very night, as the overture to the millennium.

I was still twisting the dial, still listening to the scattered snapping, popping and crackling, when I realized that part of what I was hearing was the sound of somebody pounding on the door. If it was that silly bastard from across the hall ready to hock his girl, I was going to have a fight.

He stood in the hallway in one of those yellow slickers you always associate with grade-school safety patrols on a wet morning. A puddle was forming around his feet.

—This room four fifty-one, Hatcher Hall?
—That's what it says on the door, I told him, one ear still on the sputtering radio.
—You E. M. Sentell Four? he asked.
—That's what they tell me.
—Sign here.
I signed, and he handed me a limp tan envelope. It looked as if he'd picked it up out of the gutter. I reached in my pocket and gave him fifty cents. I didn't know whether I was supposed to give him fifty cents or not because I had never gotten a telegram before. In the movies they always did. No matter what awful news the telegram might contain. It seemed the fifty cents was all right. He walked away down the hall. Dripping.

It occurred to me as I closed the door that maybe there was something on television. Sure there was. Some damned fool explaining to his six-year-old daughter why he and Mommy were getting a divorce.
—Di . . . vorce?
—Yes, darling . . .
—Div . . . orce?
—Yes.

I was trying to listen to the radio, change the television channel, and open the telegram all at once.
—We interrupt our regular programming . . .

I had to orient myself to realize it was the television, not the radio. For a moment, I thought I was listening to the telegram. Good. Anything would be better than di-vorce. I spread the limp telegram out on top of the television. Then my eyes and ears drifted down to the tube. What I saw made me feel as if a rill of pounding rain from outside had spilled down the back of my shirt. I felt my breath catch.

—Major offshore disaster. Men lost. Omega Oil's Okeanos Platform Number One has been rocked by an explosion which one observer described as lighting up the Gulf of Mexico from the mouth of the Mississippi to the Yucatán. Allowing for exaggeration, this film shot in the Gulf by a Channel Nine crew coming back from work on a documentary about shrimp fishing gives some idea . . .

Yes, it did. The grainy black-and-white film showed a patch of hell in driving rain that the Reverend Bywater had never guessed at. I closed my eyes, stuffed the telegram in my pocket without reading it, and started packing. I knew what it said.

Before the news announcer could finish his spiel, I was running for the door, a rutsack under my arm. I didn't slow down even when I reached the outside door of the dorm and the rain, turning to sleet, pushed me backward as if it knew my name and where I was headed.

The Omega plane was at Ryan Field when I got there. Not the executive plane. Some ancient anonymous Cessna that had already crashed once going into an airstrip near Lake Charles. It looked like it wouldn't glide on a soft spring day—much less fly on a night like this. The wings were beginning to ice, and Charlie Mangum, Omega's air-arm, looked frightened as he opened the door and pulled me in.

—Hey, Sonny, Charlie said. —Nice night.
—They're not going to let you fly, I told him.
—Yeah. Right. That's what they said when I landed. FAA this and CAB that . . .
—We can go get something to eat and wait it out.
—Haw. The old man called.
—What's that got to do with the weather?
—Not dipshit. They just put down that I never landed here. If we was to go down and buy us a farm, you and me was just flying out of Shreveport.

I thought he was joking till he revved the engine and started taxiing out onto a runway neither of us could see.

—Nobody fucks with Omega Oil, Charlie bawled at the top of his voice, and he pushed the throttle all the way forward.
—They leave us to do it to ourselves, I yelled back, and closed my eyes, thinking insanely of Heraclitus: *The way up and the way down are one and the same.*

Don't ask how. We touched down at the old Shreveport Flying Field three hours later. Charlie looked like a ghost pilot from some past war.

—Hey, good-lookin', whatcha got cookin', he intoned in a soft, fragile voice. —How about cookin' sumpin' up with me . . . ?

Singing Hank Williams is Charlie's approximation of religion. There seems to be, in his mind, some connection between those words, that music, and the Deity. When he is running lucky, he refers to the Lord as good-lookin' or pure white dove; when everything goes to shit, he sings "Cold Cold Heart" or "You Win Again", and any sensitive theologian would know at once whom he is addressing.

I left Charlie limp in the plane and clawed my way across the field to the Omega Motor Pool. That's what they call it. What it is, is a shack with an ugly old bastard sitting in it, and a handful of ratty cars out back for salesmen, land men, and crews passing through. Once in a while you could get something sporty if one of the wheels had flown to Chicago and left his company car—and if your name was Sentell.

When I asked for a Lincoln, the old spider handed me the keys to a surplus 1947 Jeep. I gave him hard Sentell eyes and asked where his own car was.

He pointed to the Jeep, giving me back a stare just as hard.

—That over there is it, he said.

Then he walked back to his office to get out of the sleet and freezing rain. So he could watch while I tried to crank the goddamned thing up.

After ten minutes, with maybe one more jolt of battery left, it turned over. Somebody had rigged a radio up under the dash, and the first thing I heard above the roar of the motor was that same hard-breathing announcer repeating the fate of Okeanos Number One, and telling that there was yet no count of the men lost to the storm and the Gulf.

Now I'm sitting here in this crummy-looking Jeep in front of Shady Grove Sanatorium west of Shreveport. Waiting. Waiting to pick up my uncle, Samuel Shadrach Sentell. Called Shad. They've had him inside for weeks, supposedly drying him out. Joke. I know him. He probably hasn't missed a drink or a piece of ass.

The telegram I got in Baton Rouge is limp and sloppy in my pocket. I can just barely make it out with the flashlight they keep under the dash on field cars.

OMEGA PLANE BATON ROUGE 2000 HOURS STOP GET SHREVEPORT SOONEST STOP GET SHAD OUT NUTHOUSE STOP NIX HIM OUT OF SIGHT STOP NO BOOZE EVEN IF BEGS OR THREATENS STOP OKEANOS NUMBER ONE BLOWN STOP EIGHTY THOUSAND PER DAY UP OLD BAZOO STOP CALL RUPRECHT SHADY GROVE

SANATORIUM STOP BRING SHAD CASABLANCA HOTEL NEW ORLEANS FASTEST OR FIND PENCILS DARK GLASSES TIN CUP STOP

It's signed simply SENTELL. There are a number of Sentells around here. My mother, my uncle, me—plus a few cousins scattered here and there. But there is only one SENTELL: Edward Malcolm Sentell III, Sentell par excellence. *The* Sentell.
E.M. III is my father. He wants me to get my uncle Shad down to New Orleans fastest. Which is kind of funny, since he's the one who put Shad in the nuthouse in the first place. Not personally. E.M. III does very few things personally. He sent a raft of lawyers and private security people after Shad and had him interdicted. Interdicted is something your kin can do to you in Louisiana if they think you've slipped your knot and the parish coroner agrees. Some judge says you can't handle your own affairs, and they hand you over, body and soul, asshole and appetite, to what they call a Curator.
The Curator owns you. He can do anything he wants with you. He can put you in and pull you out. If you get interdicted in Louisiana, you better hope your Curator isn't pissed at you.
You wonder who Shad's Curator is? How about E. M. Sentell III, my father, his brother, chairman of the board and CEO, Omega Oil International—and Shad's sworn-to-God, blood-certain enemy. E.M. III does not own the State of Louisiana, its courts and judges. That wouldn't be cost-effective. He just rents them when he needs them.
Ah, some imaginary auditor in my head says, What a peculiar family. Pigshit, I answer. You don't know what a strange family is. My father sends me to get his brother so that my uncle can go down and put out the fire on Okeanos Number One that has already killed more than half the people on it. Would he rather have the fire out or Shad blown to hell? Don't ask me. How would I know? I haven't seen my father since I was a kid. My father loathes my mother, who cannot stand being in the same room with my uncle.
It's not quite six o'clock in the morning. The rain is still falling in sheets. The radio says it's forty-three degrees. The roof of this goddamned Jeep is leaking like a sieve. I've got ice water running down my leg into my boot. I swear to God this is the last shot. Everybody in this family thinks I'm a servant, some hired

hand to do their dirty work. I'm sick of being a servant for this collection of North Louisiana Goths.

I stopped by the house before I came out here and got on the phone to this Dr Ruprecht at Shady Grove. He was relieved to hear I'd be picking Shad up at six. Ruprecht said in a mean, judgmental, and unshrinky tone that my uncle's conduct had been . . . what was the word? Execrable.

I hung up to keep from laughing in the dumb bastard's face. Execrable? That's the kindest description of Shad's conduct in the past thirty years.

Just as I was ready to move out, my mother had come downstairs. I felt that little catch in my throat. I do not have an Oedipus complex. I have a Jocasta complex. It was a little after five in the morning, and she looked as if she'd just stepped out of a Paris salon. Ritual embrace, loving, cool smile.

—And how are the Pre-Socratics, she asked in a not quite mocking tone.

—We must not speak and act like men asleep, I said.

—That's so, she answered. Then the niceties were done, and her expression changed —You bring him here as soon as they turn him out. No pauses, no side trips. Then we'll just take him out to the airport, and the Omega plane will fly us to New Orleans.

Us? I thought. Holy Christ. Not Mother and Shad on the same plane. I've seen sleet and I've seen ice tonight, but we'll never make New Orleans with both of them on the same plane. No side trips? No pauses? In a pig's prostate. Shad pauses. His life has been one lengthy side trip.

—Remember, now, she said as she stood there reading my mind. —Straight back here.

—Yes, ma'am, I told her, lying in my throat. Then I went out through the garage, grabbed some of Shad's stuff, threw it into the Jeep, and started out.

Almost six-fifteen, and the rain has slacked off. Now it's only cold and miserable, and all the trees around Shady Grove look like they ought to have nooses hanging from them. Over the radio, they're saying that at least six men died on Okeanos. Uncertain how many more missing. They say it's an inferno, totally out of control. The man who takes care of infernos for Omega Oil International is Shad Sentell. Who is also out of control.

That's why the telegram. Why Mother was up so early. E.M. III and Mother have the notion that Shad is partial to me, that I can manage him. That's why I'm sitting in this frigging Jeep with rain water puddling under my crotch. Handle Shad? Christ, he's ... execrable. They're lucky he hasn't wiped the place off the face of the earth and turned all the feebs and crazies and perverts and stone drunks and criminally insane loose on a helpless public.

On the other hand, he's not out yet.

Chapter One

> ...meet the barbarians who came from Okeanos...
> Pausianias X.20.3

Now the foyer of Shady Grove seems suddenly to come alive. A single dim night-light within is replaced by a vast, cold blue-white region of illumination. As far as the Jeep, one can hear something: a single and uproarious howl of exultation, triumph.

Like a smash cut in an action movie, the foyer is full of objects, white figures here and there, moving apparently at random under the cold, lucid light. The particles of white seem clustered about a central point, moving in upon it, thrust away, some falling to the dark shining floor.

That central point is dark. It is in motion toward the doors. It seems to shift and turn, spinning away the pale figures in its path—in fact, punching, kicking, shattering everything in its way past the wilderness of light, through the electronic doors, into the hard dawn shadows toward the parked Jeep.

When the charged madrigal reaches the doors, they fly open as if the moving presence of the dark figure has conjured them. So close to the world outside, still bathed in fluorescent glow, the particles of white reveal themselves as men in clinical coats. One sits in the foyer, head down, the front of his coat slowly turning from white to red. Another leans against the glass next to the doors, both hands covering his face as if he has seen something too awful to contemplate. Then he begins to sag, leaving a trail of blood on the glass as he falls full length, crooning, sobbing, pawing at the remnants of his nose. At the open doors, the figure dressed darkly takes one final swing, sending another attendant stumbling into the foyer in the antic posture of one doing well in a hundred-yard dash—backward. The attendant hits a fawn-colored sofa and a coffee table covered with magazines. He is elevated for a moment, then drops to the shining floor with a disgusting and terminal sound.

—All right, motherfuckers. Anybody else want some?

Now he is outside, and between the glow of the foyer and the rising natural light one sees a tall, thick-bodied man in khaki work pants and shirt, a draggled and stained canvas jacket, and a dispirited Stetson of no certain color, fouled, shapeless, the front of its brim turned down as if in a half-hearted effort to obscure the face below.

Imagine a fresh side of beef, quivering, flushed, still hot with the glow of bestial life. Place sharp green eyes and a thick slash of mouth in it. Meet Shad Sentell. Not in an alley, not in a blind tiger in Mississippi, not in a brawl dockside in Houston. Not in any sort of struggle for mastery, physical or psychic. Please, God, not in anger.

He sees the Jeep, its motor now turning, and starts for it down the path of concrete covered by a canvas awning that leads in and out of Shady Grove. He sees who is inside, and for a moment he smiles. He says something which Sonny cannot make out.

If he'll just get in the fucking Jeep, Sonny thinks, we might make it. We might get out of here before every sheriff's deputy west of Shreveport and south of Texarkana comes barreling in, gun-grooving and kill-crazy to defend the surrounding area from this hulking mad dog.

As he is almost to the Jeep, there erupts from the foyer a soprano howl that would give pause to Wagner. Another figure in white runs past the obstacle course of broken furniture and sprawled bodies, pointing, gesticulating, screaming words no ear pitched north of Memphis could possibly decipher. Epithets in unbroken stream, the kindest of which is: low-down yellow dog piss-swilling son of a mangy street bitch.

Shad appears to pay no mind, but his eyes harden. This is not a style of conversation he is accustomed to. He gestures Sonny to open the passenger door of the Jeep, then throws in a faded, patched, played-out tote bag upon which one can barely make out the vanishing legend: SHREVEPORT SPORTS.

As Shad is about to climb into the Jeep, the harridan from inside the sanatorium reaches him. She is small, slender, red-headed, remarkably good-looking, within that range of age where the battle is still being waged, passion yet unspent. She grabs his shoulder. One supposes that a shrug will send her reeling. Not so. Shad is turned as if by some invisible hand much stronger than hers. Up close, her voice is astonishing in volume and depth.

—... hell you think you're going?
—What's it to you, Anna? Any damn place away from here.
Hey, Sonny...
  —Sir?
  —You got a...
  —No, you're not. Not again. Her expression is one of absolute and maniacal determination as she runs at him once more. This little woman has her own brand of luck. She hits Shad just as he is about to climb into the Jeep, shoving the door closed on his leg, trapping him there, half in, half out.
  —Goddammit, you got my fucking leg.
  —Good. That's the one I was going for. I'm gonna talk, and you're gonna listen. You know what you did to me all those years ago in Tulsa?
  —I ain't never been in Tulsa. You got stabbed by some other shitkicker, sugar.
  —You vicious shit, you're not going to march away on me again. Can't you tell when somebody really loves you?
  —Lots of regrets, girl. But time passes, don't it? Hell, it's passing right now.

He has broken her grip at last and lifts her up as if she were a rag doll. He starts to carry her back under the awning, perhaps as far as the foyer where the recumbent orderlies have begun to stir. Then, as Shad nears the door with his howling, cursing burden, a single solitary figure all in white, a halo of colorless hair around his head, appears there before him.
  —You, sir... Stop where you are.

That, Sonny considers, recognizing the voice, must be Dr Ruprecht, commendatore of this loony bin.

Shad regards the figure with mingled anger and contempt. He puts the woman down, her yelling only interrupted by a moment spent rearranging her nurse's uniform.
  —Old man, stay clear of me, hear?

But the wraith moves through the doors, his finger raised as to a small boy, his thin face pale, outraged.
  —Troublemaker... animal...

Shad faces away, and Sonny sees his expression is flat, lethal, murderous. He moves back toward the Jeep.

—Oh, no, you don't. The time for walking away is past. You'll wait for the authorities. You're no longer a patient, and if what this poor woman says is true . . .

—It's true. Whatever she says, it's true, says a tired, irritable, disgusted voice from within the Jeep.

—Goddammit, Sonny, shut up, Shad rasps. —What the hell kind of kin are you?

In the moment that Shad's attention is distracted, Dr Ruprecht pounces upon his back as if taken in some transport of madness, as if he supposes surprise will enable him to bring Shad down. Had there been any lingering doubt on Sonny's part that this is a madhouse, here is proof positive.

Shad turns, takes Dr Ruprecht by the throat, and throws him some twenty or thirty feet back into the glass doors, through which rousing and angry attendants are about to burst in full cry. The old man's body smashes into the electronic doors, addling their circuits, blocking the way, trapping the massed orderlies inside. Dr Ruprecht moans as the redheaded nurse, tranced by this turn of events, kneels to help him.

—Ah, God, someone help . . .

—I told you I'd had enough of you, you nutless old bastard.

—I think . . . my . . . I feel something . . . broken inside.

—What'd you jump me for? After all them electric shocks, and your hired help whipping up on me.

— . . . only doing what . . . we could . . . for you.

Shad leans down, stares coldly at the old man's agonized face.

—Well, that's just what I done for you.

Shad straightens up, glances at the frenzied attendants who beat helplessly on the glass. He grins, gives them one and all the Ancient Manual Salutation, and walks back to the Jeep with measured, unhurried stride. As he climbs in, the nurse turns from her mission of mercy and emits a howl of rage as the Jeep pulls away, gathering speed near the end of the long circular driveway, narrowly missing a stray orderly who has had the presence of mind or mindlessness to seek another exit. In passing, a single hairy fist reaches out from the Jeep and decks the attendant, leaving him to mull over his unwisdom sitting in wet leaves, bleeding freshly in the dawn rain.

—Say, Shad says, putting his enormous hands on Sonny's head, tousling his hair, pinching his ear till he squeaks, all by

way of greeting, —you got a drink in this run-down wreck anywhere?
—No.
—Shit. Get this damned thing pointed toward whiskey.

—You know how to handle women, Uncle Shad used to say down at the Glass Hat on Texas Avenue. —Shit on 'em. Don't ask 'em nothing, don't answer no questions, don't smile at 'em. If you got to talk to 'em, lie. If you buy 'em something, make sure it's something you can hock. Don't put no initials on nothing. So you can give it to the next one when the one you got goes flat.

—Or starts to swell, somebody else would bawl, and everybody would roar with laughter all around.

In a triangle formed by Kilgore, Texas, Texarkana, which is not precisely anywhere, and Bossier City, Louisiana, Uncle Shad has always been known as a Mean Ass. With the possible exception of Bad Sonofabitch, that's the most honorific title a man can hold in this part of the country. It signifies that the one so called is solitary, vicious, merciless, incapable of charity or the most rudimentary civilized acts and attitudes except within a small circle of friends and kinsmen, dedicated to every form of hedonism this side of necrophilia, not necessarily excluding certain forms of violence known only to people who have passed from hogs and cotton and whiskey making to drilling, dusting, and bartending in less than a generation. Shad is celebrated wherever drinking, whoring, stomping, and wholesale outrage are on the blue-plate special.

—Treat a whore like a lady, Shad would lead a chorus at the old Skyway Club out on Highway 80.

—And a lady like a whore, all the Omega roughnecks and tool-pushers would yell back.

—And the world's best snatch is gonna fall open for you like a sailor's satchel.

That's how Shad is. That's how he's always been. There are things he loves and things he hates, friends and enemies. He loves Louisiana and Texas. He wouldn't leave the border for any amount of money someone is likely to offer. The last figure he turned down was three hundred thousand a year to honcho damage control in what he likes to call one of those chickenshit heathen A-rab kingdoms down in the Persian Gulf's steamy crotch.

He hates my mother. No, that's wrong. Despises her. She makes him shudder. Why does he loathe her? She is very good, and very beautiful, sophisticated, witty, and deeply religious. Her name is Marie-Claire, pronounced as in French.

—Bullshit, my uncle would pronounce when the subject of my mother would come up. —Her goddamned name is Mary Clare Fontenot, and she grew up in a cornfield two miles out of Kilgore, Texas, without a pot to piss in or a window to throw it out of, and her old man was some coon-ass drove crazy in the First World War. Your mother, she went to work at Effie's Grand Café and met your daddy, who was two years ahead of me gargling drilling mud, and who got lucky on account he had a head of naturally pure silver hair when he was only nineteen and got in thick with old man Clint Robinson of Robinson Oil —which wouldn't of happened if I hadn't turned up. But that don't matter, because your momma ain't a damned bit better than our folks. She just thinks she is.

It's even more complicated than that. If Shad has no use for my mother, she can hardly bear living on the same continent with him. He is, according to her, the living, brawling, cursing epitome of everything that is wrong with my gender. It is her deepest desire that her son have as little to do as possible with Shad Sentell, and be devoted to whatever Shad is not.

That being the case, naturally, when I was younger, Shad used to come by Byrd High School and pick me up after school. To introduce me, as you might say, to honky-tonk living.

We would do the Bossier strip. Across the Red River from Shreveport, and meaner than the twisting bowels of hell. When I failed to show up for supper, my mother would hit the phone. She knew what was up, and she'd call the Bossier Parish sheriff's office and start some song and dance with them about letting a minor frequent barrelhouses and gambling hells in company with a known dangerous madman, blood kin and local custom aside.

Seeing the kind of money Omega Oil spread around North Louisiana, the authorities tended to give her heed, but as far as the Bossier sheriff's people were concerned, it was a no-price, no-win game. There was a Sentell on both sides of the argument —and a little towheaded Sentell in the middle. On the other hand, those old boys knew how to bridge a gap. They'd come looking for us.

But they'd start at the nearest bar to the Red River, just across the Texas Avenue bridge. That would be the Hurricane Bar, where they knew we weren't, because Shad would start at the other end of the circuit, the Mistletoe, all the hell and gone out the highway. By the time the heat touched base at the Ming Tree, we'd be at the Wooden Shoe, and when they dropped by the Shoe, we'd be lolling and sipping at the Tower Motel and Grill. The whole thing was kind of Chinese, you could say. Sooner or later, we'd all come together at some dump like the K-9 Bar, which was indeed a deadly wretched dog of a place where the barmaids were too far gone in age, vice, or disease even for the Mistletoe or the Tower.

—Thanks be to Lord Jesus for cold beer, Shad would mutter, studying the one-eyed girl who brought over the cold six-pack he'd ordered. With a Seven-Up for me. —If it wasn't for cold beer and hot pussy, life wouldn't hardly be worth living.

The girl would try to smile, never quite sure what Shad's speculations might lead to. Then he'd drop a twenty on the table and wave her away. She'd be smiling for the rest of the night.

About then, Deputy Pritchard would arrive. He was short, bald, mild-eyed, and faintly ridiculous in his Stetson and boots, with one khaki pants leg in and one out. There was no way on earth to see Deputy Pritchard as dangerous, which was peculiar, considering he had killed six or eight men in roadside shootouts over the years—in fact, had done a day's work over at Arcadia, Louisiana, one afternoon when he was young and Bonnie and Clyde made their last wrong move.

—Pritch, Uncle Shad would say, cold-eyed, mean-voiced, —you can have this here beer or kiss my ass.

Deputy Pritchard would shake his head and lift his belly as he slid into the booth beside me. —It ain't no contest, he would answer. —Why don't you hand me that beer?

And they would talk. It was a ritual almost without variance. Uncle Shad would ask questions and Deputy Pritchard would answer. Then Deputy Pritchard would ask and Shad would answer. How are things? Making any money? Been fishing? Who you fucking? When are we going after some dove or deer or squirrel? There was almost no exchange of information at all. Which was all right, fine. Because they were not talking to exchange information but to touch one another with words, reassure each other of continuing amity and respect. They had grown up on the rigs together, and one had saved the other's life or something which I never was quite able to make out. Then when the beer and the talking were satisfactorily done, Deputy Pritchard would turn to me as if he had only then noticed that I occupied the corner of his booth.

—Son, he would say gravely, —your momma give us a call. She seemed to think you had gone off with some lunatic.

—His momma can fuck a bull baboon, Uncle Shad would mutter.

Deputy Pritchard was always amazed. —I'll let that kind of talk pass, seeing it's your own kin. But I never heard such talk about a lady . . .

—You'll let it pass 'cause if you don't, I'll pull off your goddamned arm and stuff it up your dying ass, Uncle Shad would grin.

Deputy Pritchard would purse his lips like a bank teller and shake his head. —I believe your momma was right, boy. This here man is clouded in his mind.

—No, I would answer, making one of my first sallies into the rough, stylized banter of men. —He's my uncle.

—You mean, Deputy Pritchard's eyes would widen, —this here is the widely known bad man, Shadrach Sentell?

—The same, Shad would answer.

—The one without no brains, no guts, no balls? The one they call the Living Miracle?

Then Uncle Shad would reach across the table and put a necklock on the deputy, or they'd grip for an arm wrestle. People sitting at the tables around us or dancing to the jukebox would pause, gawk, and move out of what might arguably be the line of fire when Pritch got his hand free and went for his .357 Magnum. They mostly all knew who Deputy Pritchard was, and that nobody had ever manhandled him and lived. Some of them knew Shad and had never seen him carried out till all the other bodies were removed. A few people knew both of them. You could tell which ones. They would pay their checks and leave. Or just leave.

After a little fooling around, Uncle Shad and Deputy Pritchard would break it off, grinning, finish the last of their beer, and we would leave.

It would be late by then, and cool, and we would stand outside in the gravel of the parking lot a little while longer, the two of them swapping stories of sexual heroism or reports of new degeneracy they'd heard about. They would talk about women they had known and legends of endurance and cruelty from those old days. Shootings and cuttings, accidents and assassinations, wells that had gone bad, friends who had died in one sorry way or another. Deputy Pritchard would chronicle the latest wave of whores known to be working the town, and oftener than not, Uncle Shad would evaluate them one by one for Pritch, listing them according to his own arcane system.

Then, finally, it would be time to pull the other end of the Sentell string. Deputy Pritchard would load me into his patrol car, and we would head back across the river toward that enormous house on Line Avenue where there was no talk of whores and stabbings or the old days on the rigs. Rather an oboe concerto of Albinoni playing softly on the expensive sound system, a copy of the *New York Times* on the hall table, fresh flowers in every room.

—When will you come by school again, I would ask Uncle Shad almost desperately as he leaned in the window of the patrol car.

—Can't say, boy. Don't know. I got to go to Tulsa in the morning.

—Something burning up there, Deputy Pritchard would ask deadpan.

Shad would grin a little. —Red hot and waiting, neighbor.

—When? I would repeat.

—Soon, Sonny. You behave yourself. Don't give your momma no trouble.

Then I would watch him walking away under the buttery light of the parking lot to where he'd parked his Omega pickup. And I would know that it was going to be dull and dumb and decent until I saw him again.

They are in Shreveport now, and the rain has faded to a mist. The clouds are breaking up, and pale sunlight glitters softly on the asphalt streets. Six bottles of Jack Daniels have been added to their supplies. Shad takes a hit from one of them.

—You seen about Okeanos Number One, Shad says grimly.

—That's why I had to come up, Sonny responds. Neither of them wants to talk about the platform. Both know why.

—I knew everybody on that rig, he says. —Russell Whatley was out there. You remember Russell . . .
—No.
—You ought to. He give you that twenty-two long rifle with your initials on the stock when you was nine, ten, whatever.
Sonny's face falls. —You mean Uncle Curly?
—Yeah.
They fall silent again, but Sonny can see that Shad is fidgeting.
—Lemme drive, he says.
—No way. You can't drive. You're interdicted.
—Right. I ain't responsible.
—Not till that shrink you just broke up sends release papers to the court. Till then, you belong to my father.
Shad shudders. —You could of gone all week and not said that. On the other hand . . .
Shad hands Sonny a balled-up piece of flimsy tan paper. Another telegram.

OKEANOS NUMBER ONE BLOWN TO HELL STOP SONNY ON WAY STOP GO JACKSON STREET WHARF NEW ORLEANS STOP CREW BOAT EQUIPMENT WAITING STOP HUNDRED GRAND PER DAY UP IN SMOKE STOP DONT FUCK AROUND STOP GET DRUNK NEVER SEE LIGHT OF DAY AGAIN STOP KILL FIRE OR DIE WHICHEVER STOP

The telegram is signed simply CURATOR. Even more economical, more pointed, than SENTELL.
—I'd been lying low, hoping to get sprung for good time. When Okeanos blew, I knew that was my ticket to ride. E.M. can't get nobody else to work that burn. Ain't nobody ever done a deep-water rig fire before. It's gotta be me, and the miserable sonofabitch knows it. So I took to whipping the piss out of everybody in that sanatorium I could lay hands on.
They both fall silent as Sonny drives up Market Street. Sonny reaches for the open bottle, drinks. It scorches his throat, but a moment later, it feels just fine.
—Where to now? New Orleans?
—Hell, I just got out of the hospital. I need to rest a little. You want to run me down to the Caddo Hotel?
—No use.
—Huh?

—They closed out your suite down there when you got interdicted.
—Boy, you joshing me?
—Conserving your resources. Curator has to do that. It's the law.
—Motherfucker . . . That's another one I owe your daddy. I had them rooms for twenty years. Longer.
Sonny glances at Shad out of the corner of his eye. He looks suddenly old, exhausted. Shad does not like change—unless he initiates it.
—Shit . . . What'd they do with my stuff?
—I got most of it in back. Your guns, your rutsack. They've got the rest out in the garage. You want to go back and get it?
—Your mother home?
—Yes, sir.
—Forget it. Head west.
—But New Orleans . . .
—Fuck New Orleans.
—You're not going down to work Okeanos?
Shad cuts him off.
—My blood's down, and I've had them goddamned psychiatrists up my butt for a month. Head west. I want to go to the Old Place.
—Don't you have to do something . . . ?
Shad takes another pull from the bottle. He regards the label with something like reverence. —All I *got* to do in this café is drink whiskey, get pussy, and die. The rest is all optional.
Shad grins to himself. —I believe there's probably winter ass out on State Line Lake.
—You're gonna let Okeanos burn?
—Yeah, Shad drawls easily. —I believe that's just what I'm gonna do.

She sits in the library of the house on Line Avenue, a glass of brandy in her hand as she waits for Sonny and Shad, thinking that the problem with creation of mind *ex nihilo* is that there is always something prior to mind, something to achieve the creation. This something did not greatly trouble Descartes, but it vexes Marie-Claire. This mind of hers she has wrought seems to define its limits when it encounters a certain breed of men named Sentell. As if the something behind mind were allied to whatever drives Sentells. Before Zeus, there was Kronos; before Kronos, Ouranos, the shining sky. Before Ouranos, darkly, Okeanos, the river-ocean. Is it that behind all the nuances of mind there lies pure force? Pure will? She would prefer not to think so.

It would seem that Mary Clare might manage easily this Marie-Claire she has created through an incomparable act of will and intelligence. After all, she has managed very well indeed for over twenty years. Not just in the sensibility, the artistry required to master alien tastes, or even to convince herself that she must pay a great deal of money for, work hard to understand that world of culture so much richer than what she might have had by simply reaching out. Nor even in regard to the relatively primitive moves needed originally to obtain the name Sentell in the place of Fontenot. Any woman bold enough, beautiful enough, might have done that, done it all.

No. The master struggle has been more profound: to forget utterly the dusty streets of Kilgore, the ranks of oil wells that sprouted up in the very streets of the town, near the Krim Theatre, in the side yard of the First Baptist Church; to conjure for herself the Boulevard Haussmann and the Rue Raspail; to put out of her mind the smell of country sausage and frying eggs on a frosty morning. She has purged her sensations and her memories so fully and so thoroughly that all she can remember clearly is her first taste of porridge in London, her first aperitif in a café near the Luxembourg Gardens—that moment of awe when she first entered the soft ambience of a double suite at the George V. She has no recollection at all of the flavor of home brew straight from a Mason jar, two days out of the still, or the dusty stamp-sized front porch at Darby's Modern Auto Courts. She listens now to Massenet's *Werther* and hears beneath its lushness no hint of Bob Wills and the Texas Playboys.

She has made this transformation of herself and done it so well that even those who knew Mary Clare in the old times are in some subterranean sense unsure if their memories of her reflect past reality at all. Marie-Claire has always been ... Marie-Claire. Hasn't she?

The phone beside her rings. Then it rings again. She always lets it ring again. Then she turns down Massenet.

—Yes?

— ... Clare? You there?

—It's quite a bad connection, Eddie. I wonder . . . never mind. Sonny picked him up, but they haven't come back here.
—. . . ofabitch . . . hell out of Ruprecht . . . Hear that?
—Shad did? Surely not Sonny?
—. . . damned straight Shad. We're . . . our collective ass, you hear? Gulf . . . bright as day . . . middle of the night. If he . . . call Judge Crater and . . .

She arches her eyebrows. There is a certain flare required to understand a phone call from E. M. Sentell III. He has never had a decent phone connection in his life. Perhaps it is because, as a rule, the calls have come from Teheran or Djakarta, Oman or Buenos Aires.

—That's not smart. He'd as soon rip out your heart as look at you anyhow. You—we—need him in New Orleans. Not in a mental institution. He'll want the interdiction lifted, you know.
—. . . uck what . . . wants. The goddamned . . .

Marie-Claire stares at her perfect fingernails for a long moment. There is nothing but static on the phone line. She does not bother to ask E.M. where he is calling from. It doesn't matter. For all the difference it would make, he could be in the next room. The transmission would still be garbled, cryptic.

—Eddie, you've dealt with him all your life. That's not the way to go about it. You thought putting him in Shady Grove was clever.
—. . . got to end sometime . . . Did at the Florentine Club . . . 's wife. On a table . . . Holy . . . it . . .
—I received a full report on that, Marie-Claire says wearily.
—. . . hire a hit man . . . Detroit. Blow the . . . ucker away . . .
—Clever. The Board would love that. You'd look splendid in chains . . . But first I suppose you'd better tell them that Shad is the only man on this continent who can save Okeanos. They may have *you* committed.
—. . . uck 'em. One and all . . . Thought could count on . . . sorry little bastard . . .

At that word, Marie-Claire's face tenses, then relaxes again.
—When you and your insane brother are bones, Sonny will be just fine. But possibly not until then. I knew when you sent him after Shad, it wouldn't be simple. Shad won't leave him alone.
—'Course not . . . hell do you expect? They're . . . and . . .
—Oh, shut up. You want Shad in the Gulf, don't you?
—. . . !

—Very well. I'll see to it from here. He'll be down directly.
— . . . ucking better be. Hundred and . . . a day, woman.
—That's rather a lot, isn't it?
—Tell . . . his life isn't worth a . . . ucking nickel if he . . . down there . . .

Marie-Claire shakes her head. E.M. III is capable of something like that. For all she knows, he may have done it in the past. Actually, he may do it on a regular basis when the competition becomes intense—with the Board's approval. She has never looked into fatalities among oil executives.

—I'll never know. I'll never understand why I allowed myself to get involved with you and your monstrous family . . .

She knows. Or used to, and as she hangs up, she has, for the smallest portion of a second, a beautifully detailed recollection which passes without Marie-Claire acknowledging its existence.

The picture is of a blonde girl in a cheap cotton dress. She is scraping bits of ground-meat leavings from an enormous grill. She is very tired. She has served breakfast from 5:30 to 8:00 A.M., lunch from 11:30 to 2:00 P.M., and now with an hour's break, she is serving supper from 5:30 to 8:00 P.M. She does it six days a week, fifty-two weeks a year. She is eighteen. She makes twenty-five dollars a week, possibly twelve dollars more in tips. Her mother is dead; her father is what polite people call "shell-shocked." No one is bothered much by that. The people in town simply consider that he is peculiar. There are many peculiar people in East Texas.

She is scraping down the grill, but the shards of meat stick to it as if welded there. She is very tired, and there comes to her as it has in the past the idea of suicide. Not melodramatically. Practically. This is not her world. She hates it, and in return, it must surely hate her. Then she hears from behind.

—Hello, baby . . . the time is now . . .

She turns wearily to face a slim young man in what once was a spotless Palm Beach suit. Now it gleams with black sticky gunk. His hands are filthy, his hair bright with crude oil which runs down his forehead. His face is square, and one knows immediately that the range of its expression is limited. He radiates health and strength and self-possession. Under the muck, he is smiling with what, for him, must be uncontrollable exuberance. He does not, God knows, look sensitive or intellectual, but there is in his eyes a certain naked hungry shrewdness that should not be ignored. Perhaps he has still all the wisdom of the world to learn. But he will learn fast, and those who choose to oppose him are likely to regret it, wondering afterward how such a country boy would manage to best them over and over again.

—What do you need, Eddie? the girl asks, her voice low, flat with weariness as she looks up from the grill.

The flash of memory stops there. E.M. III's answer and its consequences become the shape of Marie-Claire's life from that moment forward.

Now she holds the phone in her lap and taps her finger on the receiver. From the concealed speakers drift the notes of the *Goldberg Variations*. She closes her eyes and smiles. She is considering how best to manage a Sentell. This has been her destiny in life. She is good at it. No one is a master of it. That something, that force, is not to be mastered. Like the great platform in the Gulf, like the river-ocean after which it was named (at her suggestion), it can be dealt with, not dominated. Less poetically, she considers how she will get Shad to New Orleans. If one wishes Shad to do something, one (a) states that he is not to do it under any circumstances, or passes a law against doing it, and (b) states that it is obvious he is unable to do it, and probably not man enough to try, or (c) places a beautiful woman somewhere in the vicinity of what is to be done, and has her make the doing a condition of her favors. Some variation on one or more of these tactics will get him there. If she can find him. She ponders this. Concretely, he has been known to disappear, turning up in Alaska or Ceylon. He has, if not friends, at least co-conspirators or accessories in every oil capital of the world. Wherever he is, she *will* find him. Even insane rednecks have habits. They are not more intelligent than other creatures; they are simply more complex, their motives pitched deeper, the metaphors through which they live their lives more primitive. Wherever he has conjured Sonny to take him, the two are engaged in archaic things. This is their way.

Then another concern strikes Marie-Claire. Her ironic smile fades. She dials the phone.

—Yes . . . Roland, this is Marie-Claire. I . . . think we'll have to change our plans. Will you come by?

Chapter Two

Okeanos is the father of Nemesis . . .
Pausanias, I.33.3

The wind has moved to the northeast, and above the sun is diffused by a slurry of high clouds. There is a headwind that buffets the Jeep from side to side. The light is sharp, astringent, and Sonny squints to see the road ahead, still shining with the early morning rain. On either side of the road, tall pines, green and fresh, stand like those of old Rome. The Jeep is warm now, and Sonny finds his mind detaching from its necessary work. He daydreams, feeling himself free from school, family duties.

Shad is slumped in the passenger seat, his battered Stetson pulled down over his face. His knees are propped against the Jeep's dashboard, and the bottle of Black Jack is caught between his legs. He appears to be asleep, but Sonny knows better. Shad sleeps awake.

An eighteen-wheeler slams past, headed back toward Shreveport on the narrow road. The Jeep skitters and rights itself.

—Not too far now, Shad says.
—How do you know?
—Been along this way for forty years. About a mile up, you take a left. Dirt road. Runs up to the Old Place.
—How can you even tell where we are? Sonny asks. —You've been under that hat since we left the city limits.
—We just come through Greenwood.
—Right.
—Highly developed sense of smell. Left three-quarters of a mile. Little old farm road. Runs back all the way.
—We're getting low on gas.
—Got a Billups station right at the junction where you turn. Just pull in and fill 'er up. Old man Claiborne runs it. Known

him since just after the creation. Must be ninety. Man full of meanness and vices. Never could stand the old sonofabitch. Your grandfather was partial to him.

—If you don't like him, why deal with him?

—'Cause he's there. Anyhow, I take it back. He had two virtues. A beautiful daughter and went to bed early.

—The daughter?

—Claiborne. Daughter went to bed at all hours. With me, anyhow.

Shad is still under the hat. There is a moment's silence, then Shad rumbles again.

—Old bastard was a red. Voted for Debs in 1924. Lived over in Winn Parish then. Whole damn parish went to Debs.

They reach the crossroads. The filling station is an *objet retrouvé*, a segment of the past jutting into the present. An old frame shack with oil drums all around, and a deep pit for oil changes and undercarriage work. The pumps are gravity pumps. Someone must use a lever to force gasoline up into a large glass cylinder at the top. Then it runs down again through the hose, and into the gas tank of an auto. In front, there is a large sign hung on a rusting metal post. It is crudely painted, chipped, and faded. In the middle is an oval with a huge hand outstretched inside. Around the hand is painted:

FILL UP WITH BILLUPS
Your Friend

—Is this where old reds retire? Sonny asks sardonically.

Shad frowns thoughtfully. —Hell, you can come across 'em anywhere. Slinging hash, pumping gas, working poor land. I believe they're partial to funeral homes . . .

Shad sits up slowly as they pull in to the station. His Stetson falls away, and he lifts the whiskey for a quick drink.

—I never seen one of the sonsofbitches didn't have a broken heart. Like queers. They know they been had. Too late. If a woman puts it to you, the next one'll do you all right. There's always good whiskey if you can bum a dollar somewhere. But it's hard to change religions.

—You got a religion, Uncle Shad?

—Nope. Never did.

—You're not an atheist, are you?

Shad smiles to himself as the Jeep grinds to a stop in front of one of the tanks.

—You don't want the regular. You want the premium. Less water. He starts to get out of the Jeep. —I got to go shake my lily, he tells Sonny. —You want anything?

—No, sir.

—Then fill it, and we'll get on up to the place.

Sonny watches Shad go. He walks a little stiffly. Sonny can remember when Shad moved as if his boots did not touch the ground. Now that he thinks about it, Shad is aging. He had never considered that as a possibility. He takes a drink from the bottle Shad has left on the floor of the Jeep.

Someone taps on the side curtain. —You want gas?

Sonny nods. —Fill it. Premium.

He watches the man amble to the rear of the Jeep and begin to lever gasoline up into the cylinder atop the pump. The man is gray-haired, sallow, resembling an albino except he lacks the pink tinge to his hair, his eyes. He wears overalls and a dirty long-sleeved cotton undershirt. He moves as if he were tranced, hands managing the pump without attention. His lips move constantly, but there is no sound. Now he holds the hose with one hand, rubbing the other across the bib of his overalls ritualistically. Something is on his mind.

Sonny gets out of the Jeep and inches closer. He takes money from his pocket as an excuse, counts it. Then he realizes that the man is talking to himself.

—If Christ Jesus comes . . . If Christ Jesus comes, what will you say to him? Yes, that's what I want to know . . .

Sonny's eyebrows raise. He looks away quickly. Staring at loonies enrages them. As to the question on the old man's mind, Sonny has not given it much thought. He has not reached the Christian era in his own musings. He is still concerned with *Adikea* and the *Arche*. But it seems the old man has pondered this question long and hard. He seems to have some firm conclusions.

—I'd say, Come, sweet Jesus . . . Long time a'waiting. Come, I'll show you where the sinners is, where the fornicators lie in their own sweat, the connivers, liars, sodomites. I want to see the cocksuckers burn, you hear, Jesus? I want to see New Orleans inundated. I want to see Dallas on fire. I want to see the earth swallow up San Francisco, and New York topple into the sea . . . That's what I'd say. Get on with punishing sin. Surely all who sin must face the judgment. That's what I'd say.

Sonny backs away slowly, then turns toward the shack. He'd rather pee with Shad. This joker has loose rods.

—Hey . . .

Sonny pauses, a sudden line of chill between his shoulder blades. Has this night crawler suddenly decided that Sonny is the Prince of Darkness?

—Yeah?

—Check the hood?

—Right. You know where the dipstick is?

—I know.

Sonny watches him lift the hood and go to peering into the steaming engine, plumbing deep into the filthy, oil-soaked entrails of the Jeep. Sonny hears him muttering on, and considers that if he ever was a red, he has changed hue. But then half the fun of being a damned fool is converting to some other kind of damned foolery. He realizes that Shad has been gone quite some time, and starts for the shack. As he nears the door, he glances in through a dirty window patched with black electrical tape. It is larger in there than he had guessed. It is a small general store. Shelves filled with groceries, a cold-food locker, shotgun shells, and fishing lures. And Shad passionately kissing a woman. What? Right.

Sonny glances behind at the old man servicing the Jeep. Now and again, he shouts the name of Jesus in a peculiar lilting style. But for the most part, he seems engrossed in the privates of the Jeep. Sonny eases over to the door of the shack and enters quickly.

Shad has let the woman go, but her hand still toys with his leg.

—It's like . . . saying a prayer, and what it is you want, there it is. Dropped out of the sky. Lord God, Shad, if you only knew . . .

—Now, honey, you're saying more than you mean. It's been a long time. What? Ten years?

—More like twenty. When I went and visited you in Kilgore. My daddy told me it wasn't no use, that I couldn't trust no pervert.

Shad frowns. —Where is that old bastard? I'm gonna whip his scrawny ass. I don't take kindly to being called no pervert.

—Don't talk ill of the dead. My daddy's been in the ground seven years.

—Hell you say? I thought they'd take him over and stick him in the Kremlin Wall along with Big Bill Heywood and that silly little pimp from Harvard.

—My daddy didn't mean any of that. He was disappointed.

Sonny listens to all this in mild amaze. The woman is perhaps forty, but an excellent forty. Sonny looks at her appreciatively. She has dark blonde hair, green eyes, the body of a girl. She wears an old shirt and jeans, her thighs bunching the fabric tightly, her breasts causing the shirt fabric to shine where it is pressed outward. Sonny likes her mouth, her low woman's voice. There are moments when he wonders if he is Shad reincarnate, the genes pressing onward, abstract configuration of a pecker swinging in mythical time.

—That old man out there, Sonny asks. —He's not Claiborne?

Shad turns, surprised to see Sonny. —Old man's dead. Saves me the trouble of throttling him. This here's the girl. Elvira Claiborne, meet Sonny Sentell.

—Uh . . . yes, ma'am . . .

Sonny takes her hand and holds it overlong.

—My nephew, Shad says. —Mean little sonofabitch. Quiet. Very worst kind.

All this by way of compliment. Shad's way of saying that Sonny is to be taken seriously.

—Hi, Sonny, Elvira says with a quick smile. Sonny is taken aback to see that Elvira is looking him over much as he has been her. But her attention shifts quickly back to Shad. Her hand toys with his leg, her rapt gaze warning that whatever there has been between them is still flickering.

—E.M.'s son, Shad says to fill the silence. —You remember E.M.

—'Course I remember him.

—Who's the old man? Sonny asks, glancing out the unwashed window to where the man in coveralls crouches under the Jeep's hood, diddling with the engine.

—That's . . . my husband, Elvira says, an edge of sorrow and contempt on her voice.

—Husband? But he's . . .

—You got it. That's what it says on the paper. Parish of Caddo, State of Louisiana.

—I thought it was . . . your father.

—Cecil wouldn't make a patch on my daddy's ass. It was a *mistake*. Lord God, it *was* a mistake.

Shad is over among the shelves, pulling down boxes of twelve-gauge shells and pushing them into his pockets.

—Cecil? Shad says, then comes over and looks out the window with Sonny. The hood of the Jeep is down now. The rain has started again, and Cecil stands stiff as a mummified Indian under the narrow, leaky roof which covers the pumps. His lips are moving furiously, and he seems to be staring directly at the dirty window. His hands, slick with oil, move compulsively across the bib of his overalls. As if he is trying to clean them. His eyes narrow, and his stare appears to intensify. Reason tells Sonny that the old man cannot see them, but in some remote but puissant region of his mind, he is becoming convinced that Cecil sees all, knows all. Idiots, cripples, blind men, albinos, and all women have powers. Everyone knows that. For everything taken away, something is given. Arrant bullshit, no? No.

Shad turns from the window, his expression changed wonderfully. The look of mild disgust becomes one of pity and terror.

—My God, he says, —that's . . . Cecil Miley. Cecil . . . *Miley*? That's awful. That's the worst I've heard in years.

—I been *trying* to tell you, and you wouldn't pay no mind, Elvira snuffles.

Sonny is listening to all this with both ears, but his eyes are fixed on Cecil out by the gas pumps who has now stepped out into the rain. He begins to gesticulate, apparently invoking heaven, pointing toward the shack, staring at the inoffensive Jeep, conjuring a curse on its occupants—or is it simply an imprecation general to mankind? Sonny is tense. There is, he suspects, no good way to deal with crazies. Ignore them and you're dead meat; hole them and the ACLU will piss and moan and call them harmless eccentrics. Like Charles Starkweather.

—How the hell could you go and marry that sorry sonofabitch? You're a fine-looking woman.

—Shad, help me?

—Honey, I will. I never thought . . . Listen, I got to get a little rest. I'll be back to you in a couple of . . .

—Horseshit. You told me that twenty years ago. One night it was forever, and the next night it was a phone call from Caracas.

Meanwhile, Sonny watches nervously as Cecil staggers a few steps toward the shack. His eyes are a little mad, and he is staring upward into the cloudy sky, striking himself on the breast as the rain courses downward through his thin gray hair. Now, suddenly, he falls to his knees, his mouth wide open in a vast round O, a howl of desolation that Sonny can almost hear. Sonny wonders if he is armed, and as quickly as the thought crosses his mind, he looks about for something. Close by on a dusty shelf, near paintbrushes and toilet plungers, he sees tire irons laid out. They have been there an age, covered with dust which has stuck to the thick grime with which they were coated to begin with. Probably army surplus. Sonny takes up one, keeps it in his hand down by his side. This wacko is going to get it just as quickly as he comes through the door armed with anything more dangerous than his index finger.

—Uncle Shad, that bastard is going crazy out there.

Shad squints out into the rain, nods slowly.

—I believe you're right, boy. 'Vira, is that sonofabitch epileptic?

—Hell, no, Elvira says, staring at Shad accusingly. —You ought to know what's wrong with him. He's been like that ever since graduation night . . . when we . . . come out of high school together.

—No shit, Shad says in quiet wonder. —Now, that's a caution, ain't it?

—Huh . . . If someone was to hit *you* in the head . . .

—All right, drop it, Shad rasps summarily. —Reckon he recognized me?

—How do I know? I ain't heard a sensible word out of him since . . . you know when.

Sonny grabs Shad's arm. —That loony is on his feet . . .

Sure enough. Cecil is risen. He is approaching the door of the shack, face bathed in rainwater and a smile. Sonny holds his tire tool firmly. All Cecil has to do is frown. Sonny is tight as a full tick on a yellow hound.

—I'd watch him, Elvira observes. —Some say he knows . . .

Cecil enters, his eyes wild, hair splayed across his forehead by the rain. He is soaked, his overalls stained with mud, knees baggy and dripping. He comes up to Shad quickly, his smile set as if in the harsh ragged concrete of madness itself.

—You owe me, he says, and up from his side comes the barrel of something aimed straight at Shad's gut.

Sonny hits him with the tire tool so quickly that he is almost unaware of having done so. Cecil drops like a rock, blood appearing suddenly in rills down his forehead. He looks puzzled as he folds slowly to his knees, the oil spout falling from his hand.

—Shit, Shad says. —I reckon I owe him for a quart of oil.

—Two, Cecil says, and falls forward on his face, the blood flowing freely now, soaking into the floor, mixing with the water draining from his hair.

—Holy Christ, Sonny blurts out.

—Shut up, Shad says as the three of them contemplate Cecil stretched out at rest before them.

—Don't you worry, honey, Elvira says coolly. —I won't tell if you don't.

Shad has leaned down, putting his fingers on Cecil's throat. —He's alive. Just cold-cocked, that's all.

—You-all go on now, hit the road, Elvira says. —I'll bring him around.

—He's gonna remember us, Shad says thoughtfully. —Reckon we ought to finish him off? Little favor for you, 'Vira. I don't like a sonofabitch walking behind me alive with a grievance. Sonny, you want to give him another couple?

Sonny's eyes widen. He cannot tell if Shad is serious or not. He would not bet his Loeb Classical Library on it.

Elvira nods, understanding Shad's view. —Never mind. I'll tell him he fell down. What? A stroke? Maybe epilepsy . . .

—I thought you said . . . , Sonny begins.

—He's got what I say he's got, Elvira says fiercely. —I'm the one's got to take care of the dummy.

—Well, let's move, Shad says, and steps over Cecil on his way to the door.

—Going to your daddy's old place? Elvira asks.

Shad looks surprised. —I ought to tell you no. We're headed for Texas.

—You'll stop over. I know you.

—Nobody knows me too good, Shad grumbles. —But I ain't gonna lie. We'll stop over.

Sonny skirts the recumbent figure and skips to the door, tire iron still in hand. He looks for a place to set it down. It is now grimier and stickier than before.

—Hang on to that thing, Shad says. —You never know. We might get us a flat tire.

Chapter Three

> ... And the ship was borne down the stream
> Okeanos by the swelling flood ...
> *Odyssey*, XI, 639–40

Best advice one man ever give another was: *Forget it.* Never mind what. An insult, a bad debt, some woman who pulled you in, then pushed you out. Mainly, a man does better looking forward than back. What's that Sonny says? Can't fall into the same river twice? That Greek had hold of something. You look back, you get to thinking you can *go* back, and then it's all downhill. 'Cause there ain't no *back* to go to. It's gone. It wasn't all that wonderful anyhow, most likely. But it doesn't matter 'cause it ain't there, and you best get to moving on. And that's the second-best advice a man ever got: some cop hitting him on the soles of his boots with a nightstick, saying, *Move on, move on.*

Like most advice, good or bad, there's times when you can't take it. Some things just stick in your memory like a burr in a saddle blanket. Like for example, you always remember your first piece of ass. Whenever you think back and find you've forgot most everything you ever come across, there she is, coming alive in the arms of your memory just like she'd never been away.

Which ain't to say necessarily the first one was the best. May seem that way looking back, but Number One wasn't necessarily so hot. Special, yeah. But that's something else. I knew a guy got it the first time rolling in chickenshit in a henhouse late one night. A bad omen. You wonder what a man like that has to look forward to. I had me a nigger friend worked the rigs with me for a while. He got it the first time from his sixth-grade teacher on her desk after school while he was being kept in for calling her a cunt in class. She punished him for hitting it right on the head, and then proved it to him just as soon as the other kids was gone.

But that experience fucked him up bad. He never could make out the difference between reward and punishment after that. I remember how he went: down in Galveston one time he tried to help out this white cop who had four other niggers whipping him to death. Cop shot four times. The other niggers scattered. My man took all four in the head. Don't tell me there ain't a connection.

Not that it matters. When I was sixteen and come into my manhood, I was whacking off five, six times a day. I'd be working a field for my daddy in the middle of the day, pull the mules off to the side of the tree line, and go to flogging it. Reckon why young folks get so solitary? But I seen that couldn't go on. I was gonna jerk my root off if I didn't make some arrangement. It like to drove me crazy to think that any hour of the day or night, people was doing it by the thousands, tens of thousands, millions, all over the world. Why, Christ, they was fucking in London and Buenos Aires. They was doing the deed in Dallas and Bombay —especially in Bombay. There wasn't hardly a dirt shack in Senegal or Montenegro where it wasn't being done constantly. Jesus, I'd think, where's mine?

Well, one fine morning, there mine was. Elvira Claiborne had come home. Her old man run the Billups station up the road from my daddy's place, and she'd gone off to St Louis or Minneapolis or some other Yankee town after her momma died with a fit. She'd gone off a kid and come back Something Else. At the school-bus stop, right in front of the filling station, she come up and hugged Cecil Miley and me. She had a catchy new smile to go with her new way of walking, and she told us she'd had a fine time up there in New Jersey or Milwaukee or wherever. She was going to ride to school to see everybody this last day before summer vacation. She'd had herself a nice time up north, and it was gonna be a long, lonely summer. Cecil and I kind of looked at one another. I could whip his ass, and he knew it. He didn't like me, and I didn't like him, but hadn't anything come of it cause it wasn't anything he wanted that I wanted. Up till then.

At school, as soon as I could get that report card, I was back outside with Elvira. Half the damned Greenwood Consolidated football team was around her, and Cecil had her hand in his like they was already on the way to church. I kind of pushed in between 'em. Cecil started to say something, but I just grinned at him, and he got the message. He kept giving me hard eyes, but

I was talking to Elvira by then and didn't pay him no mind. Elvira and I rode home on the bus, talking about how summer was so fine and this was gonna be the very best summer of all.

That night, she come out after her old man had gone to bed. It was a full moon that night, and we walked and talked in the moonlight till we found ourselves down by the creek.

In the west, there was summer lightning and you could see the thunderheads building up against the moon. The crickets was going after it, and the grass was fresh and soft, and the two of us was talking like we'd just met that day. We talked about how nobody paid her no mind when she was a little kid, before she left for the North. And how time does change things.

—I always wanted folks to notice me.

—Honey, I believe you got your wish.

She smiled. —Those old boys at school . . . They kept touching me.

—I seen that. Part of being noticed, I guess.

—I thought I'd like it. Maybe I'm gonna hate it.

—Shit, Elvira, you got to make up your mind.

She smiled again, and stretched out on the grass, looking up at the moon. She raised one leg so that her skirt kind of fell away. I thought I was going to have some kind of attack. I swallowed hard.

—You can't have it both ways. You want to be left alone or not?

She reached up and pulled me down and kissed me. I think that kiss lasted fourteen years. It wasn't long enough. Our mouths opened to one another, and it felt like the single nourishment we needed to live was in that kiss. Then we broke off, out of breath, and I found I had me a hard-on tough as an axle shaft.

—Maybe I don't want *you* to leave me alone, she said.

—Uh . . . Then I won't.

I reached down and touched her leg. For some reason, I wasn't in a hurry anymore. I wanted to touch her everywhere. I run my hand up her leg real slow. It was like satin.

Then, all of a sudden, she was standing up, looking down at me. I couldn't make out her expression, 'cause the moon stood just behind her shoulder.

—I don't know that I want this, she said.

I thought, Go jump in the bayou and get it over with. Tie a

rock to your neck so you'll stay down. If you miss this, you're gonna beat yourself to death anyhow. Below the belt.

—You never paid me no mind when I was a little girl.

—They put you in jail for paying mind to a little girl, I said.

—Now *you* can't keep your hands off me.

—I ain't got my hands *on* you, 'Vira. You're up there, and I'm down here.

In the distance, out to the west toward Texas, I could hear thunder. Sooner or later, sometime tonight, the rain was gonna come. I thought about that. I had to think of something else, or I was gonna drag her down, take her till mine fell off or hers caved in. Then she moved to the side so the moon was on her face. I could see she was grinning with devilment.

—Tell you what, she said. —I don't know it's what I want, but as long as we're here . . .

She unbuttoned her dress and then kind of shook it off her shoulders. In the moonlight, her brassière was blinding white. There was another band of white below her waist. I felt like I was paralyzed. I hadn't never seen a woman with that much of her clothes off before, and the sight of it goddamned near killed me. A breeze blew up from the west, and behind her, you could see lightning closer now—as if the sky itself couldn't believe what it saw down there on the earth below, in that Louisiana pasture near the Texas line. She did something, and that brassière fell away, and then she hooked her thumbs in her panties and slid 'em down real slow. She did a turn in the moonlight, and smiled down at me.

—I used to stand waiting for the school bus, and when I saw you coming up the road I'd pretend you was in love with me. You'd tell me you couldn't stand it anymore, you had to have me, and you'd ask me to meet you that night over to Mr Petrie's cottonhouse that he don't use anymore. And when I snuck out and got there, you'd have it cleaned out with a nice pallet and all. And we'd do it and do it till neither one of us could move to do it again.

I thought about that. —All right, I said. —I guess that's where it was when you left. Now you're back, and you sure as hell have got my full attention. It's nothing I can do about the past.

—You're right, Elvira said after she thought about it for a minute. —Let's fuck.

Then, just as she had me half crazy and ready to spike her for sure, that thunderhead come right overhead blotting out the moon and letting go a bolt of lightning that seemed to light up the whole parish. I saw her body outlined stark naked and white and beautiful above me, and on beyond her the shadowy trees jumped into relief like it was high noon. We heard the crack and sizzle as the bolt hit a tall pine in the woods, and we couldn't help but pause and watch as the tree swayed from side to side and its top fell down into the darkness below. The thunder clap come right behind, loud enough to kill the living and wake the dead.

The rain started then. It fell in sheets, and there was more lightning and thunder, but we didn't pay the rain any mind. We just laughed and held on to each other like we was afraid this couldn't ever happen again. I felt her body twisting in my arms, cool now and slippery, like a mermaid trying to escape the grip of something that had pulled her up from the deep.

When the rain passed and the moon come out again, we lay there in the thick summer grass, too tired to talk, too full of each other to need to. After a while, we got up off the ground, our hands still exploring each other. We carried out clothes in our hands and walked across that pasture that gleamed from the rain just like it was the Garden of Eden and we hadn't heard about the Fall.

It had turned cool. Elvira shivered and held on to me. Our clothes was soaked, so when we come to the edge of the woods, I hung 'em on low limbs of a dogwood to dry while Elvira pulled together a pile of pine needles.

—It's not Petrie's cottonhouse, and it's not much of a pallet, and I made it for you, not you for me.

—Aside from that . . .

She laughed and lay down, beckoning me to her again. I thought to myself, this girl is trying to see if she can kill me. She is deep and permanent pissed 'cause I didn't used to pay her no mind when she looked like a little old tomato stob with blonde hair, and she's gonna even the score by fucking me to death. All right, fine, I thought. Why not? Being as wise in the ways of the world as any sixteen-year-old in them woods that night, I reckoned it was all going to be downhill from here on out anyhow. No sonofabitch living ever has *two* nights like this. So let her put me away with that sweet ass of hers. If she can. Then I kind of grinned and went down on her again. I pushed and jammed, and she kept pulling me closer, whispering in a harsh voice like a witch, —Deeper, deeper . . .

I can't say when we finally give it up and fell asleep, but I know it was broad daylight when we woke up. We come awake at the same time, kissed, and started touching again. It wasn't no way we could get enough of each other. In daylight, she was even better than in the dark 'cause she was so good-looking and 'cause she'd close her eyes and bite her lip and whisper stuff and look like she was hating it even as she was trying to drag me inside of her cock first.

Then, when we were done that time, it dawned on us that we was lying buck-naked in a little patch of woods along the road between her daddy's filling station and my daddy's farm. A lot of people passed back and forth on that road, and every damn one of them knew Elvira and me. I got our clothes. They were still soggy, but they'd sure as hell have to do.

—Your old man, I started.

—I'll see to him, she said, looking at me real intense, as if she wasn't sure in her mind what come next. —Tonight. When you get done working. I'll get some stuff from the store. We'll have us a picnic. That way, I can bring a blanket . . .

—Better bring some vaseline, too.

—You hurting, honey?

—Naw, but I don't want to wear it down to a nub.

I was pulling my shirt on, and she caught me by the cods, pulled it close to her, and kissed it. —*My* nub, she said. —And don't you forget it.

I was quiet for a moment, sort of feeling what the whole night had been. —I'm not gonna forget it, I said. —I'm surely not ever gonna forget it.

And that's one promise I've kept over all the years between then and now. Lord, that summer. We was together all that year and the next, too. We stayed tight till it was time to graduate from high school. I guess we was what you would call talked about. It didn't make much difference, 'cause her old man, old man Claiborne, used to allow as how he believed in free love, being as he was a stinking socialist bastard and all, and there wasn't anything anybody could tell my daddy about me or E.M. that he wouldn't believe and ignore. In his view, neither one of us was worth a shit, and the rest was just details. One time I had in mind to get tatooed. I was thinking of "Born to Be Hanged".

The old man heard me mention it. —Go ahead, he said. —Why not? Every poison package ought to have a label.

With me and Elvira it was every night, rain or shine, hot weather and cold. It was as bad as playing football. I mean I had to stay in shape. I'd chop cotton, slop hogs, see to the cattle, tote feedbags, and not even notice 'cause all I was thinking about was that next night.

It come to where we hardly talked. We'd meet in the woods, get out of our clothes as fast as we could, and land on that poor beat-up blanket of hers steaming. We'd grapple like wrestlers, seeking that hold that give us the most pleasure. Elvira was better all the time, patrolling out to the very edge of what bodies can do together. She'd show me what she wanted, and I'd do it. Hell, it got to be like a gym class except at the end you'd been in paradise for a little while.

But a strange thing come up as the months went on. We seemed to get sullen with each other. As if somehow we was chained together. Like we was old married people with nothing but one another, no place to go, no one else to go to nor even any idea of something else. But resentful, tired. Like it was a marriage holding us together.

That sounds silly, but that's how it was. Then one day, I was out back seeing to daddy's beans and peppers when it come to me. It was our bodies holding us together. We'd said all we had to say to one another in the first week or so. There wasn't nothing new between us. Old married folks who never had got round to talking about getting married.

It seemed to me both of us had took the bloom from the rose. We was restless, wanting to go see what else there was in the world. But we couldn't. We neither one of us could even imagine that some certain night we'd fuck for the last time. The last time I'd slide into her, the last night she'd twist under me and hold that thing in her hand. See? More to lose than we could possibly gain. So we just come together every night and did what had got to be our business with each other, and went our ways not even saying anything about the next night because it was taken for granted. And ain't that a hell of a way to live?

It got solved for us. Graduation. June of 1934. You know how it goes. Some folks go right on doing what they done before. Some go away to college, some to a job in another town. Better or worse, things got made new.

E.M. was gone then. He'd been working in Texas for a couple of years. He'd been a tool-pusher with Robinson Oil, and old man Robinson had taken a shine to him. E.M. was that kind. People liked his looks so much they let the rest pass. And he was fine-looking with a straight, narrow nose and cold blue eyes, a dark country tan skin, and hair so light and shining that it was closer to silver than gold.

I guess it always pissed me a little that E.M. looked so good. I had a face like hamburger, mean green eyes, and where he had that tan, I was beet-red. I was built good and solid, and I was going to last like oak or hickory furniture, but they wasn't gonna carve no Looie Keenze out of me. Wasn't any oil man and his old lady gonna see me as the son they wished they'd had.

I'll give E.M. this. Back in those days, already slicker than greased owlshit, he stuck by his people. Later, it was gonna be different. But that summer he turned up in a white Palm Beach suit, a white Stetson, and a pair of black water buffalo Justins from Fort Worth. When I come down from the platform with my diploma, there he stood with daddy. They was both staring at me. That was our way. We wasn't given to back-slapping and funning much.

—What do you say, little brother?

—Goddamn, I said. —What are you doing in them clothes? I know . . . You gone to pimping in Dallas.

Whatever kind of smile he'd been trying went down like a overloaded barge. Then it come up again, with an edge of meanness on it.

—No, no, he said. —No way I'm gonna get in the way of your operation. By the way, where is Elvira?

Well, she was about ten steps from us, just barely out of hearing. Which saved E.M. a lot of dental work.

She come up to us in her white dress, eyes wide when she saw E.M., who tipped his hat and told her he was rig super now, and old Robinson was gonna move him into administration when he had a good hold on the business down where business gets done. As he talked in a low tone, I could see he was looking Elvira over. Hell, so was I. That graduation dress of hers was enough to make the rest of the senior girls give it up right then and there. You could make out the curve of her breasts under white lace, the swell of her hips under white organdy. Lord God, we'd screwed as much as most folks married for twenty years. I knew her body better than my own, and still there was mystery. I still was hungry for her. I wanted her right then. I didn't have a word to say to her, but I wanted to drop her to the ground and fuck her right there.

E.M. was jawing about how he wanted to talk about my future. I hadn't never thought of having a future. What I wanted right then was to shuck my old man and E.M. and get out to the woods with a bottle of whiskey I'd bought, and do it all night long.

So I said, All right, fine. Maybe we could talk about my future in the morning. Right then Elvira and me had to get ready for the dance and all. No, he said, still smarting from that stuff about him being a Dallas pimp. Right now. Come on. He and the old man started walking to E.M.'s car. Elvira was looking hurt.

—I thought we was . . .

—We are, honey. Look, give me an hour. You know how family is . . .

—I know how *your* family is.

—Honey, my damned brother come all the way from Kilgore.

—If he matters more than me . . .

I kissed her to shut her up. Lord, she was lovely. —I'll be by the station. In an hour . . .

She turned away from me and started walking away. —Don't bother, she called back over her shoulder. —'Cause I won't be there.

I just stood there, and she walked on over to join a bunch of the boys and girls who'd just graduated with us. Cecil Miley was there, and Elvira walked right up to him. He looked over at me, but she said something, and he smiled. I should have gone over right then and busted his goddamned nose, but instead I climbed into E.M.'s car. I'd pick up on Elvira later. What the hell? Maybe I'd ask her to get married.

—Nice you'd offer him a job, the old man was saying to E.M., that stain of irony always in his voice. —Youall ain't been tight.

E.M. stared at him. —No, none of us has been that close. But when you get where I am, you see how things are. There's nobody you can trust. Nobody.

—You reckon you can trust me? I asked him.

—Don't be a dumb asshole, E.M. said, unsmiling. —I can trust you. You're my brother.

The old man and I looked at each other. Something was

coming over E.M. He didn't sound like no recognizable brother of mine.

—If you was to do me, he said, —it'd be *personal*. I can look out for that. I know you. But I got to have somebody I can trust.

He frowned and stared on down the road ahead, looking almost bewildered. Made me wonder just what he'd come up against out there.

—Everybody's got to have somebody he can trust.

In a little while, it was all settled. I'd be leaving with him the next day. I said, All right, fine, yeah, sure. Whatever it was out there had to have more to it than screwing around with that damned postage stamp of a farm. I wasn't sold on going, but I reckoned that must be what was next. Then I got loose as quick as I could and walked up the road to find Elvira.

On the way, I got to thinking about that getting married stuff again. I looked at it one way and then the other, and I guess I stopped still in the road when I realized I was going to ask her to get married. Once you've had a prime woman every damn night for a couple of years, there's no way you can look up ahead and see nothing but crap years and empty nights in a cold bed. I hated to ask her, 'cause it seemed I was closing doors I hadn't even looked through yet, but you got to be a realist. Long term, the root rules. The dick disposes.

I cared for her. I really did. But what I was afraid I might be losing by marrying her was that first night. That's what I really wanted. That night. The rain and the thunder, and that edge on everything that still stood in my mind like it was etched into the meat. Well, I thought, maybe you was right in the beginning. Maybe a man only gets that night once. The rest is choice, but it's only prime one time.

She wasn't at the filling station. Old man Claiborne didn't know where she was. I didn't make too much of that. She'd be around. I walked down to the creek, through the pines and on into the pasture. I tried to remember just how it had been that night, and I got me a hard-on just concentrating. What the hell, maybe we could get it back if we worked at it, and storms came through on a regular basis.

I come to the edge of Petrie's land then and was about to start on back and wait for her. Then I remembered what she'd said about dreaming I'd fixed up that old cottonhouse for her. I could see it out in the middle of the field amidst the ratty little crop

Petrie was making. Run-down, empty, kind of falling apart under the hot sun there. I walked over toward it. Rusty lock on a hasp against the gray wood. Everything about it gone gray. Just a long dirt path to an empty shed. That had never had us in it at all.

I was almost to the shed then, when all of a sudden I thought I must be out of my mind. I thought I could hear Elvira sobbing, moaning, asking for more, more. Holy shit, I thought. Not only can't you go without for a night, you can't even make it through the day. Lord, is it a sign? If it was a sign, and I was supposed to marry her, well, hell, I would. I don't ever argue with God or with no sure sign. I do what He says do. But He's got to say it to me. Loud and clear. No written communications through no third parties.

By then, I was close up on that cottonhouse, and it was plain all that noise wasn't in my mind. It was in my ears. Right off I wondered if she'd got carried away and come out to this old shed and gone to jacking off, thinking of me. I kinda smiled, and moved over by the shed and looked in through a crack between two weather boards. It was dark in there, and I knew it was hotter than the hinges of hell. But I could see Elvira. She was on her back, of course. The top of her dress was down, and the skirt up, making it look like she had a wide white belt around her middle. But she wasn't by herself. Some sonofabitch had his head between her legs, and she was loving it.

I felt cold all over. As if I was out of my own body, standing there like some kind of ghost in that summer heat looking in on Elvira and me. This is what you-all look like, I thought, standing there tranced, frozen watching. But that didn't last long. First thing you know, there's Cecil Miley coming up for air, grinning, shaking his head how good it is. And there *I* was, outside the crack looking in at what should of been me. And grinning, too. It's good, ain't it, Cecil? Never had anything in your life that good, huh?

Which is when I found myself backing off in the dirt looking for twigs, pieces of soybean stalk, a couple of busted boards off the shed. Pretty soon I had me a nice pile up against that shed. Then I lit it. The shed was bone dry, and it come up burning pretty quick. I got around by the door and waited. I knew what was gonna happen like it already had. Sure enough, in a minute or two that door came creaking open and Cecil, buck-naked, showed his head out to see where the smoke was coming from.

So when I hit him up side the head with my fists clubbed, he was off balance, helpless as a damn pig in a slough. That's the best way to get 'em. Fighting over a woman ain't like a prize ring. Different rules. Bite off noses and ears, thumbs in eyes. And there's stomping. I always dearly loved to stomp. Boys in school used to yell when I got in a fight, —Watch Sentell. He's a stomper.

Old Cecil hit the ground and tried to turn over and roll. Forget it. I had kicked him in the face once and in the side of the head a couple more times before he even knew he'd been hit. I doubt he even knew then who'd done it to him. When he woke up, he'd have other stuff to think on. Like a broken nose, and whatever that boot toe in the eye had done.

When he was down and out, I went over and kicked out the fire. I kicked hard and loud, and then went in the door quick and threw out Cecil's clothes.

She was back in a corner away from where the wall of the shed was smoking. There was a pile of croaker sacks under her, and her body was shining with sweat. She was trying to cover herself with what was left of that graduation dress. She had the top pulled up, but the skirt was still around her waist, and her panties around her ankles.

I stood looking down on her for a minute. I thought maybe I ought to whip the shit out of her, too. Lay 'em out side by side and burn their clothes. But just as I reached over to bust her jaw or something, she put up her hands to protect herself, and the top of her dress fell. That done it. I got out of my clothes, and went for her.

She fought and scratched as I shoved her down, her legs pumping around me, her face dark and red and angry.

—Get off . . . get off me, you cocksucker.

Well, I thought, there goes marriage and all that stuff. This is a hell of a way to say goodbye. But while I'm at it, I might as well get everything she's got to give this one last time.

—You're a dirty nigger pimp, she was shouting.

—You got me mixed up with my brother.

Then I got off of her. But as she started to rise, I pulled her over on top of me, her face real close to mine.

—Listen good. You know what happened to old Cecil?

—No. What? Oh, shit, you fucking animal. You killed him, didn't you?

I kind of let my eyes go funny and giggled. —I broke him all up. He ain't never gonna be right again. And that's just what I got in mind for you.

Her eyes widened. She just didn't know. How was she to know? Hell, I didn't know myself. All she'd had from these hands was pleasure. It's got to be hard to get into your head that somebody you've screwed for two years is gonna kill you. She couldn't decide, so I helped her. I slapped her kind of easy, and gave her one in the ribs at the same time. The slap drew a little blood at the corner of her mouth, but the one in the ribs hurt. It took her breath away, just like a good stiff length of cock. She tasted the blood, and her eyes got wider still.

—You . . .

—Don't say it. Don't even think it. I ain't decided whether to maim you or kill you. Doing what you was doing with Cecil, I think I'm gonna kill you . . .

—They'd catch you.

—They'd catch old Cecil. You got in a few licks before he wrung your neck. Sex killing. Happens all the time. Things get out of hand. Cottonhouse love nest . . . teens drove mad with lust . . .

I smiled real crazy and reached for her, but I don't think it would of worked if it hadn't been for what happened just then. The door of the shed caught a little ripple of wind and eased open real slow, making a creepy sound like in a horror movie or something. I looked around quick so as to see if Cecil had come around, and I was gonna have to do another number on him, or maybe even whip old Petrie who'd come to see who was burning his cottonhouse. Nope. Just the wind. But Elvira looked past me and out the door and saw old Cecil lying out there in the sun like a sack of shit. And you can believe this or go squat on a hornet's nest. Right on the sonofabitch's chest was a big black crow. When she saw that, it made up her mind.

I'll give her this. She didn't go to screaming. She got real quiet, kind of studious. She wiped the blood from the corner of her mouth with her finger, looked at it, and then said in a real matter-of-fact tone:

—You *did* kill him . . .

—I didn't want you to know.

— . . . and you're gonna kill me.

—I believe so.

She nodded. —Come on. Let's go.

Then it started, and I can't hardly remember the details. You better believe this. A woman fucking for her life is a prime piece of ass. I had her every way a woman can be had, and the longer we did it, the better it was.

—You're gonna kill me anyhow, she whispered, wiggling her ass so fast I could barely keep it in.

—I reckon, I said, and kept on pushing.

—Don't stop, she breathed. —Do it while you're fucking me. No . . . fuck me till it kills me.

Hell, I thought, that's what I had expected the first night we did it. I hadn't known it then, but that's why I couldn't get that night out of my mind. Somewhere in me so deep I couldn't dive and find it, I was expecting—no, shit, wanting one of them lightning bolts to hit us right at the peak, drive us on upward past flesh and pleasure, over the top of the world and beyond the stars to someplace where all it was was nothing but coming forever.

—All right, I whispered back to her. —That's just what I'm gonna do.

Our bodies was running sweat, and it was so fine. Whatever we did was smooth, like pistons working together, frictionless, a perfect match. It was so hot that I couldn't get my breath, and I got to hearing this ringing in my ears even louder than Elvira's breathing, moaning under me. I thought, maybe this is heaven's gate, and all the preachers and grade-school teachers know it, had always known it, but couldn't get there themselves, and was bound and determined nobody else would, either. I could hear that thunder again, and colors started flashing across the inside of my eyelids when I closed my eyes, and Elvira had done run out of anger and fear and kept saying over and over again:

—Kill me, kill me, kill me . . . I don't want to live . . . Kill me, kill me . . .

Sometime about then, I kind of lost out. One minute, all the lights in the world was on and banging around in my head. Then somebody pulled the cord. No pain, no strain. On and off.

When I finally came around, it was dark. I'd come out fine. I hadn't never felt better in my life. Till I tried to move. There wasn't a muscle in my body wasn't stiff. My nuts felt like they was about to fall out my ass, and my ass hurt, too. I couldn't feel no sensation in my pecker. Seemed like it might never peck again. When I managed to roll over, I roused Elvira. She turned to me, took one look, and give me the prettiest, most loving smile you ever saw. Made me glad I hadn't killed her.

—Shad, honey, she whispered. —Oh, baby, it was so good. I thought I *was* gonna die.

I tried to get up. No use. The small of my back felt like a snake run over by a tractor. I kind of fell back, and she was on me, kissing me.

—Oh, shit, baby, you're so fine.

—Yeah, I said, not paying any mind. My thoughts was suddenly on old Cecil. Was he still out there snoozing, or had he come to, just waiting out there with a plank or whatever he could lay hands on?

But when I crawled to the door and eased it open, there wasn't a thing to be seen but the dark sky overhead and streaks of red and pink and yellow on the clouds to the west where the sun had gone down. That, and a white moon and one hell of a lot of soybeans. I breathed that cool night air and smiled to myself. With my luck, you don't need no brains. It looked like Cecil had come to hisself and decided he'd had enough of me. I kind of wanted to think that was the end of that.

Not likely. Cecil was a miserable little chickenshit, but he wasn't no Yankee or anything. I expected I'd be hearing from him somewhere down the line. You don't kick the shit out of a North Louisiana boy and just leave him lay without he comes back on you. What I didn't reckon on was how soon he'd be back. Which is when I heard the shotgun.

Elvira jumped over beside me, and we stood up and craned our necks over to Petrie's house and barn. Whole lot of noise over there on the far side of a piece of woods toward the road that run up to Highway 80. Some kind of party? Not likely. Petrie was a widower like my old man. Anyhow, it wasn't no music. Just yelling and hollering. Then I seen a pair of headlights coming through the woods. Over the engine noise, I could hear somebody yelling.

—Goddammit, don't you sonsofbitches go into my soybeans . . .

—Shut up, old man, somebody yelled back, and then I heard what sounded like a shotgun again. Jesus, you reckon one of them bastards shot Petrie? Whatever, I'd of bet you a gold

Hamilton railroad watch to a pickled pigfoot I knew who was in that pickup that was raising dust so it looked like fog at the edge of the soybeans. And me with nothing in hand but a limp dick. It was gonna be a long night.

—Come on, I told Elvira while I pulled my jeans on.

—What? Oh, honey, not yet. Couldn't we . . . just once . . .

—No, but you can stay just like you are, and get gang-raped by Cecil Miley and the Greenwood Consolidated High School football line.

That got her moving, because she knew those old boys like I did, and when they're drunk and hurt and mad, you don't fuck with them. No, old buddy, *they* fuck with *you*. She was trying to pull the remains of that graduation dress over her, but it wasn't any good. All tore to hell. What Cecil had started, we'd finished.

—Shit, Shad, I can't go off . . . like this.

—However you go, you got to go now.

Well, she found her brassière, and her white high-heeled shoes, but that was it. No panties anywhere, and my damned shirt was gone. Reckon it crawled off to couple with her panties. And my boots was stuck in my belt, 'cause the way that truck was coming, I didn't have no time to pull 'em on.

We was moving then. Not away from the truck, but ninety degrees to it. North toward the highway. There was a good piece of woods over there, and the pasture, too. Where Elvira and me started out. Reckon if they caught up to us, we might as well get it there. I guess we'd made nearly half a mile on our hands and knees down below the soybean tops when we heard that pickup reach the cottonshed. Elvira was already wore out, with her hands and knees rubbed raw.

—Honey, she said, —maybe I could talk to 'em . . .

—Sure you could. Just before they went to fucking you to death, like you was wanting a while ago. Stand up and hail 'em, baby. But give me a head start.

Just then they set fire to the cottonhouse. They'd pushed all kinds of field rubbish and stuff up against it, and poured gasoline on that. They didn't need to bother. It was so old and so dry, it went up with a touch. I looked over at Elvira as she was catching her breath.

—There goes your love nest, honey, I laughed. —Old Cecil's back, and breaking up housekeeping.

She just sat there with no pants on, rubbing her knees.

—Nothing seems to last anymore, I said. —Here today, gone tonight.

—It didn't mean anything. I told you that.

She looked away toward that old shed burning against the night sky, and she looked so sad I was sorry I had gone and teased her. She stood up, staring at that smoke and them flames like fingers probing the night. And all of a sudden, one of them bastards spun that pickup around, and the headlights caught her square on. She stood out like a salt lick in a corral, tall and slender with nothing but that damned white brassière just reflecting the light right back at 'em.

I could hear 'em crank that pickup, and it wasn't anything else to hang around for. I figured we had us about a fifty-fifty chance of making the woods. That is, if they wasn't drunk and mad enough to go shooting at us from a distance. I'd already heard a shotgun, but I didn't have no insurance policy said they didn't have a Winchester, too.

We was moving then, standing up and running. Elvira kept tripping, slowing me down. I just yelled at her over the whine of that pickup slipping into second gear.

—They're gonna rape them high heels off you, baby. That's all your Commie daddy's gonna have to remember you by.

Next thing, she was running past me barefoot and butt-bare, moving like a deer with them headlights dead on her sweet beautiful ass.

Now them woods seemed to be pacing us. Hard as we ran, they looked to be retreating at just that speed. But that truck was coming at five or six hundred miles an hour, slashing through the soybeans, engine roaring, headlights bouncing. It seemed I could feel the heat of their motor on my tail.

Finally, I could see we was gaining on them trees. But even so, the tracks of them headlights was moving up on either side of me, setting out the soybean plants like they was etched against the darkness just beyond. I could make out the dirt clods down below. Christ, I believe I could see cutworms on the leaves. My wind was going by then, but when it seemed I couldn't make another ten steps, I looked up and saw Elvira right ahead, legs pumping, her sweet ass bouncing so I could hardly take my eyes off it. I thought, Reckon nobody was after you? What if it was just you after her to pull her down and pile it in? Could you keep going then?

It gave me second wind to think of that, and before I knew it, we'd gone through some brush and plunged on into the woods.

Not that we could stop. I figured we'd better get a couple hundred yards in there before we started hide-and-seek, and then cut west and double back to Petrie's. But a little ways in, Elvira fell down breathing so hard she sounded like dying, and I was right beside her.

—I don't care what they're gonna do. That's it. I can't go no farther . . .

—Breathe, I said. —Don't talk. We ain't out of the woods yet. We're barely in 'em.

So she lay there dragging air into her lungs, and I was looking all over the ground for a nice big fallen branch from one of them hardwood trees around us. I didn't even have my head turned that way when we heard the crash. I snapped around, 'cause it sounded like the sonsofbitches had parachuted in on top of us. But no. The dumb bastards had run full-tilt into a big oak stump at the edge of the field. The headlights went out, and the yelling commenced.

—Motherfucker, you thrown me clean out of the truck.

— . . . the hell *was* that? Reckon Sentell tripped, and we run him over?

—Naw. I had my eye on him.

—Liar. You was just like the rest of us. All you had your eye on was Elvira's twat.

—Gonna have my hand on it soon as I'm able.

There was a lot of fumbling around then while they tried to regroup. The truck was canted over with water and oil dripping out and the engine mounts and shocks kind of sighing since the pan was sheared off and the motor block was flat on a white oak stump then.

Elvira was pushing up to where I was looking through the branches.

—What . . . ?

She saw for herself. And took to giggling. We wasn't more than ten or fifteen yards from them murderous sonsofbitches, and she had gone to giggling. I grabbed her to shut her up, but I caught her by the ribs under her titties, and she only giggled louder. We fell down in the leaves with me damned near busting out laughing, too.

—What's that sound, Millard?

—Shit, it's her. She's in there, Cecil.

—Well, come on. I been wanting some of that for two years. Tonight's the night.

Elvira stopped giggling. That was personal. We went to crawling, but we hadn't got far when we heard 'em all thrashing through the brush behind us.

—Man, Sentell's in there just waiting. I don't want to come up on that big ugly bastard without I know . . .

— . . . get hold of Sentell, I'm gonna nail his nuts to that goddamned oak stump, set what's left of my truck on fire. And throw him a knife.

Seemed me and Elvira both had good reason to keep moving, and we did. When we got a little distance, we up and run, bouncing off trees, caught up in bushes and berry vines till all of a sudden we come to what looked like a burned-out clearing. There was one big old pine standing right in the center, but its top was gone, and most everything around it was knocked down or burned off. We was out in the middle of that mess before either one of us realized, and them boys was moving right along behind. If they caught us, I didn't figure to be going to Kilgore in the morning, and I didn't expect Elvira would be able to walk for a month.

I was squatting and looking back when my hand run up on something. It was a pine limb. Three, four feet long, burned black, hard and dry, but not brittle. It was like stone from the fire, and I figured pretty quick that it was the best I could expect. Not much against a shotgun, but something. I never asked the Lord to open up the ground and swallow 'em. A fair chance was all I wanted. This here limb was close enough.

I caught hold of Elvira and told her what to do. She just shook her head. Like any sensible woman would have. But I told her it wasn't no other way. Do or Die. Now or Never. Shit or Get Off the Pot. Finally, she nodded and went over by the big pine, kinda shrugged out of her brassière like she always done, and stood there as I eased over to the edge of the woods where we come out—and where old Cecil and his buddies was just straggling in.

—Shad, Elvira called out in a little scared voice. —Oh, honey, please don't leave me. I'll try to keep up . . . Please . . .

Here come Cecil and Millard Troy into the clearing. They had 'em a big flashlight—one of them eight-battery jobs—and they stopped about three feet from me. There was another one breaking branches behind 'em, still coming on. There was three of 'em altogether. I could handle that. If things come down just right.

They swung that light back and forth, looking for Elvira. It would of been easy to cold-cock both of 'em, but that other one was coming up right behind. I had to let it simmer a while yet.

—Shad, where *are* you . . . ?

They caught her in the light just as the other bozos come crashing through the brush. It was Ferd Cox. I could take any one of 'em man on man, but if I wanted all three down, I had to get 'em split up. Let it simmer.

The three of 'em moved in on Elvira. She stood there naked, trying to cover herself, tired, scratched, and damn near dead from fear. I didn't blame her. You could smell the whiskey on 'em from where I stood. And they moved on her like critters after food, not like men.

—Lord God Jehovah, Ferd said, just looking at Elvira. —I never seen anything like that.

—How we gonna figure who goes first and who gets seconds? Millard asked, kinda businesslike. As if he managed weekend gang-rapes for a living.

—Shad, Elvira moaned, turning her face from the flashlight beam. —Honey, please come help me.

Cecil come up to her and pulled her chin around. —You better be talking to us, sugar. Your boyfriend's done hit out for high cotton.

—No, he's not. He's out there . . .

They looked at each other. Cecil had the shotgun. Ferd had him a baseball bat, and he was reaching out caressing Elvira's bush with it, handle end first. Millard had a handgun.

—What do you think? Millard asked, real serious. —I mean, if he's still out there . . .

—He ain't got no gun, Ferd said. —If he comes back, I'm gonna blow him off. My goddamned pickup's fucked. That's his fault.

—Listen, Cecil said as he started feeling around on Elvira like she was a hunk of cheese, —if he's around, we got to root him out. Don't low-rate him. That bastard come on me like a tornado today. He's crazy, and he's dangerous. Whey don't youall take a look around?

There was old Cecil complimenting me. He was right. But he

was mainly trying to get the rest of 'em off on any kind of hunt at all. So he could finish what I'd interrupted. He looked like hell. Had two or three bandages on his face, and one eye swelled shut. But Cecil was gonna get his pussy first. I appreciated that in him. You can always get revenge. —Youall scout around, he drawled. —Then pull straws or whatever for turns.

—You mean for the first round, Millard said soberly.

—Sure, that's what I mean, Cecil said. —We got her for all night, ain't we?

—We could take her back and lay her in the truck bed, Ferd allowed.

—First take care of Sentell, Cecil said. —I don't want that fucker wandering around behind me whilst I'm having my pleasure.

So they started on out into the woods on the far side, leaving Cecil there with Elvira. I wanted to go for him right then, 'cause I'd been standing like a stone for five minutes. But I had to wait till the other two got well clear. That meant Elvira was gonna have to work a little.

—Cecil, she said in a shaky voice, —I'm sorry about all this. But you come from a good Christian family, and . . .

—You're gonna suck my cock till your eyes fall out, he told her.

—Please, Elvira started, and Cecil slapped her. Then he pushed her down on her knees and brought his body up in front of her face.

—Eat it, he said, and held out his rod, stiff as a drive-shaft and on the long side of medium, I guess.

Elvira started to fool with him, playing with his balls, trying to keep him interested.

—Come on, girl, he said, cuffing her again. —Get to gobbling. I can play with myself.

I could feel my body trembling like a race horse, and I waited just a fraction more. Ferd and Millard had to be maybe a minute away by now, and old Cecil was what you'd call involved. When I couldn't hear the rest of 'em threshing around in the brush anymore, I moved.

Did you ever step into a pitch knowing that it was gonna go all the way before you ever laid wood to it? That's just how it was. It was three steps and swing from the ground up. I knew it was a homer, 'cause every one of them muscles of mine I'd been misusing all day screamed and twisted. Christ, I swung so hard the muscles in my ass clenched.

And my old burned pine limb caught Cecil full in the back of his head. Solid, where the hair comes down. He never made a sound. Just lifted up off the ground, soared three or four feet right over Elvira without touching her, and bounced off the big pine. When he hit the ground, it sounded like a bag of old clothes. He never stirred. I reckoned I'd killed him, and that was all right, fine. I didn't have no elevated view of Cecil's humanity right then. Like they say, better be judged by twelve men than carried out by six.

Elvira grabbed me like I was salvation. —Is he . . . ?

—Who gives a shit? You start yelling for them boys as soon as I get over in the shadows by them little slash pines.

—You're nuts. Let's run. You really *are* crazy.

—Well, I just kept you from having to bite off more than you could chew, sis.

—You gonna lie in wait and kill the other two. That's all you want. I don't mean a damned thing to you, do I?

—We can't outrun em, lumber-brain. We ain't go no clothes for you, and I ain't gonna play chase through these woods all night. We're gonna do it my way, or you're on your own. Root Hog or Die.

That pretty much saw to the philosophy of the thing, and she allowed she'd do what I said. I got over in the saplings, and she went to yelling. While she was hollering, she was down stripping off Cecil's shirt and pulling on his pants and rolling 'em up. I purely admired that. Girl wasn't but seventeen, cool as the knobs on a sea horse, taking care of essentials whilst the fight was on.

—Help, oh, God, youall come back. Something awful's happened to Cecil . . .

That was fact. Cecil had had him a hard day. He was lying over on his back, breathing hard, buck-naked, nose broke, eye swollen shut, and either a fracture or a concussion—sure to have a month-long headache and a life-long recollection of me and Elvira. I thought about that while Elvira was bawling, and I heard them boys breaking up the bushes getting back to where we was. I didn't much like leaving Cecil out behind me for the rest of my life. With me gone to Kilgore, all this was gonna work on Cecil's mind. People would know what I done him. He might burn my daddy's house down. I didn't give a shit for the old man, and he couldn't stand me, but you don't let nobody mess with your people. Maybe I had best go over and push a handful of dirt down his throat and up his nose.

Right then, Ferd come out of the trees with his baseball bat. He took one look at Cecil laying there looking plenty dead, and he started for Elvira with his bat raised.

—I don't know how you done it to him, but I'm gonna kill you, Ferd said. Truth is, he was the worst of the bunch, and I was glad he come out first. He was big and just as strong as I was. Dumber than dogshit, but he could bite through a sixteen-penny nail. Right then, all he had in mind was Elvira, and I knew I had me one clean swing.

—You bit off his dick, didn't you?

Elvira shook her head and started backing away. I come up behind Ferd and let go. Dammit, I ain't no Indian, and even in those days I was two-twenty. He heard something and come around just as I let go with my Piney-Woods Slugger. Call it a double. I took him full in the side of the head, and he went down on his knees. But he wasn't out. Probably his goddamned big ears. He grabbed his head and kinda whimpered. The next sound we was gonna hear was a scream they'd pick up in Minden and Gladewater. It never come out. 'Cause as I was rearing back to take another cut, Elvira come down right on top of his head with his own baseball bat he'd dropped. Turn out the lights, the party's over . . .

We spread him out alongside Cecil. Elvira smiled at me.

—Not bad for a girl, huh?

—Listen, honey, we ain't got no time for . . .

—All right, Sentell. You put that gun down and step out where I can see you, hear?

Me and Elvira hit the turf, and sure enough, comes this shot that whacked into the limbs above us, scattering leaves all over. It was Millard checking in.

—Oh, damn, Elvira said. —You mean we done all this for nothing?

—Horseshit, I said. —That's Millard Troy. He's a piss-ant.

—That piss-ant's shooting at us.

I went to fooling around by Cecil. Sure enough, propped up against the big pine, I found his sawed-off shotgun. Looked like an old Savage somebody took a hacksaw to. You could hide it under your coat and when you got in a tight, it just says, "Surprise, folks." I felt in Cecil's pockets—which was now located on Elvira.

She kind of kissed me and tongued my ear. —Reckon you could hold off on that just a little while, she asked.

—Dammit, woman, I'm looking for shells.
—What are you gonna . . . ?
—Wait about a minute, hear?
—All right.
—Then take this here piece, and cut loose where you see that tree with the wisteria.

I pointed the shotgun for her, and then took my pine limb and started skirting the edge of the clearing toward where Millard's voice had come from. It got the wind up me to be going blind against a handgun, but Millard *was* a piss-ant. He sure as hell wasn't no woodsman, and I figured he might be dumb enough to shoot and stay in one place. If he did, and Elvira shot right where I said, she was likely to blow him away. I didn't give a damn if she did.

—Sentell, I can see you. Come on out in the clear with your hands up or . . .

Elvira couldn't have picked a better time. That shitkicker didn't see nothing. Hell, he was looking away from me, and sure enough, he was pretty close to where the first shot come from. Close enough so that when Elvira cut loose with that scattergun you could hear the screaming and hollering all the way back to the highway. I couldn't tell if he was hit or scared shitless, but whichever, he was sure as hell occupied. I pushed on toward where the scream had come from. It kind of trailed off into a gurgle as I went for it, but I had my pine limb ready. Then I come by a big cottonwood, and there he was. On his ass, leaned up against a tree with his flashlight on, pulling up his shirt where it was all bloody, looking at the two holes where the shot had nicked him in the side.

I couldn't help but laugh. The miserable little bastard had been stalking us all night, figuring to gang-rape Elvira and do for me. Now he was down, and it was all king's X.

He saw me. —I'm hurt, he said. His hands was trembling, and his eyes was watering. I didn't see no gun.

—Yeah, I said. —I see that. And hit him in the face with the pine limb.

He kind of fell over on his side like a rag doll, and I picked up the old Smith & Wesson from beside him whilst he went to gagging and spitting out teeth. I broke his gun against the tree and hit him in the head again. More I thought about it, the more I wanted to do the whole bunch of 'em. In for a penny, in for a pound. If I wasn't gonna kill 'em, I was sure gonna mutilate 'em some.

—Come on, 'Vira, I said. —I believe I'll break his goddamned legs and let him lie in the . . .

—Do it by yourself. I've had enough, she said.

Just then Millard started crawling off real slow, like he was hoping if he went slow enough, nobody would notice and stop him. I hefted my pine limb. Elvira watched him as he inched off into the woods like a busted tortoise.

—Let him go, she said.

—All right, I told her. —I reckon I've had my fill. You want to stroll on by Petrie's to see if they done for him?

—I tell you the truth, Elvira said. —I don't give a shit if they did him or not. I want to go home, and I want a bath. I never had such a day in my whole life. If this is what graduating from high school is the commencement of, I don't believe I can handle the rest of it. I really don't.

We walked out through the woods, leaving the raiding party there to sort it all out when they come around and got back together. Cecil and Ferd was still laid out as we passed through the clearing, and when we reached the truck, it was still skewered on that stump with everything busted and leaking. So it went up easy when Elvira tossed a match on it.

We walked across the soybeans in the track the pickup had left coming in, a pillar of fire from the burning truck behind, a pillar of smoke rising off the ruins of Petrie's cottonhouse up ahead. The moon was down by then, but it was getting gray in the east. I could see tears running down Elvira's cheeks. She stopped by the cottonhouse and just stared at the ashes. Hardly a glow left. Just a curl or two of light smoke fading into the windless sky. No clouds up there. Today was gonna be just as hot as yesterday. But not much else would be the same. I didn't say anything while she cried to herself. It'd sound silly to tell her I was going to Kilgore after all this. And the marriage thing had kinda faded when I seen her in there with old Cecil.

Then, like I heard a call, I turned and looked back the way we had come. It wasn't light yet, but, past the soybeans and standing out over the woods, I saw the broke-off ruin of that tall pine tree. All of a sudden, it hit me. That wasn't only the tree at the clearing where all the crap with Cecil and his boys had happened. It was the same damned tree that had got busted by lightning the night Elvira and me had first got it on. I stared down at that burned pine limb I was still carting. There had to be a message in all this, but I'll be damned if I could make it out. It sure as hell wasn't Love Conquers All.

Old Petrie was all right. Seems it had been the pickup backfiring that I heard. He was kind of surprised to see us. Said he hadn't wanted to mess with them boys, drunk like they was, but he'd gone down to the filling station and called the Caddo Parish sheriff. He didn't need the cottonhouse anymore, but it was the principle of the thing.

—That's just how I feel, Elvira told him, still kinda weepy.

—They're gonna need a wrecker and an ambulance, I called back as we left.

It was dawn now, with the sun just below the trees when we got to the Billups station. Old Claiborne was out filling his radiator buckets and pumping up the day's first gas sale before ever a customer showed up. He took a look at us, and just turned away. He was going to mind his business to the end. Reckon he thought that was proletarian virtue. Sure had been a pussyhunter's convenience.

—Well, I started to say to Elvira, without another word to put behind it. She just stood there.

Even those clothes of Cecil's didn't take it all away. There was still her hair, still her tits almost busting out of Cecil's shirt, and her face was just as beautiful, just as innocent as the first day I had ever seen it.

—What do you say we forget all this, she said, taking my hand.
—I never give a damn about Cecil Miley. I was just so mad at you and that chickenshit brother of yours. I had gone out and cleaned up that cottonhouse the night before. For you and me. And when you drove off with E.M. . . .

—Put it out of mind, honey. We all make mistakes.

—But I don't want to make all mine lying on my back. I love you. You know I do.

I nodded and started off toward the dirt road that led home. I was kind of light-headed by then, and it was coming over me that if I stayed, I'd try to talk her back into the shed behind the station where they had the minnow tanks. I could feel sensation in my prong again. Same old sensation. But I had to get back by the time E.M. was up and ready to move. Anyhow, I was so tired I couldn't focus my eyes anymore. Then, too, if I was to see her stripping Cecil's clothes off, I just might drop the whole idea of going. And something kept telling me that would be a big mistake.

So there I was, walking down the road half-backward, still looking at her, thinking that I might spend the rest of my life in my dreams running behind her like I had been half the night. I closed my eyes and there it was, that fine smooth ass of hers, with Cecil Miley's headlights playing on it as we seemed to move in slow motion across the widest soybean field in the world. I remembered us swimming in our own sweat in that cottonhouse that was gone now, and I remembered that first night when the lightning struck. I opened my eyes, and she was still back there by the pumps, waving.

—No, I said. —I'll be goddamned if I'm gonna lose her . . .

But even as I was starting back, almost busting into a trot, she turned and started into the station to get that bath. And running past me, the first customer of the day turned up in a cloud of country dust so thick I couldn't even see who it was.

—Fill her up in a hurry, E.M. called out to old man Claiborne. —And you, he said back at me without even bothering to look over his shoulder, —get in. Your stuff is in back, and the old man says you can skip the goodbyes.

Chapter Four

> Far under the wide-pathed earth a branch of Okeanos flows through the dark night out of the holy stream ...
> *Theogony*, 786–87

A blackened cast-iron pot boils on a gas burner in the kitchen of the Old Place. There is a fire in the hearth, and Sonny stands near it warming his hands. He looks around the large, austere room for something he remembers. There is nothing. It looks like a museum, well kept, very clean, with the appearance not of a location ripped out of past time and preserved, but rather of one reconstructed, accreted, its very pastness an artifice, a fabrication. The place has been repainted, curtains hung, the rough cypress floors planed and sanded and varnished, the log walls smoothed, filled in with some kind of putty almost the color of the logs. It is not the house his grandfather, E. M. Sentell II, had left behind.

On every wall there are photos of Omega rigs, office buildings, facilities—a refinery near Beaumont, a cracking plant in Kuwait. Photos of smiling groups of men in khaki or in business suits. E.M. II's last domicile has been converted into an occasional meeting place for E.M. III and his executives. It is filled now with valuable Early American furniture and Oriental throw rugs. E.M. II has been as completely effaced as if he had never existed, as if the family had commenced, looped somehow around him, and gone on.

Over the fireplace in a heavy, expensive frame is a grainy old photograph, blown up and retouched from a tintype, of a dark-eyed, handsome man in the uniform of the Army of the Confederate States of America. Edward Malcolm Sentell I, Major, C.S.A. Sonny stands gazing up, searching that face, seeking himself, seeking any of them. But the thin lips, the arched eyebrows, the widow's peak of glossy hair did not descend. There is a fineness, almost a feminity in the Major's countenance, a glow of bright and intelligent passion, banked but unextinguished. The race of heroes, Sonny considers. And this is the age of iron. In the Major's trace of hauteur, the cool and measured distance he had taken from that primitive camera so long ago, nothing is revealed.

Shad stands beside the pot of boiling oil, dropping in freshly caught bream battered and rolled in cornmeal, chunks of rabbit done the same way. There will be deep-fried potatoes, and hush puppies made of the remaining meal, seasoned and filled with chopping onions. Behind him, the old oak table is set, a water tumbler of whiskey at each plate. Shad smiles, staring at the pot, and yet it boils. He is relaxed now. He is back at the Beginning. He and Sonny have fished and hunted an hour or so in the bleak late winter afternoon. The room is warm, the smell of food rich and promising. He is drinking steadily. Tomorrow at dawn they will go out again. There may be a deer in the woods that cover land he used to farm. There could be a dove or two strayed north so soon in Petrie's withered fields, given over now to sorghum and corn, owned by someone whose name he has never even heard. This is how men were meant to live. Nothing is concealed.

—The old man was a fine cook, Shad says for no special reason. —So long as it was game. We ate good in season and out. Venison, bear, squirrel, turkey, duck. Hell, we ate like kings. Had a little garden out back. Field peas, snap beans, made our own pickles. There was figs, scuppernong. Hard work, good food.

—I thought you didn't get along with Pop, Sonny says.

—Wasn't anybody really got on with him. He'd had a crossed life. Ruined him. Couldn't shake off the old days. Kept trying to figure what went wrong, where they'd messed up.

—Who? What went wrong?

—Brotherhood. Brotherhood of Workers of the World. Folks called 'em the Bow-Wows ... One big union. Bunch of goddamned reds.

Sonny shakes his head. —He never said anything to me.

—Never talked about it. Old sonofabitch knew every damned radical in the country. He knew Albert Parsons. He was eighteen and standing in Chicago when they strung old Parsons up. Knew Joe Hill and Wesley Everest. Knew Heywood. They say he worked with Simon Pincus. Your granddaddy was as red as a Harvard beet.

—Why? Why would he . . . ?

—It was a hard world. He thought it was a good way. We never talked about it. What I know came from old man Claiborne, Elvira's father. Bits and pieces. Claiborne worshiped my daddy. Said he was a great American. You can reckon what that meant, what with Claiborne being a Trotskyite . . .

Sonny is bemused. —I didn't know we had stuff like that down South.

—It ain't common. Leave it to a Sentell . . .

Shad begins dipping into the seething pot with a three-pronged fork. He tosses fish and pieces of rabbit onto two plates. Then potatoes and hush puppies. They seat themselves, and Shad begins to eat, consuming whole perch in a single mouthful, spitting out the bones. Sonny is sipping whiskey, paying no attention to his food. Some family, he is thinking. A red grandfather, a blue uncle, a golden mother, a green father. And what color is he? They make neutral shoe polish, don't they?

—You reckon insanity runs in the family? Sonny asks at last.

Shad almost chokes on a fish bone. He claws it out of his mouth and takes a solid hit of whiskey.

—No, Shad replies with surprising mildness. —No, I don't reckon. Your granddaddy was sound in mind. Knew what he wanted to say. Right up to the end.

Shad sits doing what he rarely does and never wants to do. Looking backward. —He came home to North Louisiana in the 1890s. After them radicals had had their heyday, and folks had gone to hanging 'em and lynching 'em. He reckoned he'd as well farm down here as wander around the country blowing up factories and police stations, shooting railroad detectives.

—That's what he did?

—That's what they say. I believe he bought this land with money off a train robbery in Thayer, Missouri. Some says it was the last sure-enough outlaw raid on a train.

Sonny is silent, trying to piece together what Shad is saying with the old man he remembers as mild, quiet, always a trace of a smile on his face. Was the mildness banked ferocity, the quiet bitterness, the smile sardonic? He had heard from someone, probably his mother, that Grandmother Sentell had died by her own hand. He has never had the nerve to ask Shad—or the opportunity to ask his father. Perhaps they are all mad, male and female alike. Their thoughts are not like others' thoughts.

Outside, the sun is down, the air chill. But Sonny looks out the window into the yellow gloom before dark. The trees are etched against the sky in soft tan ink, each branch stark and alone. Who knows? Perhaps in madness is the unity of generations. Sonny smiles to himself. He feels secure here. This is his place, too. Amidst ghosts he has hardly been introduced to: a titanic great-grandfather, a fierce and malevolent grandfather, all the other chthonic kinsmen who haunt this old ground. The phone rings, but neither of them pays it any mind. Shad pushes the whiskey bottle toward him, and sighs. He is now, at long last, somewhat drunk.

—I expect, by his lights, your granddaddy was a good man.

—Except he robbed trains. And blew up factories.

—It was after the Confederate War. Now ain't then. He reckoned he had cause . . .

Shad seems to be musing to himself, but that is all right. Because Sonny is into himself, too—conjuring up the last time he had been here, at the Old Place. The day of Pop's funeral.

It had been very hot, and the church was stifling. There were old-fashioned ceiling fans in the church. Sonny watched the wooden blades spinning until he felt himself falling away from the front pew into some other place.

The minister droned on for a long while. He was uncomfortable preaching this funeral for a man who never stepped inside the Paul's Mission Baptist Church. There had been one number from a small choir. The church was almost full. A handful of neighbors were there. Old Claiborne, himself in search of a grave. Petrie, dried up, pert as a bird, unmoved but curious at a death that was not his. The rest were Omega Oil officials and flunkies from Shreveport, Dallas, Houston, Lake Charles, Tulsa. E. M. was not there. Shad sat beside Sonny, holding his hand loosely.

Afterward, he remembers standing with his mother as the coffin was brought to the grave site out behind the cabin where other Sentells lay buried, though none had been for many years. The coffin had been carried by a ragtag of Omega people, land men and clerks, minor executives commandeered by phone. Men whom E. M. Sentell II had never known, for whom he would have had nothing but contempt. Sonny remembers watching, tearless, as the plain coffin was lowered into the ground, his mother on one side, his uncle on the other. Suddenly his father had appeared on the far side of the grave, his eyes red and glaring —eyes fixed not on the preacher or the coffin, but on them.

When the preacher was done, Shad had taken a shovel from an old black man standing a little behind the mourners. He pushed it into the moist reddish soil and slowly turned a spadeful into the grave. E.M. III, his face working with rage and pain, stared over at Shad. His voice shook with hatred.

—Right. Use that shovel. Cover him up. You dug his grave for him, didn't you?

Shad had stared back at him for a long moment, his own emotions unreadable. Then he lifted his shovel and tossed the remaining soil into E.M.'s face, over his white linen suit. E.M. had jumped across the grave, trying to grapple with Shad, but Shad had dropped back, and batted E.M. across the shoulder with the shovel almost casually. E.M. III had lost his footing and fallen backward. Into the open grave. Sonny still remembers the hollow sound, the thrill of horror. His father was standing on his grandfather's corpse.

Shad had looked down into the grave, the slightest of amused smiles on his lips. E.M. III struggled for a footing, for a handhold in the soft dirt by which he could pull himself out. His motions were frenzied, crazed—as if he felt himself being held, drawn down into the death upon which he stood, from which he could find no escape. Shad offered him no help. The others seemed frozen, caught beyond response by the incredible character of the thing. Is this how funerals are to conclude? What does propriety require when one brother knocks the other into their father's grave? Who is to speak, who act?

—You coming out of there, Eddie? Or do you want me to just fill you in?

At last the minister had leaned down and helped E.M. III raise himself from the pit, his clothes filthy from his sojourn with the dead. Sonny had watched as his father stumbled away, his hired help following like the elongated tail of a Chinese New Year's dragon. Sonny remembers how close he had come to laughing. He remembers as well his mother's quick, involuntary sign of the cross. She had not looked down at Sonny, hence had not seen his furtive grin. But Shad had seen. Their eyes had met, their expressions almost identical.

After the Omega contingent vanished into limousines up at the house, Shad had turned to the preacher.

—You got anything else to say, Parson, or can I go ahead and close up this hole?

The minister had shaken his head. There was nothing more. Shad and two black men began shoveling sandy loam into the grave. Sonny had stood there as if it were his part to bear witness to the burial itself as Shad, sweat pouring down his face, threw shovel after shovel full of dirt down there to cover Pop, to efface the depth where Sonny had seen his father standing, struggling. Then, almost violently, his mother had pulled him away.

They had gone back to the house then, Sonny and his mother. There was little there beyond the necessities of a country life. Fishing gear, a Winchester Model 94. A shoebox with old photos. One of men standing together near what appeared to be a mine shaft. Short, foreign-looking men for the most part, and E.M. Sentell II standing with them, towering above them in height, his own bright, camera-directed smile in utter contrast to the hard, angry expressions of the swarthy men around him. Along with the photos were badges, a red-covered songbook, and a moldering handwritten sheet in crabbed script which began: The propertied class and the working class have nothing in common.

—Is there anything you want to take? To remember him by, his mother had asked, obviously anxious to leave, to put the cabin, even the memory of it, behind her. She had come only because she was married to one of the old man's sons. And because, despite her transfiguration from Grand Café to grande dame, she could find no way by which she might turn away from so near an obligation. But now it was done. Now she would never have to come out here to this miserable barren wilderness again. Then Shad had come in, covered with grime, the shovel still in his hand.

—I want this, Sonny had said, taking the old Winchester in his small hands.

Then they were gone, driving in the darkness back to Shreveport along the tree-lined length of Highway 80. He had played games in his mind, desperate scrapes in which the Winchester had been the difference between survival and death. But he could not quite escape remembrance of the grave, the coffin, Shad's shovel, or his father's frenzied face.

I remember that night when we got home, I was so tired I could hardly make my way upstairs, dragging my Winchester behind me. But I had to. Because my father was there before us. As we came into the foyer of the house on Line Avenue, I heard him call my mother's name sharply, angrily. I remember as I climbed the carpeted stairs, step by immense step, that I had a feeling of dread. It was not just the novelty of my father's being in the house where he spent almost no time at all. Rather it referred back to that strange, malignant look he had cast upon the three of us—me, Mother, Shad, at the funeral. As if we were his deadly enemies. Even as a small boy, I could sense that.

I reached my room and stepped inside. I did not turn on the lights, because I was captivated by the play of light and shadow on the walls, the ceiling. They were covered with a vast pattern of eddying light reflected from the surface of the swimming pool down below. It was like stepping into some strange grotto beneath the sea. The gardener had trimmed away branches of a magnolia outside my room, and suddenly I found myself in a different place. I shut the door behind me, closing out the ordinary world. The balcony windows above the pool were open, and a breeze was blowing in from the west, troubling the curtains, adding to the play of shadow and light. I smiled and lifted my arms, tired as I was. I was swimming deep in the sea, yet I could breathe. I turned and turned, moving toward my bed lying at the bottom of that green and blue mirage. I carried my rifle with me. It was no ordinary rifle, but one which could be used deep beneath the waves. Should there be some serpent awaiting me amidst deep currents there. I lay on the bed in reverie, creating, maintaining, destroying mythical worlds one after another until their human voices down below woke me, pulled me from my depths into theirs.

—Goddammit, I heard my father say, —are you going to talk or not?

The sound of water splashing, laughter. Was it the imaginary water around me, or the real water in the pool outside?

—No, I heard her say. —I don't think so.

—... damn you... demand... tell me. You know... the old man said? Dying... wouldn't go without... I demand...

—Oh, Eddie, really. Demand me nothing. What you know, you know.

I tried to sleep then, as if my hearing might somehow influence whatever was happening down there. But I could not. I stared up at the shimmering patterns on my ceiling, and it seemed as if the fleeting shadows reflected the words, the emotions playing out there, skewed and troubled, twisting on my walls.

As they argued, I found myself on the small balcony outside my room, looking down into the courtyard below. Down there, I saw my father in a fresh white suit. He was slim, tanned, his white hair shimmering against the dense background of banana and rubber trees that he had spent thousands to have planted. The lights were muted, their soft beams scattered across the water as their reflections danced across the ceiling of my room.

Lord, I am seeing all this in retrospect—not, surely, as I saw it then. What I saw is tempered, refurbished, crafted by what I know now. Because I could not have known, huddled on the small balcony outside my room, that I was witnessing the end of my family. Not then. It was simply an unpleasant evening. Among other unpleasant evenings.

—Mary Clare . . .

Then the sound of her diving into the pool at the deep end where the shadows obscured everything, and the water's surface shivering as my mother's body penetrated it. Then she swam into the light, rose from the pool, and I saw that she was nude. She shook water from her hair like drops of gold falling back into the water at her feet and moved toward my father. It seemed that he retreated from her—as if he could not bear that vision, or as if she carried with her a curse or a doom. But she walked along the edge of the pool balanced, unutterably graceful, as he moved backward into the shadows.

—All right, Eddie. What is it you want to know? Or say? What did your loving father tell you teetering on the edge of the grave? If there's something you simply have to know, I'll tell you. If I know. You don't have to depend on the dead. But don't ask unless you really want to know . . .

She was not looking at him. Rather she was watching her small feet negotiating the narrow rim of the pool. She was absorbed in it, a smile on her lips, her body taut, poised, delicate, and strong.

—I know already . . . with him, weren't . . . ? When . . .

I could not make out his words. They seemed to come from the darkness in pulses, some loud, some lost in the shadows. My mother stared at him, at where he must have been standing. Then she picked up her drink from the pool's edge, sipped it.

—Are you really asking me? Or do you just want . . . details?

She had moved around the pool then, through a cluster of lamps that seemed to turn her body into pure light. I think I held my breath to see her that way. I cannot remember thinking anything, but I remember sharply what I felt. I was seeing not mother, but woman, an abstraction as chaste and distant from the world of flesh and blood as a Mozart sonata. She turned smiling back toward my father, poised at the edge of the light, raising her arms slowly above her head like a ballerina.

—Goddamn you . . .

—No. You're the one who's damned. You did it to yourself. I knew you would.

— . . . hell is . . . supposed to mean?

I couldn't see her then. She had passed into the shadows once more, and now both their voices were disembodied. Only the motion of the pool's surface and its echoes behind me were visible.

—You went too far from me, she almost whispered. —All the way to Paris . . .

My father moved into the light from the lamps where she had stood a moment before. But the light broke on him, refracted in all its colors, harsh and unreal from his stark white suit. It made him look as if he were on fire, dissolving before my eyes.

— . . . think . . . let it stay this way? . . . let anyone . . . to me?

She laughed out of the darkness. Not in triumph, surely not in humor. —It *is* that way. Whichever way it is. There's nothing to be done. *If* there's anything that something should be done about . . .

He remained there in the light, glistening, coruscating, bursting into new patches of colored flame as a rising wind moved across the pool. I remember wondering absently if he would throw himself into the shadows to find her. I knew he would not. He would never do that. I don't know why I knew. I wished he would. I wanted to see him dive into the water, swim into the darkness and fetch her back, naked, streaming water and light in his arms. That would make everything all right. Surely in that soft rich light, doing whatever epic thing parents do, surely that would stop the quarreling, the pain.

But my father didn't move. At last his voice came back to him, almost as low, as breathy as hers. But graceless, cruel—as if he had found his own true voice at last.

—... never hear... end of this, he grated.

—No, I heard her say softly. —I'm sure I won't.

—... see you both dead... in hell...

—Go away, Eddie, she said wearily out of the darkness. —You're not going to do anything. You know what he'd do if you even thought about it... And there's Sonny...

My father said something else, short, brutal, something I could not make out at all.

—Let it go, my mother said, not quite beseechingly. —It's not worth thinking about anymore. Leave me if you want to, but let it go.

—... if it takes a thousand years, he began, moving back along the edge of the pool opposite her shadow.

—We haven't got a thousand years. Thank God...

I saw him vanish then, and a moment later the grillwork gate slammed shut, and all there was left to hear was the lapping water of the pool.

—Goodbye, Eddie, I heard my mother say out of the shadows in a tone somewhere between sadness and relief.

She swam slowly into the light then, leaving behind her a trail of roiled water rippling off her body, a river-ocean which sparkled like a nascent galaxy. She lay against the side of the pool, her long tanned legs moving slowly in the water, her breasts rising and falling, bathed by the water, by the light-spiked reflections and the blue-green shadows below, each motion of her ankles creating a trail of stars that glimmered and whirled and died away, ephemeral universes of water and shadow and light.

On the balcony above, I turned and saw the pool reconstructed waterless on the ceiling of my room. I took a deep breath and plunged into the coolness of my pillows, tranced still by her beauty, by his pain and departure. But the blue-green darkness surrounded me, and soon I was asleep.

It must have been much later when I awoke to find that she was in my bed, still nude, her body chill from late night in the pool. There was water on her cheeks, and in the silence she clung to me and kissed me again and again as if we were both lost children wandering the bottom of the seas.

This time, when sleep came upon me once more, I dreamed that I stood beside her, high in the masts of a great ship standing out across the water into the dark whirling recesses of a towering storm amidst the terrors and triumphs of the Gulf.

She sits in the music room with a Remy Martin in her hand. A double. It has been a boring evening. Dinner was boring. The opera had been boring. *The Damnation of Faust.* Wordy, pretentious, full of fustian and vainglory. Everyone is specifically and concretely damned. It is tedious to celebrate the fact in art. It has been done successfully only once. She has not heard *Don Giovanni* in years. That doesn't matter. She knows it by heart.

She listens to Roland singing lieder at the piano. She would have preferred Mahler. Roland cannot sing Mahler. Therefore he sings Schubert. Something about one who wanders high in the mountains. He will surely meet a maiden in a pasture. Her mind is the wanderer. It goes by way of Fontainebleau to Paris. After the breakup, she and Sonny had lived there for almost two years. It had been diverting at first. So many old dreams to realize, and so easily managed with Omega Oil money and connections. She had been escorted everywhere by young men associated in one way or another with the arts. They had been, on the whole, delightful. And when they had made what perhaps they had supposed to be the obligatory overtures to seduction, she had enjoyed each parley as participant and spectator as well. A very few she had accepted. Not so much for the renewal of sexual excitement but because she had never managed to put away the exquisite pleasure derived from seeing the expression on men's faces when she stood or lay nude before them. Awe, something close to what Venus must have experienced when she lowered her veil, dropped her robes, and allowed a mortal to view the divine center of love. She could not help it. She had no need to help it. The part of her life that would have forbidden it was past.

But she had never been seduced in Paris. She had been seduced only once in her life, she considers. And she had not been seduced then, either. It was something else. It was what Eddie had done to her. Or not done for her. Theirs would be a marvelous double biography. Suggested title: *We Have Everything We Could Possibly Want*, or *Smothering Together*.

She laughs aloud, and Roland stops in the midst of a particularly turgid passage:

Will kein Gott auf Erden sein
Sind wir selber Götter . . .

Her German is atrocious. German is atrocious. It cannot mean what she thinks it means.

—Did I skip a repeat, darling? Roland wants to know.

Most emphatically not. Roland would never skip a repeat.

—No, I'm so sorry. My mind wandered. I was thinking of . . . something else.

Roland smiles and returns to his song. Marie-Claire muses grimly that it is a measure of Shreveport culture that an engineer from Swabia is the most interesting man in town. It occurs to her that when he leaves, in late summer, perhaps she should import an Italian chauffeur with a decent tenor voice. Perhaps a Frenchman with a contemptuous little laugh. Emphatically not an Englishman. They go native almost immediately in North Louisiana. They sense the continuity beneath the apparent dissimilarity between Caddo Parish and the Counties. They come to lust after plantations and dogs, servants and dinner dances at the country club.

Roland has finished. He turns from the piano with that smile she is coming to loathe.

—A little soft music of a popular sort, he suggests, and begins manhandling the radio, moving from station to station, finding for the most part niggers howling and amplified guitars out to disable the transmitter. At last he comes across an oasis of strings inhabited by Cole Porter.

You'd be so easy to love,
So easy to idolize, all others above . . .

Marie-Claire had always been that, had always known it, and it had done her no good at all. Not even in Paris. Men, wherever you might find them, of whatever condition, seemed bent on ruining things. There were no exceptions. None realized that the essence of true romance is its nonconsummation.

— . . . fire rages unabated on the Omega Oil Okeanos rig some thirty miles off the Louisiana shore. The Coast Guard has called off rescue operations this afternoon, saying that there was little chance of . . .

—You don't want to hear that, dearest, Roland whispers, reaching for the dial.

—No . . . don't . . .

— . . . Company officials said today that operations to bring the inferno under control will begin at once under the direction of S. S. Sentell, one of the chief stockholders of Omega, and best known as one of a handful of international industry troubleshooters specializing in major well blowouts. Listeners may remember the series of fires in Indonesian fields last year that Sentell . . .

—He does get publicity, doesn't he?
—He also makes a great deal of money for Omega. Do you know what they paid us to send him to Djakarta?
—I have no idea.
—A million two. Plus bonus when complete. Plus, as I understand it, a mansion on an island while he was there. And all the lovely Asian maidens he could consume.

Roland laughs. —I've heard he's . . . Oh, what's the word?
—Monstrous.
—I had in mind *formidable*.
They laugh. The radio music resumes.

I cover the waterfront . . .
I'm watching the sea . . .

—Do you suppose there might be another brandy, Roland?
Roland looks at her curiously. —In this place? There is always another. And another after that. Have we ever had to send out for anything?
—No. I think that's depressing.
—I think it's . . . how do you say . . . ?
—Formidable?
Roland laughs, brings two brandies, and sits beside her.
—I wonder if I might meet him.
—Who?
—S. S. Sentell. To have worked in the company and not to know him . . .
—That wouldn't be fun, Roland.
—Oh?
—Shad Sentell is . . . He's a barbarian.
—I've heard it said that barbarian is an honorable name.
—Then Shad has ruined it. Anyhow, he really doesn't care for . . .
—Germans? He fought . . .
—Japanese, actually. He killed vast numbers of them.
—Of course. Didn't everyone? Millions of Germans. Billions of Japanese . . .

Marie-Claire can hardly contain her smile.

—You don't understand, darling. You really don't. Shad Sentell is not . . . an American.

—I thought he was born in . . .

—He is a Sentell. From the Louisiana-Texas border. He is a Southerner. He is an extremely mean drunkard who is absolutely and totally proficient with all sorts of weapons, including hand axes and singletrees. I have no idea how many decorations he won overseas, because the day he came home he was in a marine private's uniform and all the medals were in a Crisco can in his footlocker. We heard later that he'd been a sergeant-major until he reached California. It seems he thought the Pacific campaign included San Francisco. He did awful things there. Only his medals bought him out of it. If he were to tell you that he killed a thousand Japanese, it's certain to be true within five or ten, and if you doubt it, he'd as soon kill you as not.

Roland falls into Teutonic meditation.

—This is so?

—This is indubitably so, darling. The man is an uncontrolled sadist. With money enough to indulge his appetites . . .

—There are laws . . .

—Not for him. He knows every police officer and sheriff's deputy for a hundred miles around by his first name. I think they all receive whiskey from him every Christmas. Or is it every time they shoot someone?

—Something must be . . . Someone . . .

—Nothing and no one.

Roland looks dubious. —I think you don't like him. Because of the separation. He sided with his brother, naturally.

—I detest him. But no. Shad observed that the only thing wrong with the marriage was that, in his phrase, a human woman had married a legal person.

—He and Mr E. M. Sentell do not . . . comport?

Marie-Claire smiles, sips her brandy. —They have not, as you put it, comported since . . . 1946. And they comported very badly before that.

—Such a family . . .

—It could be worse.

Roland laughs, stretches. —At the office, they talk about his women.

Marie-Claire is not amused. —Then they have a great deal to

talk about. On second thought, they'd do well not to talk about their betters at all.

—Gossip, you know. Harmless stuff. Someone was at the Florentine Club ...

—Oh, that. Sweet Christ, it is there anyone in Shreveport who wasn't? I thought they had a fire code.

Roland is gleeful. There is in him a germ of disarray, a certain taste for disorder.

—You must have heard ...

—I heard nothing, no details. I asked for none. I simply agreed when Eddie had him restrained, put in Shady Grove. He was wretchedly, preposterously drunk.

—This man's wife ...

—Please ...

—Out in the courtyard, among the shrubs ...

—Roland, really ...

—They came upon them ...

She rises, walks over into the music.

... I concentrate on you ...

—I don't want to hear it, can't you understand that?

The music stops, and Marie-Claire hears herself almost screaming. Her voice trails off. The music begins again. She does not turn back toward him.

... got you under my skin ...
... got you deep in the heart of me ...

—It's not amusing. Years of it, a lifetime of it ...

Roland looks mildly sympathetic, shrugs. —I'm sorry, darling. The man is a legend ...

—The man is a beast.

—Those things are not mutually exclusive.

Marie-Claire discovers that she has an awful headache. What is wrong with him this evening?

—Legend ... Oh, my God ... You don't know ... how he looks at a woman. How he can make any woman indecent ... I mean, feel indecent.

Roland's face darkens. —He did that to you?

The picture she recalls is of herself turning toward the lunch counter in the café to find those green eyes lapping back and

forth across her, divesting her, enjoying her, touching, tasting, sniffing, listening, probing, stroking . . .
 —No. Of course not. I was . . .
 —His brother's wife.
 —Yes.
 —But they hated one another. Wouldn't it . . .
 —That doesn't matter. It couldn't matter. Anyhow, the Sentells don't . . . They don't care about women . . .

She remembers the first time she had seen him. At the Grand Café. Turning from the hot griddle with a plate of home fries, two burgers, nix the pix, heavy onions, and a bowl of chili, she had been met—no, assaulted—by a pair of green eyes of such depth and character that for the smallest fraction of a second she had believed she was looking into the eyes of a wolf or some other animal inexplicably sitting on a stool, poised now to leap at her if she should move wrongly, perhaps move at all.
 —What you got there, honey? Shad had said.
 —H-home fries . . .
 —Naw . . . not the damned food . . .
His look frightened her, embarrassed her. It was as if they were sharing some intimacy even as others watched, as if there were something a man could do to a woman without anyone else being aware of it. As if he possessed an invisible hand which he could slide under her skirt and fondle her, she helpless to avoid it, with nothing tangible to cry out about.
 She had quickly served her customer and walked to the back. She had worked in the café for a couple of years. She was not afraid of men. She liked men. She liked the oil field workers. They were rough, sometimes ill-tempered, but not like that. Not like him. Her hands were trembling. She felt sick at the stomach. Effie, who owned the Grand Café, had come back to check on her, to see what was wrong. She was too shaken to lie.
 —Him? Why, honey, that's Shad Sentell. That's Eddie's brother. You ain't met him? Eddie just brung him from Greenwood, Louisiana. To help drill over by Peterson's place. Him and Eddie are gonna be rich one of these days. I seen all kinds. They're the kind.
 —They way he looks at a woman . . .
 —Yeah, Effie had said with a grin missing two teeth. —Don't you just love it?

Roland smiles with perfect teeth. —Come, now. They say he adores women ...

—But they don't *matter* to him.

—Then the legend is a lie?

—No, listen ... Anything they say about him is true ... Almost anything ...

Marie-Claire falls silent. The picture now is of a party decades ago. The house on Line Avenue is new. On the terrace which sweeps down from the swimming pool, Chinese lanterns are hung. There are white linen tablecloths, a string quartet. They are playing Mozart K. 458. *The Hunt*. Well-dressed people mix, talking softly, laughing. It is early evening, and she is very happy. There is a lovely buffet supper to follow cocktails. Then the quartet will be augmented. There will be dancing. Only two things mar her delight. E.M. has refused to wear ordinary shoes. He does not own any. He insists on wearing his jet-black handmade Justins. And, of course, his Palm Beach suit. Worse than that, Shad is in town. He is at the party. Somewhere.

—Why did you have to ask him, Eddie?

—He's my brother.

—I'd sooner have a box of scorpions loose on the terrace.

—You should have let me know. I'd have had a mess flown in from Tulsa.

—It's not as if youall were really close.

—We're close enough, I'm not going to insult him. Whether you believe it or not, any Sentell there is, is good enough for these guests of yours.

They are her guests. An oil man or two, but mostly people she has met since moving to Shreveport while the house was being built. Through the Women's Department Club, the Little Theatre, the Country Club. Really nice people. Cultivated. With Shad loose among such people, all one could hope to do was limit the damage. She had seen him talking to one of the executives of the First National Bank a little while ago. The subject had been the finer points of gelding stallions. Earlier, he and one of the oil men had been exchanging anecdotes about unnatural acts between men and various species of domestic animals. That is supportable, she thought, her neck and shoulders tight. Better he talk chickengeeking with oil-field trash. So long as he stays away from the women.

What is insupportable is the prospect that, as the evening wears on, Shad will begin to carry a bottle of Jim Beam and a glass around with him as he moves from group to group, regaling her guests with quaint stories of their early days—including her own sterling qualities as a waitress and short-order cook. He has never done this to her, but, when irritated, he has suggested it as an amusing topic for conversation.

And one thing more: that way he has of staring at attractive women. There can be no question whatever of what he has in mind . . . only of precisely how he would require that she do it. Marie-Claire has never quite managed to get past that stare. Whenever circumstances require that they talk, she feels his eyes on her in such a way that she reddens as if he were the sun. His look makes her feel as if he has calculated to the moment when he will have her—not by force or even suggestion, but by her own failed will, her spiritual exhaustion in trying to make it not happen, not be pulled into the ravenous aegis of those eyes in that slab of a face, drawn down under that thick body. She wonders if other women feel this chill, this sense of dread.

Then she sees him coming out onto the terrace. He has a bottle of whiskey in hand. But he also has a teacup. It is gross, but not worth going to E.M. about. E.M. would smile at her discomfiture and suggest that she came back when Shad becomes loudly obscene or is in the process of whipping the ass of one of her art-loving guests. He is not going to tell any man how to drink—least of all Shad. Now, if she *really* wants a disaster . . .

She notices that Shad is talking to Lucy Ryan. Of course. Who else? Wife of a college professor who is active in local musical circles, enamored of the recorder. Lucy is young, pretty, vulnerable—and probably easily shocked. Marie-Claire passes them, smiling, greeting newcomers. Listening.

—Well, sure it's dangerous. But that's all right. You got control. For right then, you own your life . . .

—I don't understand.

—Sure you do. When you're right in the middle of one of them blowouts, you sure as hell don't worry about getting hit by a trolley or choking on bacon . . . It's you and that rig and the gas and oil spewing up like a river out of where it's been for a hundred million years . . .

—Oh . . .

—I'll tell you something if you promise not to laugh, Lucy.
—I wouldn't laugh.
—It's . . . like fighting a dragon. Like in the old days. You put on your armor, and it's one-on-one with the biggest meanest snake in the world . . .
—I think I see . . .
—Sure you do. This one's not flesh and blood. It's like a spirit . . . but you can hear it screaming up out of the ground, and you can feel it, smell it. One mistake, it's gonna kill you by fire. Just like the old days . . .

Lucy's eyes are wide. For some reason quite beyond Marie-Claire's comprehension, she seems to be enjoying Shad's conversation.

—The most alive you can be is . . . throwing your old life away. Every time I go into the fire, I come out new . . .

Absolute tripe, Marie-Claire thinks, moving away. He is utterly unchanged by those risks he takes every day. It will take killing him to make him new. And one day that will surely happen. He will be blown to hell. The dragon always wins.

Later, she finds herself with a headache brought on as much by waiting for Shad to decide what sort of enormity he will perpetrate as by the long day's preparations for the party. She goes upstairs for an aspirin. As she starts back down, she seems to hear a muffled gasp from one of the guest rooms overlooking the terrace and the pool. She pauses outside, listening. Someone is inside. She can hear harsh breathing, rustling sounds as if there were a struggle going on. If it is a burglary . . . She is about to run down the back stairway for E.M. when she hears:

—Oh . . . don't stop . . . please . . .
—I never stop, honey . . .

Without thinking, she opens the door to the guest room. And finds herself in semidarkness, tones of gray, green, and ultramarine. The walls and ceiling are stamped with medallions of light and shadow reflected from the pool below. There on the bed are Shad and Lucy Ryan. His pants are off, her dress up from the bottom, down from the top. Her bra and panties are strewn across a chair, her shoes on the floor. For an instant Marie-Claire is convinced that he is raping her, raping Lucy Ryan, taking her brutally against her will. She realizes just as quickly that it is not so, because she can see Lucy's body moving rhythmically under him, hear her breath short, unbelievable words coming from her parted lips as she throws her life away, plunging with the dragon-slayer.

    Marie-Claire stands tranced, unable to avert her eyes. Is it a sudden current of air from the open door? Something makes him turn, and he sees her there in the doorway, outlined against a soft hall light. His eyes seem to glow in the darkness as he stares at her. She cannot tell if he recognizes her or not, but she hears his rough breathing almost as if it were a communication. He is swimming there in the depth of the room, his bulk thrusting downward, downward into Lucy's slender white body, pounding her into climax, Marie-Claire as transfixed as she. His eyes are still upon her, and she becomes giddy, as if she were being pulled into the room to wait her turn. Beneath him, Lucy croons, her voice ragged as his breathing.

    —Now... Now... Now... Stick me, shove it all the way in ... Oh, sweet Jesus, don't let it stop... ever...

—Marie-Claire...?
—Yes...?
—You seem... hypnotized.
—No ... I think ... I'm just very tired. I seem to have a headache.
—Of course. Roland smiles. —Bed...?

    She closes her eyes, shakes her head. If he touches her, if he insists, she is going to be violently ill. She feels the brandy glass held so tightly in her hand that her fingerprints must be etched into it.

—Not tonight, darling...
—Perhaps it will... relax you.

    You stupid ass. That's not what it's about, is it? It isn't recreational, she thinks. No, it's a blood sport. It should always take place on a burning platform in that border stream, that Gulf at the end of the world. Or down below, in the abysm and depth whence the river-ocean rises only to turn back upon itself in that rhythm she remembers so well.

    —Call me tomorrow, Roland. We have to decide about Mardi Gras. I'll have to stay here till we locate Shad. The fire on Okeanos Number One... Things I have to do...

    Roland's smile fades. He is anxious to compare Mardi Gras with *Oktoberfest*, with *Fasching*. —These invitations to the Ball of Rex... they are difficult to obtain...

—I think that's so.
—Mr E. M. Sentell sent them to me. You're sure . . . ?
—I'll think about it.
—If that's what you want . . .
—It is, darling.
—If you change your mind . . .
—Of course.

She avoids his kiss, nods to his bow, and he is gone. Almost at once, her headache eases. She turns off the radio, puts a record on the stereo without even looking. She is across the room pouring soda into her brandy when the prelude to the third act of *Lohengrin* breaks over her like an icy waterfall.

She falls back and sips her last drink. She thinks it will be her last drink. Has it taken her so long to discover that somehow the fabric of reality is reversed? That love is always couched in violence—that nothing is more gentle, reserved, undemanding than the stillness of death?

Marie-Claire wants to think farther, to see if she can tell the difference at least along the tempo of her pulses. But it will have to wait. There is still Okeanos to attend to. Still Shad Sentell to find. She picks up the phone, dials, and listens to the distant purring, like the waves of an isolate sea lost on an anonymous shore, over and over again.

Chapter Five

> ... Okeanos, which flows round in a circle ...
> *Phaedo*, 112, E61

Sonny snaps out of his reverie as the phone rings again. Shad is washing dishes, whistling. Sonny picks up the phone. Before he can say anything, he hears her voice.
—Sonny ...'
—No. Wrong number. We don't want any.
He hangs up.
—Some silly sonafabitch selling aluminium siding, Shad mutters.
—No. Mother.
—Ummm.
—I should have let it ring. Now she knows we're here.
—All right. She knows.
—What'll she do?
—Call your daddy. Tell him we're out here fucking off whilst Okeanos is losing a hundred thousand a day.
—And he'll call the sheriff's office, and ...
—Nope. If I go back into Shady Grove, that's everybody's ass.
Shad grins beatifically. —Lord, it's good to be needed, ain't it?
Then his mood changes. —No, your old man is gonna give me rope. He knows what I know. Sooner or later, old Okeanos and me has got to get together.
—You're going out there?
—That's what I do for a living.
—You haven't needed to make a living since before I was born.
—Bullshit. A living ain't just money. It's what you *do*.
—If you're going ...
—Why not just up and go? Hell, even E.M. don't expect that. That miserable sonofabitch knows I'm ...

Shad's voice trails off. He does not usually state his opinion of his brother so frankly before Sonny.

—Why do you hate each other so much? Sonny asks. It is perhaps his most fundamental question. He has asked it *sub silentio* for years.

Shad looks surprised. —I don't hate him. How could I? He's my brother. He's sorry as sin, and crooked as a corkscrew . . . but I don't hate him.

Sonny looks puzzled. —Does he hate you?

Shad nods, his eyes not meeting Sonny's. —Yeah, he says. —He hates me.

—Why?

—None of your goddamned business, Shad barks. Then his expression and his voice soften. —Things happen in families, he says vaguely.

—Did it have to do with . . . how grandpa died? That horse you got him?

Shad reaches for his glass, throws back a little of it. —Your father never gave a damn about the old man. He just used that . . .

Shad shakes his head. —Never mind. Skip it. It's all done and buried. Don't never open up a grave, boy. It's nothing down there for the living . . .

Shad breaks off. After a second, Sonny knows why. There is the sound of an engine approaching.

They walk out the back door together and stand watching the vehicle come up the road out of the woods. It is an ancient car of indistinguishable vintage, something close to olive drab in color, its chrome and trim all vanished with the years. There are no hubcaps, no bumpers, no grille, and no trunk lid. The car stops ten or fifteen yards from the house. A little too far to seem sociable. They cannot make out who is inside because of the cracked and clouded windows.

—You want to fetch me that shotgun, Sonny?

He doesn't, but he does. He comes back quickly with the gun held unobtrusively by his side. They stand silent, watching. Sounds come from the car as if a struggle were going on inside.

—Maybe they're fighting to see who gets the first shot at you, Sonny observes.

—Then they're fighting to find out who sees Jesus first. Shad grins. —Gimme that thing

Shad takes the shotgun from Sonny and, without warning, lets go a round over the top of the car. A pellet or two rattles off the scarred and dented body. The hurly-burly inside ceases abruptly, then the driver's door seems to blow open as if from an explosion inside. Shad casually lets the barrel of the gun drift down to cover the opening as Elvira climbs out. She kicks the door and turns toward them.

—Sonofabitch embarrasses me every goddamned time I want to go someplace, she grumbles. —And what the hell you shooting at folks about?

As Elvira walks toward them, Sonny notices that Shad has not lowered the gun. It still covers the open door, which lies in darkness.

—Hello, 'Vira, Shad says. —Tell that dried-up little sonofabitch to come out of there.

—He ain't in there, Elvira replies. —He's back at the station. In bed with a bad headache. What did you expect?

She looks at Sonny with amusement. —Lord knows youall breed true. This boy is a Sentell. He's better-looking than E.M. and meaner than you.

—Who's in the car? Shad asks mildly.

Elvira looks at him strangely. —How do you know there's anybody in that car? Vibrations? You feeling something?

—Yeah, Shad says testily. —I feel like putting a charge of shot through that wreck, window to window, in about five seconds if Cecil don't show hisself with empty hands and a big smile.

—Haw, Elvira croaks triumphantly. —You got no powers.

—Naw, Shad replies slyly. —But I got a shotgun.

—Well, I got a mother's rights on *my* side. Fuck shotguns.

—Mo*ther*, a voice from the car moans.

Shad's gun slips away as a figure climbs from the car, frowning. It is a girl or a young woman. Shad and Sonny check her out. Sonny catches his breath. Shad's eyebrows rise and he shakes his head.

—I see it, but I don't believe it. A goddamn carbon copy . . .

—Would you please watch your language, mister, the apparition says, stepping close to Shad, fixing him with Elvira's very eyes, speaking in her voice. Shad is speechless. Elvira watches, savoring the moment.

—Missy, this is Mr Samuel Shadrach Sentell. The one I've told you about. Shad, this here is Melissa.

—Pleased to meet you, Melissa says, her eyes fixed on Shad, studying him at least as intensely as he is studying her.

—And over there's his nephew, Elvira goes on. —I don't know what they call him.

—Edward Malcolm Sentell, Sonny says with pained dignity. No one looks at him. It doesn't matter. There is a mysterious fragrance in the air. He feels light-headed.

She is perhaps five-seven, with a thick mane of tawny hair somewhere near blonde with highlights of a peculiar and intriguing gunmetal color shot through it. She is long-waisted, wearing a loose-fitting halter curving around her breasts and shorts that appear painted on her thighs and hips. Sonny feels that old serpent rising. It is easy to see that Elvira and Melissa bear a striking resemblance to one another. Here, in the soft diffused light that falls through leafless branches, they look like identical twin sisters. If Melissa is the ultimate appetizer, Elvira would make the quintessential main course. Sonny shivers to discover the depths and shoals of his own depravity. What he wants is mother and daughter in bed together. Right now. His mind ranges quickly over the possible combinations as Shad invites them into the house.

—We got a little whiskey in there . . .

—I'm a Christian, sir, Melissa says. Sonny considers that he would like to make his pecker her religion.

—That's all right, little lady, Shad says without changing expression. —We're gonna let you in anyhow on account of your momma.

Melissa looks puzzled. Elvira laughs. Sonny comes up beside Melissa, takes her arm. She turns her cool, encompassing stare on him. Can she be reading his mind, seeing her own nude body tied to a brass bed, bra awry, panties torn, legs apart as Sonny . . .

—We've got coffee, and maybe some Cokes, Sonny says in his blandest manner.

—That will be fine, Melissa says. As she turns to face Sonny, she leans over to knock some clinging dirt from her high-heeled sandals. One strap of her halter slips down a little, and Sonny looks into the upper story of paradise.

Shad and Elvira precede them into the house. Melissa looks after them with a frown.

—Something wrong, Melissa?
—It's Missy. Nobody calls me Melissa. And you got it. What's wrong is, I feel like a fool.
—What?'
—I'm about to freeze to death. In these . . .

Sonny pushes her inside, grins like an imbecile, and closes the door. Can she know how often she has already been possessed in the dim convoluted reptilian recesses of his mind? Down there, she has been ruined utterly. She will be no good for anyone else. Missy shivers, and Sonny guides her into the kitchen.

—Anyhow, it's embarrassing, she says. —Whoever heard of dressing like this in the wintertime?
—Coffee? Sonny asks.
—All right.

He spoons some CDM into the drip pot while water heats on the stove. He is also trying to think of something he can say to her that will not drive her screaming from the room. She sits down near the window, looking outside into the chill darkness. When she crosses her legs, Sonny feels the room shake. She has lovely knees. From a certain angle, he can tell that her suntan extends well up under her shorts. Then it dawns on him. It is no suntan at all. That creamy beige is her natural hue. He fumbles with the whistling kettle, pouring it over the grounds slowly.

—You . . . go to school around here?
—I'm out. I work at the TG&Y in Waskom.
—Ummmm. You . . . like working there?
—Are you kidding? It's a dump. You don't make any money, and the manager keeps trying to show me what he's got.
—You mean . . .
—Every time I go back in that office. I hit the door and he goes for his fly. Offered me fifty dollars in merchandise of my choice if I'd . . . Ugh. Listen, I want to go to Shreveport. I want my own place, and a nice job. And one other thing, she says. —I'd have to find me a real nice church group.

Sonny nods, pours coffee. He wonders if he might be able to create a church that would please her. Would she like to be a goddess? With one worshiper? Christ, he thinks, if anyone else looks at her, I'll crush his skull and grind Nepal pepper into his empty eye sockets. There has got to be a way to get her to Shreveport. Once she is there, alone, almost twenty miles from home, friendless, trusting, needing, he will have her whenever he wants. Which will be all the time. Till it falls off or he goes blind. Whichever comes first.

She is sipping her coffee. From the other room, they hear Shad's and Elvira's muted voices. No words can be made out, but the tone is warm. Cuddly? The whiskey is in there. Two and a half quarts left. Maybe Elvira is going into detail about how much she has missed Shad. They all miss him. If you could isolate whatever it is about Shad and bottle it . . . call it Getalot: The Tonic That Puts You Where You Want to Be.

—Why did you do it? Missy asks, her voice distant as the moon.

Sonny has considered that this question would be asked. Not by Missy. Most likely by the sheriff's deputies, medical examiners—whoever it is that comes around out in the country and takes in dangerous lunatics who get their rocks whacking harmless old men across the nob with tire tools. Shit, even out here, there has to be somebody who sees to that.

—You're not going to talk about it, huh?

It turns out there is somebody. The old nut's daughter. The most beautiful feminine thing he has ever seen. Hating him now for what he has done to a helpless old man.

—Listen, it was a mistake.

—It sure was. When Cecil gets himself together, and the Savior's Friends hear about it . . . Listen, this ain't New York, you know. They're gonna kick ass.

—I'm not from New York. I'm from Shreveport.

—That don't cut any ice. Shreveport is a lot like New York. People from those big places think they can just go out in the country and do their dirt . . .

—Shreveport's not like New York. It's a lot like Florence. Anyhow, I didn't mean to do that to your father.

—Cecil? He's not my father.

—But I thought . . .

—He raised me. He thinks he's my father, but he's not.

—How could you know that? I mean . . .

Missy nods toward the other room. —She says he's not. And she ought to know.

—But then . . .

Missy shrugs a beautiful shoulder, recrosses her legs, giving Sonny an angle on the other side of what he has already become accustomed to think of as her adorable ass.

—Everybody says me and momma are just alike. It's not so, though.

—You-all do favor.

—But I'm a Christian. Momma's not nothing.

There is a burst of raucous laughter from the other room.

—Sonofabitch deserved it, they hear Shad say. Then he coughs with laughter again, Elvira's warm contralto joining in. Missy shakes her head.

—They're talking about Cecil. Why *did* you do it?

—He was out working on the Jeep. He got to acting funny . . .

—Funny? I never got a laugh out of him in nineteen years.

—I mean . . . peculiar.

—Like what?

—Well, once he got down on his knees in the mud and started praying, shaking his arms . . . At first I thought he was having a fit.

Sonny trails off. Missy is looking at him, unsmiling.

—You don't believe in prayer, do you?

—Sure . . .

—When did you last pray?

—Well, I . . .

Sonny pauses. In his own way, he prays constantly in the manner of the Hasidim. He explains himself to God endlessly, exhaustively, trying to put the best face possible on a lifetime of confusion and recent years of the grossest lechery. He has, of late, asked humbly and reverently for one single dynamite piece of ass. Nobody ever said you had to pray for a load of cowshit. One comes to glory by degrees. It is true that he has never received a clear and unequivocal response from his Father in Heaven. But he does not doubt. In fact, he has received little more in the way of communication from his father on earth; still he knows that E.M. III liveth. There are too many strange reports to doubt either father.

—I can see you don't pray. None of youall Sentells pray, do you?

Sonny quickly checks off the family in his mind. Unless E.M. III has joined a monastery and neglected to mention it, Missy is probably right.

—I can tell they didn't bring you up right.

—?

—... because if they'd brought you up right, you wouldn't never of laid violent hands on a man of God.

—I never did that. Christ...

—Go ahead. Use His name in vain. Where *you're* headed, it doesn't matter a lot...

—Where I... Listen, where did you get the idea I beat up on preachers?

—You said it. You decked Cecil, didn't you?

—The nut...?

—He may be a nut, all right. I reckon if I was a ordinary gentile, I'd say that. But in the Spirit, he's a prophet. How does it feel to go busting up a saint?

—I thought he was going to shoot Shad. He had this oil spout, and when he came in...

Missy fixes him with a look of massive contempt. —You can't shoot nobody with a oil spout, stupid. Is that what you learned in New York? Guess they're gonna demand registration of oil spouts, too...

Sonny wants to say that he has never even *been* in New York. But he has been everywhere. Even New York. Awful canyons full of gray people running about to no discernible purpose. Diseased pigeons, whole neighborhoods full of various human beasts feeding on their own illnesses. The city should be broken up, its population dispersed, Sonny thinks. Then it occurs to him that some of them might be sent South. No, a bad idea.

—Cecil never harmed a soul in his life, Missy is saying, her expression cold, judgmental. —He can't *help* being simple-minded.

—He's... *retarded*?

—I guess *you'd* say so. The Savior's Friends call it Blessed. Cecil got touched by a miracle.

—That's why he just kind of drops down and goes to praying? What kind of miracle?

It is immediately obvious to Sonny that he has hit the button. Missy rises from her chair, the somber expression changed utterly. She begins to tell her tale richly, emotionally, but in a way not her own—as if she were reciting prose crafted by another, but fitted to a truth they share.

—Years ago, before you and me was even born, young Cecil Miley went out into the woods right close to here...

Missy comes close to Sonny as she speaks. Her tone is soft,

confidential, almost conspiratorial. This is the evangeliarion. Sonny is glad to share it. Anything that will bring that sweet body closer to his is indeed Good News. He wonders if he can touch her as she moves within the magic of her tale. Is she so taken up with it that she might not notice a hand gently, lovingly, prayerfully placed under her halter or between her legs? Let the story roll.

—The woods the other side of the old Petrie place. He was looking for a blessing. And one night . . .

She falls silent, her eyes glazed and distant, contemplating that hushed moment, distant in time and space, just before the miracle, asking within herself perhaps for strength, for the words that will reach and purify Sonny's gentile heart. Has she noticed that the hand she holds now rests on her thigh? Most assuredly not. When the Spirit claims, the body is no more than a cloak cast off, forsaken in the truth, the unconcealedness of that moment, that preview of eternity—and other coming attractions.

—One night, there come up a thunderstorm.

—All right.

—There was young Cecil, down on his knees in this clearing burned out in the woods . . .

—Did I miss something?

—Huh?

—Burned out? How burned out?

—Oh, lightning. I'm glad you asked me that 'cause it's important.

—It is?

—You'll see. Anyhow, he was kneeling down by this big virgin pine that had got hit by lightning a long time before . . .

—Because the Spirit was dwelling there . . .

—No. That's pagan. Just shut up, huh. Will you let me tell this story?

—Sure . . .

Why not? As her excitement and involvement mounts, Missy has enclosed Sonny's hand between her thighs. She moves with the story, freeing her own hands to gesture, leaving Sonny's where she had inadvertently guided it. Close to heaven's gate.

— . . . and the wind come up, and the clouds obscured the setting sun, and Cecil, he could hear the voice of the Lord in the thunder, and he knew there had *got* to be a Sign coming. So he prayed harder and harder, said let the rain come down, let me be wrapped in darkness, but send Thy Sign . . .

Sonny is now stroking the inside of her thigh. It is soft and warm, but he feels the smooth flow of muscle below the tan skin and firm flesh. He will convert, so help him God. He will convert in a Shreveport second and stay converted and give up whiskey and smoking and taking the Lord's name in vain. There are other vain names enough, God knows.

— . . . but it wasn't that easy, Missy is whispering now, brimming over with excitement. —Oh, no . . . You don't just go down on your knees and get what you want . . .

—I was afraid of that.

—No. What happened was there come a trial to him. It was a vision. Of the Scarlet Woman . . .

—The Whore of Babylon . . .

Missy frowns. —How'd you know that? Sentells don't read Scripture.

—Sure we do . . . The Apocalypse . . .

—Huh?

—Uh . . . Revelations.

—That's right. Well, there she was. Beautiful. Long red hair. Lovely limbs . . .

—Yes . . .

—And buck-naked . . .

—God . . .

— . . . showing herself to Cecil, showing him her breasts . . .

Missy gestures at her own breasts as she speaks, her eyes wide, her respiration increasing. Sonny feels his own resolve harden, and he strokes boldly, high on the thigh, his hand moving lightly around to cup and caress Missy's astonishingly firm and adorable ass.

—I mean, she was showing young Cecil everything, lying down there on the ground and spreading her legs apart and moaning and saying how she wanted him, how she had got to have him . . .

—Cecil weakened. Don't tell me he didn't . . . There's always confession, a perfect act of contrition . . .

Missy's eyes are closed. Her gift for mimicry is considerable and the story is in charge now. She moves her body against Sonny's, rising from the chair, drawing him up, too. As he rises, he takes her into his arms, moving his pelvis up and down against her. Now she is whispering in his ear, and her moist breath is as sweet as honeysuckle. Thirty more seconds of this and he is going to come stronger than the Panama Limited on an open track. If he does not faint first.

—Yes, sure, of course, Missy sighs. —He wasn't but a human boy . . .

—Good for Cecil. He'll never regret it.

—He weakened, and she come to him and offered him false paradise . . .

—It'll have to do . . . till the real thing comes . . .

— . . . and he had her in his arms, the Great Whore . . .

She didn't get that name by being a lousy lay, Sonny is thinking in his near delirium. He is kissing Missy's shoulders, her neck. The universe is condensing around them now, and the room is close, hot, as compact and dense as an ingot of freshly rolled steel. No one will find them here. This place is sealed. Sonny is about to receive a Sign.

—He was . . . having her . . .

Sonny's hand is in the back of her shorts and she is pressing herself against him, her body moving in rhythm with his, her breath hot and short in his ear. She goes suddenly limp in his arms in the abstract overpowering passion of her tale.

Suddenly she comes alive again. She breaks away, sharply, definitively, her eyes filled with fear, awe. For an instant he supposes that she has come to realize the twisted and demented nature of her would-be convert. But no. They are still within the Time of the Tale. Stories have turns.

— . . . and all of a sudden, he felt this pain. Terrible pain . . . And when he looked around, it was this awful-looking thing standing, rearing up behind him . . . the Great Beast . . .

—The Great Beast?

—In the shape of a man. It was challenging him. It was saying the woman belonged to it. She wasn't for no mortal to screw, and the thing laughed and made a sign, and all of a sudden the clouds whirled and Cecil felt something hit him . . .

—Lightning . . .

—That's what it must of been. Hit the tree again, hit young Cecil head-on. I don't know. Nobody knows. Doctors said it was a caution that anybody could live with his head mashed like that. See, wasn't nobody there. They had to get it out of Cecil little by little. I mean, you can imagine . . .

—He . . . wasn't quite right.

—Never has been. Not since that night when he come on the Scarlet Woman and the Great Beast . . .

Missy stands by the window now, looking into outer dark. She is drained, exhausted.

—When you think of it, it had got to be a miracle. Skull fractured in two places, one of his eyes near out of his head, lacerations and contusions, nose broke, ear tore loose, forty-six stitches . . . Might as well of done ten rounds with a gorilla.

Missy turns to Sonny. —You hadn't ought to of hit Cecil. He's had a head like an eggshell since then. She moves back as Sonny approaches.

—If I'd known . . .

—You hadn't ought to go around pounding on people.

Sonny considers this, head hung low. In fact, he does not give a flying fuck whether Cecil lives or dies. It occurs to him that were he to be executed in the morning for the old bastard's murder, he would ask for Missy as a last meal.

—I don't want to, Sonny gasps, covering his face, letting his eyes roll. Sweet wounds of Christ, he thinks to himself. It is easier to counterfeit emotion than to understand the real thing.

—I was brought up on violence, he hears himself croak. —The whole family is into it. When the other kids got a Bible, they gave me a gun. They said, If it moves, blow it away . . . Why, if I'd had my piece this afternoon . . . Cecil is lucky . . .

Sonny glances up through his fingers. —If my gun hadn't been out in the Jeep, when I saw that oil spout . . .

Missy's look is one of pity and terror. She sits down on one of the kitchen chairs and pulls it closer to Sonny.

—You poor thing . . . I guess you never had a chance . . .

The poor thing, hands still masking his red, searching eyes, stares down into her slack halter as she leans forward to comfort him. She indeed comforts him, though her words might as well be wind. He sees. His gasps are no longer forgeries. Sweet, curved, smooth, firm, darker areoles, small delicate nipples. It is as if he can taste them, can detect her scent as her hand reaches out and rests on his leg.

—It don't have to be like that always . . .

—What can I do? If somebody pisses me . . . I mean, makes me mad, everything goes red. I try to kill . . .

But not just now. Sonny feels the pressure of her hand on his leg. It is not a small, thin white hand; it is large, almost brown, beautifully shaped. And it seems to weigh five hundred pounds. If he could but move it up his leg and over slightly, he is certain salvation would be at hand.

—The Spirit can tame a abandoned heart . . .

—Too late . . . Spirit better bring his lunch on this job.

—Oh, don't say that, Edward.

—Sonny.

—Sonny. Don't say it. Despair is a awful sin.

—Who wants to help a damn depraved psycho born-killer who goes around junking simp prophets for giggles?

—There's somebody to help everybody. Jesus understands.

—How can he? I don't.

—Because he's God, silly. He'll pull you out of your slimy miserable life.

—Not me, Sonny snuffles. —He shouldn't waste his time. Too far gone . . . Find some bastard who just slices old ladies and sets fire to lost puppies . . . somebody you can help . . .

Missy smiles, her face alight with Christian love. —I can help you. Truly I can.

—No way. If you knew the stuff I've done . . . I'm not fit to live, much less to help. Even if you put aside the cannibalism . . .

Missy stares at him. —Oh, my God . . . cannibalism . . .

Too much, Sonny thinks, his heart sinking. It is his stock-in-trade. Too fucking much. Motto of the redneck nation: Anything worth doing is worth overdoing.

—Not . . . I mean, I've thought about it. When you've done . . . everything . . .

—Sure, Missy says, relieved. —I understand. You wouldn't believe the stuff I've dreamed about . . .

—You see, I was . . . never loved. My family . . . a very strange family . . .

—You can say that again.

—What?

—My momma's been telling me about the Sentells since I was little.

—She's known my uncle for a long time. I could tell at the filling station . . .

—Oh, boy, I reckon she has. She's known him all right. Just like in Scripture. In Numbers . . . that poor Levite . . .

Sonny notices that the sounds from the next room have

ceased altogether. Missy rises and walks toward the door like a sleepwalker. Sonny catches her in his arms before she can open it. He does not want her to walk in upon a Scene. Silence around Shad bespeaks mischief.

—Listen, I think you should stay here and work on me. I think I feel the Spirit . . .

If not the spirit, then the world. It is in his arms. He tilts her head back, kisses her as if they were both fourteen, home from their first date. As her lips and his come together, he feels doubt and cynicism falling away. It is as if he has been stripped of some factor in the blood that marks the Sentells, the demon down there that drives, and plunders propriety and decency as surely as the Great Beast waylaid young Cecil.

—We hadn't ought to . . .
—Missy . . .
—Don't say it. It's wrong.
—How? I care about you. I mean it.

He does. His circumstances are those of legions before him, trapped by beauty and desire, prepared to assume a life they may not really want at all. Missy smiles, goes to the stove, and turns on the fire under the kettle.

—You know, even if I am a child of sin, bond servant to iniquity . . .
—You're not.
—Oh, yes, I am . . . a bastard.
—Don't talk that way.
—It's true . . . and the truth shall make you free.
—Cecil's not your father?
—I told you that already.
—But . . .

Missy kisses him quickly, her lips, her tongue lingering. Then she moves away from Sonny, her eyes soft, sorrowful.

—I'm glad and I'm sad, she says, something like a smile on those full, sweet lips.

—Listen, Sonny says, trying to pull her back into his arms, —I could go off any time . . . mass murder, burning convents. The shape I'm in . . . only love soothes me.

—Christian love, Missy replies kindly. —Sonny, it can't be nothing else, dear heart. Not with your own cousin . . .

I knew when Elvira come out of that car it was gonna be three ounces of old times and twelve tons of horseshit. Had to be that way. We hardly got into the house before it started.

—Same old sorry sonofabitch, ain't you? she asked me with a long-suffering, bittersweet smile.

—Yeah, I told her. —Same old shithouse slut, ain't you?

—It was a cottonhouse.

—Right. Burned to the ground. Couple of lifetimes ago. What'd you bring that pretty little girl here for? Without clothes enough on to keep from freezing.

—Thought you'd like a look. Brings back memories, don't she? You still like 'em young, don't you?

—She's fine. Reckon she can outrun Sonny?

—Reckon she wants to? She's *my* baby.

—You pimping her? Here's a hundred dollars. Come back by for her tomorrow afternoon.

She took a swing at me, and there it was. Yesterday today. Hadn't seen the damned woman since twenty years ago, and it was like old married folks inside of five minutes. I caught her wrist and pulled her down on the divan.

—What do you say we have a drink and catch up before we go to whipping on each other?

—What have you got?

—Same as always.

—Bragging . . .

—Jack Daniels. Neat or a little water. And I ain't bragging. Everything's just the way you had it last.

—Haw. I bet you couldn't fuck your way out of a wet paper bag.

—You want to get that little girl of yours in here with a shopping bag over her ass?

Elvira looked at me real serious. —You hadn't ought to talk that way. Anyhow, what's wrong with me?

I had been thinking about that. Damned little wrong with her, to tell the truth. But then I sure as hell wasn't gonna tell *her* the truth. I'd gone away lying twenty some-odd years ago, and I hadn't found no reason to change my style since then. Deny, deny, deny . . .

But she looked fine. Oh, I guess the baby fat was gone from her face, but that didn't hurt. Added character. She looked smarter. As if the years had somehow focused her attention, made her more aware of things. I'm not saying she looked like when we was back in school, but I knew women fifteen years younger who didn't look as good. There were lines around her eyes, and the tendons in her legs showed more. The veins in her hands stood out. Her lips wasn't as full as I remembered, and maybe the color of her eyes had faded a little. But all in all, I'd rather be tucked into her than in Philadelphia.

What I couldn't quite make out was why she'd brought her little girl along. Maybe to keep Sonny busy while she fooled with me. That made sense, but I had this feeling there was more to it. Well, I thought. Let it go by. Forget it. Don't ask, and don't hurry. Things come out by and by. Don't they?

We sat back and drank, and Elvira seemed to be getting her fill just looking at me. I ain't used to that, but I let it go by, too.

—Well, you ain't a bit uglier than the last time I saw you, she said after a while. —Little gray hair . . .

—You neither, honey. 'Course you had a surprise for me . . .

—What?

—Don't give me that shit. Cecil. Sonofabitch looks seventy.

She laughed kind of sorrowful. —Poor Cecil . . .

—Poor hell. I should have stomped him to death when I had him down in them woods. If I hadn't had a pussy for a heart, that's just what I would of done.

—You'd of destroyed a legend.

—Huh?

—Cecil is . . . a prophet.

—Yeah, right. He can foresee what's gonna happen if he ever messes with me again.

Elvira set down her drink and looked right at me like she was a lawyer with a sure-fire case. She pushed the glass over for a refill.

—Folks around here see Cecil as . . . touched.

—Sure. I touched him. So what?

—The story got around God touched him . . .

Then she went and told me all this crazy stuff that had come out of the night Cecil and his buddies went for the two of us. It pissed me off when I heard it. The reason Cecil Miley can't count past six is that he messed around with me and I busted his head for him twenty-five-odd years ago.

—What I can't understand is why you'd go and marry that sorry sack of shit, I told her.

—Listen, you don't know what loneliness can do to you, Shad.

You kind of get to where you shrink inside. You wonder if you're still alive.

—Hell, you had that little girl. You should of run off . . .

—You like her?

—Elvira, she's fine. That's not what I'm talking about. I mean all this loneliness crap. You had her to look after . . .

—Yeah. I sure did. That's how come I got married to start with. I'd of let it go, just lived to myself and run the station when daddy got feeble. Except for my baby.

Right then, with what she was saying and how she was looking at me, I should of got the whole message. You'd think at my age and considering what I've been through, I'd be shitproof. But nobody gets that old. You think you've learned every kind of shit there is and some sonofabitch will toss Tasmanian devil shit at you. I guess I lived with blowed-up wells for too long. You get moved away from normal living and workaday bullshitting when every morning looks and feels like a fair shot to be your last. You don't pay no mind to that midget world where the stakes never amount to nothing. They can put some shit past you.

—So old Cecil knocked you up, and the rest just kind of followed.

—No, you low-life. He never done no such thing. I never let Cecil get near me.

—All right. You never did. But you sure in hell had to get near somebody.

She just laughed and reached past me for the bottle. She poured herself a shot that would curl the eyelashes of a coon dog. Then she tossed it down like she knew what she was doing.

—Oh, yes. Oh, Lord, yes . . . I got near somebody, all right . . . You remember Kilgore? The time I came to visit you?

—I guess.

—Guess hell. You never forgot a good piece of ass in your life.

—All right. Am I supposed to tell you it was fine?

—You don't have to tell me nothing. I was there.

We laughed and I drank and just ignored what Elvira was trying to lay on me. Back in the kitchen, I could hear that pretty little girl talking to Sonny. She sounded excited, telling him some kind of story. If she was what she looked like, her mother's natural daughter, old Sonny had better get hisself ready for a fancy turn or two. And shameful as it was, I had the thought that

I was going to get into that sweet thing, too. First chance ever I got. I never saw nothing wrong with a man my age laying it to a young girl. Why should some silly bastard with a pimple problem get all the choice ass?

—Hey, Elvira said. —You there?

—Sorry, I told her. —I got stuff on my mind. Got a well gone bad down in the Gulf.

Elvira grinned and handed me a telegram. —They dropped it by the station, she said. —Man had a whole handful of 'em. Seems somebody was paying him to paper Caddo Parish with 'em. You're a big shot now, right?

—Same old sixes and sevens, honey. E.M.'s real nervous.

—Always was. I remember when he came to fetch you graduation day. Does he still fetch you, Shad?

—Still tries.

—Then you'll be going. You went then.

—Wasn't no money in soybeans, sweet thing.

She lit a cigarette and crossed her legs. She had on this short skirt, and I could see she still had fine legs. Tiny ankles, smooth full calves, and I could just barely remember the rest.

—You tend to get quiet.

—I guess I do.

—Tell me something, she said, watching me watching her. —Did you ever go a day of your life without thinking of getting laid?

—I surely hope not, I told her. Hadn't gone too many without *getting* laid.

—It ain't the only thing in life, Shad, she said, looking thoughtful.

—Last time I heard that was from an old man got hisself castrated in a railroad accident.

—Lord, just look at us. We've got one foot in the grave and the other on a banana peel.

—You sick? I mean, you got a disease?

—If you mean, am I dying of something, no. Not especially. I've just had plenty of time to think about life . . .

—Bullshit. Think long, you think wrong.

—You old bastard, she said, leaning over to kiss me. —You ain't a damned bit better than that poor half-wit I got at home.

—Oh, yeah? At least I can undress myself.

—Reckon you can still undress me?

—Honey, I never got out of practice. I can't tell you how many times I've undressed you since Kilgore . . .

—That's sweet. I wish I'd been there when you did it.

About then we got to fumbling each other, kind of checking out the equipment, you could say. We was laughing together, playing. Lord, it did feel comfortable. Seemed like old married folks was creeping up on me despite everything.

—You want to ease on back to the bedroom, honey? Take hold of that bottle, and I'll bring the glasses.

—You in a hurry?

—When I ain't in a hurry, it's 'cause I just done it. Always was anxious to get to the far side of my next piece of ass.

Elvira laughed as we went back to the bedroom

—You can't go on like this forever, she said.

—Where'd they write that down?

—Physically . . .

—I do exercises. Drink like a fish, work like a dog, eat like a pig, fuck like a goat . . . and lie like a sonofabitch.

She was a little drunk. I knew she was trying to get that way when she kept slamming down that Black Jack neat. I closed the door, and she fell across the bed, giggling.

—Man like that *could* go on forever . . .

—Damned straight.

She sat up with her skirt around her thighs. Everything I could see looked to be about the best there is.

—I wouldn't be here but for two things . . .

—One . . .

—You're the best cock I ever had . . .

—Right. Two . . .

—Oh, honey, I haven't had it in so long . . .

—What's the matter, 'Vira? Caddo Parish swore off adultery?

—Cecil . . . He used to be all right . . .

—He wasn't *never* all right.

—I mean . . . in bed.

—I'd rather fuck a dead lizard.

—That's you, and I believe it. But right at first, he was fine . . .

Well, I thought, that's what living on subsistence will do to you. I try not to even remember what I fucked in the South Pacific during the war. A man will do with damned near anything before he goes without. Now, I never went as far as you could go, but I knew old boys that did. Beasts of the field, the lately deceased. Never mind. I climbed up on that bed and went to kissing her legs. She still had that naturally tan skin, and her legs was sweet and fine. She had some kind of bath oil that smelled like orange blossoms, and it just kind of welled up around me when I drew down her panties and went to kissing her belly. I had this notion to chow down on her, just as a kind of celebration 'cause it was so fine to see that body I had cared so much for a long time ago. She was pretty drunk by then, but still talking. That was all right, fine. It was my body meeting her body again. After all, we hadn't never been soulmates.

—... Just crazy in bed. Fits. Visions. He'd come in from the station and just naturally wreck me. My God, I'd be so sore I went to limping. I'd have bruises. Then it all came to an end. He told me one day I was dead.

I kind of lifted my head up. That caught my attention.

—Huh? I missed that.

—Said he had a vision I was dead, even walking, and it wasn't no use messing with me anymore.

—Ain't they got a coroner in this Parish anymore?

—There is those living in the Spirit and dead in the Spirit, and ... Oh, honey, that's so good ... yes, don't stop ... uh ...

We kind of cut off regular communication about then, I mean with words. Lord, how our bodies talked to each other. There wasn't nothing a man and woman can do for each other that we didn't know just how. In our minds and hearts maybe we was nearly strangers after so long. But our bodies remembered. I thought right then it was a lot like being married with all the pain and lies and heartbreak and bullshit took out.

Say we'd been married all those years. You know how it would of gone. What we was having right then was the best of it. What had we missed? Some sorry tired make-do screwing and maybe a damn divorce down at the wick end when the lies and the pain and the bullshit got too heavy to carry.

But right then, sliding up her body to plant it once more, it was as fine and fresh as if we was back in that meadow, too young to know what was coming and too hot to care. No rain, no thunder, but her eyes was closed and she was biting her lip, and when she felt it between her legs and moving in, it was homecoming, reunion.

—Oh, honey, I love you so much ...

I believe I got carried away when she said that.

—Yeah, me, too . . .

You can believe this or go shit in your hat. I hadn't never said that to but one other woman in my life. I didn't believe in it. You get to lying about something trivial like whether you love 'em or not, and you get to going a little farther, lying about money and business, and when it all gets to seeming about the same, you're gonna end up cheating at a hand of poker or something really important like that and get your ass blowed all the way to San Diego. Anyhow, right then I meant it. What the hell, the only thing I had ever really give a shit about was women. What I wanted, what I naturally yearned to reach, to touch, was just the damned core of what was a woman. I wanted to find that distillation, the brandy of women. I'd had every wine there was. Wasn't a kind of woman out there I hadn't had. But for once in my life I come to a woman where I wasn't looking forward to the next one before I was done with her. Once I'd had her—a woman so right that everything afterward seemed kind of second rate.

But even then, even on the down side of the road, one night's perfection aside, there was some sliver of it in every woman I ever laid it to. A certain smile, a way of using her hands, a mean disposition you couldn't help loving, a little girl lost and wandering around in the body of a beautiful woman. There was eyes and laughs, ways of talking and ears and ankles, asses and upper arms, insteps and voices, hair every shade you can find on a head. Blue-black like lacquer on an Oriental woman. There's breasts like you dream about, a shape you don't reckon really exists. There's roan red hair and freckled shoulders and thighs like the deck of a carrier. Women so tall and broad that making love to 'em was like exploring a continent. Women so small you could slip 'em on like precious clothes. Wasn't a woman you could find didn't have something, some treasure that was hers. I lived with a fat woman for a couple of weeks who only had one eye because of her mouth, her lips. Some woman in Butte, Montana, kept me around after the well was dry on account of her legs. No tits, face like a carp, but Christ, those legs. Thin golden anklet I bought her against pale skin, ankles I could get my fingers around, smooth, curved calves, thighs you wanted to see every morning you woke up for the rest of your life. Touches here, hints there. Only a young man who hadn't had it much could expect to find it all in one place. Then, if he did, there'd have to be something wrong—something to make him move on.

If you ever come up completely happy in this life, it's 'cause you're pretty damned easy to satisfy.

Truth to tell, though, back into Elvira again, I wondered why I hadn't just packed her up and took her with me. She sure beat hell out of the average. Me and her had been carrying on for quite a spell, working our way through the repertoire, when I heard something behind us at the door and saw Elvira's eyes go even wider than when she felt a yard of cock up her. What I heard was this terrible gasp like a critter's last breath, and then somebody say in a muffled voice, Aw shit.

Now, my bare ass was broadside to the door, and I had to kind of crane my neck around to see, but it was just what you'd expect. Elvira's little girl standing in the doorway looking like somebody had shoved a dirty sock down her throat and then tickled her. And that dumb bastard Sonny right behind her, kind of covering his eyes with one hand, trying to pull her back with the other.

—Motherfucker, I yelled. —Ain't it no privacy around here? Can't you sees folks is getting reacquainted?

Door slammed, and I turned back to comfort Elvira. I figured she was likely to be upset having her child see her fucking a strange man.

Did I ever say I understood women? Bullshit. I never did. You don't listen. Hell, no, I don't understand 'em. I love 'em. When I turned back around, her eyes was closed, and she was moving her hips up and down like it hadn't been no interruption at all.

—Come on, honey, she was saying, —I'm too high now. Don't let me down, hear?

—Your little girl's used to this stuff, huh?'

—Far as I know, that child's a virgin.

—Hell, 'Vira, she must be close to twenty.

—Right. But she's picky. Like her momma.

—Goddamn, if you had as many pricks sticking out of you as been stuck in, you'd be the queen of the porcupines.

—And ninety-five percent of 'em was yours . . . Never mind. Missy understands . . . I told her a long time ago.

I was still tending to business and loving it, but that kind of got me curious.

—Told her what?

—Oh, Shad honey, it's not like when we was growing up.

These is enlightened times. Even a nice Christian girl's not gonna be too shook up seeing her mommy and daddy in bed together...

Chapter Six

> The origin of all things is Okeanos ... and nothing is at rest.
> *Theaetetus*, 180, D4

Missy sits on the divan, her face pale, eyes turned away from Sonny—who busies himself at the radio, looking for KWKH. A hundred thousand watts, clear channel. At night, the station fits over the Southwest like a cheap suit.

This heart of mine could never see
What everybody knew but me ...

Ancient Hank Williams. Balm to the redneck soul in all its manifestations. Sonny listens, eased a bit, as he tries to think of something to say.
—You don't really believe Shad's your father, do you?
—I got no choice but to believe it. I been hearing it from momma since I was twelve years old.
—Your mother told you?
—I guess you could call it a private witness. Right about then, I was real down on Cecil.
—Down ... ?
—You know. I thought, it's a awful thing to have a daddy who's a plain-out retardate. I tried to feel Christian about him, but it was hard.
—I guess I see that.
—No. You really don't.
—All right.
—I mean, do you see coming home from school in the third grade and finding the filling station full of folks listening to your father talking in tongues?
—Talking ...
—Tongues. Yes. He's got that gift. When he sets his mind to it.

They used to come from as far as Archer City and Little Rock and Fort Payne to hear him.

—Wow...

—Preacher from Selma wanted to buy him... Wanted to give my momma two thousand dollars for Cecil. Let him take him back to Alabama. Said he could translate the tongues, and that Alabama had a heavy need for prophecy.

—What did he...?

—Most of it was against the niggers, according to that preacher. Said Cecil was just a avatar of Saint Paul come to warn against race mixing, and that the niggers should be got rid of.

Sonny shudders. It appears Cecil has a bad mouth, even if just one Alabama preacher can make it out.

—What... I mean, how were you supposed...

—Send 'em to New York.

—Oh.

—No, don't laugh. I kind of believed that part. Every now and then, Cecil says, "New York New York One Oh Oh One Six." Mystery numbers. Preacher said that was the number of niggers to be shipped from Caddo Parish. Seemed to make sense.

Sonny says nothing. There is something fiercely depressing in perceiving transcendent beauty combined with the intellect of a horsefly. On a table, he spots a half-empty bottle of Black Jack and quickly pours a couple of shots that would stun a truckstop whore. He passes one glass to Missy, who takes it without paying much attention.

—But that wasn't the worst of it. Reckon you're in the fourth grade and you come home from school and there's the man you think's your daddy way out back, behind the grease rack and the air compressor. And he's got this chicken...

—Got... this... chicken...

—Oh, Sonny, you know... Is that any kind of thing to let your little girl see?

—No, Sonny says firmly. He still cannot make out what the feeb was doing with the chicken, but it doesn't matter. Whatever, one doesn't let his daughter see. Conceal the chicken.

—Lord, Missy says suddenly. —I believe this is hard liquor. She takes another purely experimental sip. —Hard liquor hasn't passed my lips before.

—You never saw your mother in the sack with a strange man before, either. Drink up. It'll take away the sting.

—Well, it was a shock. But I got to get used to it, don't I? I mean, momma used to say, Cheer up, baby. That feeble-minded old bastard ain't your real daddy. Your real daddy is Samuel Shadrach Sentell, and he's rich and smart, and one of these days he's gonna come back for us, and he'll know he's your daddy 'cause you're so beautiful . . . and everything's gonna be all right.

—You really believe it, don't you? he says at last.

Missy kisses him on the cheek. She is past the shock and seems to be happy. Sonny considers that swapping Cecil for Shad as a father is a mixed bag. There are all kinds of nuts in the world.

—Tell me about him, Missy says. —I want to know all about . . . my daddy.

Sonny closes his eyes. She could have gone a lifetime and not asked that. He would as soon hand her a copy of *The Hundred Days of Sodom* and provide a commentary on the difficult portions. Should he tell her the truth about his kinsman? Or lie like a low-down sonofabitch?

—Will you?

—That's . . . not easy, Missy.

His mind processes the matter at infinite velocity, all factors weighed and tested. All right, fine. This is one of those times for desperate, self-interested measures. He will tell her the truth.

—Is he a nice man? I mean, most of the time?

—Uh . . .

—What he's doing tonight . . . does he do it a lot? I mean, with other women?

—Uh . . .

—I know he uses foul language.

—Well . . .

—And I doubt he's seen the inside of a church since he got baptized. He *is* baptized?

—I wasn't there. Can't say.

—And he's a chaser.

—No. He's a catcher. Never misses.

—Now, I think you're making it worse than it is, Sonny.

Sonny rises wearily, goes over to Shad's rutsack, and draws out a time-worn, disintegrating leather book. He has not seen it in years, but he knew that it would be there. In another man's luggage it would simply be an address book, a record of those one knows and how they may be reached. In his uncle's case, it is a little more complex. Sonny sits down beside Missy again, flipping open the book at random. The entries are scrawled with No. 2 pencil in a hand that would flunk a second-grader in penmanship.

Elin Willis, 1029 Govermint St. BR 869-4515. 29. Skltchr. 105, blnd. Hr. Lgs+, A+. Fk 6, Sk 8. Hsbd wk 3–11 pm Ethyl Corp. Golf Sndy 8–1.

Sonia Wells, 49 Kent Pl., BR 499-2137. 26. Sec. 120. Blnd. Skn+, Ft, Arms, Skny A w pim. Fk 5, Sk 8. Hsbd wk 8–5 Esso. Crzy Mean. Gn in car. *Stomp.* Lst. Rsrt. BR.

Donnie Webster, 4002 Highland Rd., Apt. 14, BR 494-1626. 19. Stdt. LSU. Brnt. 115–120. Lgs v. bad. E. H. T.+ A++. Funny. Drnks a lot. Fk 8, Sk 7. Ftr in Angola til 5-62. AR-Mrd. Lay off after 12-61. Fr. sd wd kl any MF messed w dau.

Sarah Ann Welborne, 229 Florida, BR 494-2627. 40. HW. 125. gt tall, brnt. A+ Bel. T.++, Hr. Lgs bad. Fk 4 (but wks hd), Sk 6. Hsbd Tr. Slsmn, gone 1st 3 wks Mo. Calls hm a lt. Small, C.S. but dnt tk ch. Nxt to Lst.Rsrt. BR.

Roberta Weller, 1121 Drouet Dr. BR 482-9161. 25. Some knd exec. Phn Co. Brnt. 105. Lgs++, A+++, Ft, T+, Bel. but fc thin. H. Fk 8+, Sk 5. Tks too much. Hsbd knows but dont care. Got smthng of his own. Dont tk ch. Wks pot chp co. Bad habits. Knf in back of belt.

Page after page of it. This much only the W's in Baton Rouge. There is no end to it. Every country where oil is found, all major cities in the US and abroad, every color and ethnic origin is represented, analyzed and rated. There are tiny cramped notes of every kind strewn on the pages, even wallet-sized photos here and there—some of a woman alone in various states of dress or undress, some with Shad, some without. Some in which the woman is nude, committing gross acts while smiling at the camera. One naked at the front of a small yacht with the unmistakable profile of Diamondhead in the background, another taken on the crumbling porch of an abandoned cabin in some swamp, the subject lying unclothed, legs parted, a small Texas flag covering her most consequential place.

—Lord God in Heaven, Missy moans.

—Twenty in Arkansas, from Hoxie down to Taylor, nine in Memphis—unless you count West Memphis, then it's twelve.

Sixty-nine in California ... like you might expect. He even found eleven heterosexual women in San Francisco.

Sonny leafs through the pages dully. —London, twenty-one. Frankfurt, seven. Sounds like football scores. Rome, thirty-three. Beirut, forty-five. Athens, eleven. Djakarta, Hong Kong, Singapore ... Fourteen in Phoenix, seven in Tucson, Tulsa, Indianapolis... Can you even imagine getting laid in Indianapolis?

Missy stared at him somberly. —I can't imagine getting laid at all. 'Cause I haven't been. I'm a Christian.

—I believe you mentioned that.

—Well, I take it serious. What do all those abbreviations mean?

—You don't want to know.

—Yes, I do. 'Cause when I talk to my father about this book here, and the way he lives ...

Sonny pales. —That's a bad idea. I wouldn't do that.

—I never asked you to. But it's my Christian duty, and I can't shirk it. Not to my own daddy. So tell me what all that stuff means.

An ungenerous notion stirs in Sonny's mind. He recalls one of his uncle's ungallant observations about women: if you can get 'em to talk about it, you can get 'em to do it. He nods to Missy. If there was ever a chance to try the theory out, this is it.

—Okay, pick one.

—This one ... here.

—Thelma McDonnell, 421 DeSoto Street, New Orleans. 656-4000. Wtrs. She's a waitress. 110. Brnt. She weighs around a hundred and ten, and she's brunette. A+, Lgs+, T, E, ... She's got a really good ass, fine legs, tits are all right, nice eyes ...

Missy stares as Sonny translates. —That's what all that means? Why, he's ... his mind has to be gone. He's crazier than Cecil. What's that? Sm bd?

—Thelma ought to bathe more.

—Fk 4, Sk 6?

—Look, it's enough. No need going on with it ...

—Sonny ...

—It's ... her rating. On a scale from one to ten. How well she does ... things.

—What things?

—Things men and women do.

—And he puts it down right there?

—Yep. And when he gets to town, he just figures out what he wants and phones for it. Shad's organized.

—He's a pervert. Sex isn't nothing without love.

—You and your dad go different ways on that.

Missy rises a little unsteadily. —I don't feel too good. This hard liquor . . .

—Want to lie down? Sonny asks quickly. —There's another bedroom.

Would he undress her, peel away garment after garment, and take while she is helpless and unconscious the very flower of her maidenhood? Give him the chance.

—No, I believe I need some fresh air.

—You can't go out dressed like that. It's cold as a polar bear's tool.

—Sonny, I can't stand that kind of talk . . . I'll just put on this coat . . .

Missy slips on Shad's canvas jacket, which engulfs her. They step outside into the vast yard. The moon is high, and bright as a flare. Clouds race across its face. The air is still chill, but somehow it seems warmer than earlier. They walk across the yard hand in hand.

—I thought it was bad to have a half-witted daddy. Now I end up with a sex fiend. I believe I was better off before. I wish momma *had* been lying all those years.

They walk in silence, Missy trying to absorb what she has learned, Sonny feeling like a miserable back-shooter for telling her. Still, he wears his cravenness well. The end of the path is in her drawers, and the fastest route is the best. Shad would push him into fresh lava for a shot at something like Missy. It is time, Sonny feels, to let the blood go. Every Sentell's hand is turned against every other's. Why should he be the exception?

—You know, Missy says thoughtfully, —I wouldn't be surprised if my momma was in that book. We never looked up Greenwood.

—I did, Sonny says.

—Well?

—A+++, Legs+++, T+++, H++, E+++, Fk 9, Sk 9. Next to the highest overall in the book.

—Next to?

—Some woman with no name or address. Maybe it's nobody

real. Maybe he just put it in there to show what a perfect woman would be. Miss Absolutely Perfect.

—You don't even mind that book, do you?

—It's Shad's, not mine. If I had one, it'd be the shortest book in history. No pages. Not even endpapers.

—But you wish you were like him, don't you?

—I am . . . in some ways.

—You mean . . . you're a degenerate, too?

Sonny hears himself respond and cannot believe what he hears. —I think about it all the time. Even when I'm doing something else. I wake up with it on my mind, and when I go to sleep I think of it till I doze off. Then I dream about it. I'm outside some palace in a city near the desert . . . I sneak in over the rooftops, I get past the eunuchs and steal the pasha's pride. F 10+, Sk 10+, and all that Turkish stuff . . . I leap off a balcony with her in my arms, land on my Arabian, and we're off, hell-bent, over the chill sands under a porcelain moon . . .

He pauses a moment, an idiot grin on his face as he does an instant replay in his head. —There's the tent. In the oasis . . . We're inside. I'm undressing her. She struggles. This is against her religion. Never with an Uncircumcised One . . . I show her she's got nothing to worry about. That puts another face on it . . . her face. It's push come to shove . . . She faints from fear and ecstasy.

Sonny turns, takes Missy's hand in his, draws her close, croons in her ear. —Blue heaven, and you and I . . . sand kissing a moonlit sky . . .

Missy stares at him in bewilderment. —I got to tell you the truth 'cause you're my kin. I mean, I don't care if you're circumcised or not. That kind of thinking's filthy, and it'll drive you crazy, too.

—If God didn't want us to do it, why did he make us out of meat? With all the equipment and the urge?

—It's all right for married people. In moderation.

Missy stops her recitation, glances at Sonny sharply.

—You already got me in that oasis scene in your mind, don't you?

Sonny looks back in surprise. Actually, no. He has not had time as yet to insert her into that particular fantasy.

—Do you want me to?

—Tell me what you do.

—We swim in the pool under the moon, waiting for the sunrise. We hold each other. Like this . . .

—Uh-huh . . .

—We take each other's clothes off . . .

—How can you imagine doing that with me? You've never seen me with my clothes off.

—Extrapolation . . .

—Huh? Never mind. You just stand there undressing your own cousin in your mind . . .

—I don't know that you are.

—Would it matter?

—I don't think so.

Sonny has his hands inside the canvas jacket now. He caresses Missy's waist, feeling her warm flesh beneath his hands, moving them up toward her halter, down toward her hips. She lets him kiss her, and to his surprise, returns it. After a moment, their lips part. They stand breathless. Missy smiles.

—I guess we could be kissing cousins, huh?

—We can do better than that.

—We'd have idiots. I been through enough of that already.

Sonny has hooked his fingers into the waistband of Missy's shorts. They are coming down. If it were not for the goddamned jacket, by now he could see her A+++. He hears the distant sound of an engine, but pays it no mind. He brings down the shorts another peg or two, and slips his hands inside.

—Sonny . . .

—Uh-huh . . .

—I believe we better go back inside. It's awful cold out here . . .

—It's not out yet, he begins, and stops himself. —You're right. There's a nice warm bedroom right next to where your mother is . . . and they're going to be in there all night long.

Missy sighs. Is she coming around? Sonny holds his breath. One night of love? He begins constructing the oasis in his mind, like a mad set-builder for a sub-C movie. There, sailing above, is a moon+++ already. A moment more here, then back inside. He is about to take the plunge, reach down for two handfuls of treasure, when a pair of headlights laces across his back. The vehicle is coming up the old road that cuts through the Petrie place, and it is coming at flank speed.

—Shit, Sonny says. —More telegrams.

—You mean like the one we got at the station?

—They're touching every base six or eight times.

Missy squints toward the lurching headlights. —It's hard to make out, but I believe I recognize that truck . . .

Sonny's squint matches her own. It is a van or a pickup with one of those detachable hutches that fits over the bed. And it has to be making a good eighty down the road straight for the house.

—I bet that's Cox's pickup . . . It looks like . . .

The truck has arrived, skidding loudly and assertively to a stop just behind Elvira's old ruin. There is silence for a moment, then the truck's door opens and a man gets out. He studies Elvira's car carefully, kicking the tires, feeling the hood. He seems oblivious of Sonny and Missy who stand near trees perhaps fifty or sixty yards from the house.

—You was right, Prophet, the man says. —It's her car.

The speaker is tall, weighs well over two hundred pounds, and looks meaner than a bulldog with mange on his balls. He looks like Shad, Sonny thinks. But then most thoroughbred rednecks look much alike. Another man, smaller, but looking even meaner, gets out. He peers around, stares at the house for a moment as if he is planning a campaign. Then a voice issues from the darkness of the truck. It is not a young man's voice. It is hardly a human voice: bass, distant, commanding.

—You sure?

Missy starts forward, her mouth open to call out, but Sonny grabs her. Of all the things he knows, Sonny is past master of but one: he understands redneck nuances. He learned them when he was sent to school after returning from Paris. His classmates kicked the shit out of him on a regular schedule until he demonstrated the same kind of carelessness for life and person that they all seemed to possess. In a bar or on an open road, young or old, quiet or loud, Sonny knows his own people. This bunch gathered around Elvira's car, these are not happy, jovial country folks. They are stressed, tense. They want desperately to relieve themselves by whipping ass.

—Sonny, that's Mr Cox, and . . .

Sonny puts his hand over her mouth, pulls her behind a thick, tall sycamore, and whispers in her ear.

—I don't care if it's the pope. Let's watch them for a minute or two. Somebody said something about Prophet. That's Cecil?

—They wouldn't bring that old man out into the night air.

As Sonny and Missy dispute, the big man has made another circuit of the car. —Hood's cold, Prophet. She's been here awhile.

—Even a minute's too long, says the deep voice from inside the truck cab. —So he's back.

—I guess.

—What year you say it was?

—Nineteen and sixty.

—I been owing him for twenty-six years.

—Who's that talking? Sonny asks Missy.

—How should I know? I mean, he sounds kind of familiar, but . . . oh, sweet saving Jesus . . .

They watch mutely as Cecil climbs out of the truck with a large white bandage around his head. It is hard for Sonny to believe he is looking at the same man he dropped earlier at the Billups filling station. This man stands straight. Even from a distance, there is some indefinable quality about him. When he moves, the others watch.

—You suppose he's having a lucid spell? Sonny asks.

—Cecil don't have no lucid spells. Missy whispers back to him.

Still, Cecil paces around the car, stares at the dark, silent house, his eyes focused and burning, his expression no longer slack and vacant.

— . . . stole my damned life, he rasps, clenching his fists. —What do you do a man done you that?

—Lynch him? Ferd Cox asks with an expectant smile.

—Don't be dumb, the other man says. —We're *gonna* do that. Prophet wants something else.

—Oh. Castrate him.

—Whack it off and feed it to him. Make sure he eats . . .

Cecil raises his hand. —Now, this is gonna be the Lord's work, and it's gotta be done right.

—Amen, the smaller man says.

—'Cause this here animal has got money and connections. He's got to go all the way down . . . without a sign.

—No sign, the others repeat.

—You know, Missy says conversationally, —I just can't hardly believe any of this.

—I'd as soon not, Sonny whispers back.

—Well, I mean I haven't never heard Cecil go on like this.

—He's out to murder Shad—and Shad's in there screwing or sleeping.
—But those folks . . . they're the Savior's Friends.
—Then He sure as hell can't use any enemies . . . Come on . . .
—Where?
—Around front. We've got to go in and wake him up. Or pull him off . . .
They go through the shadows quickly, skirting the trees as far from the truck lights as they can. When they get beyond the edge of the house, they pause. It seems plans are in the making.
—Youall go around front, Cecil growls. —Go to hoorawing him, telling him to come out. He's gonna try to make it out the back or one of the windows. I'll be there . . .
Cecil reaches into the cab of the truck and draws out a shotgun.
—That's his old double-twelve, Missy says. —Hadn't been shot since I was born. He's gonna blow his fool head off if he pulls that trigger.
—Come on, Sonny says. They start to run, coming closer to the house. But before they can reach it, Ferd Cox and the other one are there, facing the front door.
—That's Millard Troy, Missy whispers. —Got kicked off the Caddo Parish Sheriff's Department last fall. Seems he was pulling ladies over for parking violations they never even done, and trying to get 'em to . . . Can you believe that?
—Sentell, Ferd Cox shouts hoarsely. —Come on out here, you low-life bastard.

Before it all started, I had just rolled off, shaking my head. I wisht right then that I hadn't never seen Elvira down at the Billups station. It come to me that here was solid proof of my notion that three days with a woman was fine, two days was great, and one day was best of all. Here's one I ain't even seen since before the damned World War, and she's out to stick me with paternity. Well, shit.
—Come on, honey. Don't stop. We can talk about it later . . .
—Bullshit. Looks to me like you're gonna go a while longer without no satisfaction.
—Oh, Shad . . . come on . . .
She went to fooling with me, but I just couldn't find no more

interest. Maybe I thought it might be true. I got up, lit a smoke, and started to pull my pants on.

—How old's that girl? I asked her.

—Be twenty this year . . . Honey, I didn't tell that child to come barging in here. I reckoned your nephew could keep her interested. Please, baby, just a little more . . . I was rounding the corner for home . . .

—I think you better go back and change Cecil's bandage.

—He don't need me. I'm dead. Anyhow, he's got the Savior's Friends.

—?

—I told you. He's a prophet. There's this religious group . . . Used to be the youth section of the Paul's Mission Baptist Church.

—How the hell did a youth group get on Cecil's case?

—Well, they're not youths anymore. It started with Ferd Cox and Millard Troy.

—Haw. Covering their asses. Didn't want nobody to know what happened that night. It was that miserable little piss-ant Millard Troy. He's the only one smart enough to come up with all this bullshit.

—I guess. They told me if I was to tell a word, they'd baptize me. Total immersion for thirty minutes . . . They'd of did it, too.

—I expect . . .

—So what with one thing and another, trying to cover and explain what become of Cecil, they got up this group, and it just kept on going. They'd come sit with Cecil, and there'd be prayer meetings on a Wednesday with witnessing and tongues and prophesying . . . They talked a lot about you.

—Me? Some religion . . .

—No, you was important. Cecil prophesied you'd come back one day in your True Colors.

—True Colors?

—Antichrist. Great Beast of Revelations.

—I been called worse.

—I guess. But you got to see how it was. There ain't a lot going on in Greenwood. Savior's Friends gave 'em something to do. Oh, they said you was to blame for the war. You and E.M. had a deal with the Japs. Then, afterward, youall made a deal with the reds. They had a scrapbook of church burnings and stuff queers did and race mixing. Saw your hand in all of it. They got some of the kids involved . . .

I was dressed then, and had hold of my whiskey again. Here I was, not fifty yet, and a devil in some dumb bastards' religion. Them old boys hadn't changed. They'd still blow you away for a silver quarter. It come to me I didn't have time to get blowed away.

—Why don't you head on back home, 'Vira? The boy and me has got to head back to Shreveport. I've got some work down in the Gulf.

—Shad, you made a mistake twice on me. Don't go do it three times. My Christ, you realize how old we are? How long you reckon we can go on like this?

I started to answer her, but then I seen lights from a car outside. Another goddamned telegram—I hoped. There's worse things than telegrams can get laid on you.

—Honey, Elvira started in again, —you got to talk to our little girl.

—*Talk* to her?

I guess I meant two things. *If* I had in mind to stay around, and *if* I went to spending any time with that little girl, I wasn't gonna talk to her. I was gonna probe her. I reckon it crossed my mind what if she really *was* my daughter. But I didn't wring my hands about it. Folks always said it was wrong to slip it to your near kin, but then folks said a whole lot of shit. Over the years I had heard niggers was a separate species, Oriental gals had cunts running sideways, aspirin in a Coke turns women on, vodka won't give you no hangover, LSU was gonna win every game in 1956, and the A-bombs on Japan was a mistake. You can't believe nothing people say.

—How about she visits me for a while, I said. —Lake Charles. About two weeks . . .

—You goddamn animal . . .

—You're getting ahead of yourself.

—In a pig's ass. I tell you what, the Savior's Friends ain't hard enough on you.

I was listening to her with one ear, and outside with the other. Men's voices. I could pick out maybe two or three. It wasn't cops and it wasn't robbers. I didn't know what it was, but Cecil's crowd had better odds than the pope sending to make me a cardinal. I wanted my goddamned guns, and I wanted 'em right then. I headed for the kitchen to find my stuff and to tell Sonny we might have us some heavy weather. You know Elvira. Right along behind, her mouth going like a cotton-candy machine.

—I ought to call 'em, she was saying. —Tell 'em you're back.

—What do you bet you can save the call? I said, finding my old rutsack.

—What?

—You deaf? Somebody's outside, and it ain't the Greenwood Welcome Wagon.

I couldn't find my damn jacket. The .38 was in a pocket. All I had was the twelve-gauge and a bunch of boxes of double-O buckshot. I like a sidearm, but I been caught shorter. I started breaking open boxes and stuffing shells in my khakis and my shirt pockets like ammunition was going out of style. I didn't need no trouble but it felt good. I mean in the blood. Comes down to it, your ass ain't worth a nickel if it ain't on the line now and again. I was checking out the gun when them boys outside sounded off.

—Sentell, come out here, you bastard.

Now, that annoyed me. I wondered if they had old Cecil out there with 'em. Like a totem pole.

—Sentell, you bugger, send that woman and that little girl out here. Then you and the punk come out hands high. You hear?

—I believe they're paging you, I told Elvira. —You go on out there and tell 'em how bad I am. Tell 'em you come to give me a try, and I'm meaner than twenty-five years ago.

—Hell, she said. —You *are* worse. At least twenty-five years ago you finished what you started.

—Well, there you are. I'm just an old man. About to be gathered to his fathers.

—I bet your fathers ain't in no hurry.

—You want us to come in and drag youall out?

That come floating in from outside. I liked that. The idea of them shitkickers trying to come in made my night. Like swatting flies. But I was worried about Sonny and that girl. They wasn't in the house, I could tell that much. Which meant they was outside. But Cecil's crowd didn't have 'em, and I'd as soon it stayed that way. These boys didn't have too much control even when they wasn't pissed.

I moved over by the window in the back where the car had come up and took a look out. You could see a truck with the lights aimed at the house. Nothing there but an old man. Then I took another look. The old man was Cecil. And somehow he looked like he knew what he was doing.

—You reckon Cecil's been funning you all these years about being mental, 'Vira?

—You're as far gone as he is. Who'd play like he was a feeb for twenty-six years?

—Wouldn't be as hard for Cecil as for some.

Just then, all hell broke loose. I heard one shot, then another, and all of a sudden the only light out there was the moon. Old Cecil's truck had just got its eyes put out. I wondered if one of them monkeys with him had lost control, but I heard one of 'em yell something like "He's out"—meaning me. Right then I got this glow. I believe there was tears in my eyes. It was Sonny out there. He had my jacket with the .38, and he'd gotten it going on his own.

—What's . . . , Elvira started off, but I was already on my way. I hit the little hallway running, and climbed up on some antique chair Mary Clare had stuck in the house after the old man died. Chair was probably worth more than the old man had paid for the house. I got me and my shotgun up into the little attic amidst the rafters. An old trunk and busted furniture and three tons of birdshit up there, but I pushed open the dormer, and I was out on the roof.

I didn't have to wait long to get my night vision. The moon was going down, yellow as butter, and everything just jumped out at me. I knew that land and those trees. I knew everywhere you could find a twig to hide behind. I hiked up to the roof peak real quiet to get me a look around. Wasn't too bad. Out front was a pair of old boys. I could see a baseball bat, and what looked like three feet of gas pipe, but no guns, so I figured they'd be easy. In back was Cecil, and he had him a double gun like mine, and that was it.

It made me ashamed to be took so lightly. Seemed I'd earned better than that out in the woods graduation night, but there you are. Shit, I guess I had too high an opinion of myself. I guess I reckoned Cecil would of brought half of Greenwood armed to the teeth, and still figure to need reinforcements before they brought down Shad Sentell. See? If you don't get your ass kicked up around your shoulder blades once every couple of years, you get to thinking you're a bad sonofabitch.

Well, we was fixing to see. I might be over the hill and fair game for a couple of old boys with clubs and one nut with a shotgun, but they was going to have to show that. We'd damn soon see.

I let go a shot right in front of 'em. Must have lifted twenty pounds of turf and magnolia leaves and whatnot. You never seen such scattering. Then it was down off the roof and in amongst 'em.

It was time to sow panic. I caught one of 'em up side the head with my gun barrel and fired off the other barrel maybe six inches from the next one's ear. He dropped like a load of gravel with a face full of wadding and powder and no hearing left at all. Then I come around on that first one again, the one I'd dropped with the barrel, slipping a pair of fresh slugs in as I turned. All he had to do to get a gutful of double-O was look like he wasn't convinced. No sweat.

—No, Sentell, listen . . . I didn't mean nothing . . .

He sort of coiled up in a knot on the ground with some blood running out of his ear. I kind of thought I recognized him, but I couldn't be sure. He resembled Millard Troy, but he looked old and broke down like he was about run out of gas. Then I heard a yell from the other side of the house.

—Sentell, I got your boy . . .

It put a chill through me. Wasn't nothing serious over here. Just a bunch of fools out for a hooraw. But that voice of Cecil's was like a call to judgment. If he done something to Sonny, he was gonna wish I'd seen to him that last time.

—I hear you, Cecil, I yelled back.

—I been dead a quarter-century 'cause of you, that voice called out. —I ain't got a thing to lose.

That told me one thing for certain sure. Old Cecil had done come out of his dream. One way or another, the sonofabitch was back amongst us. Back in cold reality after a tour as Saint Peter or Saint Paul or whatever he reckoned in that defective mind of his. And he was fucking outraged. I understood that. Just the kind of thing I always feared when I left somebody behind maimed but not dead. Cecil was a loose end I should of tied up back in 1934. Right. 'Cause if I'd killed his ass back then, all he'd have to resent was eternity. Not some certain term of years. But this was here and now, and he claimed to have my boy.

I managed to climb back up on the house, getting madder as I went. If he had hold of Sonny, this wasn't old country messing around no more. This was war. And I got to tell you this much, neighbor. I ain't never lost a war.

—Drop whatever you've got . . .

Sure, Cecil. You go on playing like it's 1934 and we're all fooling around in the woods. And when I'm done, you're gonna have nine assholes and no balls at all.

—I'm gonna let this boy run . . .

Well, he ain't gonna run. Sonny is too smart to run. No, you fucking weasel, he's gonna stand, and I am personally gonna run up your goddamn ass. You want me? You're gonna get me. I was going up the slope of that roof like I never moved before. It felt like the old days, and that was fine.

—I ain't gonna stand here all night with my gun at this boy's ear, Sentell.

Bet your ass, Cecil. You ain't gonna have to stand there any time at all, I thought. I come up over the peak of the roof, and there was that sapsucker standing out beside his truck with his shotgun in his hand. I couldn't see Sonny, but I reckoned he was down around there somewhere. Best way to get him clear was to get Cecil's attention.

—Hey, Cecil, you want your shot, I yelled, and let go right beside him with both barrels.

Took the front of that pickup apart. Shit, it was lovely. Pieces up in the air, noise enough to make you piss in your drawers, steam coming out of the busted radiator. I couldn't even see Cecil for the dust and smoke and steam. I loaded up again and like a damned fool stood right up on that roof peak looking down. A blind nigger with one arm could of brought me down with a brick. But when I get going like that, it's hard to pull back and use my head. Something gets hold of me. So I let go again, and took the driver's door off and the seat out. More noise and smoke and all kinds of hell.

—Dammit, Cecil, I can't wait all night, I yelled at him.

Wasn't a sound. Maybe something falling off that truck, but the rest was silence. Looked like Cecil had took off after the rest of 'em. Lord, I wish I could tell you how it felt. Like I owned the goddamn world. Last time I'd felt like that was just after a mortar attack on one of them damned little atolls with no name. We was bogged down in the sand with the wide Pacific behind us, and here come the fucking marines. Only it was the wrong marines. Japanese Imperial. We didn't have no place to go and nothing else to do, so we killed all day and half the night. I don't give a shit what nice folks say, men was born for that. Give 'em the chance, get 'em past being scared, let 'em go crazy, and there ain't a man born don't love it. Right then, standing on top of that old house my daddy and my granddaddy had lived in, wasn't a decent impulse in me. Didn't matter what happened next. Jesus, it was so good. And I'd been thinking women was better than this? Weakness of character, I reckoned, and took myself a flying leap off that roof.

Well, no fool like an old fool. I like to of broke my right leg where it had been broke a couple of times already, and did awful things to my back. I was sprawled out on the ground like a gutted perch, and it come to me why I'd leaned toward women. If old Cecil had been out there, that'd been the ball game. But he wasn't, and after I lay there ten or fifteen seconds, I kind of got it under control. I been shot at and missed, shit at and hit all over, but it ain't nothing worse than pain in the lower back.

Finally I come up with my shotgun ready, wondering where all the action was. I knew the front was pacified. One was knocked on his ass, and the other one was stone deaf. But where was Cecil? By then I was hurting too bad to fuck around with that Alamo crap anymore. Somebody was fixing to die if he showed hisself.

Then I seen him. Back over by the graveyard. Cecil with that shotgun of his kind of tucked into Sonny's ear, and looking around for me. I threw down on him, aiming high. He was maybe sixty yards away. No problem. I was gonna take his head off or push his chest out through his spine. But before I could pull the trigger, I heard this thump like somebody hit a cantaloupe with a ball-peen hammer, and Cecil fell out of sight like a stone down a deep well.

—Honey, I heard Missy saying to Sonny, —you all right? I crawled over as fast as I could, but what with this old fool Cecil blowing everything to hell . . .

She had my .38 special by the barrel, one foot on Cecil's back like a game hunter with a bear. Over next to him, Sonny was kind of stretched out, too. I knew damned well Cecil hadn't shot, but then how come Sonny was down? I tried to get up and fell down again. Damned near busted my nose on my gun butt.

Things was coming in and out of focus, and the way it looked, if any more of them Savior's Friends showed up, Missy was gonna have to manage 'em alone.

Chapter Seven
29 February 1960

> The sun was now just striking on the fields, as he rose from softly-gliding, deep-flowing Okeanos . . .
> *Odyssey* xix, 434–36

A shaft of sunlight cuts through the kitchen window and burnishes the top of the stove. Outside, a light mist hangs across the yard. The distant trees look as if they are etched against a gauzy drapery that fades almost imperceptibly under the rising sun.

—You want yours fried or scrambled? Elvira asks Sonny.

—Any way I can get 'em, ma'am, he responds.

Elvira smiles at Sonny, who sits at the rough table, his chin on his arms. He manages something like a smile in return.

—You ain't a thing like E.M., she tells him, and breaks more eggs into a big black skillet.

—I never had much chance to be, Sonny replies.

Elvira looks over at the couch where Shad lies, Missy beside him, obviously having found her heart's desire. Neither Sonny nor Elvira seems much pleased by this turn of events. Shad apparently finds it supportable. He and Missy are talking softly. Missy holds his hand close to her breast. Sonny's back is to them. He prefers not to look. Elvira tends to her cooking. After all, this strange reunion of purported father and putative daughter is her doing.

—Does it still hurt, Daddy?

—I just hit wrong, baby. It's gonna be fine.

—Daddy . . .

—Uh-huh.

—I'm glad you didn't do it.

—You're glad this morning. I hope to hell I'm glad by tonight.

—I mean even though you was raised a heathen, you know killing in cold blood is wrong.

—I take exception to all that, sugar. I mainly raised myself, and it wasn't nothing but hot blood out there. Them fools was here to hurt somebody.

—I know. It seemed like Cecil blamed you for . . .

Shad laughs and Elvira shudders. —Yeah. Like I was the one who . . . touched him. Ain't that something?

—You want to butter these biscuits, girl?

—Yes, ma'am.

They eat in silence, and when Shad has finished, he rises and makes his way painfully to the phone. He dials slowly.

—That was a good meal, he says. —We got to be moving on.

—Where are we going? Missy wants to know.

—Sonny and me has a job to take care of. You and your momma had best get on home.

—Home, Elvira bleats. —What's that supposed to mean? We haven't *got* no home.

—That's right, Daddy, Missy says somberly. —I believe if we turned up at the filling station, Cecil and the Savior's Friends would . . .

Shad motions her to silence. —Mary Clare, Shad. I just come round to thinking I better get down there to Okeanos . . . What? I don't give a shit whether you like my timing or not, hear?

Sonny rises and walks outside. It is still quiet, less chill than the night before. The air is wet, and the grass looks as if a shower has passed over. The truck stands in the yard surrounded by pieces of metal. It looks as if it has fallen out of a passing plane. Elvira's car is gone—mode of egress by a stunned Cecil and the Savior's Friends. Sonny almost smiles as it strikes him that the truck serves well enough as a monument to one of those insane redneck passages-at-arms that frequently take place in trailer parks, roadhouses, repair shops, auto parts stores, motels, the streets and back alleys of small towns. Anywhere and everywhere that this peculiar branch of humanity has planted itself.

Sonny does not know why, but he feels depressed. Last night, caught by that lunatic Cecil, he had thought he was likely to die young. He should feel fine. It is said that when death comes close and passes on by, one is elated, renewed. He has heard people say that. Not true. Having survived, you find life coming at you again, not threatening with knives and guns, but with trash in the yard and chill mornings and arid time stretched out ahead as planless as a Monopoly game with Boardwalk and Park Place missing. Everywhere you land is Baltic Avenue.

He is concerned about Missy, but it is no use. She believes herself Shad's daughter; Shad believes otherwise. Shad does not want a daughter; he wants a whore. Would Missy play the whore to be the daughter? Such things happen. She has seen the book. She knows. But she supposes it will be different with her. Thinking it will be different is how you get into the book. A+++, Lgs+++, T+++, E++, H++ *ad infinitum*.

Sonny feels himself shiver. Not from the cold, but from something he knows or does not know. Something he cannot call up from that vast desert within, from which the oasis has disappeared. History is what we do to each other. History is the life of families writ large. Isn't it?

He finds that he has walked to the back of the wide yard, into a small grove of oaks and magnolias planted regularly. What is this place? He walks a few steps more, turning from side to side until through the eddying mist he sees a mass of stone, a monument of some kind. He moves closer and sees that it is a large pylon of granite that he has never seen before. Atop the stone, there is a bronze oil derrick with Ω emblazoned on its side. Below, in great block letters: SENTELL. Has he shivered in precognition, sensing without knowing that he has come upon that place where Sentells rest when they have at last ceased troubling the world?

EDWARD MALCOLM SENTELL
1820–1880

The Major. Who had fought until he promised he would not fight, then fought no more. And came back from Vicksburg to Shreveport, to hatred and obloquy from both sides. Who learned, it was said, to play the violin in his latter days. And mastered serenity.

Sonny stops beside the more recent stone. His grandfather:

EDWARD MALCOLM SENTELL II
1870–1946

Not Sentell Junior. There are no juniors among them. They are numbered even as the Lord bade Abraham to number the stars.

The old man had never once mentioned the past. Or for that matter much of anything present but the weather and how it affected his small crop, the fishing, and the hunting. Had his grandfather, even as they fished the lake when he was small, been filled with the angry vision of Parsons and his other friends hanging, having lost still another small war against distant alien power? Have Sentells lost every round since the first Edward Malcolm?

Sonny walks back out into the yard quickly, thinking he has lingered too long. There is no treaty of peace with Cecil and the others, no lesson taught them. They might return at any time. He tries to clear his head. He has been too long awake, too long immersed in this seedy old country he longs for and despises. He is halfway back to the house when he decides he must be hallucinating. Because poised in the sky just above his head is some kind of immense flying object, and a distant alien voice calling out over and over:

Sentell... Sentell... Sentell...

The helicopter has taken off, and Elvira and Missy are aboard, arms full of the impedimenta Sonny and Shad had brought out to the Old Place in the Jeep.

—Goodbye, Joe, me gotta go, me-o, my-o...
—Shut up, Charlie, and head for the house.
—Yes, sir.

They clear the yard, and in a moment the Old Place, the wrecked truck, the slender thread of road, the distant filling station—surrounded by broken trucks and old-model cars—all vanish into the uniform green of pine and magnolia and oak which ignore the seasons and keep this region of the world as uniform and unchanging as the human substance that prowls and roisters in it.

Down below, the outskirts of Shreveport spring up almost at once. Sonny finds himself somehow surprised that the night's events had come about so close to home. Under the veneer of a prosperous Southern town there remains in its people the last resonant echo of some unquenchable drive that had brought them all south and west, untempered, unsatisfied, a century and more before.

Sonny smiles wryly, recalling that at the back of the yard at the house on Line Avenue, there is a circular concrete pad long disused. It was one of his father's affectations. Long before the helicopter had become a standard tool of the oil industry, E.M. had owned an autogyro. E.M. had liked the vision of himself stepping out of the exotic vehicle, clad in white, at the offices and estates of those with whom he did business. But there had been a minor crash, and that had been the end of that.

—You know, Charlie, this thing would be nice in a war . . . If you was to armor the underside . . .

—You reckon, Mr Sentell?

—Look over there. Highway 80. Couldn't we interdict that road from up here? Recoilless rifle, .50 caliber . . .

—Maybe we ought to send some to Indo-China . . .

—Not worth it. Nothing'll come of it. Be over before you get 'em there.

Sonny stares somberly down into the center of town. There is the Beck Building, the post office, the library, the Texas Street Bridge, and at the far end of the street, the First Methodist Church with its enormous white neon-lit cross—a call to drunken prayer for all those driving back to town late from Bossier City. Now the helicopter crosses Jordan Street and parallels Line Avenue, its shadow falling across Congregation Agudath Achem, stippling the sunlit treetops as it moves southeast over Byrd High School, the Glenwood Drug Store. From here on, Sonny knows the streets by heart, and someone who lives on almost all of them.

They begin to descend between Ockley Drive and Longleaf Road. The yard comes up as quickly as the yard of the old man's place had fallen away. Suddenly there is the reverberation of silence as the engine is cut off, the blades stutter to a stop.

They cross the yard, reaching the terrace and the pool. Sonny and Shad look across the pool, upward at a balconied window —then at one another as if each has caught the other in revelation of a Masonic gesture. The pool is quiet, its water cold. Leaves float on the surface. Other leaves lie on the bottom. Shad drops into a lawn chair, motioning the others toward the house.

—Youall go on. I just want to sit here and get my bearings.

In a moment, Shad is alone, his eyes closed. He has not seen this house in years. He might even enjoy a moment of nostalgia just now—if his memory were not full of reasons to avoid it. Still he takes a chance.

The picture is of a certain night in Kilgore. The year is 1934 or thereabouts. He is at the lunch counter at Effie's Grand Café. He is exhausted. He has been at the rig on the Peterson lease for over thirty hours without a break. He has at last come in to town to eat and get some sleep. E.M. sits beside him, nervously explaining that his own place at Robinson Oil depends on bringing in that well by the end of the month. Loans are due at the bank on the first. They must be extended, rolled over, even expanded if the field they are sure lies out there is to be developed by Robinson. Shad nods mechanically. He is so tired he can barely make out the menu. He knows everything E.M. is telling him. He knows also that there are sharks at Robinson who resent E.M.'s style, and hate him even more because old man Robinson has said that he will bankroll E.M. on an independent basis if he brings in the Peterson lease.

—If we don't get down this month, we're gonna be a long time climbing, E.M. is saying. —Maybe I promised too much too soon.

—Bullshit. It's down there. You can smell it. Like some big snake trying to get clear of his hole. When it blows, it's gonna throw that pipe all the way to Oklahoma.

—Well, if it don't happen till next month, it just as well not happen at all.

Shad nods. E.M. is not being a horse's ass. He can't help the pressure. He is not making it. He is simply sending it on down. There is resentment on the rig, too. E.M. has made Shad the youngest foreman in that part of Texas. He is there for two reasons. He is E.M.'s brother, and he can beat the cringing shit out of anybody in a radius of a hundred miles, and is ready to prove it anytime, night or day, drunk or sober. But he has not yet brought in his first well. If it is not Peterson Number One, it will be a while till he gets another shot. If he does bring it in, his next shot will be a Sentell well. He nods again, and drops the menu. He wonders if hoeing soybeans had been such a bad idea after all.

—I don't want to go in there and tell old man Robinson . . .

—Shut up, Ed. We been throught it over and over . . . If it comes in, it comes in.

E.M. subsides, looks at the menu. He always examines it carefully, and always orders the same thing.

At that moment, Shad lifts his drooping head from the countertop. Directly across from him a girl is moving from the grill with plates in her hands. He looks at her body as she is turned from him, and even through his fatigue he can see that she is exceptional. She has perfect legs, the legs of a dancer with tiny ankles, rich, full calves, thighs that press against the cheap cotton skirt of her uniform. Her hips are wide, her waist very small, her shoulders broad, arms full and lightly muscled. She is turning then, and he sees her profile against a light placed behind the grill. It is the profile of a goddess, serene, removed, beautiful. Now she faces him, her eyes not yet upon him, eyes large and lustrous. Her nose is small and straight, her lips full, curled upward ever so slightly at the corners. Her hair is a gleaming dark blonde, the color of antique gold touched with copper. Her breasts are not large, but they strain against the blouse of her uniform as if seeking to be free.

Shad recalls his feeling of awe, of hunger. She could be the one. Maybe she could carry him where he wants to go. He feels himself leaning forward, wanting to touch her, already half healed, the exhaustion fallen away. He wants to say, I believe you're it. What say we check it out? But such things are not said. In East Texas, what a man feels is presumably no different from what men feel elsewhere. And that is all right. But you do not express certain feelings, especially in public. On pain of finding yourself considered odd, unstable, unworthy of trust.

He cannot now remember what he said in lieu of what he meant to say. But the girl's eyes widened, and she had turned away quickly to vanish somewhere in the back of the place.

E.M. laughed. —Why would you want to scare anything that cute, bruh?

—Cute? My Christ, Ed . . . she's . . .
—Well, yeah. You could say beautiful. Same thing.
—Naw. It ain't the same.
—Screw it. I want the ham steak and eggs.
—I think I need a drink.
—Bullshit. You can't hardly walk now.
—I know.

Shad is stretched out in the lawn chair, the late morning sun warming him. A smile starts across his face. It is not nostalgia, he tells himself. Just recollecting.

He had brought the well in. It had blown away half the metal up above, and sent pipe flying all over the lease. It could have been controlled with a few extra days of cautious drilling, but old man Robinson seemed to want drama. Bankers understood the arc of black oil fanning out against the wan East Texas sky. E.M. had brought the money men out to the rig along with Robinson.

—I wouldn't smoke if I was you, Shad told them.
—We're two hundred yards away.
—That vapor is all one big cloud, and the wind keeps changing.
—What's it gonna cost spud it in?
—That's a whole nother deal, E.M. told them. —We had the drilling contract.
—Youall blew it out.
—You wanted it in a hurry.
—We're losing money. We can't sell what's up in the air. And Peterson's carrying on about his land . . .

E.M. shrugged. Shad recognized that mousetrap smile on his lips. One of the bankers, irritated, forgot himself. He tossed his cigar away. It landed in a settling pond covered by oil and gasoline carefully leaked from a generator that morning by E.M.

Shad's smile widens. He can remember the cigar in flight like a magic wand. As it landed, the gasoline vapor touched off, heating the oil to flash point. The falling shower of crude direct from the wellhead went up like a nascent volcano. The rig, the shack—everything for twenty yards around wrapped in dark oily smoke, recrudescent flame. And Omega Oil was born.

—Well, E.M. had said quietly, his tanned face somber and collected as he watched the bankers and old man Robinson staring at the blaze. —Well, sure, my brother can handle it. He's been thinking of going on his own. He's a born fire-eater . . . worked down in South Texas, Mexico, Oklahoma . . .

That's me, Shad remembers thinking. The low-life sonofabitch has brung me over here to get burned alive or blasted to hell. Some fucking brother. No way in hell he's gonna get me into that . . .

Later, as he was suiting up, the tool-pusher twisting the asbestos under his arms, as they were checking the helmet with the isinglass panel, as he wondered if this is what a medieval knight felt like being prepared for his chance at the local dragon, E.M. had nervously explained to him that this was the main chance. If Shad could cap this runaway whirlwind of smoke and fire, and start it producing, *this* would be their first well.

—The old man was screaming, but the bankers said make a

deal. Nobody else in a thousand miles wants to walk in there.

—Shit, Shad had told him, —nobody here wants to, neither. I may be a little crazy, but I ain't stupid.

—You'd have to be stupid to pass this up. That well's all right up to the platform. All the damage is from the derrick up.

—Do I get me a Palm Beach suit and a pair of buffalo hide black Justins and a new Stetson out of this?

—Is that what you want?

—Naw . . .

Into the inferno. A world where metal glows and five-inch pipe wilts and breaks like a flower stem if you touch it. Hell in a protective suit. Shit, maybe I had better see they bury me in one. Flames soaring all around, and the sound alone enough to drive off anybody with the smallest parcel of brains and a lick of sense, he had thought. A primal sound having nothing to do with machinery, industry, any work of man. The howling, roaring, insane keening of the beast that drives everything. After a few moments, he had become disoriented. He could no longer remember which way he had to turn to get out. But it didn't matter. There was no outside. Only this. The heat, the fumes, that rumble of archaic frenzy became his atmosphere.

—Aw hawwwwww, he had heard himself yell as he wrenched the valve into place at last, closing it before it could become white-hot and fall into pieces. An instant later, he could feel the flame dying around him, hear the sound depart as if, for a moment at least, the beast was satisfied. He stood bewildered, that glowing world fading like an illusion around him. He came to himself in East Texas again on a crumpled platform, smoke and steam blowing away in a summer breeze, water from a pump playing on him, a twisted clutch of steel teetering above, and up there, beyond even that, a real sky fitted with a faded and pastel sun not half so bright as the fireball in which he had lived off and on by then for almost a week.

He remembers shambling down off the wrecked rig, too hot still for anyone to approach, awkward as a knight dismounted, his dragon fled below ground once more to slumber until the next excursion up into the light of day.

Then E.M. was helping pull off the asbestos armor, grinning in utter triumph. —It's gonna be right at thirty-six hundred dollars a week. From now till doomsday, he shouted in Shad's ear. —Can you hear me?

—Hell yes, I hear you. Quit yelling. The goddamned fire's out. Somebody fetch me that Early Times out of the truck . . .

—You don't understand. We're gonna be rich men. I'm gonna buy you that white suit, and I'm gonna get married . . .

Shad had tried to clear his head. One thing was clear already. He didn't want a white suit. What is a rich man, and what is he obliged to do? And that last . . .

—What? You lost your grip while I was in there?

The job had taken the better part of a week, sometimes sixteen- and eighteen-hour days. Shad had not left the well site. E.M. had brought food to him from town. Once or twice, amidst the sweaty haze of dismembered time as he went into the flames and came out again, Shad recalled seeing some girl standing off at a safe distance. His eyes had been too full of soot, too weakened by the fire within to see her clearly, but still somehow she had seemed familiar.

E.M., his white suit now black with crude and ash, helped him over to the running board of the truck. Shad had gotten his whiskey and burned his throat with it. It was fine. That must be what a rich man does. Only all the time, in clean clothes, and with good-looking women.

—It's Mary Clare Fontenot . . .

—Who the hell is . . .

—The girl at Effie's, the Grand Café.

—Shit, Ed, they must have a dozen . . .

But before he could complete the sentence, he knew who E.M. was talking about.

—You were right, E.M. went on. —She's a lot more than cute.

Shad had taken another drink and sat staring at the ground. He had not known her name, but he had thought of her amidst the flames, pretending in some fashion that she was the reason for all this. He had thought he would go back to the Grand Café and see her when this was done. Well, it was done and there was nothing, no one to go to. He felt tired, used up. No use dreaming about some certain woman, reckoning you'll find the right words and one fine day . . . because your brother is already there, and he always has the words.

—You all right?

—Sure, I'm fine. I just got to clean my throat out . . .

—I know it was bad in there.

—It would of been better if I knew what the hell I was doing.

—You did real good. Anyhow, next time you'll know.
—Next time my ass.
—Listen, there's a lot of money in this.
—All right, fine. You get the next one. I'll see to the one after that.
—Shit, Shad, I'm . . .
—What?
— . . . an administrator.

The way E.M. had said it was all right. It was an admission. I am a chickenshit, and there is no way yet devised by man that you can get me into a rig fire, but I am also the one who can sell what you've learned to do. Why, my brother handled Peterson Number One. Threatened the whole damned field. Shad laughed, handed E.M. the bottle. E.M. drank long and deep, as they stood, arms about each other's shoulders, watching the men working again on Peterson Number One.

—Now, that's what I call having the last word, E.M. laughed.
—How about calling our outfit Omega?
—What?
—Omega Oil . . . We're always gonna have the last word.

The picture is of an endless Texas plain, grass almost yellow in the burning summer sun, a single twisted derrick like a broken finger set against the sky. Men in clothing of umber and sienna working quietly, almost passively on and around the well, a single thin stream of water playing on the hot spots, and beyond, the prairie itself pulsating under the sun, cattle grazing near a line of spindly cottonwoods, a 1933 Ford truck parked near a colorless shed, two men standing beside it sharing a fifth of whiskey, as nearly loving then as they had ever been or would be. Even the leaves of the sparse trees are wilted in the heat, and there is no sign of rain coming. There is about the scene a sense of changelessness as if it were etched into the very substance of the earth itself, the men and their grubby enterprise coregnant with nature now, no longer invaders or even ephemeral presences but part of the original sketch from whence this tableau was carved.

Shad's smile fades. His back is still throbbing. He hates to acknowledge the pain. It is unmanly even to be aware of it, to admit that pain can control, govern, claim the attention. He tries to heave himself up out of the lawn chair, but he falls back, his face twisted in what, for lack of a better word, he must call pain. He closes his eyes for a moment and wills it down within bearing.

And when, a moment later, he opens them, there she is. Unchanged in twenty-six years, looking down on him, as always, frowning.

—You're hurting, Marie-Claire says softly.

Yes, he thinks. —No, he says. —I'm just fine.

—Your . . . women said youall had trouble out at Pop's house.

—They ain't my women, and we didn't have no trouble worth talking about.

Marie-Claire smiles, sits down beside him. —How old are you? she asks.

—What the hell has that got to do with anything?

—I'm forty-four.

Shad is silent. Call him stunned. Somehow, in the back halls and silent chambers of his mind he has supposed her still . . . what? Eighteen? All right, given everything, in her late twenties.

—It gets away, don't it?

They exchange a look. She nods.

—We can't go on forever, can we?

Shad's smile has no humor in it. Not just now. He rises almost easily from the lawn chair, no acknowledgment of pain in his face. None. Not the slightest sign.

—Oh, I don't know. I got a few good years left.

—Shad . . .

He turns back to her, triumphant, aware that the blazing pain in his ankle and back is buried completely. —Pretty thing, I don't know about you, but I'm gonna be moving till there's nothing left to move.

—I want to talk about Sonny.

—He's a fine boy. He did real good last night . . . I ain't told him that. Maybe it's better we never know just how good we're doing. We might let up . . .

Marie-Claire stares at him angrily. —If I wanted barroom philosophy, I'd be knocking a few back at the Hurricane.

—Well, ain't that too damned bad? I didn't send for you. I didn't ask you to come out here and trouble me. I stayed out of your goddamned house . . .

—Stop it.

—You're fixing to ask me for something, ain't you?

—Yes.

Shad walks toward the pool, turned from her so that she will not see what each step costs him. He knows she cannot tell he is in pain. She does not know him that well. She might have, but she does not.

—All right . . .

Marie-Claire stares at his back. She is just as glad that he is turned away. Otherwise he might detect something in her expression. Life is very long, and very complicated. No one could wish it longer. Or more complicated.

—You're going out to . . . Okeanos . . .

—That's what I draw my pay for.

—You won't take Sonny . . . My son is . . .

Shad's expression is one of anger and contempt. —Your son?

—Yes, damn you. Mine . . .

—You can damn me as long as you want. But don't you give me none of that absolute possession crap, you hear? We been through all of it before.

—Promise me . . .

Shad's sudden laughter echoes across the pool. —Promise you? I wouldn't give you the time of day.

— . . . you won't take him . . . out with you.

Shad's eyebrows raise. She has brought it off. He is no longer aware of the pain. It is there, but no longer of consequence. He walks around the pool toward Marie-Claire, who stands her ground despite his lowering presence. He pauses, reaches out his large hand and lifts her chin, touching her for the first time in twenty-one years.

—I promise you this, he says softly. —Your son ain't going anywhere he don't want to go, don't choose on his own to go . . .

She pulls back from his touch as if it burns her. —You know what he'll do.

—And I promise you this, too . . . Ain't nothing gonna keep your son from doing what he's *got* to do.

He sits alone behind the cash register with a book in his hands. The others are gathered in small groups out among the quick-service shelves. A few have brown sacks from which they take a drink from time to time. One or two look the worse for wear. They are all talking in low voices, glancing back at him from time to time.

He turns a page in the dog-eared book:

1935. The Huey P. Long Bridge completed December 10 at Metairie, Louisiana is 4.35 miles long. The world's longest railroad bridge.

Cecil frowns. He has never even heard of that bridge. But then, hell, what *has* he heard of? He stares grimly out at the men, who stare back at him. Everything is different. It had not been so bad last night when he first awoke. Ferd and Millard were there. They looked like hell, but he had supposed that was just from what Sentell had done to them. He had reckoned it was the evening of the day after graduation. He had a terrible headache and generally felt like homemade shit. Then he had looked around and generally started to realize that something was god-awful wrong.

1935. Beer in cans is introduced for the first time by Krueger Beer of Newton, New Jersey.

He holds a can of beer in his hand, staring at it in numbed astonishment. Nothing is the same. The trucks and cars parked outside look like something out of that Buck Rogers serial he had been seeing of a Saturday at the Joy Theatre in Shreveport. There is not a bag or can or bottle on the shelves of the station that he recognizes. Hell, he doesn't even recognize the shelves. In fact, he hadn't known why he was at the station when he first awoke.

Now he has been told everything. Half the people he knew are dead, all his friends have grown children. He's been married for years to a woman he was about to rape in that last split second before the lights went out. They say he has a daughter, he has been a most potent prophet of the Lord, the filling station belongs to his wife—except Sentell has turned up again and taken her off, along with his daughter. The only thing he seems to recognize are the fucking trees around the place, and all of them have grown four or five times larger while he has slept. It is a lot to digest.

He stares down at the closely printed pages of the *20th Century Chronicles* someone has given him so that he can catch up. Tons of stuff have come and gone while he has been out of it.

1936. The Cord 810 introduced by Auburn–Deusenberg–Cord of Auburn, Indiana, is a sleek modern motor car with advanced features that include disappearing headlights.

For some reason this entry especially angers him. He had been promised a job with the International Harvester dealer when he graduated. He was supposed to turn up for work the day after graduation. He could have gotten himself a Cord. But the job is long gone, the International Harvester franchise has been out of business for years and . . . His thought trails off. He closes the book and walks over to a mirror behind the counter. At the top there is the tiny figure of a diver, a line of small bubbles. Seven-Up, it says. You like it. It likes you. Cecil has never heard of Seven-Up. The face that stares back at him is that of an old man, pale, loose flesh, wens, and wrinkles. Hair lank and scattered almost to his shoulders. Only the eyes proclaim seething life behind and within. His head is wrapped in bandages as it must have been twenty-six years before. There is a touch of the Islamic cleric about him—even to the crazed, unfocused look in his eyes. Cecil groans, and the others fall silent.

—Where'd you say he was? Cecil asks in a deep ageless voice.
—What's that? Ferd asks, cupping his swollen ear. —I missed that . . .
—Man on the radio said he was headed for New Orleans, Ferd's son Wesley says. —Some kind of trouble with a oil rig . . .
—Sodom, Millard Troy corrects him. —We don't call it New Orleans.
—Sodom. Right.
Cecil nods thoughtfully. —We better get ready.
—Huh?
—Sentell ain't ever gonna see that rig, Cecil says softly.
—Uh, Prophet, what are you gonna do?
—We're gonna see to him . . .
—We . . . ?
The others have gathered around him now, and he looks from one questioning face to another. Several of the young men watch him intently. Ferd squints, tries to make out what is being said.
—I said we have got to go down to that place . . .
—What's he saying? Ferd asks Wesley.
—Seems he wants to go find Sentell.
—Shit, Ferd says loudly. —I done found all of him I can use.

—Prophet, Millard says with a weak smile, —maybe we ought to wait for him to turn up here again, and . . .

Cecil stares at him out of the dark caverns that are his eyes. —I tell youall this. I ain't gonna go through the rest of my life getting hit in my head every so often when that sonofabitch decides to do it.

—I appreciate that, Millard says somberly, —and I don't blame you . . .

—It's got to be a habit with him, Wesley says. —My daddy ain't never gonna hear nothing quieter than a jackhammer if he lives to be eighty. He can't hardly work down to the gin no more. You got to write out on a piece of paper what you want him to do, and Jack Lacy over to the gin can't write. Everybody knows that . . .

—It's got to be punishment come down, Cecil intones. —A river of blood . . .

—What's that? Ferd asks. —I didn't catch that . . .

—River of blood, Millard tells him.

—All right.

Cecil takes a Big Chief strawberry somebody hands him. He takes a long draught and wipes his mouth on his sleeve.

—Who's going down to that place with me? he asks.

No one stirs. There is shuffling and shame-faced murmuring, but there are no volunteers.

—Times is hard, Millard says. —I don't know as I can drop a paycheck just to . . .

—What'd he say? Ferd asks one of the others.

—Said times is hard.

—Right.

—We can get ready for him right here, Wesley says. —And when he comes back . . .

Cecil finishes his drink and sets the bottle aside. He looks out a dirty window. Spring is on the way. It is not yet visible, but the pulse of it is stirring. He puts his copy of *20th Century Chronicles* into a small cardboard suitcase beside his Bible, a couple of shirts, a shotgun, two pistols, and three concussion grenades, old army surplus ordinarily used for fishing.

—He ain't coming back, Cecil says. —He's got what he wanted. He's got my woman and my child. Never mind him coming back. Youall can stay if you've a mind to. I got to get on the road.

Millard shame-facedly holds out a sheaf of worn bills.

—What's that? Cecil asks with a frown.

—This here is the Savior's Friends' Benevolent Fund, Millard says. —What we took up over the years. Been in a interest-bearing account. Six hundred sixty-six dollars . . .

Cecil takes it, stuffs it into his pocket, pulls on a faded and disreputable black hat over his bandages. He walks past the packed shelves and out into the sun. The bus ride to New Orleans will be a revelation. There is a quarter-century of past that needs recapturing. And down there waits the Beast who has taken it from him. That which has been lost will be found.

The others watch as Cecil trudges out to the edge of the highway and stands waiting silently for the bus into Shreveport to begin his journey down to the lair of the Beast.

—If I was Sentell, I'd shoot myself before he got to me, Millard says slowly. The others nod.

—Huh? Say that again, will you . . . ?

Chapter Eight

> But when thou hast crossed the stream, beach
> thy ship by the deep eddying Okeanos, and go
> then thyself to the dank house of Hades...
> *Odyssey*, X, 510–11

The city of New Orleans lies athwart swamps and ridges, between a brackish lake and the last rushing miles of a great river. Ordinarily it is steaming and stinking or cold and clammy. But there are moments, spring and fall, in which popular folklore about the town is actually true.

Just now is one of those moments. It is not yet spring, but a cold front has passed through some days before, bringing with it torrents of rain, tornadoes in southern Mississippi, flooding on the West Bank and such. Now the air possesses a cool crystalline quality which makes the sunlight seem almost like that of the Mediterranean. The weather is not muggy and obscure, nor is it chill and damp. It is just right. The camellias and azaleas are blooming, and the live oaks are presenting their first new leaves.

Even the French Quarter, center of things hateful and deranged, seems pleasant now, and one can, if he stays well off Bourbon Street, evoke another time when coffeehouses and vegetable markets and carts selling fresh fish characterized the place.

Only a few years ago the Quarter had been a dismal embarrassment to the better classes of New Orleans society—such as they are, its history lost and wandering in the corridors, spaces, and alleys of what had become flophouses, warehouses, whorehouses. There had been talk of leveling the whole area in the hope that Yankee money might come in and extend the central business district over the bulldozed blocks of land, some of which had not seen the sun since the 1720s.

Now things are looking up. Some parody of a sense of tradition has risen among certain segments of the populace determined to preserve lest New Orleans commit a second crime like the destruction of Storyville, the most noted whorehouse district in the nation's spotty history. Old wrecks have been repaired and painted. Bankers, suddenly discovering that styles of architecture lately despised are becoming national treasures, have bought up entire blocks. New buildings have risen on the ruins of those brought low by the worst of local natural disasters, the insurance fire.

There are, most notably, new hotels in the Quarter. Some are gross, with national corporate names prefixed or suffixed to some presumably native appellation: the Thus-and-So Creole, the Maison Whatever, Le Bon Contratempts Dumafiggy. There are others of smaller pretense and local origin, owned by politicians, mafiosi, businessmen, stylish sodomites—the classes not being mutually exclusive—and tuned to a more intimate scale.

Such is the Casablanca: one hundred rooms furnished with things referred to as antique, though for the most part they are merely old. The Casablanca possesses what aliens from far places like Omaha or Columbus might call atmosphere. There is no settled definition of the term, but at the Casablanca it includes ratty old furniture, bad reproductions of anonymous nineteenth-century paintings, intricate mouldings and trim on the walls and ceilings, very large framed sepia photos of the city in earlier times, refurbished old plumbing fixtures just purchased from wrecking yards which had obtained them free from renovating owners uptown for the favor of hauling the rubbish away, archaic ceiling fans creaking, rumbling, swaying, and in constant danger of falling into the beds or onto the tables below. And one thing more combining all these and other elements: Sam's Bar.

Words fail. Sam's might well be the archetypal design of a night spot for the blind. Eyesight is of no use here, the lighting of such character that even those who have worked in the entrails of the place for months are reduced to using a sort of large-form braille in order to negotiate their way from bar to some certain table and back again.

Here the furniture is incredibly tacky, the ceiling fans ubiquitous, the paintings and photos even more obscure and desolate since, rather than representing some presumed aspect of New Orleans taste, they illustrate frames from a well-known Hollywood epic two decades old. As one enters Sam's, it appears for a moment in the profound gloom that the patron is to be greeted and seated by Paul Henreid in a white suit.

Time stands still at Sam's. Nothing changes. It is now late in the afternoon. It is all the same in Sam's. A few tourists seem to be enjoying the atmosphere—which approximates that of an Etruscan tomb yet to be unearthed. The hotel's manager sits at one end of the bar sipping one of the obscenities known as a specialty of the house. It is called the Bogey: two shots of 200-proof rum and a shot of Southern Comfort. The effect is unpredictable, the taste disgusting.

The hotel's manager is listening to the jukebox, which glows sullenly in a distant corner. There are those who maintain that the records had not been changed in a decade. They underestimate.

. . . same old story, a fight for love and glory, a case of do or die . . .

—Sonofabitch, someone says at the door. —Can't find your ass with both hands in here. Where the fuck is the lights?

Christopher smiles. His special guests have arrived. He walks through the darkness and holds out his hand to Shad.

—Shad Sentell . . .

Shad squints at him. —Who the hell are you? Do I know you?

—Christopher Neiman . . .

—You're a lying bastard . . . No, you ain't. I guess you *look* like him. I believe you *are* him. Why the hell didn't you never come back home?

Christopher draws in his breath. It is not Shad's way to dabble in delicate shades of meaning. Nuance is not his preferred mode of expression. If he is going to say it all, he will drop it before you like fresh giblets on a linen tablecloth. In fact, it is a long time since he, Christopher, considered that question. He would as soon not now.

—I mean to, Christopher tells Shad. —What are you drinking? Black Jack, all alone and isolated . . .

—That's the whiskey, Shad grins. —Me, I'll take some company.

—You've got it, Christopher says. Just behind Shad, another figure hovers like an unidentified specter.

—This here is my nephew. Sonny, meet Chris Neiman . . .

They shake hands and move inside. Shad sees a picture on the wall. It is of a beautiful young woman who, according to the myth, is torn between love and loyalty, a former lover and a husband she deeply respects.

—I know that girl, Shad says.

—Casablanca, Sonny says.

—Naw, I ain't never known a girl named that. Helga? Karen?

They sit at a table in back, in the very heart of darkness. The gloom is palpable. Sonny looks around uncomfortably. The place makes the Pastime Lounge in Baton Rouge seem like a youth hostel. He wonders how many stabbings take place here on an average night.

—Chris and me used to fish up on Lake Bistineau, Shad is telling Sonny. —Him and his uncle Charlie and me. See, he was in the preacher factory back then, over in England, and . . .

—Preacher? Sonny echoes.

—Priest, Christopher says, staring at Sonny. He seems to recall looking like Sonny once, long ago. As if he were carrying a great weight. Does everyone from Shreveport carry an inexpressible burden within? Is it the water?

—Yeah, all we ever did was fish and drink whiskey and talk about God . . .

Sonny's eyes almost cross. This is a new wrinkle as far as he is concerned. —Talked . . . about God?

—Well, don't act like I never done that, Shad replies sullenly.

—A quart behind, and I'll talk about damned near anything.

Christopher laughs in remembrance. —A piece you miss . . . is a piece you'll never get.

Shad smiles as whiskey arrives. —You remember that? I warned you, didn't I?

—You kept telling me not to go back to the seminary . . . I don't even like to think of what I missed.

Shad looks suddenly serious. —Well, don't take it that way, Chris. Some of 'em ain't much to miss, believe me.

The barmaid comes back to the table. —Mr Sentell? S. S. Sentell? Phone for you . . .

Shad pours a glass from the fresh bottle of Jack Daniels. He is just relaxing from the flight down. There is no one he wants to talk to. —Sonny, you want to catch that for me? It's either one of the women don't like her room or Boudreaux about the damned platform . . . No, it ain't Boudreaux. He don't like to use the phone.

—Uncle Shad, I . . .

—Go on, boy. Tell your momma I'll talk to the manager about it. If it's Elvira, tell her to sit still till I show up. But if it's Missy . . .

—I'll see to it, Sonny says grimly before Shad can say more. He vanishes in the gloom before he has gone more than a few feet. The barmaid points out the phone sitting on the corner of the bar.

—Hello . . .

— . . . sonofabitch . . . About time you . . . down here . . .

—Who the hell is this?

— . . . hell . . . think it is? E. M. Sentell, you motherf . . .

—Well, so is this. Shad says tell me what you . . .

There is a moment of silence. All Sonny can hear is a strange hollowness on the phone line. As if the call were coming across some vast interval of space and time. From Casablanca?

—You . . . What are . . . doing down . . . ?

—I came down to see the Okeanos.

— . . . murderous lunatic wants to . . . out on that rig? Shit, where's . . . mother?

—Up in her room, I guess. What do you want?

Again that long silence. Only static, sizzle, and crackle to be heard. Sonny is not going to speak first. Not if it goes on for the next hour. He cannot help being curious about the man at the other end of the line. Not intensely curious. Not as if he were kin. A distant, bemused curiosity—what he might feel in regard to an interesting historical figure.

— . . . still there?

—Yes.

—Tell him . . . want to . . . him.

—He's busy.

— . . . drunk? . . . sack with some two-bit . . .

—Sober. Talking to a man named Neiman.

—Haw . . . go . . . confession. Do . . . both good.

Still another long pause. The voice at the other end, arguably that of his father, is curiously distant, very tired.

—Get him . . . phone, boy. You hear? No more . . . king around. Now.

Sonny turns in the darkness toward that middle distance where he assumes Shad and Christopher still sit drinking.

—It's . . . your brother.

—What?
—Your brother...
Then, almost as an afterthought, —My father. He wants to talk to you.
—Fuck him.
—I can't tell him that.
—What's he want?
—To talk to you.
—Horseshit. Ask him if he'd like to come in to supper.
—I don't want to ask him that.
—Do it, boy.
Sonny shrugs, feeling some unaccountable chill stirring within him.
—He says—Shad's asking, not me—do you want to come in for supper?
This time the silence seems to last for an eternity. Sonny wonders if the connection has been broken. No. The deep sullen emptiness, resounding hollowness of distance speaks of presence at that far end. Then:
—Yes...
And the line goes dead.

My back was better by the time we got into New Orleans. Everything else was worse.
 I knew how come Elvira had wangled herself into this trip. That woman was just like a Dalmatian. If she didn't see me for twenty years, that was all right. But every time she laid eyes on me, there went the firebell. Wasn't anything unusual about it, I reckon. Women generally hate it that a man gets away. But it had got to be more than that. I guess I would of just smiled and tipped my hat and stepped off again with Cecil knocked silly. That was her problem. But Cecil knocked back to his natural self could be downright dangerous. You had to know that bastard to appreciate him. Him and his crowd in high school used to set stray dogs on fire with cleaning fluid. If Cecil wasn't hurting something, his life was a torment to him. No, after what had passed, I couldn't leave her and the girl there. And that pissed me. Why the hell did I have to take her on? It wasn't any law said she had had to stay in Greenwood, Louisiana, and marry the first sorry demented freak that crawled past. She had the whole world to choose from. She could of gone to Gladewater,

Marshall, Tyler, DeKalb, Carthage, Mooringsport, Mansfield, Minden, Homer . . . there wasn't no limits to her horizons. But she just stayed in that little chickenshit hole in the woods. You reap where you sow is what I always say.

Now, the girl was something else again. Seemed she thought I was her daddy. I had rode all the way down up beside Charlie Mangum listening to his goddamned off-tune Hank Williams so I wouldn't have to jaw with nobody while I thought about the girl. First off, I reckoned if I was her, and I had the choice of me or Cecil for a daddy, it wasn't much choice. A cockroach would of picked me.

But when I thought of it, if I *was* her daddy, and the way I figured, the dates was about right, I had probably ought to leave her alone. Not because everybody said so, but because I figured if you go to sleeping with your own daughter, that kind of builds up trust. First thing you know, you got yourself where she depends on you. And since it wasn't any way I was gonna hang around like clothes in the closet, I reckoned I better pass. At least for now. Never mind later. Shit, if I come off Okeanos alive, I might take her down to Mexico, acknowledge her as my daughter, and then marry her. How do you like that for a shithouse dream?

They had some limousine at the lakefront airport for us, and they whipped us on down to the French Quarter. What a ride. Missy was sitting next to me, asking about my back and did I want her to massage it when we got to the hotel. I had been drinking Black Jack all afternoon, and if my back still hurt I be damned if I could feel it. As far as the massage went, that sounded all right.

But Elvira and Sonny had their eyes on us like a pair of matched crows. Sonny was sweating Missy, and Elvira was sweating me. I knew what Elvira had on her mind. Old bait and switch. Get me hard and fast with this little doll, and just when I'm up and marching, slip into the sack and tell me it's my own child—but Elvira's there, willing and better than ever. So I get my next-to-favorite all-time lay, and a nice little family to boot. If I was ready to settle down, it's a hard package to beat. But I ain't. Not yet. Not just yet. Anyhow, even if I *was* ready, I'd have a different package in mind. But that's a whole nother thing. I got to hand it to Elvira. It was a nice play.

When we hit the Quarter, there was flags and bunting and crap strung over everything. Missy give it all the big eye. She hadn't never seen anything half as big as New Orleans.

—Is it always this way? she asked.

—It's Carnival season, the driver said, scandalized that somebody was country enough not to know. —Tomorrow is Mardi Gras.

—Momma, Missy whispered, —we're gonna be in New Orleans for Mardi Gras.

—What do you know . . . ?

—Daddy, Missy said to me, —will you take me to see the parades?

I saw Mary Clare's head jerk around at that. She hadn't heard Missy call me that before. I guess she thought Elvira and Missy was my usual traveling supply of pussy or something.

Anyhow, we come to our hotel, the Casablanca. It was a rathole, but it beat a Holiday Inn or a Hilton. Small, but okay. They had a nice patio and a pool and this bar where, if you went in, you might never find your way out. So long as they had whiskey, that was all right with me. If I could get lost in there, maybe Okeanos would burn out before anybody found me.

The women went to their rooms, and me and Sonny had us some drinks in the bar with an old boy whose momma I used to fuck up in Shreveport, Chris Neiman. He ran the place, and we was old friends. That's when E.M. called, said he wanted to talk to me.

I guess that rattled me some. I told the boy to ask him in for supper. Hell, it never occurred to me he'd do it. I hadn't seen him face to face since 1946, and I didn't want to see him now. Too late. He said yes. Wasn't no help for it. No way to dodge him now, what with Okeanos all over the front page and the Coast Guard and Interior and every stupid sonofabitch in Washington and Baton Rouge running their mouths off.

After a little, I asked Chris to get us reservations for supper, and left it with him and Sonny. My room was all right, and they'd put my stuff in there, so I got out a fresh bottle and a glass from the bathroom and sat out on the balcony that looked down to the patio and swimming pool. It looked nice. There was some man with his girlfriend in the pool. It was too cold for that, but they seemed to be having a good time. I got to thinking that twenty years ago I wouldn't of taken a moment's thought about jumping into ice-cold water with a good-looking woman. I wondered if I was losing it.

I just couldn't get the picture of that burning rig out of my mind. Every fire I'd gone into had took something away and left something behind. I was a lot smarter and a lot cooler than twenty-five years ago. But I guess I had got cautious, too. In my line of work, too much of that can kill you quick as stupidity. Think long and you think wrong.

I liked it out on that little balcony. They kept the rooms too close. I started to pour another drink and ended up with a crotchful of whiskey. My hands was shaking. Jesus Christ, I thought, is this how it starts? I remembered my old man falling out of his fishing boat and damned near drowning when he had his first stroke. Old bastard had swum to shore with one arm, cursing and spitting water, and then dragged hisself all the way up to the house. Told me he had the worst headache since a yard bull had swatted him in the Nonconnah yards at Memphis back in 1891. I had always thought I was made of the same stuff. Looking at that hand and the whiskey shaking in the glass, I wondered.

There was this feeling of dread. Not death. Dread. Like it was something back in the room about to spring on me. Like I was already on my way to drowning and there wasn't no way back. Like there was invisible water rising in the room, and the next breath I drew would be salt water. I laughed as loud as I could just to hear my own voice, and threw down the liquor. I thought maybe I ought to get serious with the drinking and get pigshit drunk and pass out. I do that now and again. Always works. Next day you got a hangover too bad to let anything else disturb your mind.

Lord, it come to me the last time I had done that, I'd dealt myself out of the action for a week or two. I'd had reason then. I didn't have none now. Anyhow, it didn't matter. I couldn't do it. Boudreaux was on his way from somewhere, and I had me an engagement for supper. And even beyond that, Okeanos was waiting for me. Out there. In the Gulf.

There was a knock at the door. I didn't hear it at first. I had just turned on the TV to kind of fill up that silence. Then the knock come again. I turned the volume off and went to answer it.

—Are you alone? she asked me.

—Yeah. Come on in. You want a drink? There's another glass . . .

—Yes.

I kind of pulled around at that, but I got the other glass from the bathroom and poured out a slug. Mary Clare Sentell drinking straight whiskey out of a water glass? What's society coming to?

—He's coming in.

—That's what I hear.

—He sent his driver for Sonny.

—What?

—Sonny's on his way to Covington to ride back to town with him.

—What do you reckon that's all about?

—I think you and that . . .

— . . . that other low-life Sentell sonofabitch . . .

— . . . are . . .

—Up to something?

—Yes.

—No, you don't. I got no idea what you *do* think, but you don't think that. You know better. Nobody knows better than you.

She held out her glass. —Sonny is still a little boy.

—No, he ain't. And you know that, too.

—Shad, please. In the name of God . . .

—Mary Clare, what the hell's wrong with you? This ain't you. It hadn't *been* you since I got sprung from that goddamned funny-farm by E.M.

We was standing there on the balcony. The sun had dropped down behind the far building, and the shadows was stretching out below. We still stood up in the light, but the darkness was reaching up toward us. It was beginning to get chilly. I looked at her, and she was still the most beautiful woman I had ever seen in my life. Hell, you look at a woman long enough and you always find something wrong. Maybe her hands are thin and weak. When her hair's pushed back, she's got big earlobes. The hair on her arms is a little thick, a little coarse. Not Mary Clare. She was the one.

—Shad, if anything happens to him . . .

—Sonny? It will. Sooner or later, it will. But you and me will be long gone by then.

—You know what I mean. Out at the Old Place. There was violence, shooting . . .

—Nothing serious. Everybody got up and walked away.

—He's going to ask to go out with you. I know it.
—Maybe.
We walked back inside. She was shivering, but I couldn't tell if it was the cold or the worry. And there it was on the TV screen. Okeanos, smoke standing five or six thousand feet into a blue cloudless sky, black and thick and greasy down at the base, and the Gulf flat and almost waveless all around. I leaned down to see what kind of detail I could pick out. Not much. The pilot and cameraman hadn't wanted to press things. I didn't blame 'em.

The sound was off, but I could supply it in my mind. That picture seemed to trance me, to draw me down toward it as if deep inside those flames was the last best answer to everything.

Mary Clare's gasp pulled me back to myself. There I was with my nose about three or four inches from the tube. I could feel the electricity or whatever it was on my face, tugging at my eyebrows. Like Okeanos was reaching out past the dingy, blurred picture to touch me, to invite me. I turned back to Mary Clare, but the image of that platform on fire was still in my eyes. She looked terrified, helpless.

—I love him so much . . . I know I should have done better. He needed . . .
—His daddy . . . ?
—Yes . . . maybe . . . I thought I could . . . that he'd be better off if just the two of us . . .
—I know what you thought. You wanted him sealed off in that damned world you built. Not to be any kind of a Sentell, not any kind at all.

She had her control back by then. She was weak and hurting and ready to say what she had to say, do what she had to do to get past this. But that dream world of hers wasn't gone. It wasn't even breached. Not yet. Not just yet.

And then it come to me it was all right, her world and all that Shreveport Country Club crap. We all live in some kind of dream. I looked back at the TV just as they took off Okeanos and put on this nice-looking girl showing how she used deodorant on her armpits. The picture was gone, but Okeanos was still out there, screaming, howling, pulling at me. From somewhere I got the message. If you want to straighten anything out, now is the time. This one coming is your last go-round. Do I put any stock in premonitions? Shit yes. You think I'm fucking goofy?

—All right, I said. —Put it out of mind. If he does ask, the answer is no. Not this one . . . not now.

She looked at me for a long moment with what, if I didn't know a hell of a lot better, I could of took for love. I believe I blushed a little. Any man would, to have a woman like her look at him like that.

Then she nodded and snapped out of it. It was Marie-Claire again, walking away with what she had come to get. From S. S. Sentell, the mortal bane of her existence for a quarter of a century.

—Supper is at Antoine's. Eight, I think. Will you be bringing your women? Your . . . daughter?

—No, I said, too loud. —And she ain't my goddamned daughter.

—How could you possibly know? she said, and went out the door before I could think of an answer.

I closed the door to the balcony after she left. I kind of laughed and felt better than I had before on account of two things. First was Mary Clare's performance had took my mind off that damned fire out in the Gulf. Second was harder to put into thought, much less into words. It was just a way of feeling. Like this: same old Mary Clare. Twenty years and nothing changed. I hadn't been close to her in all that time, but it was some kind of a joy to see her skin as firm and soft and glowing as Missy's. Her hands looked like they belonged to a girl of twenty-five or so. She hadn't never dyed her hair, and it was still that dark blonde with highlights of copper. I just smiled and drank and thought that maybe it wasn't that time had been kind to her. Maybe in some way time had no control over her at all. There's women like that.

Which, along with another drink, put me in mind of another woman, years ago, at some damned party in Houston E.M. had got up when Omega was just getting started. I didn't want to take off from Kilgore just then, but E.M. raised hell, and I ended up in Houston. I had me some drinks and sported around with old boys I had got to know in the fields. We bullshitted each other about one thing and another, but I got to noticing how everybody kind of made it a point to drop by and say hi to this old gal sitting in a chair who looked to be about the same age as the Smoky Mountains. She didn't pay a lot of attention to the folks coming by, and at first I thought she was either senile or asleep.

Somebody told me she owned pieces of land from San Antone through Center, over to Carthage and up into the Arbuckle Mountains. She had to be worth twenty million or so, and E.M. told me to get next to her. He said if she liked you, she'd give you leases real cheap. I looked at him like he'd slipped a cog.

—You surely ain't saying what I think you're saying.

—Shit I'm not, he answered. —Whatever's right.

—You mean that old woman over there? The one that looks like a tanned lizard?

—I never known you to be so particular. I thought you wanted to get every goddamned one on earth at least once.

—It only looks that way sometimes.

—Well, she's still on earth. Go to it. She's outlived four husbands. First one was at San Jacinto with Sam Houston . . .

—Bullshit.

—That's the God's truth. Second one walked to Appomattox Courthouse—and then back to Texas . . .

I just stared at her. E.M. laughed. —Yes, she's a monument. It was that third husband who bought everything out from under a bunch of Apaches before they stopped that kind of dealing . . . That gal's been around.

Just for the hell of it, I went over and passed the time with Miz Lamar. She looked at me for a minute, and I got the notion she liked me. First thing she asked was where did we keep the whiskey. I asked if she'd like a glass of sherry.

—No, she said. —My goddamned great grandniece feeds me that. With water in it. Why do you reckon I came to this damned party?

—Well, ma'am, I can't say.

—So I could get a decent drink or two without a lot of bullshit.

I guess I looked kind of funny. There she was, deep in her nineties, thin gray hair, but fixed real nice, silk dress that didn't cover the fact that she was all skin and bones. Her hands looked like they belonged to a damned mummy, and she didn't hardly move as she sat in that corner. But her eyes was a rich dark brown, and they wasn't faded at all. You could see right off that she was wise and kind and had a lot of stuff left.

—Ma'am, you name it. If they ain't got it at the bar, I'll send out.

—Well, they ain't got it. 'Cause you can't get it anymore.

God love her, she wanted corn. Said the end of Prohibition and the goddamned Yankee government had ruined the whiskey business. All you could buy was labeled crap they made in New York, and it was so weak she couldn't even taste it.

—Ma'am, I told her,—you stay right where you are, hear?

—I sure as hell ain't going anyplace unless Henrietta comes back and takes me away.

I went out to the truck and found a jar of Roy Polk's latest makings. Back before I took to Jack Daniels for the sake of a sure supply, Polk's stuff was prime. Smooth, but hard as granite, with this smoky taste on the back of the palate and a rib-cracking feeling going down. It could cure a cold, and I never knew anybody to get a hangover from it. I don't believe anybody could drink that much. Roy got six dollars a jar when a good man earned five dollars a day. I stood there at the truck thinking about it, wondering if I was doing the right thing. I didn't want to kill that old lady who'd seen four husbands into the grave. Then I thought, Shit, whiskey ain't gonna kill her. Boredom is. Somebody said she'd raised nine children and fought Red Indians. Roy Polk hadn't never hurt nobody. So I took the jar inside, set it on a shelf in the kitchen, and filled two teacups.

—A spot of tea, Miz Lamar?

—It better not be . . . Oh, my God . . .

She had thrown half the cup down—the way I drink blended whiskey when I can't get anything else. Now, that way of drinking *might* kill her. She just sat there with her eyes closed and I thought she'd had her a stroke. Then she give me the sweetest smile I ever seen.

—Where's the bottle, son?

—It don't come in a bottle. It comes in a jar.

—I believe it does. Can you get it for me?

—Well, Roy Polk mainly sticks to central Mississippi and a few friends in Louisiana.

—You tell him he's got a new friend in Texas. I hadn't tasted nothing like this since Tad Skinner died up in Chickasha.

We settled down for the evening then, with me going back for tea about every twenty minutes or so. I was getting pie-eyed, but Miz Lamar was just fine and getting better. She was sitting up in her chair and laughing, not sunk down anymore. The rest of 'em went in to supper, but we just stayed there in the solarium or whatever amongst the plants and minded our business. I could see E.M. passing by now and again, looking concerned. But then he always looked that way when he wasn't counting hundred-dollar bills or fixing to steal some mineral rights.

—I hadn't *really* had nothing approaching this in forty years, Miz Lamar told me. —Tad Skinner was so-so.

—That's a long time between drinks, I said. —Glad I could serve . . .

She kinda looked me over in a certain way. —I just bet you could, you big, good-looking sonofabitch.

That got to me. I had been called everything from asshole to Zulu, but I hadn't never been called good-looking before. Nor since. All of a sudden, I realized that that old lady didn't look like no lizard. I could see inside her then, and it was pure gold.

—You know, she told me, —it ain't hardly anything worse than being old and broke down. I got all the money in the world, and I can't do a damn thing. They won't let me eat, and I don't have no appetite anyway. I can't go no place, and if I could, I couldn't see where I was cause my eyesight is going. I been operated on for cancer twice, and the stone and cataracts and something to do with my females. Last time, I thought I was off to Glory, but that damned quack brought me back and reckoned I ought to be grateful.

—Well, I heard myself say, —it can't be much longer.

—No, she agreed, hitting that tea again. —And you talk about good riddance. A woman ought to get her kids up and be on her way.

—That's hard, I started to say.

—No, it's true. I never cared a damn for business and all this oil crap. Truth is, I never had a hell of a lot of use for the children. You know what I really liked? What I liked all along?

—Well, I grinned, —you was married . . . what? Three times?

—Four. I don't hardly count Charles Willis. He got killed on our wedding trip. But I expect my oldest boy was his.

—You didn't seem to get discouraged what with 'em popping off regular.

—You're right. She smiled back at me. —Lord save me, I did love men . . .

—You've stopped?

She looked kind of surprised. Then she smiled twice as big, leaned over and took my hand. —Hell no, she told me. —I never did stop. Why should I stop?

I looked at that ruinous old hulk again, and this time my eyes had the scales lifted away altogether. Dear Jesus, there was a fine, strong, lovely woman trapped in there. Like she was in a cave where the rock had closed down to just a slit. I wanted to bring her out, make her one of the rest of us again.

You see, time had caught up to her at last, and it was cruel. She wasn't no old toad who'd always been that way inside, just waiting till her body aged and wrinkled like her soul so she could give the whole world a bad time and not get her ass kicked. She was a whole woman still, but it was like we was on mountains somewhere, separated by a deep gorge. We could see and hear each other, but it wasn't any way we could pass over, either one of us, to the other's side.

—I always loved 'em, she went on. —I loved the look of 'em riding, the way they all used to walk. Like whatever piece of land they was standing on was theirs.

I noticed that people had started to kind of ease back into the room where we was. Somewhere, in another room, they had a little string orchestra playing. A lot of those folks coming back in had their eye on how we was hitting those teacups.

—I loved a man's arms around me. I loved the smell of a man. I . . . I loved the short-sightedness of 'em. How they went out to work or out to die just the same way.

Her voice got low. —I died along with 'em. Pieces of me breaking off and into the grave . . . four graves . . .

Just then this woman about forty or some come pushing through the rest of the crowd. She give me this evil stare and then kissed Miz Lamar.

—Auntie, sweetest, I think it's time we made our good-byes . . .

Miz Lamar looked scared. Put out, but scared. The way she was looking at me, I could see she was pleading. What the hell could I do without making some kind of a scene? Well, I could by God try.

—Miz Lamar, I believe you promised me a dance . . .

This younger one, Henrietta, give me a look like a scorpion.

—Really, she started off.

—Yeah, I said, —Really.

—That's so, Miz Lamar said, recognizing salvation when it come by, however short.

Well, she couldn't hardly walk. But that didn't mean a thing cause she wasn't no bigger than a minute. I just picked her up

and carried her in the other room where they had the orchestra.
  —You boys play a waltz, hear, I said. And they did.
  And we danced. We danced for San Jacinto and Appomattox Court House and all the years between and after, for the ghosts we both loved and honored. Lord, we danced for what it was to be a woman, what it was to be a man. We danced for the time between us and what there might of been had I got myself born fifty years earlier. All those dumb sonsofbitches who'd come to make deals just stared at us, and E.M., who'd been romancing old Henrietta all evening as I heard afterward, looked like he had done pissed in his pants and was about to shit in his socks. But they all kind of faded away. It was just Miz Lamar and me. I couldn't dance worth a damn, but it seemed like I was dancing then. I believe it seemed that way to both of us.
  —Goddamm it, I said to her.
  —Why are you cursing, boy?
  —You know why, don't you?
  Her face softened, glowed. I think there were tears in her eyes.
  —I guess . . . Oh, I tell you, if I had just one more go-round . . .
  —That's good enough, I told her, kissing her on the cheek. —I wanted you to say that . . .
  All right. By then we was both skunk drunk. You can't hold Roy Polk back but so long. He don't put out rosewater. But that wasn't it. Whiskey don't make you feel a damned thing. It just lets you say what you feel.
  —I could of done anything your men done, I said.
  —I know. And I could of made you happy. You ever been happy? Really happy?
  —No, ma'am.
  Miz Lamar smiled and kissed me back. —Honey, I'm sorry for that. Don't you be afraid of love. You find it, hear? You find it any way you can. I could of give up after Charles Willis was laid in his grave. But I said no . . .
  I believe Henrietta had got to somebody, 'cause the band stopped playing, and we was standing in the middle of the floor all by ourselves. I didn't want to let her go. Yelling from one mountain to another ain't much, but it sure as hell beats the silence. I wanted to find a place for her somewhere and go see her every day. Somewhere her snot-nosed uptown niece couldn't find. I know it sounds silly. Who gives a shit?
  I took her back to her chair in the solarium and set her down in

it. I could see she was wore out, and I hated it. We had a lot more to say.

—Cassie, I said (her first name was Cassandra), —you're about to fall asleep.

—I don't want to . . . Shad, they use me like a dummy in a showroom window. They're just waiting for me to die . . .

—Fuck 'em, I whispered. —Leave your money to a nigger college.

We laughed together, and I leaned over and kissed her on the lips.

—Cassie, you ever decide to get out and mess around . . .

—I'll beat your door down. She smiled.

They came and got her then. I followed her to the door and they put her in a big LaSalle, stacking the blankets around her like she was an egg. They pulled out of the drive, and I knew right then I wasn't gonna see her anymore. Even if I'd tried, Henrietta would make sure I didn't get in.

—Well, hoss, E.M. said right behind me, —I hope you had yourself a sweet time dancing and farting around, 'cause you just clowned us out of three-point-two million worth of leases for half that . . . I had Henrietta over the sawhorse and her drawers down till you . . .

—Ed, what do you say we go home, and you let me be. All right?

We drove back to Shreveport then, to E.M.'s house on Line Avenue. I had myself a few drinks more, took a swim, and went to bed in one of the guest rooms. The lights from the pool down below reflected up on the ceiling like I hadn't never noticed before, and it made me giddy to watch that ceiling flutter and sway as if it was a pool itself. As I drifted toward sleep, I couldn't help thinking on Cassandra Lamar again.

It come to me that who we are and what we love ain't much more than a matter of the time and the place we find ourselves in. If I'd been born in Texas in 1840, one way or another, me and Cassie would of come across each other, I was sure. We would of been happy, too. For however long we had. We would of both understood that every day was a new gift and tomorrows was scarce back then. All right, fine. Look how I felt after just one night, and her fading toward eternity.

I dreamed I was out on the Texas frontier. I had me a spread, and these Indians raided the place for beef, and Cassie and me figured to set them savage sonsofbitches up and blow 'em away. Right then, E.M. woke me up.

—Christ, he was babbling, —you're not going to believe this...

—Try me, I said, barely awake. —I can believe nearly anything.

He handed me a telex from Houston. Six tons of legal junk. I looked up at E.M. who was smiling like a fox with the deed to the henhouse in his hand. —I can't believe it if I can't understand it, I said.

E.M.'s voice got low. Like he was witnessing to a religious experience. —Any Lamar leases we want, any. At ten cents on the dollar down, and ten percent of profits till payout.

He shook his head. I had never seen him speechless before.

—I believe it, I said.

—We just got to be big, he said. —Very big. I can borrow half the money in New York on this, he said, waving the telex. Then he stared at me. —I watched you all night long. How the hell did you do it?

That almost made me mad. —I didn't do nothing, I said. —But you ought to send Roy Polk a case of Marsh-Wheeling cigars.

When I got back to Kilgore, there was this special delivery package for me. I opened it up. There was a note on top.

Shad Sentell,
It was a good evening. The best I have had in almost forty years. Thank you for reminding me. I had almost forget.
Cassandra Lamar

With the note, there was a picture. It was in a solid gold frame that must have weighed a pound. The picture was of a beautiful young woman standing alone in one of them old-fashioned dresses—long skirt, narrow waist, bosom raised and tight. Her right hand rested on some kind of broken column, and her face was turned toward the camera smiling and without care. No, maybe not just without care but beyond care. So purely full of herself and the person she was just then that there wasn't no room for fear or foreboding or care.

On the back, it said in beautiful Spencerian script, Cassandra Wellbourne, Galveston, 1868. I wondered if that was her maiden name, if it was a picture made before she was married. If there was such a picture, that's what she would of sent me.

I turned it in my hands. There was Cassie, a young woman looking out at that anonymous camera and past it to the world, her eyes bright and hopeful, her body strong and untouched. Ready for whatever the world might offer. There she was, three hundred miles and seventy years out of my reach. And yes, Lord, I would have turned my head had she entered a room where I was talking with the boys. And yes, I would have wanted her as much as a man could want a woman, not even thinking of a deal or money because any woman worth wanting at all is worth all the deals and all the money that's ever been dragged together. There she was, looking out of 1868 into my world, smiling, saying, Here I am with all the world and all my life before me. Please, let me know how it will be. Please, somebody, reach out your hand.

I closed my eyes and thought, here I am having done stuff that no other sonofabitch on this planet would even try, much less succeed at, ready for anything. And I can't do it. I can't push time aside. And put out my hand.

The next year I spent setting up new drilling sites on the leases E.M. had negotiated with the Lamar interests. Then, when I was dog-tired and ready to drop, things broke for a while, and I went on back to Shreveport. I remember it was late summer of 1939.

Everybody was keyed up by what was going on in Europe, but it looked like the oil business was gonna do just fine. I went by E.M.'s office, but one of his secretaries told me he was out of the country. He had left me a letter, though. Except when I opened it, it wasn't no letter at all. Just a clipping from a Houston paper.

It said Mrs Cassandra Lamar had passed away, aged ninety-six, cremation and deposition of her ashes in the Gulf as she had wished, and some crap about her being a Texas pioneer and on and on. I sat down at E.M.'s desk and stared at that clipping for a long time. Then I went over to my luggage and found that picture she'd sent me. I shut the door to the office because right then I didn't need any interruptions.

There she was, freed of time at last. Twenty years old or thereabouts. There she was still, her eyes fresh and young, her body at an angle to the camera so you could see how fine it was, her hand on that plaster pillar that had broke up and dissolved in rains in a backyard somewhere before I was even born. There she was, standing against some painted pastoral backdrop that no one could find in a hundred years of looking, for any amount of money whatsoever. Cassandra Wellbourne, a daughter of Texas, at the very moment of her entry into the world. Now, almost a century later, she was gone from it, and good riddance, like she said.

And here I was, up to my ass in the stock of Omega Oil, making money I couldn't even imagine spending, with a iron-clad lock on Lamar leases that Henrietta couldn't bust loose from in a month of Sundays. And down there in Houston an old lady who had long outlived her men, her time, and most of her children had been gathered to her ancestors. Now ain't that the way things go? And ain't that the way they're *supposed* to go? Sure. Of course. Why not?

Except there was one mourner who couldn't make the funeral and pay his last respects because they had already had the funeral, and I wouldn't have gone anyhow.

What I did was drive out Kings Highway and on out Highway 1 past Dixie Gardens where I could take the last jar I had of Roy Polk's fine whiskey and climb up over the levee and stand on the bluffs of the Red River. I took as long a drink as a man could, and then I threw the rest of the jar out spiraling under the summer sun until it hit the slow, shallow brown water down below and started its long journey through all the waters of the world until in course of time some trace of it would touch some trace of her in tribute and remembrance. And if I believed anything at all, I did surely believe that. I needed to. I just flat had to.

I drove back into town then, hardly paying any attention to where I was going. Halfway back, it started to rain real softly. In the distance, I could hear thunder, and I could smell that clean, crisp aroma of fresh rain on hot concrete.

When I looked around, I was at Pierremont and Line Avenue, wore out and needing a drink. All there was there in those days was a Holy Roller church, and the nearest whiskey was a couple of miles up the street at E.M.'s house. Never mind how I could have drove back downtown. I pulled up into the drive and knocked on the door. What the hell do I know? Maybe Cassandra Wellbourne hadn't done with me yet. I waited there, too tired to feel, too down-hearted to care. After what seemed a long spell, with the rain soaking through my shirt, Mary Clare came to the door.

Chapter Nine

> We pour an offering to Okeanos . . .
> *Georgics,* IV, 481

We pulled into this long driveway. It was still daylight, but not there. The oaks were tall and gnarled and older than the path we were driving on. You could see that whoever carved out the roadway had been careful to display the live oaks with Spanish moss dripping down from them. Then, out of the gloom, the better part of half a mile away, standing unconcealed in the late afternoon sunlight, I saw the house.

It looked to be as wide from side to side as a football field, blinding white frame with square pillars across the front. There was a balcony at the second-floor level that seemed to run all the way around. Within a few yards of the house, on both sides and out into the distant sloping backyard, there were magnolias as thick and tall as the oaks.

A Southern castle, the kind of place we all dream of. Where all our people lived, every last one of them—the blacks' were a little smaller—until we were burned out by Yankee greed and envy.

We drove up in front, and the driver turned off the engine. Then he just sat there. Hell, I thought, I could starve to death looking around this place for another living soul. Do I just walk up and ring the doorbell, walk in, or wait to be summoned? Sorry to be so maladroit, but you see . . .

—He'll be out back, the driver finally said. —He's always out back this time of day.

I got out and started hiking down the front of the house and around the side. Like an ant doing his constitutional around the Washington Monument. It was still pretty warm. Down here, you could count on the sixties when Shreveport was fifty. The sun was low in the west behind the house, and the area shaded by trees was already close to twilight. I walked through that corridor of shadow and came out into the weak sun again, shivering. But I thought it wasn't the temperature. It was that other thing. Some kind of foreboding. I shouldn't have come. I should have told the driver to go back and get him and bring him in. That I would meet him along with Shad and my mother, who, if they had done a few numbers on my head over the years, had at least been there. Bullshit coming all the way over here. I wasn't his servant. It seemed as if I wasn't even his son.

The backyard, when I finally reached it, looked to be about twenty acres—maybe fifty. It wasn't even a backyard. It was a park. Grounds. Estate. Off in the distance, you could see a lake or a river. There was a dock with boats tied to it. Halfway down that long slope to the water, on the left, I saw what looked like a pin on a golf green. The tennis courts were closer, near the swimming pool with the three-meter board. The whole place made me think of a painting. How about English Estate: Teatime. 16 June 1904. Everybody is inside. Tennis is done for the afternoon. It is not quite time to dress for dinner. Please do not press against the guard rail. Then I turned back toward the house and saw the terrace.

There was an arbor thick with old vines, some of them inches around. They were leafless and looked dead, but in a few weeks, a month at most, they would be alive again. Inside the arbor there was a table, and through the vines I could see that there was a sparkling white tablecloth on it. There were bottles, glasses, and what looked like an ice bucket. There was a lawn chair, too. At first I thought it was empty, but then I saw a hand on the armrest.

I say hand. Try claw. There was skin and plenty of bone to it, but it seemed there was nothing but a gray mist between. I wondered who might be staying with my father, who could be so old. Then I remembered what Shad always said. Most of the rich are old. Because only an old man is fool enough to save it for a rainy day when it is likely as not he'll be nice and dry underground when the rain starts to fall.

What the hell? I might as well start playing E. M. Sentell IV. That's the role I had decided to take on. Cool, distant, ironic, laconic.

I walked around in front of the arbor so that the sun was behind me, my shadow falling across the occupant of the chair, who squinted up into what must have been a dark, looming shadow cutting off the last light.

— . . . there . . . ?

No, I almost said aloud. This isn't him. I don't know who it is, but somebody will come and tell me. Some great-uncle I never heard of, some pensioner that helped him get started right at the beginning. But it isn't him. It can't be. I know how old he is: two years older than Shad, which makes him forty-six. He isn't eighty or ninety.

— . . . here . . . boy . . . ?

I still didn't answer. Because I couldn't. I knew why I had come now. It was as clear and mean as a quick knee from low down: to tell him to go to hell. Whatever had gone wrong that he couldn't abide, that had driven him from Shreveport all the way down the state, didn't matter anymore. I was beyond caring about it. I had gotten this far alone. I was all right. The next disaster in my life was going to be caused by me—not by my mother, and sure as hell not by him. So what was holding me back?

Have you ever seen a photograph of the mummy of Ramses II? That was what I was facing, and I knew it was him, my father, because, above the emaciated face with skin stretched so tight that it seemed about to burst, above great hollow eyes that seemed to glitter like x-ray machines in B-movies, penetrating to the core of things, there remained intact that sweep of gleaming, perfectly cut and combed silver hair.

— . . . You're the . . . boy . . . Sonny? Yes, you're a . . . Sentell . . . Can . . . see that.

I had said nothing so far, still wide-eyed, still staring at this ancient, debilitated figure in a white suit cut for someone twice his size, sitting with a glass in his bony hand. There was an expression in his staring eyes as if he were at every moment face to face with something unspeakable. Did he always look that way? Or was it me?

— . . . drink . . . gin? Any way you like . . . gimlet . . . tonic . . . fine martini . . .

He seemed irritated by something and fumbled with what looked like some sort of a signal buzzer on the edge of the table. I heard nothing, but almost instantly a black man wearing a white coat came out from the back of the house.

—Fucking . . . martini. This . . . Sonny . . .

The black man smiled at me and offered his hand. —Don't mind Mr E.M. He gets pissed off, and when he does he has a little asthma. I'm Henry.

I knew the name. He had been my father's valet. Maybe I even remembered seeing him long ago. He had left with my father. Despite the fact that he had been courting one of the maids. Henry Tobias. My mother would speak of him. A man of unusual imagination, she always said. If Henry sees something in him, Eddie can't be all bad.

We shook hands, and Henry made martinis by rote, looking out at the setting sun. —I believe, he said, his words directed to no one, talking to himself aloud in case we chose to pay him no mind. It was a nice device. —I believe on the far side of these here martinis, we're gonna go in and get ourselves ready for a big night in town.

—Goddamn clothes . . . scarecrow . . .

—I got one back from the tailor.

—Ah . . .

—You're gonna look fine. All things considered.

Henry handed each of us a crystalline martini in a glass so cold it chilled my fingers to the bone. My father threw his down before I could get mine to my lips.

— . . . Blood to . . . vampire. Remember . . . said that? Damn runner on . . . blocks. Wait all day . . . Ahhhhh . . .

—He likes his liquor. Henry smiled indulgently. —Gets stone drunk every night. Can't hurt . . .

—He's . . .

I tried to whisper as my father pushed his glass back to Henry again. But Henry shook his head. —No need of that. Mr Sentell suffers from cancer.

—No one told me . . . I don't think anyone knows . . .

—No one has told no one, Henry said serenely. —That's how he wanted it. If not for Okeanos, I believe he would have got clean away before anyone knew up home.

— . . . own goddamn . . . siness. No family . . . ything gone wrong . . . years . . .

He began to cough harshly, and Henry held his fresh drink until he was done. Then he gave him the second martini. As he ministered to my father, Henry kept glancing at me from the corner of his eye. I couldn't tell why. Maybe he was just curious, trying to see if he could find anything left of the child he had known so long ago. Don't sweat it, Henry. Mostly boiled away. The rest is going.

—Well, there it goes, Henry said cheerfully as the sun was lost below the far shore of the lake or river, whatever it was. —I believe we are due at Antoine's at eight sharp, Mr Sentell. Would you be ready to . . .

—One more . . . No . . . fix a shaker . . .

Henry smiled and took out an enormous thing that looked like a gallon pitcher with a chrome cap. —He gets through a quart or so of Bombay between five and ten, he told me, as if it were a matter of family pride. Maybe it was.

Henry took him inside then, carrying the big shaker with him. He nodded that the small one was for me. I followed them in and strolled around the house while Henry was putting him together. I left my glass behind and started drinking straight from the shaker. They were the best martinis I had ever had in my life. I was convinced that if I could get through the shaker, I could get through the night.

I walked into a room that must have been his study. There was an old roll-top desk covered with papers that looked more like a museum display than a place to work. I expected Henry had arranged things months ago and they had not been troubled since. On the walls were old photographs and plaques and framed stuff like a special commission in the state police signed by Governor O. K. Allen. There was a faded old photo of E.M. and Shad standing on either side of Huey Long, who was smiling at E.M. with his arm around Shad's shoulders. There was the brand-new state capitol behind them, and they all looked pleased with themselves. New men for a new time—all up in a hurry. Another picture of E.M. and Shad standing in filthy clothes near a shack with a primitive, burned-out twisted derrick in the background. They are sharing a bottle of whiskey and grinning like apes. They are covered from head to foot with crude or burn-off, and look like a pair of comics from a Mack Sennett quickie. But they know. Not in detail but in general. They know, because, lettered along the bottom of the picture in faded ink is: PETERSON NO. I OMEGA OIL.

There are dozens of other pictures. Some of the Old Place, one of the graveyard. A picture of Pop on what looks like a stuffed horse. He is surrounded by men who look like Mexican bandits. For all I know, they *are* Mexican bandits. Pictures everywhere

—but not one of Mother or me. All right, not Mother. I could understand that. Something had happened between them. But not one of me, either. It was as if E. M. Sentell had never married, had never had a child. It was about then that I began disgusting myself. I suppose I had been looking for a secret: my father had always loved me, and when he left us, he had taken with him bronzed baby shoes, pictures, crude little drawings, a fragile old baptismal gown. Over the years, he had drawn them out from time to time to weep over. Horseshit. There wasn't a secret in sight. My mother and father couldn't stand one another, and my father didn't give a damn about me, either. Not then. Not now. Just then is when the self-loathing began. Gazing at the endless array of pictures and mementos on the walls of the study, finding myself nowhere, I felt my eyes mist up. If you drink a large amount of gin scarcely troubled by vermouth in a short time, that can happen. An old song, a forgotten name . . . No, that's no excuse. Shad could drink a quart in half an hour and laugh at an execution. I don't know where the cheap sentimentality, the hunger for feeling, comes from. It must be bad blood.

—I beg your pardon, Henry said at my elbow.

—Huh?

—Your . . . Mr E.M. is almost ready. He's had his medicine, and he's just sprucing up.

—Medicine? Does anything help?

—Well . . . Henry smiled serenely. —That depends what you call help. He's not gonna live an hour or a minute longer on account of it.

—Oh . . .

Henry glanced around as if he was concerned that someone else might hear. —It's dope. Some stuff with numbers and letters. Experimental. Absolutely forbidden to be used by folks. But we got connections.

—It helps . . . ?

—Helps? Man, if that stuff was legal, I'd use it in whole-hog sausage, and the entire country would be happy. You not gonna believe Mr E.M. . . . Makes him a new man.

—How much can he . . . ?

—Take? You concerned about this evening?

—Henry, I'd as soon go spend the night up an elephant's ass.

Henry nodded, shrugged. —Well, he was still on his morning

dope when he made that call, you know. Said your . . . Mr Shad Sentell invited him in for supper. Said he'd rather drink muddy water, sleep in a hollow log than miss it . . .

—But if he just goes in and . . .

—This substance concentrate him powerfully. As do thinking of Mr Shad Sentell.

—God, they hate each other.

—Ummm, Henry said, and took the empty martini shaker. —You had enough?

—I don't think so.

—We'll fix a bunch to take along, huh? I sometimes drinks with him. What the hell? One get soused, we all get soused.

—You'd as soon he didn't go to that supper.

Henry was leading me back to the kitchen. It was enormous. The pantry could have housed a platoon. Filled with mostly liquor.

—I tell you this much, Mr Sentell. It can't make no difference. If it was me, I'd go in red-eyed and come out red-fanged. So to say. See, where he is now, he can't win. Can't. Not unlikely or mean odds. Can't. Ain't. Not gonna. Now, you have got to see the advantage there. If you *can't* win, why, you can't *lose.*

I didn't follow that for a moment. Then there arose on the skewed and weatherbeaten stage in the theater of my mind the image of E. M. Sentell III, at some certain point in the supper upcoming, reaching in his pocket, doing something obscure with his hands below the level of the table, and then placing a live grenade, pin removed, in among the carrots and peas. I struck the sets quickly, refunded admission to all, and got out of there.

Henry had a fine, fast, light touch with a drink. When he had done with the Bombay and the vermouth and the ice, he took a small bottle from his pocket and with immense care let one drop fall into the shaker.

—What's that? I asked. The martinis were superb. I wanted to know.

—I had governors and A-rabs ask me that. I don't tell nobody.

Then he handed me the little bottle. —Now you and me knows. You tell anybody else for less than a couple of big ones, I'll come at night and haunt you.

On the bottle was a crudely printed label. It showed Confederate infantry assaulting, the battle flag borne high. Dr Tichnor's Antiseptic.

—Takes the edge off cheap gin, puts a sweetness on good stuff. Never had a complaint.

—One drop . . .

—Two, and you fucked up. Pour 'em out or gargle with 'em.

—Maybe I'll be a bartender.

—No. Maybe you'll be a rich young college man with the whole mess right under his thumb. You gonna be The Sentell.

—The . . . whole mess . . .

Henry looked at me strangely. I guess he was smiling.

—You going to be a man of means, throw a lot of weight up in Caddo Parish. One way or another, things going to get straightened out with you.

—Straightened out . . . ?

—You know what I mean.

— . . . ?

I make Henry leave after the medicine. I do all right then. I do fine. I can pull on these pants, tie this black tie—a color I have never worn before. Saved for tonight? Because there had to be a tonight before there comes that last and lasting night. Not seeing the boy. I hadn't even given thought to that. But seeing my brother. Seeing my brother after fourteen years. I knew I would see him one more time, and that I would have to do nothing at all to make it happen. I have to see what time has done to him even though that entails letting him see what it has done to me.

I look around this room. I have lived here alone since the latter part of 1946. Women have come to this room, but none has stayed. I never asked one to stay. Now no more come. Perhaps that is a mistake. I could buy all I want. Maybe in the midst of whatever kind of orgasm I could muster, my heart would fail and I could leave these last months—weeks, days, hours—aside. No. That would be Shad's way.

Speaking of mistakes. Shad was my biggest mistake. One so vast that even now I cannot quite get hold of the scope of that miscalculation. Which is absurd when you consider that there is no mystery, no secret to Shad Sentell. He has always been utterly predictable. He still is. Perhaps my mistake was in supposing that no one, absolutely no one could be that regular, that invariant.

Never mind. I expect one way or another, the old man ruined us both. I despised him. Even as a small boy, I distrusted him. I can remember him sitting on the porch telling old Claiborne that the bourgeois family was doomed, the family relation reduced to a cash nexus. I listened. I learned chess watching those two old Red bastards playing and debating the merits of Trotsky and Stalin, the glories of the Revolutionary State. I figured out early that, as Henry likes to say, money talks and bullshit walks. I knew that if I didn't look out for myself, I'd end up chopping cotton when I was forty. On somebody else's land. Or owning me a filling station. That wasn't going to happen. Not to me. The old man could live out his days in his damned silly radical dream world if he wanted to, but just as soon as I was old enough, I was determined to put distance between me and that ill-tempered old loser.

The fact is, maybe I made my initial approach to the mistake all the way back then. Shad and I should have been close. We could have been close. The old man had little more use for Shad than for me. After my mother left him—left him in the most expressive and direct manner—the old man had no interest in either of us. I think he was relieved when she killed herself. That was the end of it. Now the last thing in the world that could betray him, turn against him, twist and break in his hand, was gone. Now he was truly and honest-to-God alone. Except for us. And us he ignored. I should have taken up that slack. I should have pulled Shad into my dream much sooner. I believe we would have both been different if we had shared that dream together. But I am not a good sharer. I do things alone. I do them with great care, with silence and secrecy. I always managed myself around the old man that way. I never gave him cause to whip on me. I just stood at a distance and hated him.

Once—when he was what? Five or six at the most—Shad hit the old man. I remember it more clearly than last week's appointments. The old man had come in from plowing, staggering with exhaustion, angry, barely containing that fury that dogged him every day of his life. His dinner was on the table, but not the buttermilk. It was not there. In fact, Momma was pouring it. He spoke to her sharply, and she paused in the pouring, her head up, expression unchanged. The old man did not move to threaten her or strike her, but Shad heard something in the old man's voice as he came into the room. Some certain thing in the old man's contemptuous tone, or even more likely in Momma's straightening up, that slight stiffening in her back as if she were a bond servant who could not act and had in fact not even the right to resent, but who nonetheless could not let such a slight pass without at least some response even damped, buried in the body.

Shad looked at her in horror as if the old man had felled her with a singletree. Then he launched himself across the room at the old man just as he was sitting down and off balance, and knocked him sprawling. I did not see the old man's face because I was looking at Momma. Her eyes met mine, and she smiled. Not for the small vengeance her youngest had afforded her, but for his own sake. She knew at that moment what I knew, too, but have never been able to admit and have used every sorry excuse to avoid admitting for almost forty years. Shad was a thoroughbred. No, not a damned race horse, because however beautiful and fleet and graceful, that poor sonofabitch runs when his master says run and stays when his master says stay. Shad was a range horse, a wild stallion who will vault over a cliff at the touch of a rope; an outlaw of no earthly use to any master except in the most dangerous and venomous kind of a rodeo where it is required that somebody, anybody, be seriously hurt for it to be any kind of a crowd-pleaser at all.

That smile of hers, and already an instant's shame in me, and then I was turning, knowing that I was already too late to see the expression I wanted to see: that prophet of social justice, that tribune of the people flung on his ass by an angry six-year-old. The great train robber, the agitator, the prince of radicals down on all fours for speaking harshly to a lady. But I missed it. And missing it knew that I would never even get an adequate, much less a satisfactory, description of it from Shad—who could only say later, as I rubbed bacon grease on his butt and legs, that the old man had looked plenty pissed.

That much I had seen for myself. As he got up, caught Shad by his overall strap, and dragged him outside, catching his razor strop off the wall near the sink as he went by. Neither Momma nor I moved nor spoke. We knew what was going to happen. He would beat Shad, and Shad would draw himself inside himself and not cry, and the old man, who was already too shaky from plowing since first light to do him any harm, would give up, and Shad would know that he had won, vindicated her, and she would know—already knew—that Shad would beyond a shadow of doubt find his integrity and, sure as God scattered the stars, live *his* life and die *his* death.

Which, when you think about it, left only me with nothing done and nothing known. But then that's not altogether true, is it? I had seen it all—all but the old man's first expression. What I did not know was that I would see even that, its sure and certain reproduction, years later. Nor could I even have imagined what it would cost me.

Shad was inconsolable when she died. He loved her. I believe he truly did.

They did a strange thing, the women who came in, who had not been her friends because she had no friends, because if for no other reason he wanted her to have no friends among the peasantry who were our neighbors and whom he hated because they suffered the capitalist wage system to burgeon. The women laid her out in the same white dress she had chosen to die in. They took it from her body and dried it and hot-ironed it and placed it back upon her once more. Doubtless because it was her one nice dress. But still she lay in her coffin as she had lain in the water, as she would lie in the earth.

No one and nothing has hurt Shad from that day to this. He has been not only proof against pain since the day they folded the earth in over her, but not even concerned with the threat of that kind of pain again. And I have never told him, not in thirty-five years, that his womanizing constitutes nothing more than walking in the dark, avoiding the old man, seeking a part of her in every woman he reaches out for, draws near, absorbs, and leaves behind.

He used to keep a book years ago. He may still, for all I know. It was incredible. It was filled with all her names and all her places of residence, and all the other men who claimed her—as if, when he completed his anthology, it would be the equivalent of having possessed her piecemeal almost every night for all the nights of his life. That is his unrealized fantasy. Mine was that I could somehow avoid her, keep the search for my own integrity at bay, live some other life, dying at last no death at all, preserving myself in action from that deep yearning that drew her up one night while the rest of us lay sleeping and carried her out to the water where she would be free of him and his old wrecked feckless rage, and even of us—Shad and me—whose mute love did her no good, moved her, daughter of silences, into the Silence.

It has taken me this long to know that, having lost her, I went on to lose my brother. The first loss was no fault of mine. I owe that—among other things—to the old man. The second was my doing. I have had reason to regret it.

Not that Shad held anything against me. I expect if someone were to ask, it never occurred to him in all these years that it might have been otherwise between us. He blames me for nothing because he does not think. He is not dumb; he simply does not think. He does not need to. He is carried by the blood, sleeps well at night with whatever woman is beside him, still loyal to her, pressing on through a sea of flesh, young ones, old ones, pretty ones, brutes, still trying to catch another glimpse of her.

But something happened amidst that quest. Something I would not have guessed if given an infinity of guesses, or believed had I been told. He came upon her. He reached her. No, not her of the silences who was lost to us both in the prim decency of the grave, buried simultaneously within us both. Her. Mary Clare—who was my choice, my way of moving past the wound, the open grave, the unhealed burial plot I didn't even know was there until years after when it had all come irrevocably apart and I was here outside Covington and had begun the practice of what it is clear that I do best: analysis.

When I met her, it was as if silence had ended. She was very beautiful. I said "cute" to Shad, but I knew better. And while he was learning how to control a well gone mad, I came to know better still. Mary Clare was, you would have to say, seeking her integrity, seeking that life she wanted to live—which is of course to say the dream she carried within like an embryo, a time bomb, and a doom. There was something almost desperate in her, almost fearsome, because she knew she had no place out in the sticks and little hope of anything else. She might have any man who saw her. The cream of El Dorado and Oil City, Denton and Tyler, Pleasant Hill and Plain Dealing. Which is why, I reckon, she moved toward me so quickly. It must have seemed to her that I had found my integrity, was already living my life. I had already broken with the sticks by then. I wore that white suit I could hardly afford, and the Stetson and the boots. It set me apart, and to be apart was to be worth something. I was living the life, all right. The integrity was something else. But then how could she possibly know what I would not know until, except for the raw acrid pleasure of the knowing itself, the knowledge was worth nothing: that I wore a suit the color of a certain dress, the style of silence and secrecy, bore that improvident white as the ancient Greeks dragged everywhere the rotting corpse of one whom they had killed. Were the Master of Questions to ask me today why I have always worn the white, I would say without hesitation: Because I am afraid of water, of the great depths. Because I loved my mother. Because once, on a certain day, I did not strike my father down. All of the above.

We walked and talked, Mary Clare and I, the whole week while Peterson Number One was in the balance. And when, against all odds, Shad got it working, we got married. I did not think much about it then, but the only shadow—much smaller than a man's hand—on those days was that, for some reason, Mary Clare disliked my brother. I reckoned it was that inbred hauteur of hers. There was no place in her dream for Shad with his raw country edges. But never mind. It was me she was marrying. Wasn't it?

It was fine at first. We moved in to Shreveport. Good business would have kept me in East Texas. That was where the deals were being made. More fortunes were made and lost in that damned Grand Café in a week than in the Shreveport Petroleum Club in a year today. But we already had a stake, and I wanted out. I didn't want to make wells. I wanted to make money. You make money by dealing way up front. You lease the right land, hire the right people, find the right drillers. That's what I wanted—along with two dozen white suits, scores of white shirts, as many pairs of Justin boots, plain black every one, as a closet could hold. I wanted a cool drink prepared by another hand, and a vista: grass, trees, a pool, tropical plants. Long evenings just sitting, looking at tall, straight oaks—not the twisted yellow slash pine we'd had around the old man's place.

And we came to have it all. Today, when any chickenshit doctor who avoids being thrown out of medical school can count on being a man of property in five years unless he butchers and bakes a patient on a public barbecue grill at Ford Park, it may not seem so much. But in 1935, there were not many self-made people in their twenties who enjoyed what we did. We came to have it almost as quickly as I came to realize it was what I wanted to have. Mary Clare was very bright, very tasteful. She turned the house we built on Line Avenue into a showplace. And began, as soon as the roof was on, to fill it with antiques, paintings, and books.

And that was all right. I liked it that she stayed at home listening to Bach or Schubert or whoever the hell, reading around the clock. It beat bridge parties and charity balls. Women who spend too much of their time around other women lose their femininity. That managing streak of theirs comes to dominate, and they begin to haggle for what they might have gotten simply by waiting for it.

She was a fine hostess, too. A little frightened, a little withdrawn. But then it was quite a leap from working tables at Effie's place to managing a staff of ten. I think she came to realize that in our circle neither she nor I nor anyone else was taken for what we had been or even for what we were—but rather for what we were going to be. And just then the signs were auspicious. Omega Oil was moving on.

Now that I remember, the only shadow on those days was the same shadow that had glanced off us in Kilgore. After a lot of hemming and hawing, Mary Clare told me that Shad made her uncomfortable. The way he looked at her. I asked if he had ever said or done anything improper. No, she said. It wasn't that. He had always been all right. But he still made her feel strange. Was it necessary for him to stay with us when he came to town? That irritated me. No mystery there. My reasons were as solid and homespun as the food at a church supper: Shad is my kin. We might not frequent the same places or buddy around, but he is my brother, and that is that. And even if the old man decided against all chance to accept one of her frequent invitations to come in and spend a few days, much as I loathed him, he would be welcome, too, and treated as an honored guest. With what I was and what I was going to be, I was still going to be it here, in Shreveport. And no one would ever be able to say that I had turned from my own kin when the wheel carried me upward into the sun. That could ruin everything. None of it would work out then.

What I did not say was that Shad was the burden I carried as the Greek murderer his corpse. That my duty to the silence that lay just beyond my elbow all the time was done through him. Not that alone, surely, but that too. It had to be done. I had to do it. Because of what I had not done when I was eight years old, and the time for the doing had come.

And aside from that, it was surely the best of everything. Once another man in oil mentioned how good Mary Clare and I looked together. We seemed happy, he said. Best deal I ever made, I told him, and we laughed. But I was serious. I was taking care of her dream, and she was hostess in mine. And for then, it was just fine. And it would go on being fine until it was lost irretrievably, and I found myself back amidst the silence again.

—Henry, will you tell me something?
—I don't know.
—You're a good person.
—I had my ups and downs.
—Why did my father leave home? You were there. What happened?

Henry stopped shaking the martinis. He set them down and looked at me in awed disbelief.

—You don't know, do you?
—How could I? Nobody tells anybody anything. Everybody talks all the time, but . . .
—Seems things comes out.
—If it came out, it crawled away in the night. I missed it.

Henry came to himself, shook vigorously again.

—You know, young Sentell, I thought about you plenty . . . You remember me?
—Pony rides in Dixie Gardens . . . Watermelon at Mrs Pat's Grocery on Kings Highway . . .

He threw back his head and laughed. —You remember, all right. It wasn't much. You were so little . . .

—What happened? I remember the night after they buried my grandfather. I was up in my room. They were arguing down by the pool . . . I got up and went out on the balcony. He said he'd kill her . . . No, kill . . . *them* . . .

Henry stared out the window. I think by nature he would have said nothing at all. I think, had he been put to the torture by some third party, he would have smiled and smiled and taken what came and said nothing. Nothing at all. But I was different. There are forms of coercion beyond torture.

—He would of said that, Henry murmured. —It was that night, all right. 'Cause he woke me, and we was on the road. We made Alec by six, Baton Rouge by nine. We had lunch in New Orleans. They put me at a table in the kitchen at Arnaud's. It was all right. I hadn't never eaten like that before . . . By that night, we had this house bought . . .
 —It was . . . another man. I figured that out. Some other man . . . He found out . . .
 Henry looked shocked, disturbed. He shook his head as he shook the martinis.
 —Lissen, it wasn't that simple, you know. I mean, Mr E.M. could of reached out if it was just some man . . . He had people who did things . . . No, it was . . . awful. I can't just go and . . .
 —Well, gentlemen . . .
 We turned together, and for a split second I felt my heart almost stop. My father stood there before us. Without support or even the apparent need of it. His silver hair shone, his face full of color. He was thin, wasted, but smiling and looking like a man who has survived an awful ordeal rather than one who is amidst it. He noticed my shock, and his smile deepened.
 —I'm good for about four hours, he said. —Let's get going. We'll lose almost an hour driving over.
 —Should of called a chopper, Henry said.
 —All out. One's bringing Louis Boudreaux in. The rest are with the Coast Guard. Off Okeanos.
 He turned, and we followed as he walked slowly, stiffly toward the front. Henry looked at me as if to ask, You seen any dope like that before? No, but in pancake mix, it could make us all better people.
 In the limousine, he settled himself carefully, maintaining the smile at some secret cost. The driver who had brought me over was gone, and Henry got behind the wheel and pulled away. There was a large ice bucket in the console built against the back of the driver's seat, and the martini shaker fit into it. I pulled out one of the jump seats so my father would have room—and so that I could face him, look at him. I had no idea what I might feel later, but I wanted this time, these minutes—something concrete to base it on.
 —Well, you're a young man . . . in college.
 —Yes, sir.

—It seems . . . a few months ago I was at Schumpert Sanatorium, seeing you for the first time.

Even his eyes looked better. Maybe it was just that the pupils had contracted so that they no longer seemed to threaten to take over his eyeballs. His voice, a reedy wheeze thirty minutes ago, was still soft, low-pitched, somehow at odds with the personality it was expressing. He motioned for a drink, and I poured two. Outside, it was dark now.

—I was proud . . . very, very proud . . .

As he said it, he looked away, and I could tell somehow that he was saying two things simultaneously. Proud of having a son. But proud, too. What the Italians call with their own special knowledge carried to the heart, *superbia*.

— . . . wasn't thirty, and the first million was salted away. Not for investment. Safe. Bonds, commercial paper. Back when a million was . . . something.

He paused, sipped. —Shit, I could have walked away, sold what we had, and lived in Paris or Rome, or you name it. Because in those days, I could have bought the Pantheon and used it as an abattoir . . .

I recognized as he talked a certain way of thinking like Shad's, like what I had heard of my grandfather's. A sharp and unfeigned contempt for the world and what can be done with it. It is not so large, so fine, and only dullards reckon it wide and tall enough to hold their dreams. That colossal shrug in the voice: Sentell. *Superbia*.

—That's what your mother wanted. You know that? Once she said we could . . . buy a title after the war . . .

I could not distinguish whether his tone carried irony or wonder. Perhaps it was both: the notion that a Sentell would wish, much less pay good money for, some other name.

We were on the causeway then. On either side, I could see the lights of small boats in the distance and up ahead, to the southwest, the red glare of the city.

—There wasn't any after the war for us . . . But you know . . .

There was a silence then. I caught myself wondering what a Sentell response to that might be. Then I thought, goddammit to hell, I *am* a Sentell. Whatever I say will *be* a Sentell response.

—No, sir, I said, proud of the edge on my voice. *Superbia?* Who cares? When they want a stand-in for Saint Francis or Uriah Heep they can go look somewhere beside Caddo Parish.

He stared at me. It was a replay of Henry. If I hadn't known better, I would have thought they were toying with me.

—Nobody ever got around to telling me why my family went to shit.

He was taken aback. It wasn't a rehearsed response, some kind of catch-up he was playing.

—I reckoned . . . over the years . . .

I didn't know how to go. Because I was as surprised as he was. It seemed he felt I knew why he had never sent for me to visit, had never come back to Shreveport to see me.

—Over the years it got lonesome, I told him.

—But Shad . . . if your mother couldn't . . . Shad . . .

—He's been good to me. If it wasn't for him, I'd probably be a crummy little faggot with a French accent.

—But he . . . never told you . . .

—What does he know?

He gestured for some more of our stock. He was deadly sober, but what I was saying had stunned him.

—I always . . . reckoned . . .

He stopped talking. As if he had to work through in silence the implications of what I had said. It gave me the creeps. It made me feel as if in some way I had been thinking wrong, thinking at a tangent, most of my life.

—Well, he said at last, —then I guess you think I've been a pretty sorry . . .

I didn't answer. It was my turn to pull on my martini and stare out at the glare of New Orleans. It looked like the city was on fire.

—Bad traffic, Henry called back to us. —Parades all up and down Saint Charles . . . Quarter is gonna be a . . .

—Sonny, I'm sorry . . .

—That beats a kick in the nuts, I said, not looking at him.

—But not by much. I'll . . . speak to your mother.

—That's fine, I said. —But why don't you talk to me?

He drifted away, his eyes unfocused and distant, as if he had second sight. Don't we all? The past playing over and over again in our memories like an old grainy, sprocket-chewed film, never quite the same twice. Edited, re-edited, out-takes thrown in, master shots altered, substituted.

—Other people involved . . . things that have to be . . .

—Damn tourists, Henry was saying. Then he hit the gas and spun around a line of cars.

—Good, Henry. We don't want to be late for the . . .

—Feast.

He turned to me. —Is that what you'd call it? All right, listen . . . later on, we'll . . .

— . . . talk? I'm listening.

Chapter Ten

> But afterward she lay with Heaven and bore
> deep-swelling Okeanos . . .
> *Theogony,* 133–34

There is a small room at Antoine's, set apart from the ordinary dining areas, its walls lined with bottles of vintage wines, a single narrow refectory table set in its midst. It is reserved for certain parties; the proprietors will tell you that no such room exists. It is not for ordinary suppers.

Marie-Claire sits there alone, an untouched drink in front of her, a pack of Gauloise and a tiny, delicately wrought gold lighter beside it. She has, it seems, arrived early. There is nothing for her to do but wait. She has considered booking a commercial flight back to Shreveport later, but she is not so secure in Shad's promise that she is willing to leave Sonny in New Orleans alone. There are other considerations. Tomorrow will be Mardi Gras, and Roland had planned to come to New Orleans to see the parades, to attend the Rex Ball. Perhaps she should stay, go to the ball, and keep her eye on Sonny, too.

There are moments when she considers that she will let Sonny be, allow him to follow the dictates of his blood with no more interference from her. He is more or less grown now, and it seems clear enough that despite all her hopes, he is indeed a Sentell. She has, God knows, had her fill of Sentells, had had it long before E.M. walked away. Had had it perhaps as far back as Kilgore if she had only stopped her dreaming long enough to realize that E.M. was not inviting her to play in a dollhouse but to marry him and live his way. His way all the way. She smiles wearily and recalls the summer of 1939. E.M. had been involved with a flock of foreigners. Something about alternative oil supplies considering the world situation. He would be going to London for two weeks, Paris for a week, and then to the Middle

East, Asia, the Dutch East Indies. It was going to be a wonderful trip. Except that E.M. said she couldn't go.

—Well, I *am* going. Listen, this is what I've wanted since I was . . .

—I know all that. But this is business, and I can't do what I have to do and look after you, too. There's a war fixing to happen.

—I can do just fine. I'll stay in Paris. Maybe I'll even go to Rome.

—The hell you will. If you knew what I know . . .

They had argued for almost two weeks. Some days it looked bad, but she would win back the ground at night that she had lost during the daytime. At the end of it, she thought she had him talked into letting her go for the first three weeks, and then fly back home while he went on. But one morning she had awakened to find him gone, a note left on the breakfast room table propped against a pot of hot coffee. He could not have been gone more than a few minutes. The coffee in his own half-empty cup was still warm.

The note said he had decided to go to Europe a few days early. Things were getting worse by the hour. He would stay a day or so in New York before he sailed. No need to call. Nothing more to argue about. His mind was made up. She would understand later.

She read the note, tears running down her cheeks, crying as if her life, her chance to be happy, had ended. And perhaps it had. She took the pot of coffee he had made to the sink, poured it out, and waited, stone-faced, for fresh water to boil. For a moment, she considered buying her own ticket, flying to New York, and meeting him aboard the boat in the cocktail lounge or at the captain's table. With her own cabin and her own plans. But that notion never reached the level of resolve. She needed more than her own desire, her own dream to fuel such a journey, and now, confronted with his brief note, she discovered for the first time that whatever she needed was not in her. At least not then.

She sat and drank her coffee and looked at the front page of the *Shreveport Times*. Something about an ultimatum, something about the Russians and the Germans. Poland. Chamberlain. Deladier. It was August 31, 1939, and she was alone for the first time since Kilgore. She wanted to pick up the phone and call Effie, anybody who might understand, but she had no more will to make the call than to make the trip halfway across the world. So she sat alone, the summer morning sun streaming in the window, tears drying on her cheeks, drinking her own coffee, and naming to herself the places she would not see, the things she would not get to do. At least not yet.

—What do you say, girl?

Her reverie dissolves. It is a Sentell. Shad. He has a large cigar in one hand and a large drink in the other.

—Shad, she says softly, acknowledging his presence, nothing more.

He sits down at the far end of the refectory table, drawing on his cigar. His eyes are directly on her. They do not waver. If she looks away and then looks back, those gray-green eyes are still fastened on her as if she were a staple of his diet. E.M. and Sonny are much the same. They stare at women. All Sentells seem to have some peculiar linkage between their appetites and their eyes. They do not understand the etiquette of looking at other people. You do not stare. You do not fix them with your gaze, make them feel like trapped animals, as if there were no escape. You do not announce with every glance your readiness to couple.

She looks away, studies the racks of dusty wine bottles, hoping that Sonny will come quickly—even if E.M. comes with him. It is silly to feel this way. It is embarrassing. Think of something else. Ignore him. Act as if he is not here.

Shad sips his drink and looks down the table at Marie-Claire. He is unaware that she has noticed his gaze. Strangely, he is not thinking of her. He cannot get the image of Okeanos out of his mind. He has never dealt with anything like it before. No one has. It is an enormous platform with multiple wells rising from deep beneath the ocean floor. It is a shambles now. What if he cannot reach the controls? What if there is no way to separate the wellheads out of control from those which have not blown? Worst of all, what if one of the other wellheads blows while he is working? He has never had thoughts like these before. He has gone to the job ready for whatever might be there, waiting for the event to think what must be thought. It is, he is certain, a sign of approaching dementia. Physical, mental, and emotional degeneration. Who knows? Perhaps he has had his last erection. In which case, Okeanos holds no horror.

He comes to himself to discover that his eyes are locked with Marie-Claire's. He is conscious of it whether she is or not. And he remembers.

He stands in recollection before the front door of the house on Line Avenue. He does not remember the rain just then because he had not needed a drink so badly in a long time. She had opened the door, surprised, almost frightened. Then her expression had changed.

—What do you say, girl?
—Shad . . .

He walked past her, dog-tired, looking for a triple shot of gin on ice cubes. Skip the vermouth.

—Honey, what is this crap about him being out of the country?

He was at the bar, pouring what he needed, paying her no mind. He had tried to learn not to look at her when he could avoid it. It was better that way.

—That's right, she said. —Paris, London . . . I don't know . . .
He paused. —When's he gonna be back?
She smiled, came to the bar, and began mixing her own drink.
—How much time have you got?
—Don't play games, Mary Clare. I had some bad news today, and I ain't in any mood.

She handed him the note, which, she suddenly realized, she had not let go of all day. She had found it on the breakfast room table again this morning. She had been meaning to throw it away, burn it. Get rid of it. She looked up to see that Shad was looking at her.

—That miserable sonofabitch . . .
—Don't, Shad. It doesn't matter.
—You didn't want to go?
—It'll keep, won't it? Paris will be there.
—I wouldn't bet my butt on it.
—The war? Do you think . . .
—Gonna be ten pounds of shit in a five-pound sack.
—Shad . . .
—Sorry. I mean it's gonna be bad.

Outside, the sound of the rain increased. It drummed down on the roof, the terrace. Marie-Claire found something on the radio and came back to the bar. The music was counterpoint to the rain, fresh, cool like the approach of autumn out there.

—Would you like to go swimming? she asked suddenly, surprised at her own question.

—Swimming, Shad repeated, looking bemused. —I feel more like drinking.

Marie-Claire was smiling at the music. Or perhaps it was the gin. She had been drinking it most of the day. For several days.

Shad lifted his glass. —To a beautiful woman I'll never forget . . .

He smiled then. She supposed he was toasting her. She found that she was not afraid of him. She had always feared him. She would find him frightening tomorrow. But not now. Outside, the rain was competing with the timpani. She walked back into the breakfast room and looked out the French doors toward the terrace. The floor was wet, but it didn't matter. The humid breeze blew into the room. Shad came in carrying the gin. He was quiet, almost somber. As if he had lost something. But that was impossible. Sentells never lose.

—I'm going to go for a swim.

—It's a thunderstorm, Mary Clare.

—I don't care. This is my place, my time . . . He . . . just left me . . .

Sturm. Allegro. The wind slapped the terrace doors closed, then open again.

Their eyes locked for the first time. Never before. Not that way. Not with him staring at her, her staring back. Not since that evening at Effie's when she had turned and seen him as the Beast, he seeing her as the Woman. She was not afraid. He was not threatening. Perhaps there had never been a threat, no reason for the fear. A shower of wind-blow rain coursed around her as she walked to the shaking doors.

—Make me another drink, she said. —Please . . .

Then she could not hear the music. The storm was too loud. She stood just outside the doors. She was wearing a light cotton dress, and the rain penetrated it, pushed her roughly from side to side as the wind shifted. Perhaps she did hear the music. Shad was making drinks. He made them strong. It was going to be a long night. When he looked up, the French doors were fluttering in the storm, and she was gone.

He moved toward the doors quickly, drinks in his hands. He squinted into the darkness out there. There was thunder and lightning in addition to the heavy rain, and amidst one bright flash he could see her down the terrace in that tree-sheltered, dimly lit alcove around the pool, but scarcely believed what he saw.

Then he was outside, drinks left behind, moving against the wind, the rain no longer soft but slashing, driving against him, pushing him back, but of no force because he was determined to reach her there by the pool, outlined against the trees and the dark sky by the lightning. She stood at the edge of the pool, her dress either shrugged off or torn away, her body set forth as in a series of photographs against the shadowy wind-blown trees, her tan flesh underexposed, her bra and panties stark white amidst the darkness.

He reached her then, just as she had raised her arms, about to plunge into the vexed waters of the pool. He put out his arms and circled her, feeling even in the driving chill rain some preternatural heat at the touch of her flesh and his.

—Listen, he shouted to her against the wind, —this is dangerous.

She turned toward him, her face a mask, determined, alien, utterly unafraid. —Is it? she said. —Is it dangerous?

He drew her back from the pool and tried to say something more, but by then the roar of the storm was too much. He picked her up in his arms and carried her back into the house. Inside, she clung to him, sobbing, talking incoherently about E.M., the Place Vendôme, the storm, something about coffee.

He carried her upstairs then, realizing, admitting to himself for the first time that she was almost nude in his arms and more than half drunk and lonely and miserable. He was pushing out of his mind at all costs the thought that he had wanted her from that first instant when she had turned away from the hot grill at the Grand Café, had wanted her enough to lie or cheat or steal or whatever he had to do to have her, would have killed her husband or lover to have her. Except that her husband was his brother, who, scurvy sonofabitch or no, had at the very least the right to expect that what was happening right now not happen. Not with him. Not with Shad.

The upper hallway was dark, the sound of the rain and thunder muffled, distant enough so that he could hear her whisper, —In there. That room. I want that one. Don't take me away from the storm.

He pushed open the door, stepped inside, and closed it behind them. In there, it was like stepping into some negative reflection of the storm. The lights from the pool down below sent an agitated pattern whirling, prancing, diving, soaring across the ceiling. The lightning was close, and when it arched downward, just before the thunder, the room was illuminated as brightly as if it were high noon and some great force had pulled the roof of the house away to reveal what was happening within.

He set her down on the bed gently and was about to turn away. He had not looked at her directly since she had stepped through the French doors into the storm—except for the moment when that first bolt of lightning had caught him unawares and scorched her image not only into his eyes but into his memory. He knew he had not to look at her because if he did, something was certain to be lost: her virtue, his sense of himself, E.M.'s pride, the very teetering, shaken and disintegrating order of the world already at war with itself. He would remember later for no reason he could imagine that even as he carried her up the stairs in his arms, he had kept his fists clenched lest his open hands touch her hips, her thighs. He was turning away then, forcing his mind to think of the perils of a trip back to Texas in weather like this. Maybe once out of Shreveport, too far west to reconsider and come back, he would stop and get some sleep. But he had to get out. Now.

—Shad . . . open the window.

—The rain . . .

—Please.

He moved past the bed, lifted the window, and felt a wave of cold, misty air flow over him, tossing the drapes upward and outward as if they were alive, trying to flee the storm. Then, still pledged to leave, trying to keep his eyes away from her, he turned back. He had seen too much already, knew that he would remember her that way for the rest of his life, and that every other woman he had had or would have could be no more than a substitution for one he had not had.

But it was not going to be that way. Because when he turned, she was kneeling on the bed, slipping out of her bra, her breasts almost pale against the deep tan of her body, against the troubled shadows, the flowing patterns on the ceiling and walls of the room.

—I don't want to be alone tonight.

Now he could not look away, could not even keep his distance, negotiate within himself a passage by the bed and out the door. Her nipples were small, deep pink, raised as if he had touched them already.

—I got to go. I got to go back . . . You know that.

—Not while it's storming. Please . . . stay with me now. There's no one here.

He was almost past the bed, his body somehow achieving on its own what his will could not accomplish. But she was standing now, her thumbs in the waistband of her panties, pushing them down until they stretched across her thighs. Rainwater was beaded on her belly, her thighs. He could see the band of lighter skin where the sun had never reached, a delicate filigree of hair scrolled on the mound of Venus. Even then he tried to think about the trip back, but it was no use. It was as if the sight of her nude had somehow shorted out, confused the pathways in his mind. There was a feeling of constriction in his throat, a tightening in his muscles as when he entered the flames on a burning rig. It was a feeling of awe, of being at the brink of a mystery as ancient and precious and consuming as the sacrifice of stars in nova, or the command that began the universe. He thought, Jesus Christ, it's not just *like* the very first time—it *is* the first time. Like being about to die, about to step beyond all the limits ever set, fearful, tranced, drawn toward a triangle of darkness within which lay everything he had sought since he came to consciousness.

I'm not going anywhere, he thought. Being damned is a chance no matter what. If I'm going to be damned, at least I'll know why, know it was worth it, and not just some silly thing that happened to happen. She pulled him against her body then, and the touch of her skin was cool. He kissed the inside of her thighs, let his tongue seek her out, his hands drawing her to him so closely, so tightly that she gasped.

She was whispering then as he began to throw off his clothes, unbuckling his belt, kicking off his boots.

—I knew this was going to happen, she was saying dreamily. —Not where or when or how, but I knew it would. He kissed her breasts, hands cupping each one. —It's . . . almost a relief . . . I've waited . . . so long . . .

Then he was on the bed beside her, still struggling with his clothes, unwilling to move away, to lose her touch even for the seconds it would take to finish undressing. — . . . to be devoured . . . Just to . . .

He reached for her, lifted her up, rolling over so that she was beneath him. Outside, lightning flooded the terrace, the pool. For an instant, the room was white, and another gust of wind-filled rain passed over them. It was then that he entered her, felt her become tense, then relax as he moved deeper. They kissed amidst the racket of the wind, bodies turning and turning on the soft bedclothes.

—I'm not afraid of you, Mary Clare whispered, her arms caught under his, her hips finding his rhythm. —I don't know why I ever was.

—Me neither. I always wanted this. Used to wake up in a cold sweat in that damned motor hotel in Kilgore thinking of you with him, dreaming of this, saying, No, she don't want it and you have got not to want it. You're not supposed to want it. You can have all the rest of 'em if you can get 'em. Just not her. Every other damn one on the face of God's earth . . . but not her.

She opened her eyes to find him above her, a look of incredible intensity on his face, green eyes boring down into her as fiercely as his body. Behind and above him, the ceiling seemed to be the floor of some silent sea, its textured surface covered with ripples and eddies reflected from the pool down there. She imagined herself drowning in those great depths, held, pressed down by him. She would never be released, and this would go on forever. She smiled, closed her eyes again, leaving her body to act on its own. She could feel herself alive, all of her straining back against his force. It was as if she were discovering dimensions of herself created moment by moment. She bit her lip as his thrusts increased and felt a vast warmth moving through her, some obscure current wayward and unfamiliar entering this grotto where they had lived and struggled for eons, face to face, always wishing, never touching. The warmth rose like a cloud through her thighs into her belly, and then it was not warmth anymore but fire, and she heard herself gasping, making little sounds that were most closely hers, yet which she had never heard before.

—Oh darling, oh God, oh God . . . Ah . . .

She felt herself collapsing into the fire, felt her consciousness begin to eddy and whirl like the patterns on the ceiling overhead until it expanded to fill the universe, drawing everything else with it, turning faster and faster, contracting then into an essence that was her and not her, her and all—at last and crucially everything as her. She could remember nothing coherent for some indeterminable passage of time until his gasps brought her back. In the moment's fantasy, she discovered herself the millennial earth, him the ephemeral drill that penetrates the core, releases, and is absorbed, used up by the very force of his driving downward, the awesome counterflow of her rising up.

He came then. He felt himself go out of himself as if he were aboard some rocket fueled by its own hunger. He spun eyeless in the expanse of all space and no time at all, his only connection with the world down there the bare sense of himself deep within her. Then he realized that he was the vehicle of the journey, she the space through which he turned and turned, not expanded but contracted, that she, his universe, was bounded but unlimited, all the universe he wanted or could ever need. Then the vessel, the projectile exploded, and he felt that disembodied self flare and fall in fiery bits which reconstituted, fading back into his body again, arched above her, eyes suddenly open to her open eyes, there passing between them at last that look which she had evaded five years before, but which now shared would never really be broken off again, and which contained in it the very oppositions of the cosmos, love and strife, united for an instant as long and as short as the duration of the world's dreaming.

And then he, within himself again, was falling slowly back into the universe, that instant's mere order not faded or diminished, but simply displaced from the absolute center of duration into the frame of memory like a circle on a map evoking a point where everything that matters had converged, would now remain not in its intensity nor even perhaps in its form but surely in its meaning for as long as consciousness persisted, or longer—as long as the last reverberation of this their secret epoch flickered like radiation across the echoing cavern of their altered universe.

A waiter enters the wine room, places a fresh drink before Marie-Claire, another before Shad. Her cigarette has burned out. His cigar is a stump. They find their eyes meeting down the distance of the table which is over twenty years long. He is thinking of the waste, decades of approximation, and only finally, casually, distantly, emotionlessly, of still another approximation. Of a fire in the Gulf. She is thinking of afterward.

The thunderstorm had passed, and the rain had become a soft curtain, hazy and obscure, falling through the lights outside. All there was to hear was the sound of water dripping from the eaves and his measured breathing.

—Are you asleep? she asked softly.

—No. I ain't asleep. How could I be asleep? I got to remember this. It's gonna have to last for a long time. For as long as I live.

—No, she said. —No, it doesn't. It only has to last a day. You'll come back tomorrow night . . . and the night after that . . .

He was silent, drew her to him, kissing her, his large hands stroking her gently.

—I can't do that, he said, his voice low, harsh. Outside, the rain dripping sounded like a metronome, a clock counting off their seconds. —I can't, and you can't.

—I can, she said. —Once I couldn't. I was afraid, and anyhow, there was a world out there, and his money and . . .

She paused, remembering Paris and London, which she had never seen and would surely never see now.

— . . . but that was stupid. You have to live the life you have. You can't dream a life, can you?

—I don't know, he said, caressing her legs, her hips. —I would of said no a couple of hours ago, but now I seem to be doing it.

—This isn't a dream. It's . . . what we would have had. If I hadn't been afraid . . .

—I wish I hadn't scared you, honey. I never meant to.

—Do you remember that night?

—What night? Never has been a night like this. Not in the last million years . . . Maybe not in that long again.

—The party? All those oil men and bankers . . . some of my friends. You brought Lucy Ryan up here . . . I opened the door . . .

—It was you, he said almost wistfully. —I never knew for sure . . . There was light from the hallway. All I could see was this shadow against the light . . . some woman . . .

—It was me . . . wanting to be Lucy Ryan.

—What?

—I wanted to be her, to send her away and strip off my clothes. Take her place, slip into bed with you . . . to have you in me so that I wouldn't have to go on wondering when and how and . . . But I was frightened.

—You never said nothing. Never turned a hair afterwards.

—I thought about it. I'd watch you with other women . . . the way you could touch them as you talked to them with them not minding at all. I remembered Lucy's underthings just . . . thrown all across the floor. I wanted that.

He laughed humorlessly. —What you saw, what you thought about, was me making do without you, Mary Clare.

Somehow this did not even surprise her. She had to ask, but she knew the answer before she did so, and before she asked and he answered, she believed him beyond question. She turned and looked at him lying beside her, his hands on her breasts, between her legs, his eyes never leaving her.

—Do you love me?

—Christ, do I love you.

—No, not desire me. Not even want me alone and nobody else . . . I mean . . . love me.

Shad sat up in the bed, his brow furrowed. As if he could not find the words he was searching for even though he had recited them to himself a hundred times before. He took her by the arms, turned her toward him.

—I want to live with you and die with you. I want to have sons and daughters by you till there's no room in the goddamned house for another one and we can't keep their names straight. I want to see you naked in the morning and watch you take off your clothes at night . . .

—Shad . . .

—Just hold up. You asked me, and I'm telling you the best I can. I want to keep you from harm, and I want to see you laugh and sing for me . . . I want you to be so happy that I can't see the sun for the way you shine . . .

He had drawn her very close then, and she felt despite all she had said that thrill of fear again as she looked into those green eyes that fixed her, held her beyond escape.

—And something else. However it happens, when it comes, I want your face to be the last thing I see in this world. I want to carry you with me, into the fire and out again. When it comes, I want to close my eyes on you . . . and then open 'em up again—and you be there . . . forever.

His hands fell away from her as if he were exhausted, but his eyes held her, caressed her. —That's what I feel, he said after a moment.

—Stay with me . . . here.

—Honey . . .

—Don't leave me. Don't even go back over there. They've got people over there who can see to things. Stay . . .

—Mary Clare, you know . . .

—Wait. Don't say no. When he comes back, we'll tell him. He can do whatever he wants. He can have Omega. You'll give him that.

—I don't give a damn about Omega. It's gonna get me blown to hell one day or another, but we've got to . . .

—Shad, you do love me. You want me. Stay here with me. Tell him so. I can't do it alone. I shouldn't have to . . .

He was silent, thinking not in abstractions but in images: what would happen if he did as she asked. The thing would not pass quietly. There was no way in which it could simply be talk between him and E.M. Yankees in New York did that in the movies; they are adult about such things. But probably not even them in real life with no cameras and bright lights and directors telling them how it had to go.

There would be a fight, and not just blood drawn but all the way down. Which he could win because he always won if the matter didn't turn on business or some other kind of talk. Then he would have to face the old man. Not just having turned the tables, Abel having done for Cain, but the thing having started with him taking his brother's wife behind his brother's back. Worse still, taking her, having her in his brother's own home while his brother was four thousand miles away tending to business that belonged to both of them. No, that was too much for love or salvation—even if they were one and the same thing.

If he would do it for anyone, for any reason at all, he would do it for her. But he wouldn't. No, not wouldn't. Couldn't. Because when he thought about it, even if he was willing to try, he would be helpless before E.M., consumed by the magnitude of the hurt he had done him, hearing already E.M. saying again that he had to have *somebody* he could trust. Truth to tell, he wouldn't even be able to fight back, surely not defend himself against what E.M. would have to do whether it mattered that much to him or not, whether he wanted to or not—if he ever wanted to walk the streets of Shreveport again in the company of men.

—No, he said slowly.

—I don't think you do love me, she said bleakly.

He seemed bewildered, unable to grasp why she could not see what he could and could not do. —Mary Clare, I love you, and I'll do anything in this world for you that a man can do. But I can't stand in my brother's doorway when he comes home and say, Look, I got your house and I've had your wife. What do you mean to do about it?

—Men, she said wearily, not to him. To herself. —Sentells. And you don't love him. God, you don't even like him. Youall have never cared about each other.

—That's not it. That's not what matters . . .

—No, she said. —I see that. I don't understand it, but I see it. All I can't see is . . . why I don't matter more . . .

He was silent, defeated then. I've never seen him this way before, she mused. He really wants to stay. He loves me as much as he says. But something won't let him stay, something it would kill him to lose. And it doesn't have anything to do with E.M. Not with him as a person. Isn't that strange? Because my life isn't ever going to be the same, I'm never going to be fulfilled, happy again after tonight, and I'll never even know why.

He started to speak again, but she put her finger against his lips.

—No, don't say anything else. We both understand as much as we can. I even understand that you won't be back the rest of the time he's gone. She kissed him a long last kiss, mouth open to his, then broke from his arms, picked up her bra and panties, and ran nude down the hall toward her own room and her new life. With no final words at all.

Chapter Eleven

> Then the star Arcturus leaves the holy stream of
> Okeanos and first rises brilliant at dusk . . .
> *The Works and Days*, 565–66

Sonny comes in breathless, as if he has had to run the last few blocks through the Quarter to Antoine's.

—He's here, he says. —He's come. As if there had been some doubt about it all along.

—He may be out *there*, but he ain't in *here*, Shad replies sullenly. For all his memories, he has not forgotten the interdiction that E.M. holds over his head.

—Uncle Shad, he's . . . , Sonny begins, but before he can say more, E.M. comes in, Henry assisting, a waiter behind them.

—Mary Clare, E.M. says, pausing for a moment by her place. His expression passes for a smile because it is not a frown. Then his eyes travel down the table to light on Shad. The something like a smile widens, deepens. —Shad . . . long time . . .

—Yeah, Shad replies without inflection, his eyes turned down to the table. He does not look at E.M. until he hears Marie-Claire gasp as Henry gently guides him into the light and his appearance is manifest.

—You . . . invited me to supper.

—Right, Shad answers, elbows on the table, his eyes now on E.M.'s, his expression revealing nothing. —Sit him right there, Henry. Sonny, that other place is yours . . .

But Sonny does not move. His eyes move from Shad's face to Marie-Claire's as they watch Henry seating E.M. He cannot read Shad's, but his mother's expression is one of horror and sorrow and dismay. She's seeing her own future staring at her out of the past, Sonny thinks as he takes his seat. She doesn't care about him.

But Sonny is mistaken. Marie-Claire is not thinking of herself. She is questioning what has brought E.M. to this state. Does she bear part of the blame? Is it a curse lately arrived, visited upon ancient acts?

The poor broke-down sonofabitch, Shad is thinking. And we're all on the same track. I wonder if that's what comes of living alone in some out of the way place all by yourself, grieving.

The waiter standing behind Henry places E.M.'s drink at his elbow, and the rest of the enormous shaker next to it.

—Are those Henry's martinis? Marie-Claire asks casually.

—Yes, ma'am, they are, Henry answers with a smile. —Will you have one?

—Of course. It's . . . been a long time. Sonny . . . ?

—I've *been* having them. Sonny coughs, as if to suggest an explanation for his breathlessness.

The waiter has come around to stand near Marie-Claire. As she raises her martini, Sonny notices her hand is trembling. He notices moreover that E.M.'s eyes are upon her.

—Yes, Marie-Claire says in a voice the least bit unsteady. —Are we ready to order? She plunges into the menu's dubious French, E.M.'s eyes still upon her, predatory and unblinking.

—Steak, Shad snaps after a decent interval. His reverie has upset him even before E.M. arrived. He hates to go over the past in detail, preserving only certain erotic moments to savor in recall, chief among them those he has just relived. Now the wraith of his brother appears before him, looking little better than if he had been hoicked from eternal slumber for the occasion. If it is a judgment, Shad considers, he will just have to live with this one, too. There have been times over the years when he has thought he should have met E.M. at the Shreveport Municipal Airport when he returned home that late September of 1939, handed him a pistol just like the one he carried in those days, explained the whole thing to him, and then had at it. Win or lose, live or die.

It would have been better than lying low like a chickenshit, waiting, hoping nothing came of it. It would have been the right thing to do. And one way or the other, it would have rid him of this rich and unnatural lust he has borne for Marie-Claire every day and night of his life since the first day of September, 1939, that he has played out in stewy mime on the bodies of countless other women over the years since. He would either have been dead or married to her. Both, he reckons, are cures. At least they would not all have lived in this garish suspension for twenty years. And who knows? Perhaps E.M. might not have come to this. Shad feels his brother's condition, can guess what it is, roughly knows how much longer it will take to kill him.

He should have done right, and he would have. But he could not, for love of Marie-Claire or fear of his own life without her, frame the words to speak to his brother. He remembers thinking, Judas never told Jesus, did he? He might of kissed him, but he never had the balls to go right up to him and say, Hey, Lord, see them Jews and them Romans? I done that for you. But that is all behind him. He does not mean to show anything at all to E.M. Not pity, not sorrow, not shame, not remorse. It is too late. It is always too late. Too late for any of those things one second after you have done the thing you regret. Too late for him and Marie-Claire when he drove away from the house on Line Avenue alone that morning after instead of just lifting her up, piling her into the truck, and taking her back to Kilgore against her will—or, failing that, figuring out some way where he could face E.M. and see the thing settled once for all this side of death or the other.

—What kind of steak, sir? the waiter asks for the third time without enthusiasm.

—A goddamned beefsteak, you stupid sonofabitch.

The waiter jots something down and moves quickly to Sonny, who manages a smile of his own. —Steak, he says, before the waiter can ask. He looks up just in time to see E.M.'s eyes move from him to Shad. The waiter nods, almost asks about salad, thinks better of it, and moves on to Marie-Claire, whose nod indicates that she is ready to order, and that both Shad and Sonny are common and trashy. She engages the waiter in a discussion of certain dishes in French. He is relieved, delighted, and voluble. E.M. watches this performance with heavily lidded eyes. He has seen it all before already, all before. He turns to Shad, who is finishing off his double Jack and is obviously anxious for another.

—Mellowed, Shad . . .

—What the hell is that supposed to mean?

—Twenty years ago you would have knocked him down and gone to threaten the chef.

Shad grins despite himself, his eyes locked with E.M.'s. Sonny is watching them both. He cannot tell how they feel about one another. It is not as simple as he had thought. The antagonism is there, thick as the armor on a Sherman tank. But it runs deeper than that. They are playing with each other, feinting, parrying. But Sonny cannot make out what the weapons are, or even when one scores a hit on the other. Much less what the end of the game might be.

—You wasn't so bad yourself. Before the loot started rolling in and you got respectable.

E.M. smiles distantly, coldly. —Well, he says, —it can catch up with you. Unless you stay in the field. A man should stay close to home. London and Paris can ruin him.

All this said casually enough, but Sonny sees Marie-Claire, who has been rattling on with the waiter, turn her head sharply toward E.M., a stricken expression on her face. Shad flushes and falls silent. E.M. has scored a direct and devastating hit on them both. Sonny hasn't a clue. He looks from one to the other uncomprehendingly. There is a long silence before Marie-Claire can find her voice again. —And *pommes soufflé* for everyone, she says weakly. In English.

As the waiter passes, trying to steer a path as far out of Shad's way as possible, Shad thrusts out his empty glass, almost hitting the waiter at crotch level with it.

—Bring me two of these, he snarls. —And put a nigger at the door to see when I need some more.

The waiter looks stunned, but nods and goes out. Shad looks up then, sees Henry standing behind E.M.'s chair like a stone statue.

—Sorry about that, Henry. Nothing personal.

Henry stares at Shad, his own expression matching E.M.'s. —That's all right, Mr Sentell. I know your mind.

—I'm glad somebody does. Look . . . this here ain't a family reunion. I'm sorry as hell to see you down like this, E.M., but we got business to discuss. You want to talk or wait till we've eat? No damn talking while there's food on the table. You know what the old man said . . . When you talk, talk, when you shoot, shoot . . .

— . . . when you eat, eat . . .

—Always made sense to me. What do you want to do?

Henry leans down, whispers in E.M.'s ear. —Henry says . . . we should . . . talk until the food comes.

Shad looks astonished. —Henry?

Henry comes around the table to Shad's seat, leans down to whisper to him.

—Mr E.M. is on these drugs, you see. He's got about two hours left, and if he's not stone drunk by then, you gonna have to help me get him out to the car, because you know how Cinderella turned to a pumpkin at midnight? Well, Mr E.M. turns to shit and starts screaming and frothing at the mouth.

Shad goes pale, swallows hard. —Why the hell don't you give him some more of whatever it is you're giving him anyhow?

—'Cause it would kill him.

—Even so . . .

—Right. I know your mind, and you're absolutely right. So I brung some along and a needle, too, and you can give it to him in the men's room. See, the doctor's got his eye on me.

Shad and Henry stare at one another for passing seconds. Sonny can hear them both breathing short, hard. Like men who have been working strenuously. Or fighting.

—You'd like that, wouldn't you, you black sonofabitch? . . . No offense.

—Boy, I would. I sure dearly would . . . None taken, you white motherfucker.

It is all said sotto voce, without passion, out of some mutual loathing that has nothing to do with race or even personality.

—With your track record, Henry says, —I believe they might make a exception, forget all that money, and capital-punish you . . . I'd love to see that. For him . . .

—If youall are rattling on about the good old days, I don't have the time, E.M. says slyly, hitting the table with his glass.

—Sure, that's what we was doing, Henry says venomously, his eyes locked with Shad's. Then he moves quickly, quietly back to his place behind E.M. and pours a fresh martini, his expression once again smooth, flawless, intact.

But Shad is not looking at him anymore. His eyes are on E.M. again, and Sonny can see that he is calculating.

—All right, Shad says. —I'm going out to that damned platform as soon as I see Boudreaux and get things squared away.

E.M.'s tight smile seems to brighten. —They've *been* squared away, he says softly. —Crew boat, a little transfer tanker sitting about a mile off Okeanos . . . it's all out there, all . . . waiting for you.

He stares at Shad, as if he can see past flesh to truth, his smile becoming even broader. —The fact is, he drawls, —I didn't think you'd . . .

—Show up? Shad finishes for him. —Bullshit. You never thought that. You might of hoped it, you sorry sonofa . . .

—Shad, Marie-Claire cuts in nervously.

—All right, fine. My part's settled. Soon as I can see Boudreaux, I'm headed out. That's my part of it.

—And stay. Till it's out, E.M. says, eyes shining from the cavernous shadows under his brows.

There is silence again. —You know, Shad says in a conversational tone, —I'm beginning to remember why I always did hate your goddamned guts.

—Nobody you hate like one you've wronged, E.M. replies with equal ease. —Especially when the proof is right at the table with you.

Shad looks appalled. Sonny can hear his mother's sharp intake of breath. It is as if that sealed door is about to open, as if the dry, cloistered air of the past is about to rush out and overwhelm the room from some crypt long-hidden in the depths of Antoine's. But the moment passes as E.M. smiles at the effect of his sally and lifts his hand to Henry for that martini he knows will be there.

—In a manner of speaking, E.M. concludes, coughing a little, sipping his martini. —What's Okeanos going to cost us, brother? he asks amiably.

—It's gonna cost everybody, Shad says irritably, barely recovered from E. M.'s last remark. —First, that goddamned interdiction comes off. I'm fucking sick and tired of wandering around labeled a lunatic.

E.M. reaches back again, and Henry places an envelope in his withered hand. E.M. holds it a moment, relishing perhaps that crystalline moment when it had first occurred to him to have Shad put away at Shady Grove. Then he pushes the envelope down the table toward Shad.

—I reckoned that might come up. That unsticks the label. Not that a label is needed . . .

Shad rips open the envelope and frowns over the document inside. It is signed by a judge of the First Judicial Court in Shreveport. It dissolves the interdiction and places Shad once more in charge of his own affairs.

—I ain't never walked away from a goddamned job in my life,

he mutters as he reads, still irritated at E.M.'s earlier remark.

—No, E.M. observes smoothly. —That's so. I recall a time when you even took on my job . . .

Again that extraordinary reaction from Shad and Marie-Claire. Sonny is bemused, wonders if E.M. has some kind of an electric buzzer under the table connected to their chairs.

Shad's temper is at the end of its tether, Sonny thinks. His face is red, his lips tight. The next step, as he recalls, is ordinarily an overturned table and a chair broken across someone's shoulders. But surely not here, not now. Not directed against his own brother so sorely in decline. Sonny relaxes as he sees Shad regaining control.

—Now it's your turn, Shad says, turning to Marie-Claire. —I want Sonny emancipated.

—What? Marie-Claire asks in dismay. —What?

—You go into court and declare him an adult.

—No. He isn't . . .

—He's fixing to be in a little over a year, anyhow. I want it now. Right now. I want to know it's gonna happen.

Before Marie-Claire can refuse again, E.M. cuts in. —I believe I can handle that, too. He smiles across the table at Sonny. —I'm natural tutor even if . . . she's . . . custody. It's not as if we'd . . . divorced, he concludes, staring down at Marie-Claire, eyes luminous with some passion Sonny cannot identify, cannot even imagine. Then Sonny finds E.M. looking at him with a distant and contemplative expression that resembles affection.

—Time I did something for my . . .

His voice trails off, and he throws down the rest of his martini. Henry glances at his watch, pours him another. Shad looks uncomfortable. Marie-Claire closes her eyes.

—One thing more, Shad says at length. —We all get in on this. I want him to have his own money.

—Sonny doesn't need . . . , Marie-Claire begins.

—The hell he don't. I don't want him beholden to no one . . . least of all you, girl. What do you say, bruh?

E.M. smiles like a mandarin as he watches Marie-Claire's discomfiture. —I can live with that.

Waiters enter. They begin to serve. Shad looks at his steak without pleasure. It seems to be covered with a brown, tarry substance. His eyes meet Sonny's. Both steaks are much the same. Shad shrugs, nods. He is prepared to give it a try for hunger's sake. He has eaten some purely bad meat in his time. Marie-Claire's entrée is something French. It is formally unrecognizable, but appears to be an overcooked small bird of one sort or another. E.M. has a plate of grits and grillades. Sonny and Shad try to scrape the sauce from their steaks.

—That's béarnaise, Sonny's mother tells him. —It's quite wonderful here.

—They put it on meat that's over the hill, Sonny responds testily.

Shad finishes quickly, motions a waiter to take his plate. It is not that he does not enjoy eating. But it gets in the way of drinking, hence must be kept to a minimum. Marie-Claire works on her bird listlessly as E.M. picks at his grits, glancing from time to time at each of his table mates. Henry checks his watch apprehensively.

—Coffee all around, and a couple more Black Jacks right here, Shad barks. —And don't make me wait. The tip's still up in the air . . . Then to Marie-Claire:—Them souffléd potatoes was all right. What do they use? A football pump?

E.M. pushes his plate away. It is difficult to tell if he has eaten anything or not. He looks across at Sonny.

— . . . finished?

—Yes, sir . . .

— . . . then maybe . . . excuse us for a bit.

—Sir?

—Little bit of . . . old business . . .

—But . . .

—You ain't emancipated yet, Shad glowers. —Go walk around out on Bourbon Street and watch the fools carrying on. But look out for yourself and remember where you're from. They get dangerous down here . . . the queers go crazy this time of year.

Sonny goes out sullenly. That door on the past slams closed once more. He is convinced that he will die at eighty-five or ninety-seven knowing no more about the currents and crosscurrents which have moved his family than he knows right now.

E.M. stares at Shad, then at Marie-Claire. Whatever pretense of a smile he has worn up until now has vanished. He turns to Henry.

—Get Shad a bottle. Throw together some more martinis for me. She'll take a Remy-Martin . . . No, bring a bottle of that, too.

And a pot of coffee. When it's all here, you go out in the hall and stand in the . . .

E.M.'s voice grinds to a halt. His face twists, and he seems to begin to shrink back into himself. Henry points to his watch, his expression tight, troubled. E.M. reaches up, touches his hand, nods.

—There's . . . back way out. Better get . . . cleared. Then don't let anybody . . . Nobody . . . at all . . .

Henry nods. He has become a master of hermeneutics, of the interpretation of this esoteric shorthand of agony. He exits silently, closing the door soundlessly behind him.

—Sonny and me was out at the old man's place, Shad says, to fill the awful silence. —Over the years, you really fucked it up. It don't even look like ours.

E.M. laughs. He straightens up from cramped pain, seems to billow back out from some dimensionless cavern within, and laughs, his voice rich and deep. It is only a moment's victory, but it is formidable. Marie-Claire pales. Shad stares down at the tabletop.

—I cleaned him out of there, E.M. says, his voice level, every word filled in, whatever the cost. —I ripped the stinking evil old bastard out of there. It's the way *she* . . . would have wanted it. *I* did that. You hear? *I* did it.

Shad's eyes rise to meet E.M.'s. There is a moment of recognition between them, some sudden current of mutual recall that even Marie-Claire cannot begin to understand. Shad nods slowly, and Marie-Claire is astonished to see something close to tears in his eyes.

—Now . . . business. Old family . . . business, E.M. announces. —Come to . . . attention tonight . . . neither one of you sonsofbitches . . . guts enough to tell the boy . . . truth.

Shad flushes, says nothing. It cannot be said that he hangs his head, but the impression is much the same. Marie-Claire has regained her composure. She stares defiantly at E.M.

—I don't give a damn . . . how youall . . . , E.M. begins, then pauses. Eyes glazing, thin fingers twisting in the tablecloth, he tries again.

—He's . . . going to . . . before I go on. Youall hear me?

—You want him to know that I'm . . . Marie-Claire says angrily.

—A whore? Don't be silly. He didn't give you any money . . .

Shad never gave any of 'em any money, did you, brother?

Shad's face is purple with rage. He rises slowly from his chair as Henry comes in with a tray. He is moving toward E.M. when Henry seems to glide between them in the act of placing the tray on the table.

—No, Mr Shad . . . we can't have none of that.

The tray is on the table now, heavy with drinks. Henry has moved back from Shad and in so doing, with infinite finesse, he has allowed his black jacket to fall open. Shad sees the strap of the shoulder holster; Marie-Claire sees nothing. Shad sees, moreover, the expression in Henry's eyes. He has been waiting almost fifteen years for just this. Nothing would please him more. Shad leans over, picks his coffee, his bottle, and a fresh glass off the tray, and sits down. After a moment, as Henry serves Marie-Claire, Shad looks down the table at E.M. His voice is low, almost serene.

—You say something like that again, brother, and your nigger is gonna get his chance.

E.M.'s face reveals nothing. Henry is pouring a brandy for Marie-Claire. One would have to be standing beside him to detect the sudden infinitesimal tremor in his hand as Shad speaks. He smiles at Marie-Claire, then glances once more at his watch. —About ten, fifteen minutes, you hear? It's gonna be hell going back across the causeway anyhow.

—It . . . always is, E.M. grates. Henry steps outside and closes the door.

—In the name of God, Marie-Claire says, agitated, pushed to the edge. She had expected none of this. Not E.M.'s condition, surely not his resolve. She had come to assure herself one small victory: to keep Sonny on land, shielded from Shad's lunacy, which drives him ever closer to that inferno in the Gulf. Now she seems to stand at the edge of another gulf, a deep-flowing river-ocean which she has carved out for herself.

—I've got an interest, E.M. says. —That . . . the boy's going to inherit everything I've got. And more than just a few million, I've got the *boy's* interest at heart . . . After all, I'm his . . . uncle.

His laughter is ragged, bubbling up from a well of pain so long endured that he can almost contain it now. He looks over at Shad, his eyes bright, the pupils enormous. —You hear that, brother? I'm his goddamned uncle . . .

Then to Marie-Claire. —Is that . . . sophisticated enough for you? Don't call a spade a spade . . . Call it . . . *pique dame* . . .

He starts to laugh again, but this time it ends in a moan. He finishes his drink, puts his head down upon his spindly arms. After a moment, they hear him whispering, his voice broken, muffled.

—I can't get drunk anymore . . . Terrible thing. Last infirmity . . . I stayed drunk for . . . years . . .

He coughs, raises his head. There is blood on his lips. —You going to tell him, Shad?

Shad's face is impassive. He has seen pain before. It takes getting used to each time. He has had enough time. He is used to E.M.'s now. —I'm gonna do what she wants done, he says, looking down the table at Marie-Claire.

—What about you, E.M. gasps, staring at her venomously. — . . . Tell him? Shit, why not? You had the guts to do it, didn't you?

Marie-Claire returns his stare. She, like Shad, has found her balance. —I never said that. I never said anything. You assumed it. For fourteen years, you've lived with your own assurance of it.

—You're not going to say he's mine? They've got tests . . .

—Eddie, for God's sake, leave it alone. Let things stay the way they are. All of us have . . .

She is about to say "suffered", but her eyes focus on E.M.'s face, and her voice dies. Beyond the ravage of disease and pain, there is in his eyes a look of fury and outrage and irrevocable loss that silences her. The balance she has achieved is broken, and she finds herself weeping.

—All for a goddamned trip to Paris, E.M. says, almost dreamily. —A goddamned chickenshit trip to Paris and London. Well, you've been there. Was it worth it? Was Paris worth a bastard?

Marie-Claire stands abruptly, her chair clattering over behind her. Tears have run her mascara, and she almost looks her age. —You sonofabitch, she screams. —It was never that. Maybe I thought it was, but it wasn't. It was *you* . . . Do you hear? It was just *you* . . . and . . .

—What? E.M. demands, leaning forward, his eyes on fire. —Me . . . and what? Tell me that . . .

She is looking at Shad. He has been staring down into his drink during this exchange. But now it is as if he feels her eyes upon him. He looks up and their eyes meet. Just before Marie-

Claire runs past Sonny's empty place, pushes open the door, and rushes from the room. Shad sits somber within himself for a time. Then he stands up slowly.

—I could break your fucking neck before your nigger got through that door, he tells E.M. —And I could probably kill him too. But it ain't worth the worry just to push it up a week or two.

He stares down at E.M. wearily. —There's nothing I can do to you.

E.M. meets his eyes. —You already did it, he says.

Then he rises, too. Slowly, painfully, his teeth gritted. Having come so far, he means to get out of the room, out of this restaurant on his feet, under his own power, before he loses control altogether.

—I'll see you . . . when Mardi Gras is over, he says. —Helicopter. It's a long way out to . . . Okeanos . . .

—I'll be there, Shad grates.

—You sure? Give me your hand . . .

Shad stares at him and smiles. Catharsis is complete. Pity and terror are past.

—I wouldn't give you the sweat off my dying ass, Shad says, opens the door, and is gone.

It looked like I was going to come out all right: legally grown and money of my own. Which was to say that I had some extra stuff to throw at Missy. But I had this peculiar empty feeling. I had thought somehow Shad or Mother would one way or another manage things. But they hadn't. E.M. was the honcho. Because he was sick, dying? Mother, maybe. Not with Shad. E.M. had something on him. Something on Mother, too. With her, it was another man. I knew that. He had caught her with someone. It happened when I was five or six. That night at the pool was the last night. But that was over and done with, wasn't it? What was there left to say tonight that called for me being gone, out of their way again?

I walked back down Saint Louis Street trying not to get knocked under passing cars by passing drunks. The crowd was dense even on the side streets, and everywhere seemed to be its own small carnival. I saw the seven dwarfs with a Snow White who must have been sixty. Overslept again. Some blind guy was juggling, dropping stuff and then getting down and feeling around for it, and another one was playing a violin while his three-legged dog danced. People were cheering. Maybe that passes for entertainment in New Orleans. I got back to the restaurant just in time to see the car rolling past with Henry driving. Henry motioned me to get into the back. My father was there, curled up like a ball, only the martini glass sticking out, held steady somehow, and half full of gin.

—We gonna drop you off, Henry said. —Mr E.M. wanted a last word with you.

—I don't think he can . . .

—Just lean close. He can still talk.

I did. —Sir . . . ?

—Something . . .

—Yes, sir.

— . . . Father . . .

—Yes, sir.

— . . . not . . .

—Sir?

— . . . Shad . . .

All right. I understood that.

— . . . mother . . . lied so many . . . years.

I could believe that, too.

—Shad wronged, but . . .

His voice was reedy, whispy. What I couldn't figure was how much worse it could get. I thought he was going to die right then and there.

—Henry . . .

—No, he's just hurting. You ain't seen him when it's really bad. Lean down and listen, Sentell.

— . . . Your . . . father . . .

Why did he keep using the third person? Next the royal "we"? Did he really feel that distant from me? It didn't matter, because just then that ball he had curled up into suddenly opened up and he yelled as loud as I have ever heard anyone yell. His face was warped into a mask of agony like that of Greek tragedy, eyes squinted, rolled up into his head, mouth pulled down, and the sound went on and on.

We were stopped at a corner, waiting for pedestrians to clear the way. There was a traffic cop there. He heard the scream —who didn't, for two blocks around? He walked over to the car, looking us over.

—Hey, he said, leaning in.

—It's all right, Henry said smoothly. —My boss is having a little pain.

My father nodded at the policeman, who shook his head. —A little, he said, shuddering. Then he withdrew his head and looked about at the gawkers who had stopped to see what was up.

—Okay, move it out, keep moving . . . nothing to see. This ain't part of Carnival.

No, it wasn't. Because as I watched him there, crumpled, turning to ash in the flame of pain, I reached out and put my arms around him, tried to hold him as close as the agony did. I didn't care what he had done or why he had done it. What was done was past, behind us. I really believed that. What mattered now was that he was moving in anguish toward the goal of life. Which is death. I wanted to make the passage as easy as I could for him. There was no law that I had to like him or even be able to stay in the same room with him. Only, carved somewhere inside, that I honor him. Which might even mean love him.

He found his control again. I poured him another drink, and he tossed it down. Can you believe that he smiled up out of that dark valley at me. —No . . . olive . . .

—I believe this is your hotel, young Sentell, Henry said.

—Sir, I started, —I don't think I understand what it was you . . .

But he was passing out, trying to stay conscious but knowing that, if he was successful, pain would come back again. —I . . . your . . . uncle, he said, and slumped over on the seat.

—Sir?

I got out of the car, looking backward, but he didn't move. Henry motioned me to the driver's window. He stared at me as if he'd never seen me before. Then he said something in a low voice.

—I can't hear you, I told him.

He reached out and pulled me close, that bright vivid gleam in his eyes. —You're a better man than your father ever was, he rasped, then pushed me away. —Good night, Sentell, he said, and pulled away.

Chapter Twelve

> She came to deep-flowing Okeanos that bounds the earth where is the land and city of the Cimmerians, wrapped in mist and cloud. Never does the bright sun look down on them, but baneful night is spread over wretched mortals. There we came and beached our ship and went beside the stream of Okeanos until we came to the place of which Circe had told us . . .
> *Odyssey*, xi, 13–21

Goddamn both of them, Marie-Claire is thinking. If I'd waited, someone, something would have come along. I didn't have to get out of Kilgore that way. There were buses to Shreveport and Dallas every day. Then I'd have been shut of them, all the damned Sentells. One is dying, another one is determined to get himself killed, and . . .

She looks in the mirror. She shudders at what she sees. If I keep this up, if I let it matter, I'm going to be an irredeemable hag inside two weeks. They'd like that. They'd love to see me go down with them.

She starts to clean off her makeup, but that nagging horror returns. Did E.M. go home directly? Or did he find Sonny on his way out and tell him everything? Did he just blurt out, You're not my son. Not only are you nothing to me, you're the walking, talking, living, breathing emblem of my shame and your mother's whoredom.

No, she thought firmly. He didn't do that. He could have done that last year or the year before—as soon as Sonny was old enough to know that bastard was something other than a naughty word. Not only hasn't he done it, he isn't going to. He wants me to. Or failing that, Shad. He wants to force us, one of us, because he isn't going to do it himself. Because Sonny is a Sentell, and Eddie, on the very brink of eternity, still supposes that matters, that Sonny would feel better as an adulterous, incestuous bastard Sentell than as no Sentell at all. Oh God, who knows? He may be right. Maybe only the sire counts. It is better to be a Sentell any way you can be one than to be anything else, and even if your dam's name was Fontenot, and her father was a half-crazed roustabout, it makes no difference at all because we have conquered genetics by the triumph of the will, and we are all of us Sentells and nothing else. Jesus, I've spent most of my life with these wretches, and I don't understand anything about them at all.

Or perhaps, she thinks, all that is nonsense. E.M. *has* told him. Told him in the most businesslike way—as a matter of family history, something to be considered along with the other vagaries that abound in every family. Worse yet. Considering that E.M. is consummately underhanded and indirect, he may simply tease the matter, press it past any possible alternative but one—and send Sonny to her to force the conclusion. Marie-Claire shivers. If E.M. is not past thinking, that is exactly what he has done. It would be a classic—something to store with all the other unspeakable business he has transacted over the years.

She had thought to undress, to go to bed. But this last imagining puts that idea away. She will wait for Sonny, wait for him to come to her door wishing to see the Great Whore. He will be along any minute to ask her how she could have done what she has done. Not whether she did it. A Sentell, dying, has stated or implied that she did, and she knows that she will never be able to put off Sonny as she has E.M.

Why, she thinks, I will say, there was a terrible storm and I was afraid . . . No, that's wrong already. There *was* a terrible storm, but I was already past being afraid, and your father . . . sorry, the one who might have been your father . . . had left me again for *his* whore, Business. No, bidness, that's how he said it then, in those days, before better acquaintance improved his speech. And your uncle . . . oops, your father, was there and I was a little drunk. No, abominably, monumentally drunk, and needed more than anything in the world to think that I was the very radiant center of everything, something—anything. And you know your uncle—sorry, I suppose one accustoms oneself to the very best lie one can muster—your father . . . in a twinkling, in the storm . . . Oh, my darling, please don't hate me. It happens all the time. It happens every night in every town and village in America. Husbands have their duties, and wives have their drives, and no matter what those vicious bastards of your gender tell you, duties and drives are the same—and almost always nothing happens. Nothing at all. The lover takes what he wants, the wife enjoys the taking or doesn't, and the husband comes home. And nothing happens. Almost always. But sometimes. And sometimes was my time, and my time was you.

She looks into the mirror again, seeking there some semblance of a girl to whom the Sentells had never happened. Someone who had dreamed of lovely things—things more exciting, more intense than the thick, hot, scraggly pine woods and flat, hot plains blotched with weeds and grass scarcely fit for cattle that had been her portion from the beginning. She wonders if the first immorality had not been the dream itself. No one had warned her of that. Not even Effie. They had said it was absurd to dream, even that it was painful to dream because dreams do not come true, and the awakening is worse than never having dreamed at all. Never mind. She had gotten past all that the day E. M. Sentell had asked her to marry him and Peterson Number One had blown a black hole in the brazen Texas sky.

Dreams do come true. If you are determined and lucky and seize the moment. It is not that they don't come true, but that they do. And no one, least of all Mary Clare Fontenot, could be expected to understand in advance the economics of dreaming. There is no such thing as a free dream, she smiles to herself bitterly. The payment may be deferred, the demand note may call for some unlikely and incredible currency. But every dream is paid for at last.

Now she puts on cold cream, wipes it off quickly with a tissue, and pauses only a moment before she begins to make up again. She is remembering E.M. at supper. A figure out of Dickens. The Ghost of Christmas Past and Present and Yet to Come—all in one. Made of stone or made of mist—somehow beyond them all. As if a Great Death had come, and he had suffered it, and it had left him . . . as he is. What must he know now that he didn't know before?

Marie-Claire laughs to herself. Nothing, of course. He knows nothing, cares about nothing that could have made the slightest difference to them, to their lives. Even now, at the bourn from beyond which no traveler returns, all he is concerned with is what it means to them—to Sonny, to Shad, and himself. He isn't interested in why it happened, why it had to happen at least that once. Since it *did* happen, he can put me out of his calculations even now. Now all that makes any difference to him is working it out among them, the three of them.

Jesus Christ, I'm the ghost, the shadow, the stone—not him. They hung on everything he said all evening long. Both of them did. It has to be worked out between them, and then it will be all right. The whore's misconduct has to be corrected by some arrangement. And it will be, because all that really changes is the provenance of the next Sentell. It's irregular, it's indecorous, but it comes out the same, doesn't it? He's still a Sentell, isn't he? Only Eddie's . . . his uncle. Which she had never once thought of in all the years since 1939. Not once. It had never occurred to her to consider what relation Sonny had to E.M. Only the relation he didn't have.

She tries to hold back the tears, but it is no use. She sobs for a moment or two, manages to win back control, and surveys the damage. She takes out more tissue, thinking perhaps this is what they mean when they say that woman's work is never done. It *might* be done—no, it *would* be done. Except for men. She begins on her makeup again. It's not going to be that way, she thinks. Those sonsofbitches . . . I won't let it be . . .

—Gimme one of them pig's feet and a bottle of beer.
—That'll be six bucks.
—What?
—Six bucks. You talk English, don't you?
—A pig foot is a nickel, and a bottle of beer is fifteen cents. Didn't ask to buy the whole hog and half the brewery.
—Who the fuck runs this place, you or me?
—I never heard such prices in my whole life. You a born thief, or did your momma raise you to it?
—You miserable bastard, I'll . . .
—You mess with me, and it's certain death.
—I'm gonna mess with you all right . . . Oops . . . Now, look, put that thing away. Man, they'll put you under the jail for that. It's a federal crime to carry . . .
—It's a fucking crime to charge like you do. Now hand me over a couple of them pig's feet and a bott . . . no, two of them cans of beer.
—This is armed robbery, mister.

—No, this here is a man getting something to eat and paying a fair price for it. Here's fifty cents.

—Carlo . . . Carlo, call the heat. This redneck sonofabitch just come in with a sawed-off shotgun in a paper suitcase and . . .

Cecil is dog-tired and bone-dry, and his head is full of an incredible array of things. It is as if someone had come along and turned every shelf in the filling-station store upside down and then gone to stirring up the rubble with a spade. Dates and names and events and ideas and songs and movie stars and countries and autos and inventions and products and emotions and memories ramble about this way and that in the corridors of his mind. He is not sure whether he has been insane or not, but he suspects he soon will be if he cannot manage to sort things out. It is downright amazing all the crap that can happen in twenty-six years. You hardly dare go to sleep for fear that, when you awake, everything will have been rearranged and what you knew for sure is no longer true and what you believed is not even remembered.

He has left the Trailways bus station on Tulane Avenue and managed to get himself the first bite of food he has had since the Awakening. Everybody he sees looks crazy, talks crazy, and must be crazy from the way they act. A man on the bus with whom he struck up a conversation has told him he was leaving Shreveport because the niggers were taking over. At the first stop outside Alexandria, Cecil has used his penknife to cut a hole in the end of his cardboard suitcase. He can now insert his hand inside and grasp the trigger of the shotgun. He does not mean to be taken by niggers—nor by strange and perverted whites, either.

He has reached Canal Street, where the people look even weirder than on the bus. No one wears a hat, few wear coats. The women's skirts reveal almost all of the best of everything, one look at which may cost you salvation. Down to his left, the uproar is deafening. Cecil moves toward the noise, the milling crowds in the Quarter. He has yet to find Sentell, much less the family that he has lost without even knowing he had except for the word of the Savior's Friends. Or the Savior's Fair-Weather Friends who have wished him well and sent him on his way alone. With nothing but the church treasury of $666.00 for sustenance.

He has made his way across Canal Street now, and finds

himself at the verge of the Quarter. He cannot believe what he sees. The people wandering about, moving from bar to nightclub, from nightclub to bar, are costumed outrageously. There are men in ballerina costumes, women wearing Roman helmets and short swords. There are a pair of frogs down a way, one frog mounted on top of the other in what Cecil takes to be a simulation of frog sex. A woman on a balcony above is naked to the waist. From the bottom. She is dancing and tossing things to the people below, and they are wishing her well.

All his life he has heard this of New Orleans, but common sanity suggested it was overstated. Things couldn't be as bad as the elders said. The hell they're not. If anything, the old folks played it down. Cecil considers that perhaps this is just the way people in New Orleans comport themselves at night. Maybe it is better in the daytime. Or maybe it is because Sentell is in town.

He has finished chewing on his second purloined pig foot. He tosses it toward the gutter, but it strikes a Viking in his codpiece. The warrior is stone drunk. He looks over at Cecil in astonishment.

—You little fart, you want to die right here and now?

—No. I got important work to do. Sorry about the pig foot . . .

—You're gonna be sorrier . . .

The Viking starts for Cecil, who backs off, frowning. —Listen, you silly-looking asshole, if you keep coming, I'm gonna plant you . . .

—Haw . . .

The Viking raises what gives every evidence of being an enormous sword made of real iron. One lick, Cecil reckons, and it won't matter whether the niggers have taken over or not. He raises his suitcase in what must appear to passers-by as no more than a gesture of self-defense. But then the far end of the suitcase disintegrates, the Viking's sword falls into pieces, and a store window behind shatters. The air is filled with flying glass, bits of cloth, a couple of handguns, and assorted pieces of socks, shirts, pages from Holy Scripture, and the like. The Viking stares at his sword's broken hilt, turns, and shuffles away without a word. The rest of the crowd gives Cecil room to scrabble amidst the junk now floating back down to the street. He has his now unconcealed shotgun well in hand, and manages to snatch up forlorn remnants of the *20th Century Chronicles* before he darts down a side street and around a dark corner.

Sonny is on the house phone. As it turns out, Omega Oil is generous. Missy has her own room. The phone rings four, five times. Then it is raised slowly. Sonny waits.
—Hello...
—Missy?
—Sonny?
—I just got back.
—Was it nice?... I mean to have supper with your...
—It was terrible. I want to talk to you, see you.
—Sonny, it's... Lord, I don't know what time it *is*.
—That doesn't matter. No school, no work tomorrow. You won't have to dodge that creep at the TG&Y.

She laughs, and Sonny's heart beats faster at the sound. —I'll be right up.
—I'm not dressed.
—Good... Let it be.
—Oh, you stop that, hear.
—Where's your mother?
—Next door.
—I'll be there in a minute... Three knocks.
—Sonny, I don't know...
—I do.

He hangs up quickly. She'll have to open the door just to send him away. He will see her. How about forced entry? Into the room and then into...

He catches the elevator, still thinking about E.M. Tomorrow he will tell his mother that he plans to lose the spring semester at LSU, stay in New Orleans and Covington a while. Given even a month, perhaps he and his father can find a place to stand together. He will speak to Shad, too. They will have all day. Shad has to wait for Boudreaux, and nobody seems to know where Boudreaux is. What if he could pull the family back together? Whoever it was his mother fooled with so long ago, the sonofabitch is probably dead by now.

By the time the elevator door opens, he feels good. He has something to tell Missy, and considering that he is about to become a man of means, something to ask her as well. This could be the night. What's wrong with an engagement screw?

Cecil has tucked his sawed-off shotgun up his coat sleeve and what is left of the *20th Century Chronicles* into his pocket. The shotgun is reloaded, and he is listening for footsteps, voices, anything to warn him if the Viking decides to make another try. Nothing. Just a woman's shriek from some anonymous balcony. He walks to the far end of the block and turns the corner. He is going to have to start asking questions.

No, he isn't. Walking down the street, right at him, is the chief object of his search. Shad Sentell, eyes down, hands thrust in the pockets of his khakis, canvas jacket stretched over his shoulders, and a Stetson that looks like it was present at the losing of the West. This is the Lord's hand, Cecil considers. He has delivered the Philistine over to me. The only trouble is that the goddamned shotgun has exposed hammers, and they are caught up in the fabric of his sleeve. Cecil struggles with the barrel, twisting it this way, turning it that. Until he realizes that he may well blow himself away if he does not take care.

Shad is almost upon him. It wounds Cecil to drift back into a deeply recessed doorway and let him pass. There is no help for it. He is close enough to reach out and grab Shad by the ear, but he forgoes. One ear wrenched off, bitten through, is not enough. He lets Shad get well ahead and then walks quietly behind him —back toward Bourbon, where the encounter with the Viking took place. As he does so, he manages to free the shotgun. It is still up his sleeve, but now he can let it slide down into his hand at will. He will stalk Sentell until the time is ripe.

Up ahead, the crowd is thick again. There are Arabs and a Tin Woodman, some kind of a beetle with a blue glitter back, and young men with black leather jackets and iron crosses. No Vikings. Just as well. It would cause a stir, but if the bastard shows, rearmed with sword or mace, there is one barrel for him, one for Sentell. And one is quite enough.

—Sonny, it's so late.
—I know, but it doesn't matter.
Missy lets him in, and Sonny closes the door behind him. She is wearing what are called shortie pajamas and, it appears, nothing more. They are the rage right now. She has purchased them at a small shop on Decatur chiefly patronized by harlots of Hispanic origin. They would cause a scandal in Greenwood, Louisiana, but then almost anything would. Sonny cannot take his eyes off her. He reaches out to draw her close, but she backs away.

—I don't believe we should . . .
—You know I respect you.
—Well, sure . . . but it's late . . . Maybe tomorrow . . .
—There's no tomorrow . . . Tonight . . . is eternity.
—Is that supposed to mean something? Sonny, if anybody knew you were here, they'd think we was . . .
—Right . . . Let's do it and say we didn't.

She is pulled into his arms, and they kiss. Her response is far less inhibited than her words. Much tongue, much body, and sure enough there is nothing beneath the pajamas but her flesh. Sonny's hands close greedily on her hips, pulling her closer. After a tranced moment, she pulls away again, breathing hard.

—Sonny, please . . . We got to control our passions.
—They gave me the store tonight.
—Huh?
—I'm an adult. With more money than a Monopoly game.
—I guess that's fine.
—How would you feel about getting married?
—You . . . want to marry me?
—Missy, I love you . . . I knew I loved you when you climbed out of that crummy old car . . . I want us to be together always. You know that. Quit teasing me.
—Oh, Sonny, I'm not. I don't want you to think that. It's just that I can't go making up my mind in the middle of the night when I haven't even known you but like . . . two days? I got to think about it . . . pray over it . . .
—Can we fuck while you pray?
—Sonny . . .

Shad sits in his underwear staring at the TV screen. He is beat out, dog-assed tired, and also middling drunk. He is trying to puzzle out precisely where he has gone wrong. He is not given to this kind of venture, and the going is tough. He is used to calculating how to put down pipe and make oil flow for the cheapest possible price. Or how to extinguish a rig fire and stay alive. Or how to get a good lay with minimum complications. He is not dumb; he is simply specialized. He can sweat a squirrel around a tree or heft a bass out of an underwater thicket. He can make men work when they are too tired to count their own fingers. But he cannot see quite how it all came down to this.

The volume on the TV is off. On the screen, of course, is a

pillar of fire, a column of smoke. It is as if the whole world is watching Okeanos burn. He touches the volume control in time to hear an invisible reporter state that Omega Oil spokesmen in Shreveport have said that S. S. Sentell, the renowned troubleshooter, is now on the scene and ready to commence operations to bring the blazing rig under control. Shad kicks the sound off again and drinks. Bad news travels just this side of the speed of light.

All right, fine. He has managed to set as much of the chaos of his life right as can be set right. Sonny is going to be in good shape. E.M. is going to be dead, and Mary Clare is going to have all the money she needs to finance that dream of hers until the stage lights go out and the orchestra puts away its instruments.

He snaps off the TV and ponders. He should make a bequest to Elvira. She should have a place of her own where she can screw herself to death, educate a whole new generation of young men. She must have ten or fifteen years of prime fucking left. As for Missy, Shad considers that he will leave that one lie. There is no way to know whether she is or is not his daughter. Leave her to Sonny. It is probably a lot of bullshit about imbeciles and idiots. Sentell on both sides might well create a superman.

There is enough whiskey left to get beastly drunk. He has nothing to do tomorrow until Boudreaux shows up—probably to tell him he knows no more about Okeanos than Shad does from watching the TV. Drunk or sober, there is no way he is going to start thinking about what passed tonight. He is already too drunk to piece together what he will tell Sonny if that half-dead brother of his makes good on his threat. Typical chickenshit E.M. He has had since 1946 to find a gun and lay for Shad if that was his way. Or he could have hired someone to do it for him. Or he could have said it was all a goddamned lie and let it go. Or he could have married again, sired a bevy of sons, and named every goddamned one of them Edward Malcolm Sentell. But no. He has decided to wait until he is dying and then piss on everything in sight. He considers calling Mary Clare. Forget it. If she had a choice of who to hang first, he is not sure she'd pick E.M. Shad takes a long drink and wonders if things could be any worse.

Then he brightens. Things can always be worse. He remembers a man who had his pecker whipped off by the power belt on a lathe. He shivers at the thought and walks out on his balcony.

The moon is high and stands radiant in the untroubled sky. Clouds pass over its scarred face like small vessels on a tranquil sea. Shad wonders if there is a port somewhere amidst the stars, the galaxies. Then from below he hears:

—Lord, I never seen a prettier night.

Shad cocks his ear. Voice and accent are more than passing familiar. He leans forward, squints down into the courtyard. The pool is lighted but no one is swimming. The tables are at last deserted. He leans even farther and finds the source of the voice on the balcony directly below his.

—'Vira? What the hell are you doing up so late?

She looks up at him, unsmiling. —Well, it's sure as hell not a guilty conscience.

—What's that mean?

—Nothing. Not anything. I had dinner tonight with our little girl. She told me . . . never mind . . .

—What?

Elvira looks disgusted. —I'm not gonna get a crick in my neck standing here talking up to you.

The idea has risen in Shad's mind—and one other location—that he has perhaps been hasty thinking about his will, assuming that Okeanos is going to send him off. In any case, he has always wanted to believe that if he were ten minutes away from execution, and his jailers, in a spirit of good fellowship and scientific research, sent a fine woman to his cell, he would manage a last stand and go out with a grin. It is a splendid image to carry in the mind. It might even be true. All this business with E.M. and Mary Clare and Sonny and goddamned Okeanos out there burning like his own flame-covered cottage in hell has cost him his principles. He smiles down over the rail of the balcony at Elvira, who stands in the moonlight in a dressing gown she must have bought at some shop during the afternoon. It has surely never been seen in the living quarters behind a Billups station.

—Well, Shad says, —I reckon we can do a little better than that . . .

—Listen, we can go to Alabama . . .

—Lord, why would anybody want to go to Alabama?

—I know a guy in school. From Mobile. He's paying his way through school making phony IDs—anything you want.

Driver's licenses, birth certificates. He told me they've got justices of the peace over in Alabama who'd marry a troll to a vampire for fifty bucks.

—Ugh. I saw this movie once where this vampire . . .

There is a region of Sonny's mind which contemplates whether this stunning female can be happily married to a student of ancient philosophy. That region is located well above the belt, and its caveats are not much heeded. Perhaps he will repent at leisure.

—What do you say? I can rent a car or grab a taxi.

—I don't know what to say. Sonny, I believe there *is* something between us.

—There will be, as soon as I can . . .

—I appreciate that. But getting married is a serious thing. It really is. It can't be just on account of mere physical attraction.

Sonny looks stunned. —You don't really believe that?

Missy has said it as if she believes it. As if her observation has been delivered from a very bedrock of long-pondered and deeply held belief. Now she pauses. Sonny has his hands on her again, exploring under the shortie pajamas. He kisses her as well, as thoroughly as he can.

—What do you feel? he asks breathlessly.

—I feel your hands on my butt, and I don't think that's right.

Sonny's hands fall away as if her rear were a hotplate.

—If that's all there is to it, he says sullenly, moving toward the door.

—Sonny . . .

He turns back. Missy is smiling, holding out her arms to him. It appears the bed has lost its rock. He hesitates. Every time he is close to her he undergoes a physical transmogrification which, unrelieved, is painful and frustrating. He can feel it coming on again just looking at her. The top of her pajama is low-cut and pulls tight across her breasts. The bottom is so high that it is possible to imagine in the darkness that he sees the shadowed place he yearns to enter.

—I don't want to be mean, she says softly. —I believe I do care about you.

She holds him tight, her pelvis moving against his. She kisses him better than he has kissed her. His hands are quickly back where they were before. He maneuvers the two of them both back toward the bed, and they fall across it locked in embrace, the kiss uninterrupted.

Shad has one leg over the railing of the balcony. He is moving slowly, carefully, his agility hampered by his aching back and the bottle of whiskey he has tightly clasped under his arm. Elvira watches him with interest—as if to judge his performance.
—Room service, he hears from outside his door just as he is ready to move the other leg over. He pauses, thinking that hotels are, by nature, obtrusive, a pain in the ass. He wishes he had a dollar for every damned maid who has walked in on him as he pursued his avocation. Room service, he mumbles. I'll serve my own fucking self. —I don't want none, he calls out.
—What's that? Elvira asks from below.
—Not you, honey. I *do* want that. There's some damned . . .
—Telegram, the voice outside calls.
—Slip it under the door, Shad snarls, pulling his other leg over.
—Got to sign for it, he hears.
I'm gonna strangle this sonofabitch, he thinks. And then strangle Boudreaux or E.M. or whoever the hell has taken to sending me night letters.
—The hell with it, Shad shouts at the door. —Leave it downstairs.
He is lowering himself carefully, setting his foot on a metal brace below the balcony, his eyes still on the door when it seems to dissolve in a storm of flying fragments amidst a roar, a huge flat sound that pushes his head downward just in time to dodge flying splinters and shards of glass from the half-open panel that shatters just above him. He shakes his head and shoulders which are covered with a light dusting of wood and glass and metal. Then he lifts his eyes to see what the hell is going on.
There beyond the blasted door frame is a man who appears to be in his sixties, sharp features, clad in a nondescript black coat and a rusty black hat, with a sawed-off shotgun in his hands. He is smiling, eyes alight, coarse mouth turned up at the corners. For a moment Shad does not recognize him, and then he does. Recognizing, too, as Cecil enters the room, that this miserable degenerate means to scatter him all over Orleans Parish. It may be that all Shad's bellyaching and worry has been in vain. He

may never get out of this wretched city, out to Okeanos, which he has come to fear, but which is surely his proper and appointed place to exit this world and enter, roaring, whatever there may be in the next.

Shad lowers himself quickly, hands on the metal support, feet not quite reaching the rail of the balcony below. I'm too old for this kind of crap, he thinks as he stands on sheer air. I used to make it out second-story windows if some dumb-assed husband come home off schedule, but that was then. This is now, and I seem to be losing my suppleness.

He looks down just as Elvira reaches up and grabs his legs, pulling them to the inside of her balcony. Shad lets go, and they fall together to the floor. She is about to say something, but Shad covers her mouth with his hand and gestures above, grinning. They hear movement in the room above, then out onto the balcony.

—Elvira, baby, you say you got to have it again?

The scuffling above ceases. Shad turns to face Elvira, whose expensive robe has fallen from her shoulders. This seems as good a time as any to even that score.

—I never seen the equal of you, sugar. I done fucked you three times in the last two hours.

Elvira looks at him in astonishment. —Shad, are you all right? If you had it three times tonight, it sure as hell wasn't me . . . And what was that awful . . .

—That's all right, baby. I don't mind, Shad says loudly. —I want you. I got to have you . . .

They hear a muffled groan above, then feet running away from the balcony, across the room. Desperate feet. The tide has turned again. There are crueler weapons than shotguns.

Shad and Elvira step into the room. Shad finds two water glasses wrapped in some kind of plastic with a note that says they are absolutely guaranteed sterilized. He pours whiskey, but Elvira remains perplexed.

—What in God's name is going on? she asks. —I was taking the air, and I heard you say something about coming down for a little . . . talk, I guess. Then there was this shouting, and then this . . . Sounded like somebody slammed a door.

—Close, Shad tells her as he hands her a glass. —It was that little fuck-off you married . . . Cecil come near slamming the door on me.

Her eyes spark in the darkened room. —That weasel . . . What's he got?

—Short gun was all I saw. But then I never took time to shake him down.

Elvira starts for the door. —I'm gonna find him and take it away from him, whip his head to jelly with it, and shove it up his dying ass.

Shad restrains her. —Reckon you could hold up a minute?

—This is a nice trip. I'll be lucky if I ever get twenty miles out of Greenwood again. That piss-ant's not gonna ruin it for Missy and me.

Shad makes her take the whiskey. He kisses her on her naked shoulder. —You just ease up. He's gonna be all over the hotel looking for us. You can say what you got to say later.

—Lord God, I have surely paid. I wish I'd just stayed in Kilgore and gone to open whoring. If hell ain't in this life . . .

Shad is leaning against the dresser, his legs coming back to some semblance of their normal strength. His back is stiff and painful when he moves from side to side, but he can manage. He might even be able to do a little up and down. He notices that Elvira's fancy wrapper has fallen open from top to bottom. Under it she is nude. His eyes are at last accustomed to the faint light, but they will never become used to what he sees. Every time is a revelation. She notices his eyes on her. Cecil drops out of her mind like a sinker on a trotline.

—Maybe I better get dressed, she says softly.

But in order to dress, she must undress. The wrapper falls from her shoulders onto the floor, and she turns slowly. The shadows brush away whatever the years may have cost, and Shad moves toward her, setting down his whiskey on top of the TV. It has been a hard couple of days. Cecil is out roaming the halls, Okeanos lies out in the Gulf. Faced with oblivion, what can a quick hustle hurt?

—Elvira . . .

—Shad . . . ?

Marie-Claire stands before the door of Sonny's room. It is very late, and she has knocked three times. He is not in there.

E.M. has him, she is certain of it. He has taken Sonny back to his place and even now is poisoning his mind. For all she knows, Shad has gone with them. They are brainwashing him. It is all made up between the three of them now, and Sonny will be their joint heir.

Then something strikes a chord in her memory. There is a bare chance that he is *not* with E.M. What would a Sentell rather do than . . . shoot the shit? That girl on the plane. The one claiming to be Shad's daughter. Sonny had been mooning over her, making improvident efforts to paw her. The girl had been the very image of her mother—one of Shad's chief drabs, obviously—and Sonny had had about him the look of a pauper at a feast. If she is here, Sonny might have come directly back from Antoine's with the purpose of doing what Sentells always do whenever they have a chance to do it at all. At this very moment, he may be . . . sleeping with his sister? Christ, Marie-Claire thinks. This is getting out of hand.

She closes her eyes, trying to think. What can she do? To her embarrassment, all she seems to be able to think of just now is a large bottle of Remy Martin back in her room. That will do nicely. Later. After she has separated the girls from the boys. She is about to start for the elevator when there is an incredible sound. As if someone has opened the door to hell and slammed it shut again. Her nerves are already shot. This is no good for them. She will go downstairs and find out the girl's room number. Then she will see to it that something disgusting doesn't take place. Or is stopped if it is taking place already. It crosses her mind to consider what the child of two of Shad's children might be like. She shudders and moves on.

Marie-Claire presses the DOWN button and waits patiently. Perhaps she will have a drink at the bar while she is downstairs. God knows she needs it. But can she spare the time? Penetration may be only moments away. As the elevator arrives, an incredibly scruffy man passes her. He wears a black coat that almost reaches the floor, a rusty black hat with one side of the brim broken. He is wild-eyed, long-haired, smelling foul. He mumbles something about Jesus as he goes by and pauses at each door, placing his ear against it for a moment. He groans and moves quickly to the next. She wonders if it is possible that a convention of fallen-away Amish could be meeting in town, staying at the Casablanca. He looks criminal, dangerous, possibly demented—utterly out of place in anything approximating a decent hotel. She will mention it to the management.

Elvira stands near the bed, stretching, outlined to Shad's view against the moonlight falling across the balcony. She is still nude, very beautiful, smiling.

—I believe it was worth it, she almost whispers.

—What's that?

—Waiting twenty years for a good screw... Makes up for that little interruption out at your daddy's place, huh?

—Naw, Shad says solemnly. —A piece you miss is a piece you never get. If we'd got done out there, we'd of had us *two* now. But it was fine. You are the sweetest, wildest fuck I ever...

—Second sweetest, Elvira says mordantly, reaching for one of her new dresses, not bothering with underthings.

—What's that supposed to mean?

—I wasn't but second in your book.

—In my book, sweetheart, you're...

—Missy *saw* your book. Told me I came out second best.

—Goddamn sonofabitch, Shad roars. —How the hell did she see it? That's private.

—Sonny showed her. She said it was outrageous. Hundreds of women from everywhere, all kinds, all ages...

—I'm gonna kick his ass till his nose bleeds.

—Your daughter's afraid she'll end up in there.

—Ain't a bad idea. Youall do doubles?

Elvira shakes her head, regards him with hauteur. —I've heard of a motherfucker... but a daughterfucker is a step down. A big, long step.

She walks toward the bathroom, which is located by the outside door. She has almost reached it when she hears a peculiar scrambling sound just outside, almost inaudible. As if a large dog were rubbing its back on the door.

—Reckon you can get off that shit, Elvira? That's just what messed us up out at the old man's place. Why don't you come back to bed, and let's see if we can't...

—Room service.

Elvira's eyebrows raise. She turns and unlatches the door lock.

—Elvira... don't... Aw, shit...

—Honey, honey, honey, Missy sighs. —... Please...

—It's right. You know it's right. You're going to marry me. I'm going to marry you... tonight...

—It's... almost tomorrow.

—Lovely. Sounds like a song . . . Just a little now . . . a running start on the honeymoon. So we won't be utter strangers.

Sonny's head is buried in the front of Missy's pajamas. He nuzzles there, happy as a wolf after hours at the Piggly Wiggly. By rough calculation, it will take ten thousand years to adore each breast—thirty thousand for the rest. He wants to stop for a moment and snake out of his pants, his shorts. But he can't bear to stop what he is doing. If looking at her breasts worked a transformation, touching them, kissing them is ecstasy. How in God's name can one human being give such pleasure to another?

—Sonny, you got to hold up . . .

Missy manages to pull away far enough to draw together her tousled vestment. —It's not that I don't love you, 'cause I think that I do . . .

—Then . . .

—We're getting ahead of ourselves.

—No, it may seem that way, but we're not. It's as if we were already married. You get married in your heart.

— . . . but not in *bed*. That's gross.

Sonny's mind is working like a stockticker. He would give his trust fund and whatever Shad wheedles out of E.M. and Marie-Claire to have a good Alabama justice of the peace close at hand. A fat, ugly one with a tic at the corner of his mouth and a cast in his eye and the scruples of a graverobber would do. That would be just fine. But no. Things are not so simple. If he doesn't want to miss or postpone the lay of the century, he is going to have to improvise. He lifts Missy from the bed, opens the balcony door, and takes her outside. The breeze is wet and chill. That's all right. It will only make her want to go back to bed. With a warm body.

—Sonny, I don't want to stay out here. It's cold.

—I'll keep you warm . . . Look . . .

—I don't see nothing but the moon.

—That's it. That's it. There's our preacher.

—Sonny, sometimes I don't think you're all there.

Nonsense. He is not only all there, some portion of him is considerably distended. If this moon shot doesn't work, he is going to find a cab and move the whole operation to Alabama. Maybe he can get the money from Shad. Maybe E.M. But first things first. Honeymoon now, marriage later.

—Why can't we? In ancient times, people just . . . made their promises under the moon. It's always going to be there. At night, we can just look up, and . . .

—I think you're a common, ordinary pagan.

—They weren't . . . common. Ordinary? Heraclitus? Anaximander?

—That's different. Those are Catholic saints, ain't they?

—How did you know? Baby, let's just . . . unite.

He is about to take her into his arms again and try the body-to-body approach once more when there erupts some sort of uproar in the room next door. The balcony door over there bursts open, and he hears a voice. —Aw, shit . . .

A horrendous explosion follows, and then another. Sonny and Missy are knocked back into the room by a body hurtling through the air from the next balcony. Sonny hears a rattle of metal as well, and wonders what kind of people have shotgun battles in downtown New Orleans hotels.

—Sorry, buddy, the same voice says a little breathlessly. —See, there's this . . . Sonny, is that you?

—Hi, Daddy, Missy says. —Something wrong?

—Well, Cecil's showed up. Just like I didn't have enough on my mind . . .

—Uncle Shad, have you got a couple hundred . . . ?

—Huh? Aw, sure . . . Goddammit, it's all up in my rutsack, along with my .38 Special, which I sure could use right now. See, he kind of blew me out of my room.

Shad puts his ear against the wall. There is ferocious whispering going on in the next room, but the Casablanca is not Ramada Inn; one is not perforce privy to the doings of one's neighbor's wife. In fact, one cannot make out a syllable—only the certainty of muffled voices transacting in great passion.

—I believe Elvira's trying to talk to him, Shad says. —Seems he's wandering from room to room.

Shad picks up a chair, breaks it up in his hands. —I need me a weapon . . . Shit, this'll only make him mad. Sonny, you got anything in your room?

—My Swiss army knife.

—With the fish gutter?

—Right.

—Oh, gross. Missy shivers. —He's just an old crazy pervert.

—Ain't we all. Shad grins. —But this one has done turned ugly, sweet baby.

Then to Sonny. —Let's get the knife. If I was to hide in a broom closet till he come by, I could likely cut his throat.

—Why don't we call the police? Sonny asks, his mind on ventures other than eviscerating Cecil.

Shad stares at him in astonishment and disgust. —That's a hell of a thing to say. This is private. Cecil ain't no stranger . . . Come on, where's your room?

—From here? I'll have to think . . .

—Wait a minute. Mine's right over Elvira's. Maybe we could climb up from here and snag that .38. I don't much want to get caught in an open hallway up against a double-gun.

—Good, Missy says, hugging her legs. —You're not gonna gut him.

She notices Shad's eyes and the position of her shortie pajamas and lowers her legs quickly. L+++, A+++.

Sonny and Shad step cautiously out onto the balcony and start to climb. From the next balcony they hear Elvira.

—Cecil's gone after you. I couldn't do nothing with him. Says you stole away half his life.

—I'm gonna get the rest if I can lay my hands on that .38 Special of mine.

Shad stands on the rail of the balcony and catches hold of a metal support bolted to the balcony above. He swings up, gets one leg over the bracket. Now he has it made. He pulls himself hand over hand up the vertical rails, then over the guard rail. It is not his room, but the three or four feet to the next balcony is a breeze. Beats wandering in those dark hallways with a feeb loose and shooting.

—Sonny, you ready? Come on . . . That sonofabitch is gonna be . . .

—I'll help Missy up.

—Missy, you reckon he'd hurt you?

—Naw. He'd rape me some, I guess. He's always been wanting to, but when I was little I could run like blazes. Almost made me doubt religion, though.

—Hand her on up, Sonny.

—Somebody is gonna get killed, Elvira cries from the next balcony. —I mean, fun is fun, but . . .

Missy, lithe as a young deer, stands on the handrail of her balcony and throws her legs upward over the brace above. Down below, Sonny is looking at the door as he hears Cecil out there, snuffling at first, then pounding with the butt of his shotgun.

—Must be running low on shells, Shad says. —He's going conservative, knocking instead of blowing 'em off the hinges.

Sonny looks up to see Missy's progress. His heart almost stops. The shortie pajamas have fallen away, fallen utterly, and all is revealed.

—Jesus . . .

—Anything wrong? Shad asks.

—Uh . . . nuh-uh . . .

As Shad lifts Missy to the balcony above, Sonny notices that it is now silent out in the hall. Cecil has stopped his importuning. Is it possible he has gone away? Are all these theatrics unnecessary? Then he hears from above:

—Whatsafucksamatta . . . ?

The voice is harsh, possessed of a foul, scarcely human accent that resembles English as a gorilla might pronounce it.

—Mister, I'm sorry for the inconvenience . . . We're fixing to . . .

—Lissen, I don't like nobody on my balcony. I'm paying forty-five bucks . . . Take your chippy and haul your ass . . .

Sonny is up on the handrail, grabbing for the brace. By the time he gets up there, the trouble will be dealt with. One way or another.

—I said we're fixing to . . .

—Don't give me any of your Deep South bullshit, or I'll . . .

As Sonny pulls himself up, he hears the reassuring sound of a fist punched deep into flesh.

—Ah, God . . . Mamie . . .

—Saul . . . what? Oh, my God . . . you . . .

Sonny is free-hanging from the brace now, his hands reaching up to grab the floor of the balcony above, when he hears the door slamming beneath him. Actually, it has been blown away, pieces of wood lazily drifting through the air, slapping against the railing down there, tumbling into the fathomless courtyard below. Sonny dangles between balconies. If that lunatic rushes out quickly, he is going to have the same shot at Sonny as Sonny had at Missy a moment ago. He scrabbles upward as fast as he can, but his hands slip. Then he feels Missy grabbing at his wrists.

—I got you, honey.
—Sentell, you mangy sonofabitch, your hour is come . . . If you know Jesus, you better let him hear from you.
—Missy, baby, let go. I can't . . .
—But if I let go, you'll . . .
—Lady, just get back inside the room before I poke your goddamned eyes out.
—You animal . . .
—Aw, honey, where you from?
—New York . . .
—Listen, I'm just the hotel greeter. Here, that's right. Just drag him . . . Never mind his head. He don't feel nothing. That second one was real solid.
—Missy, I can't grab hold if you . . . That crazy bastard is . . .

That door slams once more, and the whole frame of the sliding glass door flashes past over the railing of the balcony below. Sonny watches, fascinated, as the debris spirals into darkness. Does moon-preacher know a funeral service? He shakes free from Missy's loving hindrance, and his hands move up to the rails, arms lifting him with unwonted strength.

—Give your soul to God, Sentell, cause your ass belongs to me.

Sonny stands silent on the balcony, holding Missy close. Down below, there is a moment of puzzled silence.

—Sentell, come on out like a man, hear? It'll be over in a hurry.

Inside, Shad and a redheaded woman have pulled an unconscious overweight man in a khaki undershirt across the room. They are talking animatedly. It appears there is something they agree upon. They drag the inert body into the bathroom. Shad kicks the legs inside, and closes the door.

—Come on, Sonny says. —He'll come looking for this room, too.

—He's out for an hour, maybe two, Shad is telling the redheaded woman. —You get to knowing them things.

—I think he's dead. Like I should call the police?

—I wouldn't, Shad says warmly. —You don't want to do that, honey. It'd just make you cynical.

—What do you mean?

—Sonsofbitches here ain't any better than your cops. All bought and paid for. Might as well be teamsters. Anyhow, it's

Mardi Gras. You got three days to wait? Say . . . you know something?

—What? What?

—You're one hell of a good-looking woman. I guess your old man in the john there tells you that.

—Saul? Ha. You're kidding with me.

—No, I ain't.

—Listen, can I tell you something? Three years . . . three years begging on my hands and knees for this trip . . .

Shad looks astonished. —Shit, I don't believe it.

—Believe it. And even now, he don't want hardly to leave the hotel.

Shad smiles. —Now I *do* believe that . . . Honey, if I was your old man, I'd take you to Waikiki or Moose Bay, but I'd keep you in the sack eighteen hours a day.

The woman stares at Shad in wonder. —Eighteen hours a day in bed? You got a bad heart?

Shad roars, —My God, an ass like a Amazon, tits like a tiger, and a sense of humor, too . . . Lord, I never knew they had anything up North like you.

Sonny is thinking of the scores of listings in New York, Boston, Chicago, Columbus, Buffalo, and dozens of other out-of-the-way places in Shad's book. If Shad doesn't know, it's because he's forgotten.

—Come on, Uncle Shad. That idiot bastard . . .

—He's slow, Shad says, never taking his eyes from the red-headed woman. —Took him thirty minutes to find Elvira's room. The room numbers is funny in this hotel.

—But . . .

—Get along. Here, take my key and get that .38 Special and a box of shells. I'll be right along . . . I just got to reassure, ah . . .

—Mamie.

—Right.

—Daddy, you got to . . .

—Don't meddle, baby. I *know* what I *got* to do.

Sonny scans the redhead carefully for the first time. She is perhaps thirty-five, in a scanty nightgown doubtless purchased for the trip in some bare hope that Saul could, in an exotic environment, with the proper prodding, be raised to his duty once more. Perhaps twice more. T++, A+ at least. L++. Large, frightened eyes, but already excited, watching Shad as if she expects him to attack, hoping he does not disappoint her. Lovely hands, carefully manicured. The red hair looks natural. The rear of the nightie hardly exists, and the curve of her back is visible to her hips. It is smoothly modeled, warmly colored. There is a small birthmark at the cleft where her buttocks begin. She stands close to Shad now, her voice low, soft.

—You think he's . . . all right?

—Honey, I done it a thousand times. You get where you got a certain touch.

—An hour?

—I believe so. Anyhow, if he stirs, I can stretch it out some.

—You could?

—Come on, Sonny says, dragging Missy out into the hall.

—Hold up, Missy says. —You ain't gonna leave him here . . .

—Hush, Sonny says, leaving the door ajar, determined to hear the Next Step.

—Mr . . .

—Shad, baby . . . just Shad . . . Look, when he *does* wake up, tell him it was a big ugly nigger burglar . . . cut and run . . .

—But he *saw* you.

—Tell him it was two of us . . . Mamie, you got the loveliest shoulders.

—You think so?

—Hey, has that worthless bastard took you to Galatoire's?

—Uh . . . yes, last night.

—Arnaud's?

—At lunch . . .

—Well, while you're here, hadn't you ought to sample the local cock?

Sonny closes the door quickly. Missy looks astonished.

—Did he say what I . . . ?

—Don't think about it, Sonny tells her. —Just don't.

Next door in Shad's room, they find the Colt .38 Special, a box of cartridges, and a money clip full of hundred-dollar bills. Sonny empties the cartridges into the capacious pockets of Shad's canvas jacket and then pulls it on. He is surprised how well he fills it. It makes him feel good. Anyhow, Shad has no use for it now. He has a redheaded woman.

—Sonny, Missy frets, —I don't know what you got in mind, but I can't go lunking around a hotel like this.

She is barefooted, and her shortie pajamas are beginning to look the worse for wear.

—We'll go to my room. I've got clothes.

—I'm tired . . . I just can't believe all this. It's worse than that nigger football game they have at the State Fair.

—We're Alabammy bound, Sonny sings.

—You still want to do that?

Sonny smiles as he looks both ways down the dimly lit corridor. Now that the flush of surprise is off this Cecil stuff, his mind has settled back into its accustomed groove. He remembers the fleeting sight of Missy's unclad fanny as she had swung up to the balcony above. Does he still want to do that? Haw.

—Come on, sweetheart.

He steps into the hallway with new assurance, Missy's hand in his. There is almost no feeling so full and fine, he thinks, as having a beautiful woman in one hand and a Colt .38 Special in the other.

Marie-Claire sits in the darkest corner of Sam's Bar, her third brandy in front of her. She has called Sonny's room. Nothing. Shad's room does not answer. It seems the phone is out of order. She was right the first time. They're in Covington. Gathered around an enormous table. By now the top brass of Omega Oil may have flown in. Perhaps they're having a secret ceremony of investiture. Sonny as the new Sentell. Teaching him passwords and secret phrases in Arabic, placing the mark of the Beast upon him in Saudi sweet light crude. She laughs. What a perfect description of Sonny himself. One more drink and she will go up to Sonny's room. The desk clerk knew the Sentell name and had handed over a pass-key without a question. She will simply drop by. Very casually. Just in case.

Over the distant bar, next to a picture of Sidney Greenstreet, a silent TV shows an enormous pillar of black smoke standing above the water. If Okeanos could sing, Marie-Claire thinks, it could be on the Ed Sullivan show.

—Don't stop . . . uh . . .
—Got no such intention, honey.
—Harder . . .
—How you gonna explain the . . . bruises?
—The nigger beat me . . . Uh, oh, it's too great . . .

Mamie has nothing more to say then, her words dissolved into exquisite moans. There is nothing like a neglected wife, Shad considers. The clock in his head says he has at least ten or fifteen minutes left before Cecil manages to find him out. On the other hand, old Saul could be coming around anytime. Unless he was drunk. Then unconsciousness can pass into sleep, and they would have all night but for Cecil.

Maybe when they're fucked out, they could go get something to eat, and go to another hotel. Shad has no desire to stop at all. Once in, you stay in till they shoot you off or it falls out. This one screws like her life depends on it. It is hard to believe she is from the North, where the women make you feel like a graverobber. Maybe he has been hitting the wrong cemeteries. This sweet, plump thing would put a Texas woman to shame. There's desire here. There's lust, he thinks. This here woman knows what she wants, and she's gonna stretch it out till the sun comes up and goes down again if she can, 'cause she knows it won't happen no more till she can talk that sorry pig into another Southern vacation. I got to remember to get her name and address. Fk 7, Sk . . . ? We ain't got around to that yet.

There is a muffled groan from the bathroom. Dingbat is coming around.

—Honey, reckon we ought to wind this up?
—Uh . . . uh . . . uh . . .
—I said, baby, your old man's having bad dreams.
—Ohhhhhhhh . . .
—I said . . .
—Go in and hit him again . . . But wait a minute first . . . No . . . don't stop . . .
—I don't reckon he carries a knife or a gun?
—Saul? Only his wallet.
—In that case, we'll give it a minute or two.

They are alone together at last. The balcony window is locked, the curtain drawn, the vanity-dresser pulled over in front of it. The lights are off. Missy stands before him, eyes glowing, arms outstretched. Sonny embraces her.

—Were you frightened, sweetheart?
—I just said a little prayer that we'd be all right, or all end up in heaven.

Sonny nods. He suspects that heaven, faced with a maiden's

prayer, considered the possibility of Shad's elevation and elected to keep them safe. On earth as it is. He picks up the phone, starts to dial the front desk.

—What are you doing? Missy asks, stretching out on the bed, paying no mind to the displacement of her shortie pajamas.

—Calling the desk. Finding out if we can get a car.

Missy reaches over, takes the phone from him, and hangs it up.

—You really do want to get married, don't you?

—God, do I . . .

She kisses him, mouth open, long and hard. —Then we can go to Alabama in the morning. Nobody'll miss us. We'll have all day.

—Right.

—Reckon we ought to practice?

—Nothing to practice. I do, you do, and then . . .

—That's it. That's the part I thought we ought to practice.

Sonny is speechless as she lifts her shortie pajamas up and over her head, then tosses the garment away. He can hardly breathe as the soft light sifting through the curtains barely illuminates her body, highlighting her hair, her breasts, her flat belly, the soft shadow between her thighs. This time it's going to be right. He is going to take his time. He pulls off his shirt, unbuckles his belt, letting his jeans fall to the floor on top of Shad's canvas jacket. Missy turns on her side to watch as he tries to draw his shorts down over an impressive erection.

—Honey, it's so big . . .

—You think so?

—I guess. I can't say. All I ever saw was that nasty old pervert Cecil shaking his at me, but it didn't seem to be anything like that. It was kind of shriveled.

Sonny climbs into bed, shyly kisses Missy. Having gotten so far, he finds himself moving in slow motion. In awe, he kisses her breasts, then her belly. Missy turns to him, her hand reaching for his rod. She holds it tight, rubs it across her thighs.

—Oh, Sonny, I do love you . . . I really do . . .

He tries to part her legs, but she resists. —Not yet, she says.

—There's plenty of time. We got years . . .

—But we've got to start, he says a little desperately, feeling his control ebbing away.

—Kiss me. Touch me . . . here. I want it to be just perfect . . . Please . . .

Sonny does as she asks, his body on hers, his hand between her legs. Her breathing deepens, speeds up. She strokes him in just the right way. He feels himself flowing into her hand. Sonofabitch.

—Sonny, I believe . . .

—It's all right. It's just that . . . touching you . . . In a minute or two . . .

Shad stalks down the dim hallway dressed only in his shorts and T-shirt. His khakis, shirt, and boots are in his room. He stands before his own demolished door, looking in carefully, trying to make sure Cecil has not returned to bushwhack him. He wonders fretfully where Sonny might be. He was supposed to get his .38 Special and wait for him. Cecil is wandering around these gloomy halls, and even if he couldn't hit a bull in the ass with a bass fiddle, he doesn't *have* a bass fiddle. He has a double-barreled sawed-off twelve-gauge shotgun. He can clean out a hallway this wide with just one barrel at thirty feet. Shad shivers. Terrible implement. No more fearsome weapon can be imagined in the hands of a manic cur like Cecil. He hopes nothing untoward has befallen Sonny. He has heard no extraordinary doors slamming. Then he smiles, remembering Missy in her shortie pajamas. By now, that boy is topping her like gravy on potatoes. That's how come he forgot the ordinance. He is about to go into his room, satisfied at the long silence there.

—Oh, my God . . .

—Listen, lady . . . Oh, hell, it's you, Marie Clare.

—Shad, you don't have any . . .

—Sure I do. I just ain't got 'em on at the moment. Anyhow, anything you see, you've . . .

—Don't say it. And not for a very long time. I think E.M. should have left you in that asylum. People aren't supposed to wander about in hotels with their . . .

Shad frowns, moves in to look closely at Marie-Claire.

—Honey, I believe you're drunk.

—Of course not.

—Hell you say. Think I can't tell?

—I've . . . had a drink or two.

—Bullshit. You're tanked. Reckon a few weeks at Shady Grove might . . .

—Damn you, stop it.

She notices for the first time the lamentable condition of Shad's door. —What happened? Some woman tried to escape?

Shad stares at her in grim irony. —I don't lose 'em that way, he says. —You ought to know.

Marie-Claire blushes. —Then what?

—There's this nut from Greenwood thinks he's got a score to settle with me.

—Never mind. What did Eddie tell Sonny?

—Huh?

Marie-Claire almost shouts. —What did he tell Sonny about . . .

—Oh, that? Nothing. At least as far as I know. Last I saw of Sonny, he had something else on his mind.

—Thank God. Can you stop him?

—Stop Sonny? I doubt it. See, he had that little girl with him, and . . .

—Can you stop E.M. from . . . telling Sonny? Marie-Claire pauses, eyes Shad narrowly. —Do you want to stop him?

Shad pauses, leans up against the blasted doorjamb. He is tired as hell, and his back hurts. He could use another drink or a warm bed.

—I hadn't thought about it.

—Think about it, damn you. If you and Eddie get together in this . . .

—That ain't gonna happen, Mary Clare. I'd like to be with my own brother when he finishes up, but even that ain't going to happen. If you're worried we're gonna double-team you, forget it. E.M. and me, whatever there was, went down the drain a long time ago. Seems you ought to remember.

Shad walks into his room, leaving Marie-Claire behind. She watches as his tall, broad-shouldered, hulking body seems to fill the shattered balcony window from top to bottom, side to side. She smiles as she sees the gray sky beyond him where the dawn will be making its way in a little while. They have never exchanged an idea, never shared more than an illicit bed and a bad conscience. Still . . .

—*Je ne regrette rien*, she whispers, astonished at her own

sentiment, swept by the brandy's sudden vertigo as she tries to remember the way to Sonny's room.

Things are again in hand in Sonny's room. Missy's hand. They kiss and kiss again in the darkness.
—You're fine, Sonny. You really are.
—How do you know? I just . . .
—Honey, please don't go quarreling with me. Not on our honeymoon.
—Some honeymoon . . .
—Sonny, I didn't expect you was going to be a stud. I mean, there's more to love than . . .
—What?
—Well . . . hey, look . . . I believe it's . . .
—You're right . . . it is . . .
—What'd I tell you? True love will find a way.
—Look at it.
—See, I said a little prayer . . .
This time Missy does not resist as Sonny rises to his knees, parts her legs, and prepares to do, if he but can, something far, far better than he has done. Her eyes are closed, arms around his neck, lips parted, hair arrayed softly across the pillow. His equipment is in order again, and his heart and hers are beating fast. He allows himself one final moment before he enters that chamber that all men seek, that grail that renders the grim world in all the mystical colors of the universe, and which, as it seems, no Sentell can long go without. Her body is rich with the promise of ten thousand nights of love like this, no one like another, and there is this key turning in the lock and the lights go on.
—Sonny . . . Oh, my God . . .

Cecil has been wandering the dreary corridors of the Casablanca for what seems years. He is now squatted down in a linen closet, tired, out of breath, disgusted. It appears the numbers on the room doors bear no relation, floor by floor, to the relative positions of the rooms. You would think room 307 would be below 407, right? Not a chance. And Sentell moves like a ferret. Cecil is fuddled by it all. His latest sally has been fruitless. Sentell was cornered, he was sure of it. But when he broke down the door, all he found was some fat man in his underwear laid out cold, and a buck-naked redheaded woman with a nasty accent moaning and calling back her demon lover or some such nonsense. Hell.

> *1939. Al Capone is released from prison, but his mind has been destroyed by syphilis while in Alcatraz. The gangster retires to his estate at Miami Beach and will vegetate there until his death in 1947.*

Cecil feels a certain kinship with Al. Vegetables should stick together. He wonders what ever became of John Dillinger. Then he closes the dog-eared pages of the *Chronicles* and surveys the contents of the closet. There are numerous piles of dirty linen and a few uniforms stacked on shelves. He decides it is time for a change. He pulls on one of the white jackets, ties a neckerchief over his stiff collar, and draws a chef's hat down over his matted hair. A moment is spent shaking shotgun shells out of his delapidated coat, drawing his diminutive shotgun up his sleeve. He looks into a small mirror on the wall. Just like Chef Boyardee on the can. Older, scrawnier, a scruffy three-day beard, blood-shot eyes, but the idea is right. What is needed now is a quick drink, and some rethinking. Sentell is in this damned hotel. Search and destroy. Easier said than done. What about that drink?

—Mother, Sonny moans as Missy wraps herself in the sheet and stares, unbelieving, at Marie-Claire.
—Oh, Sonny . . . not this way . . . and not with . . . *her* . . .
—Will you just get out, goddammit?
It is not a request. Not even a demand, but a *cri de coeur*, the broken soul in anguish screaming at its tormentor. Marie-Claire feels herself blushing, but she cannot simply apologize and withdraw. It is Sonny who must remain withdrawn. If this pretty, empty-headed thing is Shad's daughter, then . . . Sonny is about to have his sister.
—Darling, this simply isn't . . . possible. Truly . . .
—It *is* possible . . . It was damn near . . .
—You don't understand. This girl is . . .
Marie-Claire's voice fades away. It suddenly occurs to her that she is within three or four words of doing what she has feared E.M. had already done. A nice problem. Does she tell her son

what she would rather die than reveal? Or does he know his sister without knowing it?

—What does it take to get you out of here?

—I'm afraid, considering the state of things, I simply can't . . .

Missy has had enough. Or is it that she has had nothing at all? She tosses off the sheet, stands up nude, fresh, young, glorious, facing Marie-Claire. She picks up her shortie pajamas, shakes herself into them. Marie-Claire can see what it is that Sonny adores.

—I am not gonna sit here like a hamburger somebody ordered and didn't pick up, Missy says. —I just ain't.

She walks toward the door, using her body as if it were a flail and a condemnation as she passes Marie-Claire.

—You stay here with your momma if that's what you want, she says contemptuously. —I'm going back to my goddamned —sorry—room.

She flounces out, and Marie-Claire turns back to Sonny, almost ready to tell him what he must know if something monstrous is to be avoided.

—Sonny, that girl . . .

But he is already in his jeans, pulling on his boots. He picks up Shad's canvas jacket, checks a large pistol, and turns an angry frustrated face toward her.

—Never again, he shouts at her.

—Darling, be rational. There's something you have to know . . .

—No, he yells back at her, jacket over his shoulder as he starts for the door. —All I've *got* to do is get laid and die.

He is gone then, and Marie-Claire sags down on the side of the bed, suddenly much older, wondering if somehow, in some sense not clear to her, Sonny is right. And if he should be, what does that make of her life? Is it possible that, translated into civilized language, all that matters is that we love before the darkness comes? God forbid, she thinks. Because if it is so, then she has lost everything.

—Missy?

—Get out. I ain't going through all that again.

—Honey . . .

—Now, I asked you as politely as I know how to just go.

Maybe folks can't get it across to you polite. So haul your miserable ass, okay?

Missy sits on the side of her own bed sobbing. Sonny stands in the doorway, forlorn, shirtless, Shad's canvas jacket over his shoulder. There is the first shadow of a beard on his cheeks, and he looks tired enough to fall over where he stands. She knows she should not even look at him. It is a misery to look at what you have come to want and cannot have.

—Sonny, please . . .

Then he is sitting beside her, kissing her. —I'm here with you. Get dressed and come on.

—I'm too tired. I really am. I thought we could . . .

—We can. We're getting out of this loony bin.

—Huh?

—We'll get a cab, go to Mobile. It's all going to be different in Alabama.

—Will it?

—I swear.

Shad is dressed now. He would like to go to sleep, but that is not wise, what with Cecil running about. It might occur to him to go back over old ground once more, and since Shad no longer has a door, that could prove fatal.

The room is a wreck, walls pocked by shot, chairs broken, the balcony awash in fragments of wood and glass. But the TV still works. One of those dawn shows is on now. People who look as if they were made out of cereal boxes chatting away. A weatherman who is a laugh a minute. Then the news segment. You guessed it. Shad turns up the volume to find that the death toll on Okeanos Number One out in the Gulf of Mexico now stands at eleven, with nine men missing. Hope for their rescue is now fading, despite the fact that weather in the Gulf has calmed, and the Coast Guard and Omega Oil helicopters have been combing the area.

He turns off the volume again, stands up slowly, and starts for the door. The liquor is gone now, and Cecil or no Cecil, he must go downstairs and see what he can find. For himself. For some small toast to his friends who have found final shelter in the Gulf.

When she awakes, she remembers everything. Some vacation, Elvira thinks. You can go one thousand miles, but your past is like your shadow. Caddo Parish, in the form of Cecil Miley, has come roaring down the state and is at large. She slips into her dress and smiles without humor. If someone had told her years ago that she had been facing her destiny there on her knees beneath that big blasted pine, staring at Cecil's parts, she would have laughed. Don't laugh. Never laugh. The future is coming at you at a million miles a minute, and the last person to have any control over it is you. It's not funny. It isn't even sorrowful. It just is.

She picks up the phone, dials Missy's room. No answer. What does that mean? Either Missy will end up a Sentell, or something awful has happened. If you can distinguish between those two things. Better go find out. It's better to know than remain in doubt. Isn't it?

Outside, it is still dark. Far to the east, the first flush of gray, so faint as to seem illusory, has begun to fill the sky. The moon still stands overhead, pale, fading, perched on scattered clouds like an egg in hollandaise.

—I don't think he's coming back, Missy says.

—Sure he is, Sonny replies. —Nobody just abandons a taxicab. He'll be out by the time it's light.

—If you say so . . . At least it's quiet out here.

—Put your head on my shoulder.

—I'm just wore out. Is this the way you-all live all the time?

—You mean my family? No, sometimes it's really bad.

—I'm so embarrassed . . . I mean, your momma . . .

—Put it out of mind.

—Out of mind? My goodness, how am I gonna face her? That's gonna be my mother-in-law.

—The hell with it. We'll live in California.

—Haw. Not me. It's bad enough here. Lord, I wish we didn't have to live *anywhere*.

—Ummmm . . .

Sonny's head falls forward. Too much for too long. We must live somewhere. Inside the dubiety of our skins at least. In a moment, Missy cuddles toward sleep. She pulls Shad's voluminous canvas jacket over them and surrenders.

Elvira knocks on the door of Sonny's room. For a moment there is no answer, and she almost turns away. Then the door opens. But it is neither Missy nor Sonny standing there. It is Sonny's mother.

—I was looking for my little girl.

—She's not here. She left. With her . . . my . . .

Marie-Claire's voice trails off. There is a long silence. Elvira does not like Marie-Claire. Sonny's mother had not so much as a word to say to her on the flight down from Shreveport. She seems to think herself superior to almost everyone.

—Perhaps you'd better come in, Marie-Claire says finally, woodenly. —There's something . . . you have to know.

Marie-Claire closes the door behind them. Now that she has someone to listen, what is it she means to say? Is she perhaps going to tell a stranger what she hardly can bear to think?

—Sonny took . . . your daughter, she begins, with no clear idea of what she will say next.

—Ummm. It's no surprise. That boy couldn't hardly keep his hands off her. I guess she could do worse. She might do better, but she could do worse . . . They'll probably go to Mobile.

—Mobile?

—They say you can get married over there by accident. No blood tests, no waiting around . . . hit and run.

Marie-Claire finds herself sitting on the side of the bed again, shaking her head. —Married? Oh, my God . . . It was bad enough already.

Elvira takes this unkindly. —Melissa Miley is good enough for any damned Sentell that ever stood up, shook it, and walked.

Marie-Claire continues to shake her head. —It isn't that. She's a lovely girl . . . but . . .

—So she ain't got a dime. Hell, it wasn't any rich people *in* Greenwood.

—No, you don't . . . Sonny said she's . . . She kept calling Shad . . . daddy . . .

—Me and Shad was close. It was a long time ago. It happens. What's the matter? Is that too strong for you?

Marie-Claire covers her face with her hands. It is true. Has it come to this? It has come to this.

—Oh, God, this is . . . horrible.

—I didn't come in here to hear no shit about my little girl.

Marie-Claire settles heavily onto the bed. Incredible. She feels the carefully structured matrix of her life coming unraveled. How is it that she and Elvira stand here, drawn inexorably into one another's lives? By Shad Sentell . . . that's how.

—Your daughter is . . . Shad's?

Elvira is irritated. —I ain't got a birth certificate that says it, but I expect I know my baby's father as well as you knows yours.

—Yes, Marie-Claire murmurs. —I expect you do. But if that's so, you see, she . . . your girl . . . is Sonny's . . . sister.

Elvira's expression does not change. She is not stupid, but some things take longer to consider than others. —Sonofabitch, Elvira finally says. —You and Shad? Sonny? Lord God Jehovah . . .

Elvira seems suddenly energized. She stares at Marie-Claire in rueful admiration. —He's had you? His own brother's wife? Ain't he a caution?

Marie-Claire closes her eyes. —Yes, I suppose he is. It . . . there was . . . only once.

—Come on, Elvira says archly. —Him and me must of had each other a thousand times, every chance, every way we could. And you got knocked up the one time out? Lord, honey, you do press belief.

—I wouldn't lie, Marie-Claire replies, her voice close to breaking. —It was . . . an accident.

—Now, I believe that, Elvira says spryly. —Commonest form of accident happens to women when Shad's around . . . worse than slipping in the shower or cutting your hand on a paring knife. Not as bad as Rocky Mountain spotted fever . . .

—I was lonely, unhappy. He was there. I'd been drinking . . .

Marie-Claire feels a flush come to her cheeks. Not for the telling, though it has never been told before, but for the distortion. For the truth that, being told at long last, is yet not told as it was.

—Don't think twice about it, sugar, Elvira says, patting her shoulder. —I wasn't lonely, and I hadn't drunk a drop the first time he come down on me. And I loved it . . . He is fine, ain't he?

Marie-Claire looks away. —I . . . I can't remember anything about it.

She tries to catch a quick glimpse of Elvira as she feels these words tumbling out. It is quite true that she does not remember anything about it. She remembers everything. Elvira is staring at her, sizing her up. Maybe she has never encountered quite such an errant liar before.

—You can't be her . . .

—Her?

—The one . . . number one in Shad's book.

—I don't understand.

Elvira looks Marie-Claire over from head to foot. —Could you . . . have it?

Marie-Claire returns her look, astonished. —What?

—Oh, don't be stupid . . . What I ain't got . . . that I must of never had.

Elvira sits on the bed beside her now, her own mood not much removed from that of Marie-Claire. —You see, he's got this book, she begins in a low, monotonous voice, and keeps on talking.

Marie-Claire rises and goes to stare out at the brightening clouds visible beyond the balcony, the distant rooftops. Whatever this woman is telling her is unintelligible and unimportant to her just now. What is there to do? Sonny and Missy are off to Alabama. They will come back—what would you call it? Man and wife? How about brother and sister?

She shudders and smiles despite herself. How truly they breed. And it's not even for sexuality. That's just what it slips into because it's a challenge and it feels good, and for a moment or two each time they can believe it's an arrival. No, they're bred for penetrating, for finding the center, piercing to the core. That's why women can't walk away from them, why they always find the oil. Sex and other forms of drilling, she thinks, laughs, and leaves off. Her reveries are tending toward free association. Perhaps one more drink, and then a long, long sleep.

Shad has walked out to the door of the hotel to get a look at the weather. It is not yet full light, and the air is crisp and chill. He lights a cigar and looks at a cab parked near the door and apparently filled with old clothes. It is going to be a pleasant day. If the weather holds, the Gulf will be serene, seas two or three feet at the most. He will be able to study Okeanos from a crew boat, have pictures made with a telephoto, do the job right. Which assures him of nothing. Men die on clean jobs. The dragon down there is not mollified by a precise workmanlike approach. When you go into the flames, a sudden small change of pressure can tear the remains of the rig apart. And when the rig goes, so do you.

I got to stop thinking about it, Shad thinks. I got to put it out of mind, or they're gonna have to tie me to a plank and carry me back up to Shady Grove. That fucking doctor will electrocute me for sure.

He goes back inside and turns toward the dark entrance of Sam's Bar. The door is open, and he is about to enter when a voice hails him from over near the elevators.

—Shad . . .

—Mary Clare? What the hell are you doing still up? You *got* to be drunk.

—Do you know what's happened?

—Shit, what ain't? Tell me you heard on the news that Okeanos has done foundered and gone down. Now that'd be a weight off my mind.

—Your daughter . . . your own . . . and our . . . I mean . . .

—Go ahead. You almost said it. Say it.

—You subhuman filth . . .

—That's not what I had in mind.

—Everything's ruined. You know that, don't you?

—I tell you, I hadn't give it much thought. Let's go get a drink and you can tell me about it.

Together they enter the bar. The place is darker than Caliban's crotch, and Shad looks about for an empty table.

—It's in the blood, Marie-Claire is saying, a sob in her voice. —He's just another insane, lustful brute like the rest of you.

Just then Shad looks over toward the bar and sees there a strange tableau. Men are frozen along its length from one end to the other. And a cook seems to be babbling something about the Great Beast who consumes the honest man's provender. It must be a religious meeting of some kind, Shad considers, still looking for a place where he and Marie-Claire can sit. Then that distant whining voice breaks off. The silence is total now.

—Aw haw, Sentell . . . I'll see you in hell.

Shad does not need another look to identify the cook or reckon what is on the menu. He hits Marie-Claire as if he were breaking up an off-tackle play. She goes down under him, crying out as the buckshot chuffs past overhead to find its mark in the outsize photo of Paul Henreid, who looks amazed and saddened to find his plaster entrails tumbling down to the floor, his paper privates blown away.

The shot breaks the stasis, and a stampede begins. Tables go over, customers trample one another to get Sam's Bar behind them. The sound of breaking glass and voices cursing seems louder than the shotgun blast.

—What in God's name . . . ? Marie-Claire moans.

—Hush, he says, kissing her hair, her ear, her cheek. —You're gonna be all right. When I get up, try to run with me.

—But I . . .

—Yes, you can. I won't let you go, you know that.

—Yes . . . I know.

Then the worst of the crowd—or the best, if fleetness of foot and drive for survival be criteria—is past. Shad rises, carrying Marie-Claire with him, and barrels out the door, a handful of late leavers knocked sprawling by his momentum. From behind, he hears a final execration, and one last shot which strikes just above and behind Shad's head, leaving Peter Lorre looking philosophically at a hole blasted by a shot fired in 1960 through the wall of a set struck in 1942.

Chapter Thirteen

> And they reached the stream of Okeanos, and the Red Sea, and the race of the Lemnian wives who slew their Lords . . .
> *Pythian Ode* IV, 251–52

The dope worked fine. As soon as Henry could give it to me again. I don't remember much between supper and now. Did I tell the boy? Hell, I have no recollection at all. Worse, I cannot bring myself to be concerned. It is as if those hours were obscured, lived through behind a pane of red-tinted glass. And even with the narcotic beginning to take hold, I can't sleep. As if I had just finished putting together some new deal, my nerves hum and sing. That thing inside, that great beast consuming me at its own pace, has fallen silent. For now. I will sit here in the study and wait for the sun, and when the sun has carried away the mist and warmed the arbor a little, Henry will help me outside. I will not have to call. He knows when it is right, and he would not let me miss a moment of the light for the sake of his own salvation. This morning hour or two has become a form of worship for those who dread the business that stalks at midnight. For those at the edge of the great dark who doubt there is light in eternity.

I never did sleep well. You know how people say they sleep badly in a strange place—a hotel room, a guest room for a weekend in the country? The whole world seems to be my hotel room. I wake up in the night and remember some detail I left undone, some manner of doing what I did that might have been done better, or something certain to go wrong if I could not remember what it was and go and set it right. Of course it was always nothing, nothing at all. Just that I never slept well and required some waking excuse for it.

Now it no longer matters. I sleep no better here in my own place on the river than I did in the old man's house, or in the series of crummy tourist courts I lived in coming up, or in that damned pile of red brick I built on Line Avenue just to show the world—and myself, and her, too—that I had arrived, gotten there. What was her line the day we moved in? Standing on the front staircase, arms above her head, laughing at how quick a trip it had been from the Grand Café to the Grande Maison: *J'y suis, j'y reste,* she sang. Yeah, I answered, *Ils ne passeront pas* . . . We laughed together and I said, Let's go upstairs and screw ourselves into oblivion, honey. And she said she had to see to the servants.

I went to sleep by myself that night with her still unpacking and arranging and fussing around and just getting into that barn of a house and hunkering down. She meant what she said. She was there, and she was staying there. As for me, I woke up around three or four and couldn't sleep. I remember wondering, is it possible to have a bad conscience before the fact? I went and checked all the windows and locks as if I expected an intruder. Then, after a drink and some more thought, I reckoned that it was possible indeed, and that I was paying with insomnia for what I meant to do if ever the chance and the need arose at the same time. And as for the intruder? It was me.

Last night was the first time the three of us have occupied roughly the same space since 1946. The old man's funeral. Howling madness. My worst moment. I would give a great deal to wipe that day and night out of history, let it not have been. Then I would be able to say honestly that I have never lost control in my life. Of myself. For what that would be worth just now. And when you have nothing else so fine to say, I think it would be worth a lot.

Last night I looked at them, knowing what I know and yet even then hardly believing it. Disgusted. With myself. For the failure not of love or marital success or insight into the soullessness of women and the treachery of brothers. No, for the failure to set the net of my own calculations wide and fine enough to encompass a logic that reverses all logic: women's logic.

She was always sexually fastidious. Very good in bed, but even in the throes, only partly there, something withheld. No—not something she was holding back. Rather something holding *her* back. Therefore, because she could not give herself up utterly to one she owed abandon, I should have assumed that she would sooner or later fuck wildly and completely my polar opposite, fuck him sooner or later as certainly as the sun will rise tomorrow over the green tulmultuous Gulf, over Okeanos Number One.

What went wrong? What caused her to surrender? Not that damned trip to Paris. I do not believe that. I will not, and I cannot. That was the occasion, but the roots ran deep. Was it that I obtained her rather than loved her? I think so.

I had made a deal with Mary Clare: I will extricate you from the Grand Café and take you away from your hootch-swilling antic coon-ass father, because those are things I can do for you. And moreover I will make you flat-out wealthy because I can do that, too. And in return, you will take care of my house and bear me children, and sooner or later I will have reached that thing I am headed for that I don't yet know the name of because I started out too far down to have heard the name or even to know anyone else who had. Then, having arrived wherever it is we will have reached, we will sit down and talk and find out what it is we do when you have gotten where every sonofabitch who was ever born has dreamed of getting.

There are always unwritten protocols, aren't there? Mine, in the fine garnet print they use to record stock market quotations, would have read: but don't ask for or expect love, some sudden or even slow and certain opening to my deepest places, because I know what a woman can do when she finds the anteroom where love exists. The room has been wrecked by someone before you in a white dress, water pouring from her open mouth as they lifted her past the cypress stumps. And even wrecked, made unfit for habitation, its lodger bludgeoned and trampled, that room is still occupied. It is a grave where the rest of me visits to do whatever one does when to pray seems tendentious and silence is forced to speak.

Still, as the world measures things, I didn't not love her, and we were good in bed, and the parties were fun, and she got whatever she wanted and had no ground for complaint. Or, taken another way, if she had grounds, she made no effort to have them known.

As for me, I was distracted. You do not build an empire sitting around holding hands with some woman, and that was what I was doing, not even knowing it. I think I thought that when Omega was so big, so strong that nothing short of a worldwide catastrophe could hurt it, then I would be able to turn my mind to whatever it was she dreamed. I really planned to do that.

Because short of love, what is closer than sharing some dream not your own. There was going to be time for that. It was part of the analysis. It was in the schedule.

The next part isn't clear. It should be clearest of all simply because it began with my realizing that no matter how large I had been thinking, I still had not imagined just what Omega Oil could be. But it isn't clear. *Force majeure* tipped me off to what I had really been aiming for all the time. The sudden and irrevocable and overwhelming momentum of events that rose like a tidal wave across the oceans—even faster and more certain than Omega holdings and profits. The Rhineland, Austria, Czechoslovakia. I began to hear it early on, drinking, eating, working with oil men whose interests didn't stop at the Texas or Louisiana line or even at the boundary of the continent. It's coming. They're going to do it again. Twenty-five years after they damn near killed everybody in Europe, they've all got new teams, and this won't even be a different game. Just the second half of the same one.

And that was all right with me. Because it sure as hell wasn't going to hurt the oil business—least of all the American oil business. The small independents were going to become big businesses, and the big ones were going to become international structures that even governments would have to truckle to, because oil, and oil at a good steady price, was, as they had already come to say, the lifeblood of modernity.

But you had to get into position. Nothing just happens. Men make history—if they are where the raw materials are when the lightning strikes. I was going to be there. Be there and take advantage and construct something so powerful, so awesome that the old man would gaze upon it and wither utterly inside because it would beggar his angry imagination and all the jake-leg plots his crowd of lunatics and misfits had ever dreamed up. And perhaps from that great silence in which she dwelled now, that water-stained anteroom within and without me, Momma would see something done that Shad had not been able to do: the old man knocked down finally, not to rise again. Because one of his own blood had put together a corporation so enormous and so necessary to the survival of modern life that it would be virtually beyond challenge, and the Marxist-Leninists and the Wobblies and the Bow-Wows and the Trotskyites would see and be afraid. And then she would know that I had loved her as much as Shad did, that I had not settled for a quick gesture and a strapping, but waited until I could shape a vengeance that was total, inescapable, and sealed like a tomb.

Something like that. Not surely at the front of the mind, but present in some form for certain because now, amidst this analysis, I realize why I enjoyed it so, why it meant more to me than money or power or anything else at all.

By 1938, the drumbeat had begun in earnest. I was spending as much time in Houston and New York and Dallas as I did in Shreveport. I was dealing with Englishmen and Dutchmen and Arabs and Latin Americans of every variety as much as with Yankees and men from California. I would finish roughing in a deal in some boardroom, then leave the details to flunkies and scramble with Shad to see the deal come through. Stockpiling, research, development . . . Sometimes when I came home, I would be disoriented for a day or two, still high on the pressure and the beat accelerating now, reaching fever pitch with Chamberlain rushing back and forth inanely as if he supposed that sanity would prevail if only he could run fast enough. Those of us watching knew otherwise. Some of us knew, almost to the day, when the scurrying would cease and the blood-dimmed tide begin to roll over Europe again. How, you ask. How could you know? Because we were fueling the machine that would churn the waves.

The worst irony. The very worst. In August of 1939, I never went to Paris. I had never intended to go. But when she asked where I was headed, almost casually I uttered the magic word: Paris. I could have said Rio or Belgrade or Tannu Tuva, and she would have shrugged and turned back to her Charpentier or her expensive drapery catalogue or some absurdity by Bergson, and that would have been the end of that. It wasn't that she even cared where I was going. Our dreams had by that time already diverged so far that for her to ask where I was going amounted ordinarily to no more than a courtesy.

But when I said Paris, everything changed. It was no longer just a courtesy, a way of making conversation. It was no longer casual at all. She put down her catalogue or her book. Her eyes lit up. She said, I'd like to go. That wouldn't be wise, I said, still not quite aware of the depth of the waters I had troubled. Things are tense. The Corporal says the Polish Corridor is an infamy. The whole world could go up any time. The English and the French will have to stand somewhere. I don't want go to Poland, she said. Just Paris. They're going to go at it very soon, I said. If I don't see it now, she answered, I may never see it. It may not even be there. No, I said, and turned back to my work, insensitive enough to suppose that was that.

Or no. Invincibly stupid, perhaps, but something more as well. Trapped. Trapped utterly, because there was no way I could tell her where I was really headed. Via London, Rome, Trieste, Vienna, to a small resort town on the Bavarian border called Garmisch-Partenkirchen, where I and a few other oil men of various nationalities would be talking business with an old friend, Klaus Richter, once in the oil business himself, now Procurement Officer for the Luftwaffe. There was nothing illegal about it. You just didn't want it bruited about.

The deal was made. We would fuel the German bombers that rocked London the following late summer and fall, and continue to fuel them from what appeared to be Middle Eastern stock until it stopped making any kind of business sense at all. As we climbed aboard our return flight and I leaned back in my narrow seat, I knew Omega Oil was going to be world class. No matter what happened.

There seemed to be nothing wrong when I got home. If anything, she came to my arms with more spirit than before I had left. I thought nothing of that. The war had begun, and it had raised everyone's feeling no matter which side they preferred. It was as if that other shoe, held high since 1918, had finally dropped. This time around would end it. This was surely the biggest thing that would happen in our lifetimes, and all of us had to be somehow involved or miss out, lose the transcendent hours and days and months of our lives.

All right, fine. If Glenn Miller playing "The White Cliffs of Dover" made her more responsive, made her a better screw, why not? As it turned out, of course, it wasn't the millennium. It was just another war, and it would break Germany and England, and make the US and Russia, and clear the ground to get on with the real war to decide what system this new corporate world would be governed by.

It was a day or two before Christmas of 1939 when she told me we were going to have a baby. Or that *she* was going to have a baby. I can't remember which. This drug does not produce total recall. Just a fast float over the high spots. It would have been a nice moment for a tape recorder, wouldn't it? To have heard her exact words when she announced what, if it was not my millennium, was surely the first trump of some minor Armageddon.

By the time the boy was born, we were all caught up in someone else's dream. And on the eighth of December 1941, war was declared. It was the same day I received a check from the Credit Suisse for $2.8 million—the last payment from Klaus Richter, who was now, so they told me, an enemy.

It was not a cold day, and I walked out back and watched the baby clambering on the lawn furniture under Mary Clare's watchful eye. He was a beautiful child, and I thought, Well, son, whatever they say about it, the Third Reich just set you up in the world. When you're old enough for college, I'll tell you some of the unwritten history of this war that put us on top of the world. By then, it will be no more than another annotation in the chronicles of general lunacy, and no one will give a damn who prevailed because things will shake out pretty much the same either way. All the sonsofbitches from Maine to Madagascar will need oil, and the ones who can find it and put it in the pipeline will be riding high.

Just then, we heard a truck pull up in the drive, and I thought to myself, Hell, it seems as if I could at least take a single day off without them coming out here warting me about some problem I am paying them to solve. But it was a man in the dark green uniform of the US Marines. It was Shad. I couldn't believe it. Once more, my eyes were not where they should have been. They were on him rather than on her. I was telling him that he was a damned fool, that he was crippling the company, that they weren't just rednecks having a good time over there, but playing for keeps and using live ammunition, but all the time I was talking, he was looking past me the way he did when he either didn't want to hear what I had to say or was determined to ignore it anyhow. He was not just looking off into the distance then, but at her, at his son, telling them both in that long gaze that this was the only thing to do, the only way to solve it, heal it, put it to rest.

Then he was gone, and I had my own war to fight. I was in Washington and London, Tangier, the Pacific. On one run in 1943, Rommell's boys almost shot me out of the sky, and if the Field Marshal had known what I and some Texas boys were brewing with the Arabs, he might have used up his air force to bring down that single Grumman Norseman that almost dived into the sand to evade the casual passing attack of an FW-190.

I tried to keep tabs on Shad. I even tried to interfere with his military career by having him shipped to absurd places where he was not likely to get himself killed. It was no use. The Marines skidded across the Pacific on a path of their own blood, and where they were, he was. Guadalcanal, Saipan, Tarawa, Iwo Jima, Okinawa. It seemed that every month or so, there would be another article in the paper stating that he had been wounded again or had been cited for bravery. Three Purple Hearts and three Silver Stars, a Navy Cross, and on and on. It was good for business. Everyone liked to tell me how proud they were of Shad, and how they knew I wished I could be out there with him, and I would nod and say, We all have our duties to do, don't we?

Like hell I wished I was out there with him. The crazy bastard was *trying* to get himself killed, which was obvious after the first two or three campaigns, after which he was entitled to come home. Moreover, those other bastards were fighting with their backs to the home islands. I knew the Germans, and I was prepared to take the Japs on faith: if Shad wanted to die, they were willing and able to accommodate him.

But it didn't happen. The war ended with a bang over Hiroshima, and I was already in motion doing a fast one-eighty from war to what passes for peace. All of a sudden, a wealthy company was up to its neck in debt, leveraged to the hilt, because I was buying leases in the South Pacific where the French and the Dutch were winding it down, and the Middle East where the Brits were checking out and handing it over to those silly sonsofbitches with their burnooses and their heathen religion and their determination to live in the tenth century until a better one came along. All of a sudden, all over the world, we were making deals and trying to get pipe and lay it down fast enough to pay off the loans that had allowed us to make the deal in the first place.

Shad came home. It was a nice reunion. He played with the boy, hugged Mary Clare, and seemed to have a peculiar, almost hangdog expression on his face which, considering what I was to learn, may well have been intended to say, *I'm sorry. I went out there to get myself killed decently, to end this once and for all, but it didn't work out and I had to come back. I'm sorry.* Which sounds fine and fatal, except I have never heard it told that Shad

Sentell has apologized to anyone for anything in his life, and which, had he said that, would have been a lie because he is surely as constitutionally incapable of not enjoying a fight, and winning if he can, as he is of lying effectively.

There was the mandatory welcome home meal at the Old Place, a fish fry with a lot of people from the industry there. Shad was back, and they were glad, and it even seemed the old man found a certain glee in seeing that he had made it past whatever had threatened him. Yes, one of the living legends of the oil industry was home, and now all of us could settle down and turn our patriotism into some profit-making and restructuring. I had already sent a man into Germany looking for Klaus Richter. He would have survived, and he would still have the very best of contacts in Algeria, Libya, the Sudan, and what would become the United Arab Emirates. We would be doing business again before they hanged Ribbentrop and the rest. My man found him in a tiny Bavarian town. He was making a small living drawing up plans for stage sets in Oberammergau.

What next? Next, as I recall, the old man had a stroke. Not enough to kill him. It just crippled him a little. Mary Clare wanted to move him into town, into our house. I think his reaction was about the same as mine. I won't live under the same roof with that old sonofabitch, I told her. If you want to play Lady Bountiful and visit with him and buy him a new Philco radio and do all that crap at Christmastime, it's all right with me. But not here. Not in this house.

So we put him in Shady Grove. He had a little cottage of his own and his radio, and when I bought a chunk of Shady Grove stock and put Mary Clare on their board, they even unbent a little and let him have liquor in his cabin. And that, surely, was that.

No. Shad felt different. He was out on a survey off the coast of one of those damned South American islands—Curaçao, or something like that, and when he got back, we argued. For the first time since we had been working together. We had always managed to avoid it before. We had a custom of politeness, almost joviality, between us. We weighed our words, suggested, never demanded, never insisted. Because we both knew that just below the politeness, the veneer of bonhomie, was a bedrock of dislike and coldness between us. Mutual contempt: he for me because he despised calculation, craft, lying in wait. Because I spent my life like accumulated investment capital, placing it only where there was profit to be derived—building, always building with whatever materials I could lay hands on, escaping one by one all the nets that hold men captive within the good opinion of society. I for him because, God help me, I thought he was dumb. Not lacking in whatever kind of brain cells make us able to compete in the world, but dumb through carelessness, through inattention, through some peculiar variation of pride that presupposed a happy result to any enterprise he undertook, no matter at what disadvantage, simply because it was he who was doing the undertaking. I think we were both bemused by the other's success, by the fact that both formulas, both ways of living seemed to produce results.

The argument, when it burst out, surprised me. Shad was vehemently opposed to the old man's having been put in a nursing home. He didn't give a damn about its costing a small fortune or about its being better for the old man. I had no right to chain him up, close him off, Shad told me angrily. He ought to be back on his own place, his own land. The poorest nigger who owns half an acre has that right. He can't take care of himself, I told him. He can't move around. He can't keep up a garden, much less farm. He won't eat because it's too much trouble to cook. You want him eating cold Vienna sausages and pork and beans out of the can and stumbling off the porch and lying there till Petrie or Claiborne happens by and finds him?

Shad just drank my whiskey and repeated that a man had a right to stay on his own place till they buried him on it. Any miserable sonofabitch had that right, didn't he? You're sure describing him, I said. I don't know about the right, but he surely is a miserable . . . Shut up, Shad shot back. He's your goddamned father. Right, I said. That too. Goddamned. You want him shut up, dying as slow as he can, don't you? Shad asked me. I had never thought of that. So help me God I hadn't. I had only thought of two things: the foul old bastard will never live under my roof, and I have to make some provision for him, or people will talk. By then, the old man was just a problem to manage. Or so I thought I thought.

But even as Shad kept talking, flailing away, accusing me of every unfilial act short of ax murder, it occurred to me that, amidst a great deal of nonsense, my brother had struck home. What is it they say? Even a blind pig finds an acorn once in a while. Maybe my conscious focus was narrower than my deep intentions. Wall up the old man, immure him the way he had my mother. No friends, no relief. Only that damned radio and his memories, such as they might be. And his defeat and frustration. I had truly never thought of it. But all right, fine. One more for Momma.

Bullshit, Shad came back. You know that's wrong. Maybe he deserves that, too. But let it be the Lord's decision. He's got a right to whatever the hell life is left him. His way. On his own land. He fought like a man when he was young.

He fought us, I said. Fought common sense. Fought business. Fought every damned thing we've ever done. If he had his way and that bunch of sociopaths and defectives had won, he'd stand us both up against a wall and pull the trigger himself.

Shad looked at me strangely. It ain't a crime to fight us, he said. Yes, it is, I told him.

A month later they found the old man in the lake. Lying in shallow water not ten yards from where they had found her almost thirty years before. Thrown by a damned horse Shad had gotten him. Not only gotten him, but had taken out to Shady Grove and hobbled while he went and drank with the old man and then took him outside to help him mount up. Hell, if the DA had wanted, he could have gotten a true bill on it. You stupid sonofabitch, why did you do it? I yelled at him. The old man wanted one more ride, Shad said. Leave me alone about it or I'll whip your ass.

We took the old man to Schumpert Memorial. There was nothing to do, as doctors like to say, but make him comfortable. That will be quite an accomplishment, I told one of them, since he has never been comfortable in his life.

They said it was a matter of hours, perhaps a day or two at most. But it was strange to hear that because when I went to visit him he looked alert, even excited. He couldn't seem to stop talking. I had never heard him talk so much. As if all that he had pent up, had somehow meant to say and didn't, had to come out before his time was up. He was—the word seems absurd if you knew the old man—vivacious. Well, he said, staring at me with sparkling, keen, cruel eyes. The eyes of a train robber, a revolutionary. Well, it's moneybags. That's right, I told him. I've taken out a couple of hours from grinding the faces of the poor just to sit with you.

I take that kindly, he said. You losing money being here? No, I said, I'm past losing money. I make it while I'm sleeping. I make it all over the world. Everything I touch turns to money. How much you worth? he asked me. Give or take, twenty million the last time I thought about it, I said. It hit him like a flail. You're not lying, are you? he asked. No, I said, as slowly and seriously as I had ever said anything in my life. I wouldn't lie about that. Not now. Not to you. Not about that.

I must have smiled. He turned himself over heavily and faced the wall. I couldn't see his expression. He robbed me of that. I would have given a hundred thousand dollars to see his face as he considered that his own son had ravaged, wasted everything he cared about. But I couldn't lean over and force him to face me. The observer is part of the observation.

He lay quiet for a long time, and I just sat there thinking what a miserable, sorry piece of rubbish he was. A degenerate link between me and the past. If he had worked as hard and as doggedly as he had struggled against the system, he'd be lying there rich, with a host of friends wishing him well. Instead his life was leaking out of him with no one around but those of us who for one reason or another were saving the appearances.

It was deep night then, and I had dozed off with a copy of *Life* magazine in my lap. I woke up with a start for some reason. The old man was up on his right elbow, and he was staring at me. I had never seen such hatred in a man's eyes. You're not going to enjoy it, he said. Try and stop me, I answered. You stinking carcass. Just try to stop me. I'm not Momma. You can't do to me what you did to her. All you can do is lay there and rot and die. So that's it, he said, as if he had been vouchsafed a revelation. Well, ain't that something? Ain't that just the goddamned limit? He lay back down, his eyes bright, his face fevered. He didn't turn toward the wall again. He just stared at the ceiling with a strange smile on his lips. You stupid . . . , he began, then stopped. She betrayed me, he said slowly. I came home shot up, wrecked. Yankee capital had won every round. Between Grant and Rockefeller, every round. I didn't have anything left but that piece of land Daddy didn't sell. And I met her. I loved her. I said to myself, Look here, it's a small world but it's yours. Live in it. Do right. You can do that. You can live like other men. The new order isn't gonna happen. Not now. Maybe not for a hundred years. And . . . some damned silly clerk at Meyerling's Dry

Goods who must have pulled out and headed for Texas before the sun was up the next day because he had to know he wasn't going to see the next sunrise if he stayed . . .

You're lying, I told him. You're lying on your goddamned deathbed, lying in your teeth, making excuses for the living when you ought to be figuring out how you're going to face the dead.

There ain't no dead to face, he said, still staring at me. There are just living men. And corpses. Nothing else, you hear? Shit, I would of thought a goddamned millionaire had figured out that much. We're just chunks of matter whirling through space, nothing else.

I don't know about that, I said. I never had time to piece through theology, but one thing a businessman can tell is a low-life lying sonofabitch. My Momma was a fine person. Her only flaw in character was not using the kindling hatchet on you.

He liked that. He laughed till he choked, and I gave him some water. Yeah, well, it wasn't either one of you boys too bright. I guess you thought she committed suicide, didn't you?

I stared at him in silence. What the hell was that supposed to mean?

Forget it, he went on. After they found her, I caught that Indian pony of mine wandering in the bottoms. Saddled, with a kerchief full of her things. Her tortoise comb was in there, and seven dollars.

I shook my head, but he kept going. She didn't take her life. She fell off that horse when it spooked. Into the water. There was a bruise on her head from a cypress tree. She was going after the goddamned dry goods clerk. Died a romantic, just like you. Christ, maybe that's why we failed, why we couldn't make a revolution in this place. Even you rich sonsofbitches got illusions.

You're the one with illusions, I almost shouted at him. You see the whole damned universe as corrupt and mean as you are. You're there at the end of the road, lying about my mother, trying to smear her when she's twenty years and more dead. No, I'm not trying to do that, he said. Don't you understand? She doesn't matter. I don't matter. What did Meslier say? *Je finirai donc ceci par la rien, aussi ne suis-je guère plus que rien, et bientot je ne serai rien . . .*

I stared at him in astonishment. His French was better than mine. I had never heard him speak a word of it before. And who in hell is Meslier? "I will finish this then for nothing. Besides, I am scarcely more than nothing, and soon I'll be nothing at all..."

It's your world, moneybags, he said. But you don't understand it. It's going to break your heart. With all that money, you're already sold out, betrayed.

No, I told him, feeling his weakness, my strength. No, I'm going to prevail. I'm going to build something that...

That lasts a thousand years, he said, truly finishing my thought. You poor dumb sonofabitch. You poor dumb son...

He lay back down silent then, breathing hard. Thinking to himself as I reckoned. But no. Deciding. Planning what he was going to do next, say next, realizing that at the very threshold of death, he was still the stronger, still the father and able to change things more now than he ever had before. He knew that. He had to know that. The old man was a fool, but that had to do with strategy. He was not stupid. I was looking at my watch, wondering when Shad would get there to relieve me. Then he started talking again.

I hadn't ought to say anything about this, he said. And I wouldn't. I promised. But... you want to know the truth? Does the truth mean anything at all to you? he asked me.

I've done all right by it so far, I said. If you mean facts. Not that I expect any out of you.

All right, fine, the old man said. His voice was strained now. That wild energy was ebbing away, and he sounded reedy, distant, as if he were speaking from some far place. Still, what he said was clear, each word unmistakable.

Shad come to me the night before he went to the Marines. He drove out from Shreveport. He come to me looking for an honest witness, the old man said. He come to me because it wasn't nobody else.

I can believe that, I told him.

He said he had done a terrible thing. A thing for which it wasn't any forgiveness.

He's done that a thousand times, I said. From Texarkana to Timbuktu. Was there one little honey that he just couldn't put out of mind?

Yeah, the old man said, not looking at me, his expression

enigmatic, something almost like a smile. Yeah, it was like that.

Now that is some staggering truth, I said. Hell, if I had one dollar for everything he's hacked . . .

He lay there laughing silently, his face small and wizened and wasted away, his left side paralyzed, useless, and eternity bearing down on him at something approaching the speed of light.

You'd give twenty million and borrow some more for it not to be true, he said, his eyes suddenly on me, glaring, all the laughter gone.

I remember that instant better than all the rest. The most terrible moments in our lives are like the most beautiful: luminous, self-contained, exhaustive.

Edward Malcolm Sentell Four, he said.

Sonny . . . my boy . . .

My grandson, he said softly, his voice coming back. My grandson. But not your son . . .

That was it. Nothing more, though it seemed I waited for hours in that second or two.

You stinking, lying old sonofabitch, I said.

Not this time, moneybags. Not now . . .

I stood up and leaned over and grabbed him by the throat, but it was too late. His body was like straw, and there was winter in his eyes. He fell out of my hands and into whatever eternity may be, some odd expression of surprise and loathing on his face. I sat down again beside him and tried to draw it all together, tried to analyze, but nothing would come together, nothing would make sense. Dead men tell tales. Is that what it meant? I did not believe a word he had said, and yet I knew it was true.

After what seemed a long time, I stood up and took my leave of what remained of Albert Parson's friend, the revolutionary, the train robber. The betrayed husband? The realist. He seemed then smaller than I remembered, the hospital gown surrounding him like a cloud. My last hope for him was that there was Christ and there was judgment, and he would account in full. I did not bother to close his eyes. Let them stare for eternity.

I had a very bad headache then, and I went out to tell the nurse at the station, or a doctor or somebody. You are supposed to let other people know when a great change has taken place. Like death.

I walked out and leaned against the wall for a moment, still lost, not yet able to pull so much truth together all at once. I looked up, and Shad was there. He looked tired, somber. A man ready to do his duty.

How's it going? he asked.

How's it going? I repeated, hitting him as hard as I could, feeling the wrench of pain in my fist as a blessing.

How's it going? Your father's dead, you sonofabitch. And your mother was a whore.

Chapter Fourteen
1 March 1960

> The long night she held back at the end of its course, and stayed the golden-throned Dawn at the streams of Okeanos . . .
> *Odyssey*, xxiii, 243–45

—Shhhhhhh . . .
 —Shad, what in God's name . . . ?
 —I told you a while ago. You don't listen.
 —That man . . . He tried to . . .
 —Uh-huh.
 — . . . *kill* you . . .
 —Happens all the time. That's why I don't wear six-hundred-dollar suits.
 —I think I'm going to . . .
 —Go ahead, but shhhh . . .
They are lying side by side in an unlighted utility room down a hall just off the lobby. It is filled with a remarkable number of vacuum cleaners, brooms, mops, pails, aged and cracked chamois skins, soaps, detergents, and cleaning compounds of every description. On the floor under them are dropcloths used for painting and carpentry. All in all, Shad considers, the place is cozy, dark as the inside of Cecil's heart. The door is locked from the inside, and after twenty-one years, she is in his arms again. Frightened, trembling, almost cuddling her body against his.
 —You read about this sort of thing, but somehow you never believe it can happen to you.
 —I can, Shad laughs. —It's worse than green beer, but not as bad as the clap.
 —Do you think he . . . killed anyone?
 —Can't say. Fired about belly-high. If he didn't blow off a head or two in there, I reckon he took off some hats.
 —Ugh . . . But why would he . . . What did you *do* to make him . . . ?
 Shad is silent. Actually, his mind is focused to a fine, shim-

mering point. He is gently, unobtrusively massaging Marie-Claire's hips. He has every intention of going on with this for as long as the traffic will bear. Should day pass and the night and the day after that, he will still be here doing what he is doing or a lot better if he can. It has never occurred to him that a utility closet could be paradise. He kisses her hair tentatively, in the spirit of experimentation. She still has her mind on what has passed in Sam's Bar. God bless Cecil Miley. Let him die painfully and soon, but let his immortal soul be rescued from perdition. At the last split second. For this one good deed.

—You heard 'em say it's an old story? This one goes back to 1934. You don't want to hear it. It's not your style.

—But . . . he's waited this long to . . .

—It's the first chance he's had. He's been goofy since I hit him in the head with a pine limb in May of '34 . . . Sonny hit him with a tire tool and brought him back to hisself. I got to talk to Sonny about that.

Marie-Claire sits silent. She does not object when Shad kisses her ear, the line of her jaw, her neck. He does not feel her body tense as his hands move on her thighs. Make that five days and five nights. Just send in some liquor and sandwiches.

—You're making all that up, aren't you?

—Mary Clare, I never lied to you. It all happened the night I graduated from high school, the night before I set out for Kilgore with E.M.

—That's . . . a very long time ago.

—I guess. But not as long ago as . . . 1939.

—How can you remember?

—Don't make fun of me.

—I'm not. Elvira told me about your book . . . It must have thousands of names in it by now.

Shad groans. Go tell it on the mountain about right of privacy and all that crap. It appears his book has been published, widely advertised, and approaching best-seller status. You mean you haven't read it?

—It's a address book, is all it is . . . You got to keep track of your friends, don't you?

—Fk 10, Sk 10 . . . ? Is that a foreign zip code?

Shad is more than silent now. Even his hands stop moving. After a long while, he shrugs.

—If you was going to give that book a title, I guess you could call it What I Did 'Cause I Couldn't Do What I Wanted To.

—And what in God's name might that have been?

—I done told you once, goddammit. You asked if I loved you, and I told you what I wanted.

—As I remember, it was perfectly lovely. Much too nice to use just once. How many other women have you told the same thing?

Shad stands up, dropping Marie-Claire to the floor. The utility room seems to heat up with his rage. He paws at the lock and pushes the door open.

—That fucking does it, he says, a tincture of pain in his voice that even Marie-Claire must recognize.

—Shad . . . that man . . . he might still be . . .

—Who gives a shit, Shad barks. —If he wants me, he can have me.

She stands and watches him go with a sudden awful hollow feeling inside. As if she has just made a terrible mistake. For the second time.

Rex feels like shit. It is the first day of March, and he has been at this thing for weeks now. Since Twelfth Night. Not a party a night. Never that. How about three, four, sometimes five a night. The wretch who lives uptown from Jackson Avenue and cannot give at least one party during the Carnival season belongs in New Orleans East, where the poor whites live. Or Metairie, where Eliot Ness and the Untouchables, even now, might find much to interest them.

He rises slowly from his bed. This is the great day. This day shall be his . . . what is the word? Apotheosis? Yes. The revelation of godhead. He falls back upon his coverlet. Aching godhead foully hung over. The gods, given his circumstances, are not athirst. What does one do when the end of the road is one wretched hangover piled upon some twenty previous hangovers? One rises slowly, approaches the bathroom gingerly. One must shave, one must dress. One need not remember why.

Rex showers, shaves, brushes his remaining teeth. Then he dresses slowly, with care and circumspection. His wife must be downstairs. Preparing dark roast coffee with chicory. Humming. She always hums. This morning she will be humming "If Ever I Cease to Love", the very anthem of Mardi Gras. An old tune, a tired late-nineteenth-century tune. Tonight, when Rex meets Comus, it will be his tune. The robes, the trinkets, the costume, the endless parties. To the tune of thousands. Royalty is not cheap.

At last, he is clothed. He draws on his cloak and looks into the mirror. For a fleeting moment he considers how absurd it is for a grown man to wear the costume of an imaginary monarch. But the thought passes. Nothing is absurd if many accept it, desire it, envy it. And if it costs a great deal of money. He smiles through his pain, and walks to the head of the stairs. One can hear humming down below, and there is the smell of freshly prepared coffee. Perhaps he can sustain the day. After all, there's always tomorrow. And nothing ever happens on Ash Wednesday. Absolutely nothing at all.

1935. Louisiana Governor Huey Long is assassinated in the new state capitol. He dies at the age of 42 at Our Lady of the Lake Hospital in Baton Rouge.

My Lord, Cecil says to himself, that *is* news. I surely do hope they got the one who done that. It seems things is a lot worse in the world than before I had my accident. It's amazing what you can miss if you're not around for a while.

Cecil lowers the *20th Century Chronicles* and looks down from the roof of the building across the street from the Casablanca. The building is deserted because of the holiday, and getting to the roof had been no more than climbing a hundred or so stairs. Now he can see without being seen. Scattered out below are half a dozen police cars with their lights flashing, and several ambulances, their drivers standing around smoking, laughing, watching the increasing numbers of maskers in outlandish costumes who are beginning to move along the streets.

Cecil grins. These are more than your average dumb cops. They had come storming into Sam's Bar hot for blood, but in the confusion, he had walked right past them. Somebody had said something about a foreign plot. Somebody else said it was a uprising amongst the niggers, though there had not been a black face in sight. There is more to grin about than that. As it happens, the Casablanca has no exits in back. Its service entrance as well as its main lobby face the street below. Sooner or later, Sentell must come out. There is no hurry. On the way out Cecil has provided himself with four muffuletta sandwiches and a bottle of Early Times. He takes a bite and then a long swallow.

The weather is splendid. The crowd is growing by the minute. Let the siege begin.

Farrah Friedlander is president, recording secretary, and floatmaster of the Sabine Secretaries Society. Hers has been the guiding intelligence and shaping will behind getting the girls to hire a truck and enter it in the Mid-City parade. The Sabine Secretaries Society is made up of girls from Texas who find themselves working in New Orleans. The name implies that they are from beyond the Sabine River which divides Louisiana from Texas in its lower reaches. Other inferences one might draw are purely speculative. The group is a social club, and it is reasonable to suppose that its purposes are recreational, supportive, and inspirational.

The truth of it is that the Sabine Secretaries are lonely. Not simply because the proportion of eligible men to desiring women is unfavourable in New Orleans, but even more because, of those who might be considered possibilities, the majority seem to be wimps. The number of faggots in the male population is shocking, especially to Texas women accustomed to a particularly hardy breed of men who say little and paw much. The girls like to talk nostalgically at their luncheons of the fleshpots of Beaumont and Orange, Houston, Galveston, and north toward Dallas.

—God, they're all animals over there, Fabula often says.
—Rip off your clothes on the first date.
—Charlie used to pick me up in a cement truck, Silvia would recall. —It was a hassle at the Lone Star Drive-in. People behind us would . . .
—Jimmie Lee Transome was my guy, Farrah reminisces. —First date we had, he stopped by the Seven-Eleven and picked up a box of .22 long rifle hollow-points and took me out to the Winnie, Texas, city dump. We shot rats half the night. I'd hold the flashlight and he'd shoot, then he'd spot 'em for me and I'd blow 'em away. You talk about passion, you talk about love . . . My God, he took me the first time on the seawall at Port Arthur with the moon high and the nets out. We didn't mean it to be that way, but we got to doing it, and I dropped my string with the soup bone tied to it, and he started pulling down my jeans, and I knocked over the bushel basket, and the crabs started scuttling back into the water . . . God, what a night of love . . .

The girls are gathered around the truck. They are dressed in fake suede jackets and skirts with much fringe and dainty Stetsons. All wear boots, and the float is built to resemble a log cabin of advanced and innovative design. On top is a sign in old San Francisco-style lettering that reads:

RUN RUN GET YOUR GUN

This refers generally, one supposes, to Annie Oakley and perhaps more concretely to the collective yearnings of the Sabine Secretaries.

—All right, youall remember the rules. No getting off and getting back on. If you're off, you're off. No pulling them up out of the crowd, I don't care how cute they are. Youall got your cards?

The girls show their cards. They are beige, three by five inches, and each contains the name, address, and phone number of its distributor, along with a brief sentiment: *Hi, I'm Livia, and it's time for Carnival fun. Please no calls from freaks, heads, bi's, queens, or Tulane students.*

—Okay, Farrah shouts. —Into the truck. This year is gonna be different . . .

—Goodness, Missy says slowly, her eyes still heavy with sleep.
—Are we already in Alabama? Sonny? Hey . . .

Sonny sits up, rubs his eyes, and stares out of the cab at a vast assemblage of people pressed so closely together that they seem to move as a tide, a pulse, rather than as individual human beings. They are pressed up against the sides of the cab so closely that it would be difficult to open the doors. In the distance, he hears wild music. It is as if the Master of Hungary has returned to take his people to that New Jerusalem that so troubles us all with its absence and its promise.

—Where the hell are we? Sonny asks in amazement, watching three people in duck costumes waddle by.

—How would I know? Missy replies. —I guess it's Mobile, Alabama. It must be Alabama. You told the taxi driver to take us to . . .

Sonny frowns. —I didn't tell anybody anything. I never *saw* the driver. We got into the cab, and we waited, and I fell asleep.

—Oh, shit, Missy says, turning back to face Sonny, eyes wide with anger. —I been had again.

Sonny leans over to see what she has seen. Missy pulls back from his touch as if he were the certain carrier of some loathsome disease. There above he sees the reason for her resentment. THE CASABLANCA, the sign says.

—Honey, I . . .

—Don't say nothing, Missy says. —You don't have to. Action is louder than words. I *would* of given it to you, too. That's what hurts. 'Cause I'm simple and straight, and can't understand no . . .

A swarthy face with a patch over one eye appears at the driver's window, staring in at them. It is a dangerous, belligerent face, and it looks angry. Sonny's hand caresses the .38 Special in Shad's jacket. The face is mouthing words like a disembodied talking head. The window is up, and they can hear nothing but the rumble of the crowd and distant music.

Sonny leans forward, cranks the window down a turn. Perhaps it is intellectual curiosity or an ingrained aggressiveness of his own, but it discomfits him to have a face mouthing words at him which he cannot hear. When the window is down far enough for words to be heard, the face does not begin again. Rather it continues a stream of abuse clearly begun earlier.

— . . . doing in my fucking hack? Like you want to shack up? Okay, twenty bucks an hour . . .

—I never did, Missy puts in, surprised and irritated.

—Yeah, shit, I bet you never, baby.

—Listen, Sonny starts, —we want to go to Alabama . . .

The jaw associated with the face drops. Its expression, clearly that of a malcontent, becomes fearsome.

—When I can get this door open, he says in a soft, scary tone, —I'm gonna whip your stupid cracker ass. Then I'm gonna bust your nuts and feed 'em to your girl friend while I . . .

—That does it, Missy snaps, swinging her small metal travel case at the face in the open window. A corner of the case catches the cab driver in his good eye, and he staggers backward with a foul oath, clutching his face with both hands, his bulk overturning people behind him. It is only now, in his present condition of pain and rage that Sonny gets a look at him, full length, full girth, full bulk. He is enormous, and he is not likely to let this pass lightly. Either empty the .38 Special into his head while he is diverted or haul ass.

Sonny is pushing open the passenger door on the far side

amidst mean looks and indelicate exclamations from those celebrants struck and snagged by its edges and points.

—Up yours, Sonny snarls at the smallest complainant he sees as he pulls Missy after him. —Come on . . .

—How? Where? You reckon to walk to Ala . . .

—It might be quicker, and a lot safer, Sonny shouts as he manages to pull Missy out into the flow of the crowd and away from her vengeful victim.

Well, Elvira thinks, the kids are gone, and that's a sure thing. So it ain't a total waste. What I got to do now is figure whether I'm going to go downstairs and eat. Or drink. If it was plain choice, I think I'd go down there and get tanked and stay tanked till they had to put me on the bus and carry me home, and I wouldn't even see daylight till I woke up in the station. But that won't do. I am fixing to be the mother of a very rich young lady, and I got to start learning to handle that. All by myself.

She rises slowly, slowly opens the door, lets it close behind her, and walks down the long corridor. Slowly. When she reaches the elevator, she presses DOWN. As she waits, she glances through a large dirty window that looks out onto the street. Wall-to-wall people. Couldn't get across the street to see a parade if you wanted to. Is that . . . ? It surely is. Sonny. And Missy. Sonny in Shad's old canvas jacket. Have things gone wrong? Is it going to be a total washout? Well, he's holding on to her. I guess something's cooking. And there's Cecil. What? Sure enough, it's Cecil.

She squints over at the roof of the building across the way. The lunatic is decked out in some kind of a chef's outfit, and he is staring down at the crowd and his lips are moving, and he still has that damned shotgun and a bottle of whiskey. Best day of his life he had no business with a shotgun *and* whiskey. What is it he's screaming about?

A twinkle of rain has dampened the lawn that looks like a golf fairway, but now the clouds are parting. The breeze is heavy with moisture, lush with a coming spring. The terrace behind the house is bright and mild, and Henry has dried off the table to receive maps, charts, memos, regulations, photos, graphs, and telegrams. E.M. sits in his white suit, almost properly sized for

him. He is studying the materials Boudreaux has brought and laid before him.
—All right, what's left of control?
—Yes, sir, Boudreaux replies hazily. —See here? This picture from the chopper. You can't see nothing.
—All right. But it appears we can reach the control shack . . .
—We . . . ?
—Shad.
—Uh, yeah. If it's no east wind . . . but . . .
—Spit it . . . out.
—I think it's a bad thing. I don't like it. You look at them pictures. The azimuth . . . I think that platform's off the horizontal maybe five, six degrees.
—Ah . . .
—If that's so . . .
—Nothing will work.
—Yeah, right. Nothing.
Boudreaux's mind drifts. He is aboard a power barge. They are lifting oysters in Lake Borgne. He is with his brother, his uncle, his father. It is late afternoon. They are covered with sweat, and he is thinking of nothing but beer. It is sundown, and even in the midst of the work he can imagine what they must look like from fifty, a hundred yards away. A tableau. Men working silhouetted against the great red sinking sun.
—So you recommend . . .
—Dunk it, Mr E.M. Cap the whole damn thing. Use charges, a bazooka. Let divers cut it off and cap it. Okeanos is dead.
E.M. laughs at the image. River-Ocean, the source of all, dead? Boudreaux laughs, too. Not because he supposes he has said something funny. He just feels like laughing. Or crying. Or mainly just going to sleep. That's what he feels like.
—You're talking about throwing away . . . millions . . .
—I got that worked out, sir. Fifteen-six to just over eighteen. But the insurance . . .
—They don't write insurance for production losses, son.
Boudreaux knows that. He also knows that he is arguing in vain. Someone is going aboard Okeanos tomorrow for a survey. To check out all these photos and memos. To see how it really is out at the edge of the world. He suspects it will be Shad and him. He is not ready for it. Something about this platform has horrified him as he has flown over it, beside it, practically under

it since Saturday. It seems like a living thing, something angry and dangerous that has killed, and wants to kill more. Boudreaux has not said this to Mr E.M. You do not say things like that to him. But you feel what you feel. If Shad goes aboard, Boudreaux goes aboard. He is Shad's number two. There is no way he can allow Shad to grin at him and suggest he stay behind if the odds look long. Boudreaux considers that he has not got character enough to do that.

—Well, Louis, let's go over that control board again.

—Sir, Boudreaux sighs. They have already gone over the controls. Twice. —It's a M-60 Console with . . .

—I want to *know* that board, boy.

Boudreaux comes out of his something like a stupor. E.M.'s eyes are drilling into him, their influence flowing out of the deep caverns disease has carved and eroded in his face. For the smallest portion of a second, Boudreaux has the hallucination that he is trapped down in the deep green waters of the Gulf, somehow caught and twisted in the broken struts of the great platform—and face to face with something awful that issues up from the sea bed with a face like a moray eel.

—Yes, sir. You want to start with the rig plans again?

—That's what . . . want to do. Start from . . . very beginning.

—Yes, sir. Could I . . . You reckon I could have another martini?

They have passed over the great divide now. Canal Street and its resident howling mob is behind them. They are on one of the gray faceless side streets. Common? Gravier? People come and go, some with cotton candy on sticks, some in bizarre dress. A troup of ballerinas trips by. All male.

—You'd think they could pick costumes that suited 'em better, wouldn't you? Missy observes.

—I doubt it, Sonny snorts.

Then Missy sees it. —Lord, would you just look? Now see what prayer can do?

Sonny looks this way and that, uncertain what it is he should be seeing. The Alabama state line marvelously transposed to downtown New Orleans, a fat ugly justice of the peace with a caste in his eye and a wen on his cheek? But Missy is on the move, waving.

—Hey, you . . . Hey . . .

She is running toward a maroon car parked a little way down the block. There is lettering on the back. Sonny can barely make it out.

24 hrs. RED DEVIL CAB CO. Insured

The car is incredibly dirty, its dark color chalky and smudged as if someone has smeared polishing compound all over its paint and then forgotten to wipe it off. Sonny has caught up with Missy, and they reach the side of the cab together. Seated inside is a black in a leather hat and dark glasses with reflective surfaces, with a long, lumpy cigarette rolled in brown paper and held in a large paper clip. He does not look up at them, but seems to be listening to a play-by-play on the radio. Of the Rex Parade which is approaching downtown along Saint Charles Avenue.

—How much to take us to Mobile?

The driver fine-tunes his radio. It tells him that Rex is coming with lots of beads and doubloons for all.

—I said . . .

—Go 'way, man . . .

—You want to make some money?

—I don't know no Mobile. Must be on the West Bank.

—Mobile, Alabama.

—Man, what kind of bullshit is that? Go 'way.

Sonny reaches into the canvas jacket pocket and takes out the wad of money. He has not even glanced at it before. There must be a hundred at least. He peels back a twenty on the outside. There is a hundred-dollar bill beneath it. And another. And another. He riffles through the rest. At least thirty or forty of them. He lifts one out delicately, and slaps it onto the outside of the windshield, fixing it there with the windshield-wiper arm, which lacks a blade. The driver somberly continues his smoke until his eyes are drawn up to meet those of Benjamin Franklin. He gazes at the bill for quite a while.

—Man, where you get that funny money?

Sonny places another hundred under the rusty wiper arm. The driver sighs and sits up. He turns opaque, reflective eyes out toward Sonny.

—Ain't no bank open today. You done hit a Pak-a-Sak. You and her is from Arkansas or somewhere, ain't you? All the time coming down here to Big Easy and heisting the comfort stores.

Sonny does it again. Franklin seems to smile benignly.

—You pressing. I believe you want to get out of town. Another hundred. What the fuck? It's Shad's money.

The driver rolls his shoulders, knocks the impressive ash from his cigarette, opens the door, and climbs out of the cab.

—Hey, Missy trills. —I believe he's gonna take us to Alabama.

The driver turns his strange, shining eyes toward her. She sees herself reflected therein.

—Bullshit I am, he says slowly, reaching up and sliding the bills into his hand, into his pocket. He points to the scrofulous cab. —Youall just bought the motherfucker.

Rex is a shadow of his former self. His float is now headed down Saint Charles Avenue toward Canal Street, and somewhere in the alcohol-clouded recesses of his mind he recollects that he has to toast the mayor at Gallier Hall. It is a hoary tradition. All such essential formalities must be observed. However that may be, this very day may see the breaking of tradition, the dissolution of formality. Rex may well be raving mad before they reach Gallier Hall. His secret flasks of liquor have been exhausted. There remain bales and boxes of beads and trinkets to toss to the mob, but no more whiskey. And there are hours to go before this Calvary is done.

Rex tosses a handful of doubloons to the crowd, his eyes squinted as he stares down among his subjects, looking to see if there might be one with a full bottle. Cups, chicken legs, even a beer bottle here and there. But no brown paper sack certain to contain something of use. He sighs and throws necklaces into the far reaches of the crowd where small blacks run back and forth as if driven mad by the spectacle, the wonder of it all. The people roar at him for more. They are insatiable. His arm feels as if it is about to come off. At the shoulder. No matter how much you throw to them, they demand more. They are loud, and they are ugly. They are legion, and they betray every value but one: they betray no sign whatever of intelligence. They scramble for beads as if they were rubies. They stomp the hands of children for a worthless stamped aluminum token. He stares out at them from just below his headache. He feels a moment of vertigo, a combination of depression and euphoria. You bastards, he says to himself, if I live through this, I will volunteer for duty on the Municipal Court and send every fucking one of you convicted away for the statutory limit. This fantasy pleases him, but it does not allay the creeping fear that he may yet become sober far from his goal. What hope is there for a monarch without liquor, and miles to go before he can fall off this damned float? Miles. To go.

The two police officers stand side by side in the neutral ground on Canal Street. They lean against their squad car watching the mob cavort. Rex is on his way, after it the truck parades, then they can call it a day.

They pay no mind to the chef who has been skulking in the purlieus of the crowd, watching them for the last few minutes. No one sees when he opens the far door of the squad car and eases inside, nor does anyone take note as he studies the dashboard and controls of the car for what might appear a lengthy time in even an apprentice car thief. Then it seems he has it figured out, for he starts the car and wheels off, dropping both the officers to the ground and knocking aside a small giraffe and Goofy who is about to insert a hot dog into his cavernous, grinning mouth.

A block or so off, a Red Devil Cab is pulling out and starting to drive slowly away from the business district.

—There, Cecil roars at the top of his lungs, floorboarding the cruiser. —I knew it. That filthy nasty sonofabitch has got my little girl. He's done wrecked my life, had my wife, and now this. I believe he's got it in for me.

Cecil shakes his arm, and his shotgun does its appearing act. He drives with one hand and swings his shotgun up on the door of the car. It is a perfect fit. He can drive and sight at the same time. He will have to blow the tires off the cab and catch Sentell coming out. If he had not recognized that damned canvas jacket, the bastard might have gotten away. Now the angel of death is moving in. Cecil smiles. This could be done and him back in Greenwood for breakfast tomorrow.

—If we can just get out of town, Sonny is saying, —they have to have signs. We want Gulfport, then Biloxi . . . then . . .

—Are you speeding? Missy asks.

—Are you kidding? Look . . .

—Look at what? It's nothing showing on the speedometer.

—You're right. Why did you ask?

—'Cause there's this cop car behind us, and he's coming like a bat out of hell.

—Yeah?

Sonny frowns as he glances into the rear-view mirror. Missy is right. Are they giving tickets for driving unsafe wrecks on Mardi Gras? Cops never give cabs a bad time in New Orleans. Cabs double-park, triple-park, run up on the grass of the esplanades. Cab drivers play scofflaw as a matter of course in New Orleans. Why is this cretin coming after them, no lights, no siren, as if he meant to satisfy himself with their exhaust pipe? Sonny thinks for a moment. What the hell does it matter why? He has no plans to be stopped now. Not for a ticket, not for one miserable moment. He has a thing which he means to get done today or die trying. He hits the gas and is astonished when the wreck suddenly leaps ahead in the very simulacrum of an automobile.

—Hey, you trying to give me a whiplash?

—Wouldn't you rather have a ring?

—Funny . . . What are you gonna do when he runs this log wagon off the street and carries us down to the pokey?

—They'll never take me alive, Sonny grates.

—Oh boy . . . There was this movie and a little old towheaded guy said that . . . He looked like cat food when they was done with him.

—Was he on his way to Alabama?

—I don't believe . . . He had robbed this bank . . . Lordy . . .

Missy twists around in her seat, and Sonny glances up at his rear-view mirror. The police car has just rammed them in the rear.

—Oh-oh . . . It's worse than I thought.

—Is he pulling a gun?

—He don't *have* to pull it. He's got it perched on the window-ledge. It's a shotgun and it's Cecil, Sonny.

—Well, shit.

—I wouldn't say anything like that, but I know what you mean.

Sonny says nothing, simply glancing to the left. There is a cross street directly ahead. All he needs is something like ninety degrees. At forty-five miles an hour. He hits the sodden brakes as hard as he can and spins the wheel to the left until it hangs.

The Red Devil Cab does a smart left into the cross street, its rear bumper barely following, cutting across the sidewalk like a scythe, scattering a few pedestrians, slamming off a fireplug, which lifts out of the cement with a variety of watery effects. A man is running with a ladder under one arm and a child under the other. He manages to evade the Red Devil's bumper; a jet of water shoves him through a shop window.

The pursuing police cruiser roars by in the midst of attempting a maneuver similar to Sonny's. Its brakes are locked, smoke spinning out from the wheels as it slides by. Sonny can see the car's occupant clearly. He seems to be wearing a chef's hat and is trying to get an angle on Sonny with a sawed-off shotgun as he skids past.

Sonny guns the cab, and makes ready to turn right into the next street. —Ha, left that dumb bastard trying to find his socks, Sonny chuckles.

—I wouldn't make too much of it, Missy says. —I don't believe he's ever been behind the wheel of a car before. And if it was, I expect it was a Model A.

Sonny grits his teeth. He grabs his right turn and floorboards the accelerator. The street is almost empty. They could be on the fringe of town in no time. Then a filling station, a map, some mumbled instructions. He still has enough money to strangle a tiger. Tonight they are going to bed down in Mobile's finest. They may stay an aeon or so. No, that is arbitrary; until he has worn an inch off of it, or their eldest child is ready for college, whichever comes first.

They are coming up on Howard Avenue now. Missy glances backward to see if Cecil is still lost in his own smoke.

—Oh-oh ... Here he comes again ... You know, that's amazing.

—What?

—I mean, him being able to drive that way.

—It must have an automatic shift.

—Oh ...

Sonny runs a red light at Howard and slides into a sharp left turn.

—Goddammit to ...

—Sonny, stop that kind of ... oops ...

Ahead, a block away, the street is inundated under an ocean of humanity. It looks to Sonny as if someone has emptied out the LSU stadium into Lee Circle. Every building has people hanging out of it. They are solid around the base of the monument to

General Lee, and packed like nuts in a can on the sidewalks, in the street. And every last one of them has his back to the Red Devil Cab, which is bearing down on them at something close to sixty miles an hour. Sonny looks from side to side to see where he can turn—or even what he can hit to avoid killing half this assemblage of gawking ninnies. He mashes the horn and holds it down.

Slow motion. At first a head or two turns, then a dozen, then hundreds, and the vast waters of humanity begin to part. Cowboys, Roman soldiers, Franciscan monks, ghosts, sylphs with flowers in their hair and hair on their legs, a lizard with a notable erection—all run, stumble, lumber, scurry, hop as the Red Devil bears down on them like a judgment direct from the Company Home Office.

As the path clears ahead, Sonny realizes that there is no escape at all. Because even if he avoids dispatching or mutilating most of the mob, there before him, coming out of Saint Charles Street and into the circle, blocking any hope of passage, is an enormous float upon which is riding some damned fool in a king suit, sprawled out as if the least touch will send him, his bangles and beads tumbling down into the populace. Even a controlled skid can accomplish only so much, and the Red Devil Cab, turned sideways now, slams into the float, shaking it badly, knocking cleverly crafted pieces of papier-mâché, among them an immense crown, into the street. The crowd howls in fear and excitement. Two small blacks grab the crown and run. The police car has skidded to a stop twenty or thirty yards away, and the first shot from it tears away a whole corner of the king's canopy.

The crowd seems to dematerialize. Many of them are natives. They know the folkways of New Orleans. Gunfights on major thoroughfares are not unusual. Such things take place in front of the Monteleone Hotel and Delmonico's Restaurant. Tourists are forever being caught in the proverbial hail of bullets on Esplanade or Dumaine or Decatur streets. The local rule, upon hearing gunfire, is: when in doubt, move out. People are doing that. They are running up and down Saint Charles in both directions, ducking behind filling stations and into doorways. Those who thought they had it made by obtaining bleacher seats around the base of General Lee's pillar are diving, scrambling, rolling for anything that may give shelter.

—Alabama my . . . , Missy begins as Sonny shoves her out of the Red Devil Cab and under the float.

Lese majesty, Rex thinks, curiously dispassionate as he looks out to where a police car has stopped and its occupant, a chef by his appearance, is methodically reloading a sawed-off shotgun with an eye, so far as Rex can tell, to Assassination of the Monarch.

Rex crosses his arms, stares at his distant assailant. A dark pageant of kings looms up before him, moving fatally along, beckoning him to follow. Edward II with his wretched pathic, Richard III and his bad back, Charles I, head tucked securely under his arm, Harold, arrow planted firmly in his eye, Louis XVI and his queen, Alexander II, Nicholas II Romanov, all bespattered with blood, family gathered around him—except for Anastasia, who lives in Charlottesville, Virginia, now.

And so it shall be with Rex. He will not be moved. He will not forsake this royal place. They will find him at the end of this affray, scepter in hand, pierced with many wounds. He will not move; he cannot move. He is stone-statue drunk, without the slightest feeling in his nose, cheeks, ears, fingers, feet. His legs are useless. There is no way to flee. If the filthy sonsofbitches have turned on him, he will go down in style. He ponders his last end and considers that it may well be better to be shot off a royal wagon than die of boredom on the bench at Civil District Court.

Rex glances down at the left front of his float. There seems to be a Red Devil Cab wedged there. Perhaps it has crashed into the float to stop his progress, to make him an easy target. But no. There is a man down there, hunched behind the hood of the cab. He is firing back at the police-cook who is firing at the king. The man wears a canvas jacket, and with him is a singularly beautiful young girl. Whom Rex would like to fondle. To essay more would be pretentious given his present condition. He tries to descend from his plywood throne. He will offer her his protection. But he cannot seem to stand up. Yet his foot begins to have feeling. Now there is something worse to dread than death on a spring morning: the onset of sobriety. The shooting goes on. It is becoming tedious, because no one seems able to score, and it is holding up the parade. Rex wills that the parade go on. Drinks will be served at the Boston Club. Rex is to be toasted in champagne there by his queen. Or does he toast her? No matter.

Never mind. Let us but move on to the fucking champagne, Rex prays.

Sonny is fully occupied. The Red Devil Cab is being disintegrated by Cecil's buckshot. At this distance, it is simply tearing up property, but the din is awful. Sonny is returning fire with Shad's .38 Special. But it is too far to notch Cecil. It appears this might go on until one or the other of them runs out of ammunition. Far away, Sonny hears the howl of sirens. It sounds as if all the police cars in the world are revving up and ready to descend on Lee Circle. Meanwhile, everywhere he looks, Sonny sees human faces gazing out on the scene in something approaching awe. People are under other floats, behind a rack of tires chained down in the Phillips 66 filling station. Faces peer out from behind the monument, down from balconies overlooking the circle. Sonny fires a desultory round which seems to take the hood ornament off Cecil's patrol car.

—That's shooting, Missy says. —But it ain't going to get us out of here.

—I'm trying, Sonny says, thinking what a .357 AP round could do just now. Through the car, through Cecil, and away we go. But he suspects Missy would not want that to happen. Even if Cecil is a murderous sonofabitch. She has grown up with such people. A small thing like Cecil determined to murder her future husband and willing to take out the whole city of New Orleans in the doing does not seem to worry her overmuch. I am not a redneck, Sonny says to himself. I am not a blood-crazed lunatic living out my own private mythology right in the middle of the twentieth century. I am a classical scholar caught in a tight place. Then why, a cryptic inner voice that sounds rather like that of Xenophanes asks quietly, are you doing this? Why are you here? With the choicest of redneck maidens beside you?

—Hello, mister, Missy is saying to someone. —What can we do for you?

—I want you to know, my dear, that I appreciate what *you* are doing. This will all become a part of our history . . . the *third* battle of New Orleans.

—You reckon . . . ?

—Surely. You and that young man will go down . . .

—God knows we've been trying, Sonny mutters, his eyes on the squad car.

—... as the ones who saved Carnival ...
—What's your name, mister?
—I ... am Rex.
—Melissa Miley, Rex ... and that's Sonny Sentell over there doing the shooting.
—Sentell? Would he be kin of ...
—... of every last one of 'em. He's it. Newest of the line. Thinks he's God's gift to women, and the best news since San Jacinto.

A parcel of buckshot slams into the float above them. Rex notes that it has blown away his plywood throne. Where he sat only moments ago.

—The women at the Alamo didn't backbite their men, Sonny snarls sullenly.
—The women at the Alamo, Missy hisses, —wasn't promised a trip to Alabama.
—Listen, that's your father out there keeping us from ...
—He's not my father, and I ain't listening to nothing. Those was men at the Alamo. If they said dead Mexicans, you better dig a big hole. If they said Alabama, it was Alabama.
—Young man, I see you're busy ...
—Only now and then ...
—Would you happen to have a drink? Anything? Aperitif? Rum? Rum would do nicely.

Sonny reaches into the voluminous pocket of Shad's jacket. Sure enough. There is perhaps half a fifth of Black Jack there. He passes it to Rex.

—Good Lord, what a find. All this ... for me? I am going to knight you ... As soon as we reach the auditorium, there will be a public ceremony ... the first of its kind ... I will pay out of my own pocket.

By now the police sirens sound as if they were originating from under the float. Cars are coming up Saint Charles from the other side of Canal, others are racing down Saint Charles from uptown. There must be ten or fifteen of them, and they begin to reach the fringes of the circle almost immediately. Sonny frowns, staring over at the squad car he has holed several dozen times. Nothing but silence from there. Is it possible he has taken Cecil out? But then why are cops running past the car after a cursory look inside without dragging out the body or chaining him, wounded or not, to a lamppost?

Sonny rises, puts his .38 Special on the hood of the Red Devil Cab. He takes the bottle of Jack Daniels from Rex and throws down the last decent hit in the bottle. The sirens are hurting his ears. This is absurd. All he has wanted is to get to Alabama. Is Alabama too much to hope for?

The sirens are whimpering into silence now, and the crowd is re-forming behind a battalion of police who approach the float. The sound of their footsteps is the loudest thing he hears.

—Young man . . .

—Rex, I believe he's already drunk the last of it.

—Oh . . .

—You, with the gun on the hood. Freeze. Don't even wiggle your ears.

Sonny muses on the fact that he cannot wiggle his ears as they slam him up against the car, cuff him, and start to lead him away. The crowd goes wild.

—Now wait a min . . .

—Sir. . . ?

— . . . say you're in . . .

—Yes, sir. In jail.

—All right, fine. I can believe that. But . . . you . . . to get married?

—Yes, sir. See, we were trying to make Alabama . . .

—Met her there?

—Sir?

— . . . in jail?

—Uh, no, sir. She's from Greenwood . . .

—Louisiana?

—Yes, sir.

—Henry, have you . . . that shit ready? Put it . . . me . . .

—It's too early. You know that. Now don't give me no trouble.

—You black sonofa . . . I need it. Now. Boy's . . . on the phone . . .

—Trouble?

— . . .Jail . . . get married.

—Both?

— . . . gonna give me . . . dope or do I have . . .

—Hold still.

—Sir?

—Ah . . .

—Sir?
—Wait a . . . Oh, that's fine . . . so . . . fine . . . You want out . . . jail first?
—I don't give a shit. I'd as soon get married and stay in. Could we have a private cell?
—That good, huh? Oh, Henry, that's lovely.
—Yeah. You gonna think fine an' lovely when you start rolling like a snail in salt.
—Boy . . .
—Sir?
—Spoke to your mother?
—Uh . . .
—Well, shit, Henry. I never felt better in my life. Maybe I'm getting well.
—Mr E.M., you talk like a man with his head up his . . .
—It's got to be now? Tonight?
—Oh, yes, sir . . . I mean, honest to God . . . now . . .
—All right. Now listen . . . Henry, we run out of Bombay or something?
—Sir?
—Go to the auditorium . . . Ask for Judge Krater . . . Hello? You still on?
—You're making fun of me. I'm up to my ass with these cops and Missy is . . .
—Goddammit, boy, I can't help what the sonofabitch's name is . . .
—All right.
—He'll be there late . . . ten, eleven . . .
—The auditorium.
—He's Rex this year.
—The judge? Rex?
—You've got it. I'll see about the license and the rest . . .
—But . . .
—All right. There's got to be some miserable pawnshop that'll open to sell a ring . . . or I've got a friend in Houston. Henry will see to it.
—But . . .
—What? Honeymoon? Right. Somewhere your mother can't find you. Is she a knockout?
—My mother?
—Hell, your . . . intended. What about Borneo? It's nice. Once

during the war, I met Shad there. Coming back from Australia. He was on his way ... It must have been the Marianas ... Borneo is unspoiled ... Doing lots of business down there.
—Sir ...
—What the hell else?
—I'm still in jail
—Oh ... Who's the watch officer?
—Captain Mulvaney.
—Eustace Mulvaney? Put him on.

As far as Elvira is concerned, you can take this day and shove it. She has been wandering around in the Quarter, all along Canal as far as the river in one direction and Rampart Street in the other. She has seen everything on God's earth except Cecil, Sonny, and Missy. A while ago there had been a chorus of police sirens, but that had slacked off, and now she is about ready to cash it in and find her way back to the hotel. All she has for her trouble is a double handful of strange coins people keep throwing to her, and a dozen or so necklaces. She has been propositioned by the rear of a zebra and patted on the ass by a eunuch in the livery of the Sultan of Turkey. Something like a sea serpent has told her filthy things, and if this is what you call Carnival, and you think it's a good time, you can shove it, too.
—Hey, baby ...
—Get away from me.
—Come on ... What's it gonna hurt? Put your hand right in here for a minute.
—Huh?
—You know ...
—If that's what you want ...
—Arghhhhhhh ... !

Cecil is skulking now in the vicinity of Canal and Royal after much running, much dodging in alleys and short streets. Now and again, he still hears a siren. For all he knows, his face is plastered all over that thing they call a TV. He is a wanted man. He remembers with unparalleled clarity what happens to wanted men—or women, either. Only a week or so before his lights went out, they had caught up with Bonnie and Clyde at Arcadia, Louisiana. The butchers cut 'em down, Cecil recalls. Bonnie had a machine gun, and Clyde had him a short scattergun just like mine. We all got to go, but it's a awful thing to go without vengeance. Vengeance is fine, saith the Lord. And one way or the other, I'm gonna get mine.

Still another parade is wending its way down Canal toward him. Does this bullshit never end? Not even floats, just a line of trucks that seems to stretch backward as far as the river. A man can't cross the street without he gets run down by a bunch of perverts throwing stuff and wearing silly costumes.

Just then, Cecil sees some clown in a police suit eyeing him, talking to another joker in khaki with what looks like a state police hat on. Trouble is, you can't tell the costumes from the real thing. These two have got mustaches and hair down on their collars. It's just costumes. Cecil shrugs and turns away.

—Hey, you . . .
—Me?
—Yeah, you . . . hold it right there.
—Your ass . . .

—I never saw so many cops in my life, Livia comments as she leans dangerously far off RUN RUN GET YOUR GUN. Fabula pulls her back.

—Shoot-to-kill day. Farrah roars with laughter. She has been into the Jim Beam —Maybe it's open season on fairies.

—No good to shoot 'em, Livia snickers —You can't eat 'em . . .

The Sabine Secretaries find this uproarious. But then they have been finding everything uproarious for the past hour or so. The parade is stalled. Something broken down up ahead, they suppose. But then this is New Orleans. Something is always broken down—especially the men.

Fabula breaks out another quart of Jim Beam. It is getting cloudy. Is rain on the way? Shall they repair to the cabin and leave the mumbling crowd to its own devices? But the cabin has no roof; only sides. It may conceal, but it will not keep off the elements.

They lurch forward a few yards, stop, go on a little farther at a pace that will bring them to the end of the parade route by next spring. The crowd cheers. Beads are thrown again. Rare RUN RUN GET YOUR GUN doubloons are showered out on the waiting people. Also small rubber frogs that make an embarrassing noise when you squeeze or sit down on them. One of Livia's sometime admirers who owns a novelty shop and counts himself an inventor has developed the item. He calls it a Whoopee Frog. It sells well in the Quarter, but then what does not? As a rain of the frogs descends, the mob quickly discovers the peculiar trait of the creatures and begins to squeeze them in something like a rhythm. Some idiot begins to sing:

—The frogs of Texas are upon you . . .

—Now that's a fucking racial slur against Texans of French extraction, Livia Lemonde snaps, popping her middle finger in the direction of the singing. The crowd cheers her spunky display, and picks up the song. Coupled with the sound of many Whoopee Frogs, the effect is that of a sudden attack of mass flatulence accompanied by choral belching.

—Assholes, Livia snarls. —My folks was from Brest.

—Right, Farrah laughs. —We can tell.

—Don't start, Livia replies, fixing Farrah with a mean eye. Farrah subsides. Livia can be an ugly drunk. Farrah is no slouch at juiced up disorder herself. If this whole thing doesn't turn into a disaster, the Secretaries are going to be lucky.

Now the trucks move a little faster. There are still sirens squealing on side streets, but whatever has been holding them up ahead must be moving again.

—Now just let's settle down and drink and maybe pass out some more cards, Fabula suggests. —You know, it's going to be evening before long.

None of them notices at first that someone has clambered aboard RUN RUN GET YOUR GUN. He is dirty and unkempt, breathing hard, a smoking sawed-off shotgun in his hands. He hunkers down below the level of the bunting that surrounds the truck, snaps open the piece, and carefully reloads the empty chamber. When he snaps it closed, several of the secretaries turn to find their space invaded by what appears to be the executive chef of a restaurant one had better skip.

—Hey, Farrah yells, —what the hell . . .

—Don't mess with me, the chef gasps weakly. —I ain't gonna be messed around with . . .

Livia is, as the expression goes, dog-assed drunk. She gets down on the bed of the truck to examine Cecil a little more closely. —Aw, come on, you mess around a little, don't you?

Cecil stares at her in silence.

—He's kind of cute, Fabula whispers to Farrah.

Farrah gazes at her in astonishment. —You think so?

—Well, he just looks so fucking mean . . . and look at that toy gun of his. You ever see a chef carry a sawed-off shotgun?

—I've eaten at places where they needed to.

Cecil frowns, reaches over, and takes up Farrah's Coke. He proceeds to chug it down, seeming not to notice that it is the better part of a half-pint of Jim Beam with the merest color of cola.

—Buster, Farrah says in umbrage, —you get your ass off this float, or I'm gonna . . .

—You're gonna die trying, bitch, Cecil grates, his eyes narrow, tiny, looking somehow as if they were graven in India ink on either side of his thin nose. Farrah starts toward him. Cecil swings up the gun, the short barrel of the piece ending up about an inch from her nose.

—Take a good long sniff, Momma, Cecil whispers portentously. —That's what eternity smells like.

—I think I'm falling in love, Silvia croons to Fabula.

—Bullshit, Fabula says, —All a man has to do is threaten you, and you fall over on your back.

Farrah's eyes suddenly enlarge to the size of saucers. She stands, still bent over in something resembling an aggressive posture, but frozen now as if within striking range of a lethal reptile.

—It . . . it's not a toy, she croaks. —It's the real thing . . . and he's been using it.

—Bet your big fat ass I've been using it, Cecil affirms, his eyes depthless, with a cold, dead, exhausted quality about them. —And I aim to use it again.

—Uh . . . Farrah smiles, —I believe you must have the wrong float. I think you want, uh, HELL ON WHEELS . . . It's just past VERDI . . .

Cecil ignores her, turning to peep over the rail of the truck in the direction of police sirens passing in the distance.

—I think . . . we think you'd really be happier . . .

Cecil turns back, regards Farrah for a long moment, his face revealing nothing. He stands up slowly, then walks the length of the float like a shabby captain on the deck of a garbage scow. He returns and pauses before Farrah. She stands at least three inches taller than Cecil and likely outweighs him by five or six pounds. She is said by her friends to be statuesque. Men tend to be overawed by her, but most would concede a fugitive thought of how it might be to roam the vastness of her body, explore the curves and steppes, the smooth plains and grottoes of that immensity. Cecil picks up Fabula's drink without even looking at her. When she reaches up instinctively to rescue it, her knuckles are rapped with the barrel of the shotgun. Cecil's eyes do not leave Farrah, and she is becoming distinctly uncomfortable.

—I believe you and me has got to talk, Cecil says at last in a low, choked voice.

—That's good, Farrah says in relief. —We'll talk.

—In there, Cecil says ominously, indicating the counterfeit log cabin with his shotgun.

—In . . . there . . . ?

—I believe you got a hearing impediment, Cecil rasps. —I said . . . in there . . .

Farrah looks at the others with an expression of tragic hopelessness. She regards the fake log cabin, then squares her shoulders and enters through the painted cloth door, Cecil following. Aside from the desultory yawps of the mob, which has howled and shrieked for so long that most of its ten thousand throats are parched and ruined, and the dull swallowing sound of the truck motors edging ahead in low gear, there is something approaching silence aboard RUN RUN GET YOUR GUN.

—He's going to kill her, you watch, Livia whispers at last.

—Goddamn that, Fabula replies. —No way I'm going to watch.

—I don't think he's that kind, Silvia says. —He looks a lot like the minister at the First Methodist Church of Carthage . . .

—Minister wore a chef's hat? Fabula asks fatuously —Was that for his sermon on hellfire?

—Laugh it up 'cause you're from Houston, Silvia retorts. —Bullshit on the Bayou.

Fabula looks at the others. —When a cop comes by, I'm gonna yell . . . We can't let her . . . I mean let him . . .

—Awwwwwwwww . . . Uhhhhhhhhh . . . Ehhhhhh . . . Ohhhhhhhhhh . . .

The Secretaries stare at each other in horror as moans and keenings begin to emanate from the painted cabin.

—He isn't shooting her, Fabula whispers tremulously.

—Who said shoot? Livia bawls. —My Christ, you carry

around a double twelve without no barrel and no stock where I come from, you had sure in hell better be a bad ass, and a bad ass has got him a hideout in his right boot on the outside and Bowie on the inside and maybe a straight razor in his pocket.

—Awwwwww. My God . . .

Fabula closes her eyes, shivers. —It's either the straight razor or the Bowie.

Livia is howling now, gasping, choking, almost strangling on her tears. —We just gonna sit here and let that pervert cut on her till he throws out a leg or a hand or something?

Fabula frowns. —I seem to recall that you was the one last year that raised shit when I brought my .357 magnum with the seven-and-a-half-inch barrel for protection.

—That was then.

—Bullshit, this here is what you goddamned Dallas liberals have brung us to.

—Sweeeeeeeet Jesu . . .

—I am fixing to fling, Livia gurgles.

Fabula hands her a Coke bottle in which the Coke has been replaced by the clear amber of Jim Beam. —Take a hit of this and hope for the best. Maybe he's only torturing her a little. Some of 'em don't have to kill to get off.

As Fabula and Livia trade recriminations, Silvia has moved to the edge of the painted cabin. With fear and trembling, she lifts up a remote corner of the cloth and peers in. The others are struck dumb by her sharp intake of breath.

—I never . . .

—Don't say it . . . I don't want to know.

—He's . . .

—Go ahead, tell us all about it. I'm gonna throw up all over you.

Fabula creeps on all fours to join Silvia. She looks and turns away, shaking her head. —I guess I've seen it all now.

Livia is scandalized. She seems to forget the delicate condition of her stomach and shoulders her way in between Silvia and Fabula.

—Sonofabitch, she says as she gazes inward. —If you'd of told me, I wouldn't of believed it.

—Uhhhhhhhhhhhhhhhhhh . . . Yeah . . . !

Now they are flying above the clouds, bright sunlight streaming in the windows of the Constellation. Down below, as the pilot says, it is overcast, partly cloudy, and rain. They are over Baton Rouge, headed southeast. The stewardess smiles professionally; Roland smiles back appreciatively. There is something about American women that makes them irresistible. Physically. What is it? They are well nourished. Most have very good bodies. Many are goddesses. But as much can be said for Scandinavian women. There is something more about American women—something that separates them definitively from their European sisters and makes them perfect objects of desire.

Roland contemplates this for some while. The stewardess brings him another chill martini. Her smile is warmer. Roland watches her pert behind recede. One is permitted any number of chill martinis on the flight from Shreveport to New Orleans. If one travels first class. Roland's father, Klaus Richter, now retired after many years as an executive of Omega Oil International, has told him that first class travel always pays for itself. One is last on, first off. One meets first-class people. One eats and drinks as much as one pleases. One is perceived to have traveled first class. Things add up.

Yes, of course, Roland concludes at last. American women have always traveled first class. They have lived for decades in their own illusion of self-worth. They are not disillusioned. They have not been reduced to realism. They have the luxury, even in poverty, to suppose things might be different. Given the slightest chance, they will be imperious, demanding, contemptuous, and short-tempered. All the best qualities of vanished aristocracy. And what does every man wish for most in his heart of hearts? To overcome, to dominate, to vanquish, and to screw a princess.

Roland smiles and glances at his watch. It will not be long now. The charade of royalty in a provincial American backwater. Merchants' daughters, well-to-do Jewesses, debutantes whose fathers sell pipe and catfish and twine and base metals. But all princesses. And perhaps he will meet Shad Sentell, the robber baron his father has spoken of so often. What was it Klaus had called Shad? That was it: a barbarian throwback. To the Teutonic Knights. Very well. A great German leader has said, barbarian is an honorable name. But what must one of those be like? In the wilds of America?

—Enough is enough, Fabula is yelling. She has her head inside the painted canvas of the log cabin. In there, the President of the Sabine Secretaries is being brutalized by a chef in a filthy jacket, a sodden, loathsome hat, and no pants at all.

—I'll say when I've uhhhhhh had enough, Farrah squeals.

Fabula turns to the others. —This has been going on for forty-five minutes. It's disgusting.

Silvia shakes her head in wonder. —He don't look like he's hardly getting started.

—You'd think he hadn't had any in twenty years, Livia sniffs.

—I never knew a man who could go non-stop for *thirty* minutes, Silvia says. —And did you see the size of his . . .

—How could I? He hasn't had it where you could see it in almost an hour.

—Once, Silvia says in an awed tone. —Just once . . . I mean, honey lamb . . .

Fabula shivers exquisitely. —Well, this is what I call a new low, she says, opening the next-to-last bottle of Jim Beam and taking a long gulp straight from the source. They have almost reached the end of the parade route. The hell with Coke. It's all warm and flat now, and nobody likes it anyway. —I mean when you want to talk about vulgarity . . .

—Well, after all, he's got that weapon, Livia says.

—Lord, you should have seen it, Silvia says again, rolling her eyes.

—And he's holding it on her.

—Wow, is he ever.

—They say don't struggle against an insane rapist.

—A nice girl would puke on him at least, Fabula insists.

Silvia frowns and hiccups, reaching for the Jim Beam. —Well, youall can say anything you want, but when he gets done abusing Farrah, I'm going in there and face up to him.

—You like that kind of thing, Livia asks.

Silvia seems to nod as she drinks deep. —I just as well lay it right on the line, she says, shuddering as the whiskey finds its way down. —I hadn't been decently laid since I got in this dumb town. If that crazy bastard in there is gonna take advantage of me, I reckon I just as well make a virtue of necessity.

—Virtue? Fabula repeats. —I don't fuck no guy I don't even know.

—So get to know him, Livia says, her own interest aroused by

Silvia's frankness. —I mean, how long does it take to . . . *know* a man?

—Close to an hour, Silvia marvels.

She reaches for the phone, picks it up, pauses, sets it down again. She has been up all night and most of the day waiting. It seems she has spent most of her life waiting. Waiting for the elements of her dream to assemble, waiting for E.M., waiting to see Paris. Waiting for Sonny to arrive, waiting for E.M. to discover. Waiting now again. To hear what Sonny has done. She has called Shad's room. There is no answer. The same for Elvira's. She has tried every phone number she knows, at first for information, at last simply for some human voice to tell her that she has not somehow dropped out of the world altogether. She has even called Roland's number in Shreveport. His answering service says he is not available. There is only one number left to call. She picks up the phone, dials firmly, measuredly.

—Eddie . . . ?

—Yes . . . is it? Oh. You.

—Sonny's . . . left the hotel.

—All right.

—He's . . . with a girl.

—That's all right, too.

—Listen to me. It's not all right. It's the worst thing that's ever happened.

—You . . . hear about the Second World War?

—Stop it. Don't play with me.

—Wouldn't think of it. Haven't in years.

—The girl is . . . his sister.

—Yeah? That's rich. Thought he was the only bastard you had.

—You vicious sonofabitch. She's . . . Shad's daughter.

—No shit? Chickens coming home to roost, eh?

—I have to find him. I have to tell him. I caught them. Christ, he was . . . they were . . . naked.

—You and Shad do it with your clothes on, tootsie?

—I didn't want to call you, you pig. I knew it would be this way.

—What'd you expect? Tears? Sympathy? Concern?

—That little boy never harmed you.

—Yes, oh yes . . . hell yes, he . . .

—Goodbye.
—He called here. Seems he's not satisfied with just topping his . . . sister.
—Oh . . .
—He's fixing to . . . her . . .
—What? What did you say?
— . . . said, marry her.
—Oh, my God. I'm not going to make it through this. I'm just not. I don't even think I want to.
—Bullshit. You'd make it . . . ground zero . . . nuclear . . .
—Where? When? Please . . .
—You wanted to drop by . . . a present . . . ?
—You filth . . . Where?
—The auditorium . . . tonight . . .
—But . . . that's the Rex Ball . . . I mean . . .
—Right. Rex. All the best people. Everyone will know.
—This is bizarre, demented . . . The family will be . . . ruined. We'll be the Jukes and Kallikaks of Louisiana.
—I don't reckon to be around.
—You cowardly bastard . . . Anyhow, there are formalities, tests. They can't just . . .
—All being taken care of . . .
—My God in heaven . . . you . . .
— . . . as pie if you know . . . people. Didn't know . . . sister. A novel departure. Boy is a degenerate . . . favors . . . father and mother . . .
—Stop it.
—Not . . . your life, sweetie. You want it stopped . . . up to you. Any one . . . reasons this man and . . . not . . . holy matri . . . You'll knock Rex . . . Comus . . . a loop . . .
—You are . . . subhuman..
—Haw . . . Ought to meet my . . . wife.

Things are out of hand on RUN RUN GET YOUR GUN. Maskers on other truck floats are hearing a considerable amount of profanity and filthy speech from inside the painted-canvas log cabin, and it appears that all the Secretaries are inside. Even the crowd senses some dissension aboard, for the flimsy walls of the cabin billow and buckle from time to time, and the language has become scandalous. On board OPERAS VERDI NEVER WROTE, traveling just behind, there is a sense of outrage. Why should decent citizens have to listen to such stuff?

—I mean, like fun is fun, Un Ballo says.

—Fun? Man, I never heard such shit. Listen to 'em, Il Coarseo replies, popping a pair of Buds, drinking from them alternately.

—What the hell's going on over there? Stiffo wants to know.

—They ain't warming up Sarah Lee coffee cake, Wriggletto replies.

The yelling goes on, and it is apparent that they are engaged upon some great struggle within. The walls of the cabin shake and sag, and, as they do so, Farrah, half-naked, comes tumbling out, grabs one side of the flimsy cloth, and pulls as hard as she can. The first tug seems to accomplish little, but the next, in which she adds her teeth to her hands, brings down the cabin in awful disarray.

Those on the other truck floats stare in disbelief at the sorry spectacle which will be reported in the *Times-Picayune: Mid-City Reduced to Pornographic Shambles by Hell's Belles. Ladies from Hades Bring Smut to Mardi Gras.*

—Holy shit, Stiffo gasps.

—What'd I tell you, Wriggletto croons.

The shameful display seems to grow more disgusting each moment as the occupants of the tent begin to free themselves from the canvas which lies crumpled atop them. Livia surfaces in panties, trying to get her bra adjusted before emerging from the cloth altogether. Silvia rolls out, either unconscious or undone by Jim Beam. It appears she has, at the moment of Farrah's reduction of the cabin, either been trying to get out of her cowgirl outfit or back into it. In any case, she is disrobed but for her Stetson, and that is of little use since it obscures only her face. All the rest is on display. Beneath the quaking canvas, the action has not ceased, Groans and rough breathing still go on under there, along with language of a sort calculated to cause one's expulsion from a bordello. Farrah, all modesty, all prudence cast aside, is silently but steadily kicking and stomping on the quivering cloth. She is unsatisfied with her progress. She picks up a two-by-four which had supported the canvas and begins belaboring the remaining occupants of the collapsed fabric.

—Now, shit, I don't call that loving.

—Woman, what are you talking about?

—Don't give me that. You just hit me with . . . Ow . . . Goddamn it.

The covered figures roll out of Farrah's immediate range, and as they do so, Cecil and Silvia surface from under the threshing canvas just as Farrah is lifting her two-by-four for another swing.

—Can't nobody have any fun with you around, can they? Silvia cries as she rises to her feet and grabs Farrah's makeshift club—revealing that she, too, is in a state of nature.

—Okay, Stiffo says, drinking from a bottle in a paper bag. —I seen it all now. I mean, like you can just take me home.

—Home bullshit, Il Coarseo grates, eyes large, breathing fast. —I'm on the wrong fucking float.

—Look, Wriggletto observes, —I mean like that kind of stuff is against the *spirit* of Carnival.

—Fuck the spirit, Un Ballo roars, leaping over the side of OPERAS VERDI NEVER WROTE, sprinting over, and beginning to scale the side of RUN RUN GET YOUR GUN.

—Well . . . Stiffo frowns, his eyes on the clash of Amazons which continues only yards away. —I mean, like it's a low-down common spectacle if I ever seen one.

—Okay, Wriggletto breathes, —I guess we know our civic duty when it's right there before us, and I guess we got to . . . Hey, wait for me.

Cecil has regained some small portion of his senses. His head feels peculiar—as if everything inside were sloshing back and forth. It seems he is surrounded by naked women who are tussling about amidst a pile of canvas and one hell of a lot of spilled booze.

—This here is a awful scene, Cecil intones, donning his once white jacket and pulling his chef's cap down around his ears. He notices that his pants are off and feels about under the canvas for them. He is not quite sure how he has come to be out of them, but no matter. It is probably the work of these wanton women who are now down on the floor of the float howling and cursing. As Cecil is about to take a drink from his carefully preserved bottle of Jim Beam for his nerves, he finds RUN RUN GET YOUR GUN suddenly invaded. There is one big sonofabitch in a jester's cap and bells, another in a Protestant minister's garb, what looks like a pirate, und still another in tuxedo, mask, and cloak.

—Say, Cecil calls out.

—Shut up, turkey, the minister snarls, —you already had your fun.

The pirate, saber drawn, faces Cecil, his face flushed, excited. —We're taking over here . . . It's got to be some order restored.

This angers Cecil. In fact, he wonders if that is their purpose at all. To his horror, the minister appears to be in an advanced stage of divestiture.

Cecil's shotgun clears the canvas and swings around toward the minister. —Take this, you sorry shepherd, Cecil bawls, but even as his finger closes on the trigger, the watchful eye and quick sword of Il Coarseo see and strike. The blast is deflected over the back rail of RUN RUN GET YOUR GUN and blows into rubbish an enormous portrait of Guiseppe Verdi mounted on the float behind. In an instant Cecil is surrounded and pummeled by the collected works. Wriggletto has him by the throat. Un Ballo seems bent on smothering him in his cape.

—Throw me something, mister, someone screams. —I'll take the little blonde with the big jugs.

—Heathens, wild dogs of the desert, despoilers . . .

The mob whistles and cheers the sulking nudes, the jester and his companions, the screaming chef. They are lovers of disorder. They take it that all this is done for their pleasure, and they are enjoying it mightily.

—Rodents, vermin . . .

—You got a bad mouth, guy.

—Throw me something.

—I'll throw you something, Wriggletto yells as he and Un Ballo heft Cecil up and heave him over the side of the truck —down into the arms of the mob which raises him up on their shoulders and bears him along with them, shrieking with laughter at his indignation.

Chapter Fifteen

> And round the rim Okeanos was flowing, with a full stream as it seemed, and enclosed within the shield's cunning work . . .
> *Shield of Heracles*, 314–15

He will not wake up.
—Shad . . . Shad . . .
She has been shaking him for minutes. He sleeps in the chair before the TV in Sonny's room. On the mute screen Wylie Coyote is carefully placing dynamite in a tunnel, framing a trap for the Road Runner. The trap will fail.
—Damn you, can't you just this once . . . this one time in twenty-five years . . . You've *got* to wake up . . .
He had been striding in a sea of flames, through fiery grottoes where red and yellow and blue swirl around, enveloping him. The old man has passed by, grinning, swathed in his own eternal scarlet, and Cassie Wellbourne, strong and young once more, stripped of her infirmities as of her wealth, ready for this everlasting. And a woman in white turned from him, face obscured. The buffets become stronger, shock waves that make him break out in sweat. There in the living center of the flame is a fountain spiraling upward and outward, a serpent with its tail in its mouth. This is the one he is not going to walk away from. The one he will not even be carried away from. They will bury an empty box out behind the old man's house, simply to have a place to remember, honoring the generations.
—What . . . ? He comes to himself, suddenly, starkly awake, starting up, his face covered with sweat from the heat of those visionary flames.
Marie-Claire stands over him, an expression of surprise on her face at his sudden resurgence back into consciousness. His eyes focus on her, seem to burn into her as if he has come back from those great depths still afire.

—We're here . . . together. Sweet Christ, has it all been . . . a dream?
Marie-Claire's eyes widen. —What are you talking about?
—Did we . . . ?
His voice trails off. He is now fully awake. Of course they have not been together. This is reality—what passes for reality. They have not been together at all.
—Sorry, Shad says, shaking his head, trying to recall how he got in this room with her. —Ordinarily I sleep light. But I went way down . . . it was as real as . . . this. I was . . . on Okeanos . . . I was losing. Can you feature that? Losing. I think . . . I dreamed I had dreamed my life.
—You thought we had . . .
Shad grins. —Ain't that the goddamn limit? You and me. Write it off. I drank a lot last night, and what with one thing and another . . .
Marie-Claire is silent. What must it be like to dream that your life has been a dream? How could anyone, even in the deepest sleep, confuse life with a dream? Dreams move swiftly, from one appearance to another. Life is invested with a certain tedium that marks it as real.
—Sonny . . .
—You seen him? Where the hell did he get to?
—Sonny is . . . getting married. Tonight. At the auditorium.
—Good. He needs somebody to play with. A regular supply of ass will do wonders for . . .
— . . . to your daughter. Melissa.
Shad smiles. —Well, sure. Did you expect him to just go grab something off Bourbon Street?
—Are you still asleep? Did you hear what I said?
—Goddamnit, I heard you.
—They're brother and sister . . . or did you think you'd dreamed that, too? Your bastards are coming home to roost. Together.
—Oh, that. Forget it. If that's all your problem . . .
—Forget? Oh, my God. You're a wild beast . . . without the slightest trace of sexual morality.
—I believe that's so. But Missy ain't mine. Elvira's as full of shit as the Easter Rabbit.
—You're saying its impossible?
Shad considers, frowns. Tries it again. —Well, he says at

length, —that's a problem, ain't it? Reckon we ought to tell 'em . . . just in case?
   —Yes, Marie-Claire says, her voice under perfect control. —Yes, I really do.
   —All right, fine, Shad says wearily. —If I got to go to the damned auditorium with you, I'll go. Boudreaux's out there somewhere when he ought to be here, and by tomorrow I got to go see to that damned rig, but . . .
   —You'll need evening wear. It's the last ball.
   —What's evening dress? Women wear evening dresses.
   —Black tie . . .
   —They make you wear a tie?
   —. . . tuxedo . . .
   —Forget it. I made it this far, and the worst I ever had to wear was a business suit with a vest.
   —Shad . . .
   —Mary Clare, don't start. I'm all stove in, I got a long day coming up.
   —You don't care . . . about our son.
   Shad turns back to her. Not only what she has said, but a certain quality in her voice stuns, arrests him.
   —What?
   Their eyes lock. There passes between them some semblance of the current which on a stormy, thunderous evening broke their lives away from the day-by-day and brought them here and now.
   —What was I supposed to say? What do you want me to . . .
   —Say it again, you hear? Say it.
   —Our . . . son . . .
   Shad walks to the balcony of his wrecked room. Outside, the courtyard is falling into shadow again. He cannot understand and she cannot see the tears in his eyes.
   —I believe all that stuff last night and this morning has give me a concussion, he says hoarsely. —I feel kind of lightheaded.
   —A doctor . . . ?
   —Naw, a drink.
   He starts to the door, trying to avoid her eyes. —Where do you get one of them things? Should I call a funeral parlor?
   Marie-Claire smiles, comes toward him. —I'll call around. There must be some formal shop.

—Never mind . . . It's Mardi Gras. Everything's closed . . . Lemme see what I can do . . . What time?
—Nine of the clock, she says. —I have the invitations.
Shad leans over impulsively, kisses her on the cheek. —Okay, you got it. See you in a little while.

He exits, and Marie-Claire stares after him once more, watching him walk down the hallway, which seems too small for his passage. She touches her cheek where he has kissed her.

Cecil sits alone, dejected, in the failing light of sunset at the edge of the auditorium parking lot. The parades are mostly done. The crowd has drifted off to lose itself in a hundred bars and cafés and estaminets along Rampart and down into the Quarter. He drinks out of the bottle of Jim Beam he has salvaged from the ruin of his affairs, shakes his head gloomily. What is there left? It is all gone now. The Savior's Friends have failed him, his wife and daughter are cheerfully in the clutches of the Great Beast. Worst of all, most destructive to his morale, he is disarmed, his shotgun vanished with the madness and sensation of the afternoon. If he had the shotgun, there would be at least the options of suicide or murder. You got a shotgun, he muses, you're all right. Your soul is at peace.

He hears a peculiar sound, a scrabbling sound. Like a groundhog rubbing against floorboards, like a dog at the door. But he pays it no mind, turning his attention back to the Jim Beam and drawing out the remnants of the *20th Century Chronicles* from a torn and filthy pocket. He still has a lot to find out.

1942. La Choy food products sells its Detroit plant to the government . . . becomes the world's largest producer of canned Chinese food.

—I didn't know that, he says aloud. —It happened and I missed it. I could of bought stock.

He hears that peculiar scuttling noise again and turns to look about him in the twilight. There is nothing in sight except an abandoned car with its tires gone and the hood pulled off, and a Porta-Can standing alone at the edge of the pavement, brought there earlier to serve the needs of those parade participants requiring facilities. Is it some kind of animal? Or could some poor soul be trapped in there? Why not? Since 1934, it seems the whole world has turned into some kind of a shithouse. Of a portable kind.

Cecil pulls open the door, which seems to be stuck. A white-haired man in a lovely cloak and costume squints out at him, stumbles forth from the temporary jakes. He seems disoriented, confused. There is the reek of alcohol on his breath.

—I seem to have . . . I believe I fell asleep in that . . . convenience.

—I done that before, Cecil answers. —'Course I was feeble-minded at the time.

—Yes . . . uh, I beg your pardon . . . is that . . . ?

—This?

— . . . whiskey . . . ?

—Uh huh. See, I wouldn't ordinarily be drinking, but . . .

—I see. Of course not.

—But this is got to be the worst damn day of my life.

—The same. Those zombies, those vicious freaks . . . lunatics, screaming . . . an assassination attempt . . . Regicide . . .

—Lord, another one? You hear what they done to Huey Long?

—Huey . . . Somebody stole the . . .

—Shot him. Right in the new capitol. Dead.

—Uh . . . I believe I did hear . . . Would you take fifty dollars for that whiskey?

—No. Some nut done it. Say they tried it on you?

—Yes . . . Crazed chef, narcotics perhaps, some decision of mine . . . There was a public health case a year or so ago . . . No, that was 1942.

—Hell, in 1942, La Choy . . .

Rex holds out a soiled, crumpled, but genuine C-note. Cecil takes it, examines it carefully, then hands over the remainder of the Jim Beam.

—'Course, this goes in a interest-bearing account.

—Wise . . . very wise . . . Do you have the time?

—To do what? I had all the weird shit I can handle for one day. I mean there was this truck full of women I done shamed myself with, and that shit-ass Sentell ain't paid and ain't going to pay, and . . .

—Sentell? What about Sentell? They brought me a message from E. M. Sentell.

—Eddie Sentell? He was the dirtiest football player in North

Louisiana. Don't get in no gang tackle with him, cause he'll take your balls back to the huddle.

—His son, E.M. junior, or the tenth—I don't know how many there've been—the boy is marrying . . .

Rex fumbles in some hidden pocket of his golden waistcoat, draws out a piece of paper in worse condition than the hundred-dollar bill.

—Yes . . . Melissa Miley. I was reading this in the . . . convenience when I drifted off.

—God in heaven, Cecil rasps. —It ain't no end to this, is it? My little girl, my own undefiled baby, and a goddamned Sentell. I'd rather see her shacked up in Sicily with the pope of Rome.

Rex frowns. There is something deep here. Is this man sane? His eyes glare, his hair is lank and ugly gray, and his beard is four or five days old. He is dressed in filthy garments much like those of kitchen help—a veritable ancient saucier. But then who is sane? After a long afternoon's sleep in a Porta-Can, who shall judge this fellow?

Cecil sits down on the pavement, striking his head on the concrete like a Musselman at prayer. Rex tries to comfort him, but to no avail. He takes a long drink from the Jim Beam and smiles as a beautiful woman walks slowly toward them, stops and regards Cecil incuriously.

—How long's he been doing that?

—Madam, I am Rex . . .

—That's nice. You know how to dress, I'll give you that. How long's he been doing that?

—Not long. I wonder if I might invite you to the ball this evening . . . and afterward we could . . .

—Forget it. I got a insanely jealous husband.

—Still, if he's elsewhere . . .

—He's right there. Banging his head on the cement.

Cecil interrupts his ritual, looks up at Elvira, squints at her for a long moment through the gloom. —Don't I know you?

Elvira regards him dispassionately. —You going feeble-minded again? If you are, I'm packing it in.

The scales or whatever fall from Cecil's eyes. He starts up, clenching his fist and approaching Elvira. —You're gonna shit brickbats when I get hold of you.

Elvira stands her ground, jerks the bottle of Jim Beam from

Rex's palsied hand. —You want to find out what another good crack on the head will do for you? she asks.

Cecil pauses. —I don't think so, he says. —But that don't put you in the right, you hussy.

Elvira takes a long pull on Rex's hundred-dollar bottle.

—Wait a minute. He paid for that.

—Pay him back. I needed a hit.

—No, keep the money, Rex says cautiously, reaching for the precious bottle.

—Take a look at this, Cecil snarls, ripping the paper from Rex's hand, shoving it at Elvira as Rex recaptures his whiskey, quickly drinks.

—What does that do for you? Cecil asks Elvira in an outraged voice. —My little girl is fixing to marry that damned Sentell . . . the one who popped me on the head.

—That's nice.

—I'd rather see her in bed with John Dillinger.

—He's dead.

—Him, too?

—Look, this is the Lord's will. They love each other. It's sweet.

—Dammit, Elvira . . .

—I have to go to the auditorium now, Rex says. —Would you care to join me? There'll be champagne.

—The kids will be coming. Elvira smiles —I got to see this.

—You reckon there's any guns laying around loose in there?

Sam's Bar is packed. Christopher is taking another turn behind the bar. He has been doing Bloody Marys all afternoon. Even his eyes are red. A reporter is lifting another one, talking to whoever will listen.

—It's a bullshit job. You pour your guts out onto paper, and the next day they're wrapping boiled crabs or redfish fillets in it. I mean, who needs his work to be . . .

—Ephemeral, Christopher sighs without pausing.

—Tomorrow it's the Gulf. You know that rig that's been burning for a week?

—Since Saturday night.

—Yeah, Okeanos. I got to go out and cover some suicidal maniac who's gonna try to . . .

—He's not suicidal, he's not a maniac and he'll kick you full of new assholes if he hears you talk like that. And he might hear you because he's staying in the hotel.

—Chris, Shad says, pushing up to the bar, —I need a double Black Jack and a tuxedo.

—Tuxedo? Christ, how do you mix that? I been in the newspaper game for ten years. I thought I'd drunk everything.

Shad takes up the glass, motions for the bottle. He drinks silently as Christopher thinks about his other need.

—It's late, and it's Mardi Gras. Nothing's open.

—You got any friends? It's five hundred bucks in it if I get me a tux.

—Hey, Chris, the reporter persists. —You actually know the big bad bastard who's gonna get himself blown away out on that rig tomorrow?

Shad looks irritated by the reporter's remark. He sees that he is a piss-ant, shrugs, turns back to Chris. —There's this ball tonight, and . . .

—Ball? You must mean Rex . . .

—Where do I call him? Does he rent 'em or do I have to buy the damned thing?

—What's his room number? the reporter demands. —I want a first-person look at the dumb bastard who's gonna let big oil blow his ass from here to Dallas.

Shad turns to the reporter with an easy smile. —You looking for that stupid shit Shad Sentell who's gonna get hisself killed out on Okeanos in the morning?

The reporter squints up at Shad, who must be almost three heads taller than he, sitting as he is on his favorite bar stool.

—Yeah, right. I want to talk to that lump of . . .

—You found him, you little cocksucker.

—Hey, wait, a . . . don't . . .

—I'm fixing to die for the Company like a damn fool tomorrow, and I don't give a flying fuck how many I kill tonight, hear? I want to take the whole goddamned world out with me.

Shad reaches for the reporter with both huge hands. The reporter falls backward, legs entangled in his stool.

—Jesus . . . The reporter scrambles away into the sempiternal darkness between tables. Bogey sneers with contempt. Ingrid looks pained. Paul, his plaster innards still exposed, is thinking of other things. Shad and Christopher laugh together.

—You know something? Shad coughs, still laughing. —That bastard is probably right.
—Mr Sentell?
—Huh?
Shad looks away from Christopher. Standing at the bar beside him, staring down at him with what appears to be a condescending smile, is a great blond beast bigger than he is. The creature is immaculately dressed in a superbly tailored tuxedo, a shirt with a wilderness of ruffles. Shad's first thought is that the piss-ant reporter has a big friend. But the beast snaps its heels together and bows gracefully.
—I am Roland Richter. I, too, am a guest of Omega Oil at this hotel for Carnival. Forgive my intrusion, but I heard your name and I have been looking forward to meeting you.
—Yeah?
Shad and Christopher exchange a quick look. Christopher nods.
—This is a great honor. For many years my father was . . .
—Say, Roland, what size you wear . . . ?
Roland looks puzzled. —Size? I don't . . . No, wait. There were tables I studied . . . In America, a forty-eight long . . . But why should . . .
—Chris, anybody in the kitchen just now?
—Not a soul. All taking off to work late tonight. Like the grave back there.
Shad smiles, shake's Roland's hand.
—This here is a honest-to-God pleasure, old buddy . . . Klaus Richter's boy?
—Yes, and I am also a very good friend of your . . .
—Any friend of his is just like a blood brother to me. Listen, come on in back with me. You and me got to talk.
—Yes, of course . . . later, but now I must be going.
—Well, sure, but there's always got to be a little time for a drink between friends. Shit, life's too short not to . . .
They vanish through the doors to the kitchen, still talking. Christopher looks after them, his eyes veiled. He pours himself a drink of Black Jack and toasts the doors, which cease their swinging even as he watches.

Marie-Claire is dressed. And waiting. She is dressed in a clinging satin with a deep cleavage in front. She smiles to find how firm and smooth the skin still is. She can wear anything. For a few years yet. And she will have the taste and the character to dress otherwise when the time comes. She has been waiting for almost half an hour. She does not even want to consider that he may not come. That is not his style. Perhaps he will not be satisfactory when he comes. That *is* his style. But he will come. She rises to answer a peremptory knock at the door. She stands aghast as she opens it. He is . . . extraordinary. Tall, smooth-shaven, the slightest touch of gray at each temple. He wears a lovely tuxedo with a ruffled shirt. There is a drop or two of blood on the shirtfront. Razor cut, or is it catsup? Never mind. He looks more than presentable.

—Well, honey, I guess we're off to see Rex.
—I . . . I can't believe this.
—What? Now, goddammit, don't tell me something's wrong, cause if it is . . .
—No, no . . . nothing. You look . . . lovely.
—Yeah?
—You've . . . never looked this way before.
—You never asked me to take you to no ball. Come on, let's hit it.

Marie-Claire pulls her cape over her shoulders with a strange smile. —All right, let's, she says, still in wonderment at her escort, and at her own unsuspected power of conversion. When all this is done, she is going to have a great deal to think about.

Chapter Sixteen

> A storm wind might catch me up and bear me hence over the murky ways, and cast me forth at the mouth of backward-flowing Okeanos . . .
> *Odyssey*, xx, 65–67

It is dark now, and the green lawn leading down to the river has vanished along with the dock and the powerboat moored there that I will never board again. The expanse of the world has closed down to this swatch of grass, this square of concrete, this lawn chair, this excellent martini, that splendid drug with which Henry has just injected me.

All this long afternoon, I have been thinking on death. I am not good at such thinking because there is no strategy to death: only tactics. There is no way to outsmart it, no way to make money off one's own. One can at best do no more than smile and walk into it, looking for all the world as if he knows what lies beyond, and is as careless of it as of this ordinary darkness that comes to swallow up the light at eveningtime. What had the old man—my old man—said? How had he put it? There are no dead people. Only corpses. And in a little while there is nothing at all.

So here I am, doped to the shuddering skies above, teetering toward an Ash Wednesday that will surely rid me of my earthly sins and that temporal punishment we undergo, sinning or not. Examining, thinking, remembering, digging, and delving. Worse yet: planning. As if this life of mine stood out ahead like a great ship plowing the endless backward-flowing waters of the ocean-river. Today I have seen the details of an improbable wedding. That of my father's grandson, my nephew. It will happen because I have determined that it will. Even now I still own the means of production of events. And will. Until my mouth is stopped with good Louisiana muck, and they screw down the lid upon that bed from which I will not rise. I am not waiting for judgment. I am judging.

—What?
—It's starting to rain, Mr E.M.
—Oh...
—But you want to sit out here till the chopper comes?
—Haw... The Chopper... He's on his way.
—Ummm. I believe so, yes... Let me put this over you... No need to meet him halfway.
—Make the bastard come all the way.
—Ah ha... why not?
It is a soft English kind of rain, and the chill is within, not from outside. I remember when a rain like this meant a drilling schedule slippage. Now it means the grass will be greener. Longer. Those with death bearing down on them have had an inordinate interest in such minutiae of life. Seeds, spores, cocoons, eggs, growing, burgeoning.
—Mr E.M....
—Yes, I see.
Coming toward me with an awful rackety whirling, blades, flashing lights blinking on and off. A mechanical Kali, multitudinous arms full of knives and swords, necklace of skulls about her neck, a better than fair set of tits. Is this how that great engine will make its appearance? I'll laugh like hell. But it is only the helicopter. The beginning of the end. Not the end.
—You ready, Mr Sentell? We brought the big cargo chopper. More room, more comfort...
—Fine... Bring your kit, Henry. Plenty of Bombay, Martini and Rossi—and all the dope you've got. Can't have too much dope, can we?
—I don't believe.

The auditorium is beginning to fill up. Roisterers in every variety of finery come stumbling in from Comus, the last parade. The light rain falling seems to trouble no one. There is, in these last brief hours before Lent, an intense determination to be happy. As if, outside, the Red Death prowled. As if this were the last night of all the nights there are to be.
Rex shambles in alone by way of a rear door. He is stared at by some maskers who are aware that he has been missing since his dubious progress through the city earlier. Some have said that he was drunk on his throne; that he had cursed the multitudes; that he had vanished without a trace when the parade disbanded. It is

true that he smells of alcohol, that his gait is irregular. A tall contessa with elaborate fake diamonds everywhere notes that he carries a fifth of Jim Beam without even the decorous subterfuge of a brown paper sack to conceal it. A baronet from Baghdad snickers at the condition of his apparel.

Rex squints in the bright light, looking about, wondering where the young people might be. And the messenger with the necessary documents. All he can see is potential witnesses. But this marriage is no small matter. He has much to thank E. M. Sentell for. He hopes to have much more. Of a sudden, the long-haired creature who placed him on the float this morning materializes before him.

—Well, aren't *you* the one? What in God's name happened to you? Everyone is half crazy.

—I'm looking for a young man and a young woman, Rex mutters.

—You naughty boy . . . Can't make up your mind, huh?

Rex gives the thing a withering glance and passes on down the hallway, still looking.

Through another door at the rear, Cecil and Elvira have entered. No invitation has been required of them because, in fact, security guards at the service entrance have supposed them to be hired for the occasion—a lovely waitress and a vilely unkempt chef.

—Hey, Cecil corners a man carrying a violin case. —You seen a real pretty blonde girl about this tall . . . ?

The man looks at him as if he were feeble-minded and quickly walks on.

—It's gonna happen, Cecil. Elvira smiles serenely. —Just get set for it, and we'll find us a nice place to watch the party. You and me got to talk, anyhow.

—Talk about what?

Shad and Marie-Claire, with better credentials, have entered through the front doors and now wander down a corridor that runs beside the arena, looking for the dressing rooms.

—Where did you get it? Tell me.

—This suit? Guy lent it to me.

—It's almost a perfect fit. Oh, a little long in the trousers.

—Don't start, girl, I ain't E.M. I'll just drag you into a closet again and . . .
　Shad's voice trails off. He squints down the long, poorly lit corridor. —Sonofabitch . . .
　—What? Marie-Claire asks.
　Shad grabs her, pulls her to the side where there appear to be a number of meeting rooms. He opens the nearest door, pushes her in, and closes the door behind them.
　—I haven't said a word. What are you going to . . .
　—Hush. It ain't you. It's something else.
　He picks up a chair, smashes it against the wall, and comes away with a stout club.
　—All right, tell me . . . what is it? Something awful is going to happen, isn't it?
　—Nope. We're just fixing to take care of your problem and mine.
　—Violence . . .
　—Always pays. Even when you whip up on the wrong man. Makes the others afraid. Never you mind . . . This is going to be just fine.

—My chest hurts, Cecil is saying, —I'm purely wore out, and this damn place is so big you could lose ten acres of daughters in it. How'm I gonna . . .
　Elvira is paying him no mind. It seems they will do best to climb up into the balconies. No use looking for Missy now. If Shad and the rest are there, it could only precipitate a brawl. That can wait till afterward. Once the marriage is solemnized, she does not care what the gorillas do to one another.
　—I tell you this, Cecil is saying, —it's a terrible feeling not to know what's going on. I mean, when I come to myself over to the Billups station, the Savior's Friends had to tell me every damn thing but my name . . . Hell, I thought it was the morning after we was . . .
　— . . . Looking to murder me and Shad in the woods.
　—I wasn't going to murder *you*.
　Cecil pauses, frowns. He reaches out and touches Elvira's arm gently. He seems puzzled. —Why in hell did you marry me? he asks. —I mean, considering everything.
　Elvira turns toward him, surveying him as if for the first time.

If his hair were cut and somebody could get that frown off his face and get him in tune with the times . . .

—Charity, she answers sardonically. —Pure-dee charity . . .

Cecil smiles knowingly, scratches himself. —Bull*shit*. I *know* better than that.

Elvira tries to curtail her own smile as she walks on. —That's what it was. You had been reduced to a poor mindless creature, and I just couldn't . . .

She pauses and glances around. Cecil has disappeared. As if he has been dematerialized. Elvira wonders if it is possible he has seen a loose firearm lying about. Or whiskey. Or something else.

There is a door nearby, and she seems to hear some muffled threshing coming from behind it. The fool has reverted to type. She will find him on his knees involving Deity down on this sinful city. Here we go again. She opens the door and screams.

The picture is of Cecil looking ten feet tall against the farther wall. Because Shad has him up against it, skewered like a bug on his enormous fist, shifting him this way and that as Cecil tries to dodge the imminent blow of a chunk of timber Shad holds in the other hand, lining Cecil up for a one-shot conclusion.

—You're gonna pay, Cecil screams. —I'll come back from the fucking grave to haunt you, hear?

Shad's arm cocks. He seems to have Cecil's head just about right.

—My sweet Jesus, Elvira cries. —Don't you dare.

She dives for Shad's arm just as he brings the chair leg around toward Cecil's head. Elvira, deflecting the blow, is lifted up and bounces off the wall herself. The chair leg makes an awful sound and goes through the plaster. Elvira slowly slides down the wall to the floor.

—Dammit, Elvira, stay out of this . . . It's for your own good.

Elvira is trying to recover her breath. Shad sees that she is crying. He pauses, looks down at her with concern, continuing to hold Cecil pinned to the wall.

—'Vira, you okay?

—No, I ain't okay. I'm tired and I'm forty-four years old and my little girl is getting married and going off. I've spent most of my life with a feeb, and I'm gonna have to spend the rest of it without you cause you don't give a damn for me, and now you're fixing to break up all I got left in this world.

—Now hold up a minute, Shad says in surprise.

—Hold up my ass . . . Go ahead. It's nothing else I can do. Fracture his skull. Kill him.
—Shit, woman, Cecil chokes out as he struggles aimlessly.
— . . . Bust up his head again. Then I can live out my last days with a damned vegetable grunting and slobbering. Go ahead . . .
Shad cocks his arms again, the fire in his eyes bright. He has been waiting for a shot this good since graduation night. Elvira turns away.
—Shad, Marie-Claire begins.
—Okay, now I got to hear a piece from you, don't I?
—Don't . . . please, Marie-Claire says softly. —Don't hurt her. You cared for her . . .
Shad nods. —Sure did. But that was a long time ago. This goddamned lizard's been laying for me most of his life. I ain't gonna spend the rest of mine looking behind me.
—Great Beast, Cecil coughs out in a strangled voice. —You got to pay what you owe.
—Anyhow, he don't count for nothing . . . He ain't even the father of that fine little girl. I am.
—What? Cecil roars, almost breaking loose. —You gonna pay . . . *grawk* . . . !
Shad casually slams him against the wall, and he subsides.
—Look at this wreck. He couldn't make a baby if you was to give him a chemistry set and directions from the Lord.
—That's not so, Elvira shrieks, climbing to her feet, going for Shad. —Missy's his child . . . She is.
—Not a chance . . . Stand back so you don't get brains all over you.
—I'm not lying. I give lying a try and it didn't work. You're gonna go your own way no matter what. She's Cecil's, not yours. I wouldn't have no ugly stunted child of yours. It'd be crippled and degenerate and feeble-minded.
—What do you think? Shad asks Marie-Claire. —That satisfy you?
Marie-Claire shrugs. Her eyes are almost crossed from all this lunacy. Who can make anything out of it?
—That does it for me, Shad says, taking Cecil in both hands and tossing him most of the way across the room. He lands in a crumpled heap and tries to clear his head. Then there seem to be two Shads looming over him.
—If you ever come for me again, piss-ant, you're gonna get me.

All of me. Ain't nobody living had that much before—no woman in the sack or man in a fight. You go home with Elvira if she wants you. But if you do her any wrong, I'll come pull you to pieces.

Cecil looks up defiantly. Shad casually boots him low in the gut. Cecil curls up groaning. —You understand what I said? Shad asks. —Just say if you don't. I'll explain.

Cecil is silent for a moment. Then he sees Shad's boot drawing back again.

—Yes, he says hastily. —Yes, I believe I do understand.

Shad smiles grimly. —You been touched again. You ain't no prophet anymore. I take it all back. You're just a shitkicker that's got him a good wife and a Billups station. You hear me?

Cecil nods sullenly. —What about my baby daughter?

—Melissa Sentell, Shad says. —She's gonna get by marriage what she missed by birth. You got any objections?

Cecil contemplates that boot again. —No, no, I ain't, Cecil says quickly, with reluctance. —'Course, it *does* make us kin.

Shad's face falls. He looks at Marie-Claire in consternation. He has not taken this into account. Marie-Claire does not laugh aloud. But in this antic menagerie, we are all cross-referenced, aren't we?

—God almighty, Shad chokes.

—Hell. Cecil grins, getting to his feet, dusting off his gritty chef's outfit, adjusting his cap, and going to join Elvira. —I reckon I can stand it . . . if nobody brings it to mind.

—Youall ought to do real fine as a family, E.M. says from the doorway, standing there supported by Henry. —If you folks have gotten the genealogies and the preliminaries all worked out, I believe it's almost time . . . for the main event.

It is finished. All has been accomplished in the family way. Now Rex is downstairs at the ball, fretting his way through it until after the meeting of the courts when he will finally be free to take his ease with a bottle of Latour '47. In an upper room of the auditorium, filled to overflowing with spring flowers, there is a wedding feast in progress.

Missy and Sonny sit side by side. E.M., Shad, Marie-Claire, Cecil, and Elvira are seated around the table. Henry serves with a real smile, setting out each dish catered from a small place in the Quarter. Only he and Shad exchange cool glances each time their eyes meet.

—I just can't get over all this, Missy says. —It's like some kind of dream.

—Hallucination, E.M. wryly observes. —What the hell? You're the prettiest bride in family history.

E.M. leans over to Sonny, who sits next to him, whispers. —I hopes this makes up for something of the . . . past.

Sonny chokes up. E.M.'s soft comment even turns his mind from passion. He has not had his hands on Missy since Rex directed them to kiss chastely at the end of the ceremony. Is it that now all is permitted, nothing is any fun? No. It is the first time within memory that he has had a family. Everyone he cares about. In the same room. Celebrating his happiness. He is beyond doubt a Sentell. Tears roll down his cheeks. He reaches over and embraces E.M.

—This . . . this . . . was worth waiting for, he croaks.

Shad and Marie-Claire, across the table, see E.M. reach out his bone-thin hand and fold Sonny's into it.

—Good, E.M. says softly, his voice resonant with pleasure.

—That's what I wanted to hear . . . You're very lucky . . . Love her as well as you can, don't let anything come between you. Nothing . . . ever . . .

Shad sees Marie-Claire bite her lip as she hears this. Some things are said very late. Is it better they be so said than never said at all? Shad turns away as Sonny and Missy rise to go and dance. Everyone applauds.

—Wear out your shoes, Elvira calls after them.

—Don't . . . ever stop dancing, Marie-Claire says softly, distantly, her eyes and E.M.'s caught in chill intense embrace.

Outside, on a corner of the auditorium parking lot near a vacant Porta-Can, an Omega helicopter stands parked, several state troopers watching over it, talking softly in the cool night, watching the lights of the Quarter glow and pulse in the waning hours of Carnival.

Inside, Louis Boudreaux naps fitfully on a cargo mat. He wakes to find himself covered with cold sweat.

— . . . this heart of mine could never see . . . what everybody knew but me . . . , Charlie Mangum croons up front.

Boudreaux sits up, wiping his forehead with his sleeve. He

wonders if Shad realizes what they are up against. This is not a two-bit situation solved quickly by technology, a little brains, and plenty of guts. This is a new age, and there is a great beast named Okeanos howling and spewing fire out in the Gulf. Even as he has slept, Boudreaux has felt its power, its claim. They are being drawn to it now, and Boudreaux is afraid.

—It seems you and my brother have had . . . dealings, E.M. is saying to Cecil.
　—Dealings? I guess. He dealt me a blow up side my head, and I was daffy for . . . since 1934.
　E.M. smiles, shrugs, reaches for one of Henry's ubiquitous martinis. —You didn't miss much.
　—Hell you say. Look here . . .
Cecil draws out his ratty, disintegrating copy of the *20th Century Chronicles*.

　1938. The ballpoint pen is patented by Hungarian chemist George Biro and his brother Ladislao.

　—If I could of got in on that, got me a little piece of stock . . .
　—Oh, shut up, Cecil, Elvira says. —You couldn't hardly pump gas in 1938.
　—'Cause Sentell there had wrecked my brain, that's why.
　—I want peace in the family, E.M. says with a distant smile.
—What with you being Sonny's father-in-law . . .
　—There's *gonna* be peace, Shad says quietly. —I guarantee.
　—What do you reckon all those lost years are worth, Mr Miley, E.M. asks, taking his checkbook from Henry.
　Cecil cannot help looking sleazy, calculating. —Well, I lost the Depression . . .
　—Half of it, E.M. replies dryly, no sign of a smile. —You caught the interesting part. The rest was just a replay . . . not worth seeing.
　—Well, how about the Second World War?
　—Said they didn't draft idiots, Elvira puts in, dry as E.M.
—Though I come to wonder about that, considering the way it went. Maybe he could of got a commission.
　Marie-Claire looks from one speaker to another in bewilderment. Is this what she has raised, protected, and defended Sonny for? That he should be cast adrift on a river-ocean of madness?
　—Now that *was* a loss, E.M. is saying. —Highly diverting.

—I *could* of gone to college if I hadn't had my wits knocked out of me.

Cecil becomes more and more excited as he recounts what he has lost. No one else has ever wanted to listen, and, after all, what ceiling is to be placed on the aspirations of an American boy with a good solid high school education?

—I believe it was Harvard Medical School he was gonna apply to that summer, Elvira says. —He was a shoo-in.

—Hey, I never claimed . . .

—I could have helped you with that, E.M. tells Cecil. —They're not like the army. You'd have done fine up there.

—Well, you reckon? If I had, I'd of got me a license to steal. A Harvard doctor could pull down four, maybe five thousand a year . . . For all them lost years . . .

—How'd ten thousand sound to you?

Cecil looks abject. He has seen that figure written down. He has heard it on the radio. Usually in regard to tornado damages at a trailer park. Certainly he has never seen nor heard a number of that magnitude in any connection with himself.

—I'll take it, he says quickly.

—All right, fine. Ten thousand a year . . . since 1934.

Now Cecil falls silent, all passion spent. He has supposed E.M. meant a flat ten thousand. He stares at E.M. as if in a trance. With the assistance of his fingers, Cecil manages to add up twenty-six ten thousands. His face is ashen. —Well, I . . .

—If you wouldn't rather burn it or stuff it in a rathole, he'll take it, Elvira smiles. —We might could afford a new Billups sign.

—Yeah, Cecil says absently, then subsides. He thumbs through the *20th Century Chronicles* distractedly, wondering what Harvard Medical would have been like. Who knows? There might still be time.

—Say thank you, Elvira frowns. But Cecil has put aside the *Chronicles* and is staring down at the tabletop, overcome by the day's events.

—I believe I'll put it all in a interest-bearing account, he finally manages to get out.

—That's prudent, E.M. says, his eyes moving between Marie-Claire and Shad across the table.

—You ever played any cutthroat poker, Cecil, old buddy? Shad drawls. Marie-Claire nudges him. Elvira gives him a venomous look. Cecil smiles as E.M. finishes writing the check and slides it over to him. He stares at the string of zeros for a moment, then pushes it into his pocket covetously.

—No, I ain't, Cecil replies. —All I ever did was straight draw for pennies, and considering my luck up till tonight, I believe I'll pass. You don't milk a cow till her bag falls off, and you don't never press your luck till you lose the herd, neither.

There is general laughter. Even Henry smiles.

—All right, E.M. says in a low voice. —We've toasted the kids, and there's peace and good feeling all around.

His eyes bore into Shad, who picks up a peculiar intonation in his voice.

—It's time for the grown folks to be getting to their chores. E.M. smiles exultantly. —There's something waiting for us . . . in the Gulf.

Sonny and Missy are dancing. The music is that awful old saw, "If Ever I Cease to Love". Rex waves his wand over them as if his power were real and he means to bless every day of their lives.

—You reckon we could get out of here? Missy whispers in Sonny's ear. —I mean it's been real nice and all, but now that we're legal, I think I'd kind of like to . . .

Sonny glances at his watch and looks grim. —Not yet, he says. —There's one thing more.

Missy frowns. —Oh, hell, it was a fake marriage. I might have known.

—No, Sonny says, moving her off the dance floor, searching for an exit so he can join the other Sentells. —There's still . . . Okeanos.

—I beg your pardon, Roland says uncertainly, standing stiffly but unsteadily against the bar across from Christopher in khaki work clothes a shade too small for him. —I seem to have fallen down. Things are unclear. I require a room and . . .

—Sit down, Christopher says without the trace of a smile, pushing a bottle of exceedingly strong schnapps and a large glass across to him. He has selected the bottle some time before. Shad has paid for it. —The footing is tricky back there.

—What's the fare to Caddo Parish? the man in the filthy chef's coat asks the cabbie with one eye who has parked outside the auditorium and passed the time drinking a quart he has purchased at Sam's Bar.

—Whatever's on the meter, folks. Uh ... Where's Caddo Parish? Like I know Jefferson, Saint Tammany, Saint John the Baptist, Ascension ...

—North, honey, Elvira smiles, wresting E.M.'s check from Cecil's hand. —I'll tell you when we're there.

Chapter Seventeen
2 March 1960

> All the land seethed and Okeanos' streams and the unharvested sea. Hot vapor lapped round the earthborn Titans. Flame unspeakable rose to the bright upper air . . . Astounding heat seized Chaos . . . It seemed even as if Earth and wide Heaven above came together . . .
> *Theogony*, 695–703

It has not taken a thousand years, as it turns out. Just twenty-one. Now we are all aloft in this great noisy thing, this engine that flutters high above the Mississippi. The clouds have broken up and the moon turns the river below into a skein of silver, a great metallic thread that draws us down the continent toward the Gulf. A blast of cool air rushes in an open port, and I have not felt so alive in years. We will land at Venice and transfer to a crew boat to head out for Okeanos. We will be there before dawn.

—Henry . . .
—Sir?
—I believe . . . I'd like . . . shot . . .
—Not so soon, Mr E.M. . . . You know . . .
—It's all right . . . this . . . time.
—Sir?
—Listen to me. Hear . . . This time it's . . . all right.

Henry looks forward to where Shad and Boudreaux are going over the charts, the photos of Okeanos. Then he looks back at me.

—Ah . . .
—If not now . . . when?

He nods, prepares the injection, and I am a new man.

—Thank you, I say to him. —For everything . . . always . . .

Henry moves away, going to sit on a freight pallet with the boy and his delectable new wife. They were not supposed to be along. I had not calculated on their coming. Rooms were booked at the Monteleone for them. By now they should be caught up wholly, helplessly, in a magic that passes too soon. I am ashamed. I had not reckoned on the blood, the blood—a certain tension that seems to pass along that river-ocean of the veins from generation to generation. My grandfather must have felt it singing as he watched over the parapets at Vicksburg. It tells us when something is going to happen to our kind. We Sentells are not wiser, more intelligent than others. It is simply that our blood knows and we are, God help us all, faithful to the blood.

The boy may be happy. It is possible. When all this is behind him, his world changed utterly, he may be happy. If I were in a position to advise him, I would say: gather us all up, your fathers and mothers, all the bloodless bones, and put them out in that cemetery behind the Old Place with as much ceremony and grace as you can. Forgive us. Send into that dark soil your forgiveness. Pray for us all, all shut together in that close place, some never even having seen the others, but all linked through the generations. Then never come there again. Never come back to us until you come to stay. It is no use trafficking with the dead, attempting commerce with them, because there are no dead. Only corpses.

That day, I was still the old man's victim. He was dead. They were going to bury him, close the lid on all those archaic pasts and wasted passions. Now he was Nothing. He had assured me of it. He was Nothing, and Nothing cannot speak the truth. But I tricked myself: the truth remains the truth though Nothing speaks it.

From the hospital that night, I had gone to the Caddo Hotel where Omega kept suites of rooms. No. That was afterward. I had gone first to a place called the Glass Hat on Texas Street to drink. I was not ready to face her. Not yet. Not just yet.

I drank late that night and deep and have no recollection at all how I may have gotten to the Caddo Hotel. My sleep was dreamless as that of the dead. Next morning she called and asked why I hadn't come home, at least called. I wasn't ready for the call, for her voice. I told her I had wanted to be by myself. After all, this doesn't happen every day. It only happens once. There was a long pause at her end. I wondered if I had said too much. Then she said she understood. I wondered if she did.

She said Shad had already taken care of the arrangements. They would be burying the old man that afternoon. Out at the Old Place, of course. Was it too soon? Were those arrangements all right with me? Would I rather wait? No, I said. That will be fine. Let it be. I'll meet youall out there. You're not coming home? No, I said. I want to think. I have to think. Another long pause. Do you want me to tell Sonny? Who? Yes, all right. You tell him.

I hung up then, and my mind turned to the boy. I did not know him. I could not have told you anything about him. It might have been different if there had been no war. Or it might not have been. He was a small boy growing up in the house on Line Avenue. Like the still young pines out there on the lawn. A part of nature. Not part of me. Part of my brother. The old man had said that at the very edge of the grave. I knew he believed in nothing, feared nothing. He might have lied even then. Despite the credit naive courts of law give such a thing, a dying declaration means no more than any other. You must judge its quality, its likelihood. I had judged, and the result had paralyzed me. But if the boy was his, his and hers, whey had she become even more hostile to Shad over the years, always uneasy, irritated when he came to the house? Was it no more than subterfuge for something that had smoldered during the war and was aflame again?

No. That wasn't it. She hated him truly. Hated him because on some certain day or night at some specific hour he had taken her, done to her whatever it was he did to women, then left her there, not even attempting to make an ongoing affair of it. Because affairs were not Shad's way, were they? He might screw his own sister or daughter if he had one. But only once. Why repeat? When you have had one, you know her. When you have dipped your stick into one, you have probed her in the only way that makes any difference between a man and a woman. Time for the next one, for there lies below the belly of every woman some knowing that a man should have. That was Shad's view of it, wasn't it? And that was most certainly why she hated him now. He had poisoned my well, but he had no desire to draw water there again. And in some obscure way, the very fact that he had used her and tossed her aside carried the infamy, the base insult, closer to the heart.

I drove slowly out to the old place that afternoon. In agony. I would skip whatever parody of a church service Mary Clare had surely insisted upon and Shad agreed to simply because it didn't matter to him. His faith, his hope, his cathedral was builded between every woman's thighs. I would meet them at the house.

It was mine now. I was the Sentell, and nothing they had done or might do could alter that. After a lifetime of trimming, climbing, twisting, trading, using the law or avoiding it, I had gone beyond the boundaries of ordinary humanity in a moment at the old man's deathbed. Now I had to determine how to meet them, with what weapons to meet them. But I was paralyzed within.

Not because of the mere physical fact that on a certain occasion he had penetrated her, merged his body with hers. I was past that. I had seen it happening in the old man's hospital room as he was speaking, had seen it as if on some great stage a drama—no, a farce, a clumsy slapstick ballet of probe and pet and rub and moan had been stumbled through. Take two sides of beef from a meat-locker, push one across another, and you have as much significance. Not that, but something more. Something awful, something I could not yet articulate or call to mind. Not then at least. Not until later that afternoon.

They were there when I arrived. A small knot of people swelled in size by Omega officers from Shreveport, Dallas, Houston, Tulsa. Old man Petrie was there, and Claiborne from the filling station. Probably the only two who would miss the old man. If anyone would miss him at all.

They had just brought the coffin to the grave dug in the sandy loam. I looked quickly. His grave had not been dug beside hers, beside my mother's. Shad would have seen to that. He had put the old man where he belonged. Within the fence, within the property because he had been Sentell, whatever else. But to one side, a little isolated—the way he would have wished it himself. Alone at the edge of things, watching, jeering silently. For eternity.

Except, I thought as I walked toward them, all now watching me approach—were they jeering silently?—except there are no dead, and they watch nothing. There is no ultimate resolution, no words that are final, no acts that escape the blind push and shove of cause and effect. Like meat rubbed together in a freezer. There are only corpses.

The preacher, some old man I had known as a boy, some Baptist or Pentecostal whose church and picnics I had once attended almost surely because I was going then with some forgotten girl, paused as I came up and stood among the Omega people on the far side of the grave from Mary Clare, Shad, and the boy.

The old preacher then took up where he had left off, denying that we stand at the edge of nothing, denying that we ourselves are almost nothing, that my father was nothing now, and that the whole of us, young and old, right and wronged, would soon be nothing at all.

As I listened, mind elsewhere, trying to break through to whatever it was that so desolated me, that made my hands tremble so badly that I had to clasp them behind my back, the preacher lied vigorously, lied strongly in his country certainty, talking about those who hungered and thirsted for justice like the old man. He claimed that such hunger, such thirst, even deranged, maddened, was a vision from God and would be satisfied, reconciled—was reconciled even now in God, Who knew no time, no enmity amongst His children, Who held aloft in the eternal morning the pristine soul of Edward Malcolm Sentell Second to bathe it in His glory. And now, even now, he shouted, Edward Malcolm Sentell, who was never satisfied a day or an hour on the face of this wide earth . . . is satisfied.

I found to my dismay that I was crying. Not for the old man, God knows, satisfied or not as he might be; not for the preacher's eloquence, though it was considerable, or even for that great sadness within that could not believe a word he was saying because my father had converted me on his deathbed to another sort of belief. Not crying for any of that but for some nameless horror they had done me, Mary Clare and Shad. Someone put a hand on my shoulder. I shook it off. They would suppose that beneath the facade of my control there had always lurked love for the old man. That was all right. Such a notion could not hurt me. But the thing itself, the real reason for my weeping, so profound, so alien, so inchoate that I could not even speak it, confront them with it, was tearing me to pieces.

As the preacher was winding down, offering a similar hope to all of us, I could not take my eyes from them: Mary Clare, beautifully dressed, a dark veil obscuring her perfect face; the boy in a black coat and short pants, pale, fearful, uncertain, shaken; Shad just behind, one hand on the boy's shoulder, his other arm around Mary Clare, who seemed to lean toward him, to accept his solace for that moment at least—or perhaps craving once again in however slight a way that touching, that rubbing, that pressure of flesh upon flesh that had driven them, compelled them to destroy me.

It was a perfect family portrait, a picture made there among the bones of our dead, requiring no further touch, no detail, nothing at all, complete beyond increment: a grandfather dead, a son, his woman, and their son. Three generations of Sentells in the order of their going and their coming on that land. Anything more would have been superfluous.

I shook my head in confusion, felt my face flush with a surge of blood as the preacher finished, as Mary Clare and the boy dropped loose handfuls of dirt into the grave. I sensed that it was coming at last, taking shape in my mind like mist from a genie's bottle—the name of the horror, the thing they had done to me and which I would fling back at them. But even then it would not come. Not until Shad came forward with a shovel, aiming in some strange country piety to fill in the grave himself. Then it exploded in my head as if someone had transfused alcohol directly into my brain.

—Use that shovel, I shouted at him. —Cover him up. You dug his grave . . . now fill it.

Which was not true or, even if true, irrelevant. It was not the old man's grave I was staring across. It was mine. I was the redundancy, the element left out of that family portrait, unneeded, superfluous. What was it they had done to me? The concept, the word was on my lips as Shad and I glared at each other across the open grave. Then, as it was taking form, almost ready to be said, he threw a shovel of loose dirt on my white suit. I jumped for him, screaming what he had done, what they both had done—no, the three of them and the old man, too. But even as I reached for him, he hit me with the spade. I was standing on the mound of damp earth, my boots already slipping from under me as he swung. Then I felt myself falling, a few feet, a thousand miles. Down into that void, that gulf to which we were consigning the old man, which had swallowed all the past and is each moment reaching out for the rest of us.

I was down in the grave then, scrabbling on the lid of the coffin, which became transparent under my clawed hands, through which the old man stared up at me, his rouged and puttied face horrible, eyes unclosed, wintry, glazed, careless, dead. Calling up from the depths, commanding me in the name of blood to join him, to come down where I belonged, to fall out of that perfect picture so the Sentell family still alive could live its life. Then it burst in me like an explosion. Death. That was what they had done to me.

—You coming out of there, Eddie? Or you just want me to fill you in? Shad said from high above, Lord of the Living, of the flesh, of the sun and the morning, the moon and the soft night—looking down into the land of the dead.

They had killed me, canceled me out of life. They had made a corpse of me. I was no husband, no lover, no son, no father. I was Nothing.

In that moment I think I lost all control, felt myself slipping away into darkness, leaching down into the ravenous grave, the pitiless earth. I tried to climb back into the world, but the soil collapsed under my hands, and I seemed to hear the whispers of my near kin buried there, suddenly awake on every side. I must have screamed, because the old preacher came back to the side of the grave, gave me his hand, and brought me up into the light more surely, more certainly than had any baptism he had ever performed. I stood there trembling, a few feet from death. I was still shaking, unable to push the horror away as my eyes focused and I saw them, the man, the woman, the boy—the Sentells—standing across that emptiness in the earth staring back at me.

I looked, and I swore that I would even the score, would avenge my own murder on them if it took a thousand years. Then, I turned—left them there, close to the dead, in the midst of life.

The rough sound of the helicopter blades threshing through the thick, moist air could lull me to sleep. But not now. Boudreaux still holds his flashlight over the charts and photos of Okeanos. Shad asks him short, laconic questions. He responds. I think they are going over the control console now. All the others lie near sleep. Mary Clare is awake, having come to protect what she loves most. But what is that? The boy? Or my brother, my killer? Who made of me a corpse so that I moved down the state three hundred miles to bury myself in Saint Tammany Parish, by a river of forgetfulness, close to an alien town.

It has not taken a thousand years. We do not live so long. Only fourteen since I came to know. Only twenty-one since it was done to me. It seems a thousand. It seems that at least, but it does not matter, for here I am at the edge of the gulf, that deep and lasting grave, once more.

Shad claps Boudreaux on the back and laughs. His laughter will not last till morning. The dead remember. They reach out with their chill hands from whatever grave you dig for them. It comes to me that the old man was a fool, at last a fool. Dead, we are not corpses. We infest the sun-drenched earth. We conspire, lay plots. We plan the destruction of those who have made us nothing, who have rendered us ghosts, shadows cursed to inhabit, to animate corpses, keep them moving as if alive that we might suffer more.

And my brother? His Great Year is ended now. His thousand years is done. All his women and the legend of his strength are behind him. He talks in muted tones with an old friend, sure that he can conquer Okeanos now as he did Peterson Number One so long ago. But he will not. Before the sun stands above the Gulf, as sure as Cain found out his brother, I'll find mine. Lying here like a sheaf of dry twigs, I feel my death within me. It is towering, enormous. Too much for one alone. Hours, days, weeks away at most. The narcotic only stays the pain. It does not keep the horror at bay nor still the working of the thing inside. All right, fine. Everything is accomplished now. Time is repealed, and by morning this brother and I will have resolved all differences. We will both be what our fathers are. We will both be nothing at all.

Boudreaux and I got done, and I told him to take a nap. I had reckoned to go over and visit with Mary Clare, or maybe with Sonny and Missy if that seemed better. But when Boudreaux was finished with me, I didn't feel much like talking.

In Venice, we got onto the crew boat and took out over the water. It was still pitch black and starting to rain again, but the Gulf was as smooth as glass. It looked like you could walk out to the rig. Only I ain't Jesus.

After a while, Boudreaux nudged me. —There it is, he said.

I stood up and looked out over the bow of the boat. It was still dark, just a little gray to the east. At first I couldn't see a thing, and I couldn't figure out what he wanted me to look at. Then I realized what it was I had missed. The smoke from Okeanos. That wasn't a thunderhead out in front. It was the pillar of smoke from the rig, and it covered the whole sky to the southeast. I had thought it was another storm front pulsing with lightning down below. It was black as hell and seemed to stretch from horizon to horizon east to west as we headed south. What I thought was lightning was the glow coming over the horizon from the fire itself. My God, I thought. It's too much. I can't manage that. Nobody can. I could feel my face kind of flush. It was as if everything was taking on a new life. I could smell that cool Gulf water, feel the spray and the rain. I could feel every ache and pull and sprain and bruise on my body like they'd all just happened. I wanted to grab the wheel of the crew boat and spin it around north again and say, Folks, I don't believe the fishing's gonna be any good today. You get back your deposit, and the bus to New Orleans takes off in ten minutes. Please check to see you don't leave no personal belongings behind.

I turned away from the front of the boat and tried to get hold of myself. And was looking E.M. square in the face. Henry was giving him another shot, and E.M. was smiling right at me with that withered skull-face of his. He can read me like the *Shreveport Journal* classifieds, I thought. Sweet Jesus, he must be loving it. It must be medicine to him. That's why he came out here. Not because he's CEO of Omega Oil. Hell, he's four-fifths dead, and it don't make a rat's ass to him whether we clear this thing or blow it off at the bottom and seal it over. No. He's out here to see me in hell. And he's gonna. He's gonna see just that if I try to go up on that thing and tinker.

—It's not so bad when you get right up on it, Boudreaux said, as if he could read me, too.

—Don't shit me, coon-ass. You're scared. You got a family.

—Don't mention that. Hell, if I was to think of that . . .

—You're staying in the boat, I told him.

—Crap. You can't do nothing up there by yourself . . . You got to have two.

—This time it's gonna be one. You got Celeste and the girls . . . Just one this trip.

—No, E.M. said, beside us now, his voice strong, looking like a different man from just a minute ago. —It takes two, brother. You and me.

Boudreaux and me looked at one another.

—I believe it's the sea air, I said. —Or maybe that stone-crazy nigger give you the wrong dope.

He took hold of my arm, and his grip was as strong as mine. He was looking past me out toward the platform with that blank-eyed dead man's smile. Then, with my arm in his grip, he faced me back toward the front of the boat. I swear to God, I didn't want to look. But he was strong, and it was almost unnatural how that skinny man who looked eighty, who had once been my brother, turned me around. I was tired and a little drunk and scared shitless. Maybe, I thought, this is what comes of a lifetime spent chasing pussy. You turn into one.

—There it is . . . Okeanos . . .

I was looking forward then, and my eyes followed the column of smoke and fire upward till I was looking almost directly overhead. We had come under the cloud by then where the rain and weather held it down, kept it from rising and dissipating. I could see the platform maybe six or seven miles away. The flames must of stood two, three hundred feet high, and the platform itself was eighty feet off the water—maybe a hundred. I knew once, but right then everything I knew had kind of slipped out of my head and was running down my leg.

—It's been waiting out here in the Gulf, E.M. whispered, —waiting for us . . . all our lives . . . It's . . . penalty we have to pay . . . for the . . . injustice . . .

He looked like he was seeing the face of God. No dark glass. Face to face. That wasn't what I saw. Then I began to hear the sound.

No. I had *been* hearing it. But what with the roar of the crew boat engines and the water sizzling by, the creaking and thumping of the hull, and the endless wind of the Gulf, I hadn't separated it out. Now I did, and it only made what was bad even worse. It was a high, mournful, terrible sound. It bent your spirit. It sounded like a child in pain, a woman mourning a loss too awful to sustain. It was all the dead crying for the lives they'd left behind, the heaven they'd throwed away.

Right then it dawned on me I'd heard that sound before. What well howled and shrieked like this? One I'd got blowed off of? Odessa? Midland? No. It hadn't been a well at all. It had been some God-forsaken island in the South Pacific I couldn't even remember the name of. Rock and sand and a piece of jungle and some coconut palms. Every worthless acre covered with dead Marines. Snipers behind every rock and tree, in every crevice, every cave. My squad had a flamethrower. We come up on a wide-mouthed cave just when one of 'em had shot our platoon leader. A slender blond kid out of Texas A&M. Good heart, full of fun, cared for his men, and every damned one of us loved him, too. We went crazy. We wanted to go in with bayonets, but it was a heavy machine-gun just inside. So we brought up the torch and started pouring jellied gasoline down that dark hole until we had run through the tank and ruined the thrower.

Then that sound began to come. That distant hissing scream so awful that it quenched our anger, our craziness, sobered us even before they began running out. Somebody shot the first one, then the next two, and I took out a couple of the next dozen after that. But it wasn't necessary, and the firing died out, and we watched what we had done, what called for no shooting at all.

Tens and dozens and scores of things covered with fire come running up out of the darkness as if we had punched a hole through into hell. Falling, twisting, rolling on the ground, blackened except fingers and arms and legs with the flesh already gone and the white bone showing. Not adversaries any longer, not enemies. Not even human beings. Souls in agony, some running out of the rocks and down the beach into the sea.

—Jesus, somebody next to me whispered as one of 'em ran toward us. —Oh, Christ . . .

Because the flames had not reached her face, her hair, and for one second all of us saw one of those perfect Oriental faces, the face of a woman you could dream about every night of your life. Dream of reaching out, touching her, drawing her to you with all the tenderness you could find in yourself. And the next second the face vanished in the flames that had already claimed her body, fallen near us to emerge a blackened, fearsome thing, lipless, eyeless, that poured out past its white grinning teeth that sound like some corrosive liquid to drown us all until somebody fired his carbine not so much to end her agony as ours. Then somebody else pointed. —Oh, no . . .

Because by then we had got past the troops altogether, and the fireballs running up into the light, not to save themselves, since it wasn't any salvation for them, but to damn us, force us to see what we had done, they was mostly women. But there was worse yet, worse even than that, because by then some of them fireballs burning wasn't running, couldn't run. They was too small. They was toddling.

—Yeah, I said, coming back to the Gulf, the sound of the Pacific one with Okeanos. —I guess you're right.

—Maybe we ought to call somebody else in.

—Fuck your fist, bruh. It's our wells.

—Better safe than sorry. You're a rich man.

—No guts, no glory. I don't know about rich, but I believe I'm that other thing you said . . . How about you? You really serious about . . .

I wasn't throwing it up to him. He was in pain. He'd been in pain for a long time. I could remember when his shoulders almost busted out of those white suits of his. Now, even cut down, his jacket hung on him like it was made for a man three sizes bigger.

—I'm ready, he said. —Just like your shadow.

I nodded. It was his life, what was left of it. What the hell? The old man had wanted a horse. E.M. wanted Okeanos. Me? When my time come, I reckoned I'd rather have me a piece of ass than either. But nobody gets to fuck hisself to death. It's too good for us. We none of us deserve it. We got to go through the hot gates, don't we?

By then we were almost on top of the thing. The noise was awful, and if the Gulf had been heavy with bad gusts of wind, them flames could dip and sweep us off the water like we'd never been there. I could see details then, stuff I couldn't see in the pictures. Stuff you had to eyeball. I could see some of the casing fractures where the gas was coming out under so much pressure that it couldn't even ignite till it was ten or fifteen feet out from the pipe.

The steel was twisted, some of the light members melted loose and hanging down. It seemed all the breaks was on the side away from the direction the wind had been blowing, and above them was the crew's quarters. That's why we'd lost so many men. You could see where even the unbroken pipe was blackened, scorched, and if a strong prevailing east wind rose before we got into that control shack, the whole damn Gulf of Mexico might be covered with this cloud, and the gas and petroleum welling up in the water under pressure could burn for a thousand years.

I signaled the captain to take us around, and I kept looking, studying. There was a series of valves at different heights all the way down to the water bottom. If the linkages was still in shape, we might could just walk into that control shack and turn the sonofabitch off. I had never had that kind of luck, and I didn't expect it now, but what with my guts churning and my spine about to ravel up with fear, I sure did hope. Hope never hurt nothing. So long as you can stand disappointment.

Then it come to me that Sonny and his little girl and Mary

Clare was all sitting behind me. I plastered a big smile on my face and walked back there. The smile felt like concrete and probably looked like a job done by a cheap funeral parlor, but it would have to do. Shit, they was lucky I wasn't throwing up, considering what I was up against.

—Well, folks, I yelled against the howl of Okeanos, the hiss of the water, the motors and the wind, —welcome to the Gulf Fireworks Company. You-all known me for some time, but your haven't never visited my work place. This here is it.

Sonny was wide awake. He looked speechless. He couldn't look at me for staring at that huge cloud of flames and smoke twisting and billowing up above us. We were so close now that we could feel the heat even being upwind, feel that heat and smell the burnoff.

—Now I got to go up and see to this thing. You-all are gonna stay here. What I got to do is real simple. I got to make it stop doing what it's doing. It's just like turning off the pilot on your waterheater at home, only more so.

I could see I wasn't making anybody feel better. Wasn't no fools in that crowd, so I reckoned to get on with it. Missy was looking sick to her stomach, and Mary Clare looked small and pale and damned near as scared as I was.

Boudreaux brought out the fire suits. He looked troubled, started to say something.

—Let it be. This here ain't coon-ass work. This here is Protestant work.

—You bastard, he said, and went to hugging me like he never reckoned to see me again. It would have been better if he hadn't, I thought. Cause if there had been any doubters amongst our folks, Boudreaux had just tipped 'em off as to what we was up against. Then he looked at E.M. out of the corner of his eye.

—He can't make it up that ladder, Shad. Hell, I ain't sure you can.

—It's his rig, and it's his life, I told Boudreaux. —If he falls off halfway up, it'd probably be all right with him.

Boudreaux frowned. —You mean he don't even want to come back? Cher, I just as soon you not go up there with a man who don't give a shit if he ...

—He's my brother, I told him. —You just keep it together down here. If it goes bad, I want this torpedo boat off like a scalded-assed ape. Don't take no chances with this boy and these women, you hear? E.M.'s damn near dead already, and I'd as soon go as not . . .

—What's that suppose to mean? Boudreaux asked. —What the shit is going on? This some kind of suicide mission?

—Don't get excited. I done it all. Done most of it a couple of times, and some of it so damned often it ain't worth doing again. No bullshit rescue tries, you hear?

—I hear. *Le Bon Dieu avec* . . .

—Right. Sure . . .

I was suited up then, and Henry had E.M. ready. Oh, yeah, Henry. He was looking at me. He was smiling. That nigger hadn't smiled at me in twenty years and more. He'd of cut my throat if E.M. had only just nodded. Now he was smiling. Why do you reckon he was smiling?

The captain of the crew boat is doing his best, but the wind is rising in gusts around the pockets of rain, and the sea is beginning to run. He wonders if he can place his passengers on the small float that bobs at the base of the rig, to which is attached a ladder mounting to steel stairs that reach up into the structure itself. He would as soon write this one off and take everybody home, but Omega doesn't pay men who can't do their jobs. If you want to be warm and safe and comfortable and dry, join the navy. Maybe you can command a nuclear sub.

Shad comes up beside him. —You be ready to run, hear?

—You want me to take these folks over to the standby ship? The captain points to a small vessel anchored perhaps a mile away, its lights and the outline of its hull now visible in the brightening gray light.

—Naw, not now. Listen can you pick up these suit mikes?

—Yeah. Real good. We even tape em. In case . . .

—Yeah, I know, Shad says. —If I yell to you, don't bother to cast off. Hit the throttle and take the lines with you. 'Cause . . .

—Yeah, the captain replies. —I know . . .

Sonny has come up to join them. —How about if I go, Uncle Shad? If I'm ever going to run this company . . .

—How about if I get tore to pieces by your two women over there before Okeanos ever gets a run at me?

—It's bad, isn't it? I never thought . . .

—Naw, it's average.

Shad pauses. There is no reason for him to expect to see his son again. Unless he just goes up on the platform, takes a quick look around, and comes back down. Which would be worse than not coming back at all. Like being dead, only no one would know. Shad reckons it better if the last passage between the two of them in this world not be a lie told and believed.

—Bullshit . . . It's bad, he says with the best smile he can muster. —Biggest, ugliest dragon I ever laid eyes on. You know, there's . . . some kind of a mystery in there.

—What? Sonny asks in astonishment.

Shad looks distracted as E.M. makes his way toward them slowly, already ensheathed in his luminous white suit, strangely different from those he has worn all his life.

—Something in there to meet . . . You got any words of the ancient philosophers for me, boy?

Sonny's eyes and hands lock with Shad's, and the words come without bidding. —The way up and the way down . . . are one and the same.

Shad's smile is real this time. He embraces Sonny for a moment. —Now that's nice to know, he says.

He moves past E.M., who is pulling on his hood, over to Marie-Claire, who has not risen from her seat. She looks cold, frightened, very small. Shad is surprised to see that in the pale light of dawn she looks years older. He frowns, leans down to take her hands and lift her up.

—What's the matter with you, girl? You go over and tell Eddie good luck. Has all the woman in you just dried up and blowed away?

—Youall are . . .

—Listen to me. If it's all right and we get back, it's a damned lie and I never said it and you just thought you heard it. But if we don't, I never in my life loved anything but you and him, our boy. He touches her face with his shimmering glove as if he means to imprint it on his memory.

—Shad . . .

—Do what I said now. Go do it.

He turns away and climbs upon the gunwale of the boat as Marie-Claire approaches E.M. He looks out at her through the glass plate in the mask of the protective suit.

—Good luck, Eddie.

—His face is distant, misty, his voice muffled.

—Why, thank you. Funny you should . . . but I'm past luck. It's necessity now . . . The thousand years is over.

Marie-Claire frowns uncomprehendingly as he turns away to join Shad, who has jumped from the gunwale of the crew boat to the waterlogged bobbing float. Shad slips on the slick surface, balances precariously, then finds his footing as waves wash over the feet and legs of his protective suit.

E.M. starts to follow slowly, laboriously. He teeters on the gunwale, Henry supporting him. He leans forward to follow Shad, but it is as if he were made of stone.

—Give me your hand, Shad says over the small radio in his hood, the words tiny and echoing as if they came from across the galaxy to the transceiver next to the captain.

—Yes, E.M. says, reaching out. Shad lifts him from the boat to the float, holds him until he can catch hold of the rail and find his balance. They pause for a moment, then Shad says hoarsely, his own pain as evident as E.M.'s mirthless smile, —I want there to be . . . peace between us, hear?

—Peace? Between us? Like the peace you made with the old man? You got a horse for me?

Shad falls silent, shrugs, points upward.

—Go on. I'm right behind . . . in case you slip.

They begin to climb upward toward the platform, the source of the fire and smoke, toward the mournful howl of gas roaring upward from the depths of the earth, Okeanos called forth by Omega, the beginning sought out by the end, suddenly, inexplicably free, transformed in the instant of its escape from the depths and the ages into fire which seizes upon and judges all things.

—Which one is which? Missy asks Sonny. —I can't tell one from the other. They look like twins.

They climb the ladder slowly, rung by rung, only their breathing coming through the transceiver next to the captain. Making their way upward, they seem to shrink, to become smaller as they move toward the origin of the fire.

—Well, Sentell, Henry says to Sonny, both of them staring upward, —looks like your folks is together again.

—For now . . .

—Oh, I don't know. Maybe for longer than that.

Marie-Claire has joined Missy, reaches out impulsively to draw her close, thinking of Shad's words, certain of nothing anymore since this eminently real world has come smashing into her dream—except that the woman in her has not dried up, not blown away. The two of them watch the tiny figures in white still climbing slowly up through the crosses and interstices of broken and melted steel arrayed now at strange angles, looking like the fleshless bones of great archaic creatures torn asunder and thrown into a tangled heap by something even more powerful, more lethal than they.

—Shit, Shad's voice echoes on the bridge of the crew-boat. —I'm gonna be too tired to do anything by the time we . . .

The transmittal is interrupted by a sound from the radio like a distant gong. The captain changes frequency. It is Coast Guard weather. Squalls rising in the central Gulf, moving northeast. Small craft advisory, seas running eight to fifteen feet. All shipping interests note. Small craft should remain in port . . .

—Now, that's just what we fucking needed, the captain says to Boudreaux. —Want to call 'em down?

Boudreaux frowns, squints at the tiny figures, who have almost reached the underside of the platform, who are obscured and revealed alternately by billows of thick black smoke.

—Let 'em go . . . It'll be hours.

—Nope. Maybe an hour.

The captain nudges Boudreaux, points. Far to the south, a little west, tall ridges of cloud are building, mounting, white at the top, deep gray below.

—Okay. Ten minutes. At least they can see what's what.

—Your nickel, the captain answers. —I guess we can handle that even if it catches us. But there's gonna be some sick folks before we make the river.

—So they find out how you and me make a living, Boudreaux says, with more bravado than he feels. —We all eat out of the same pot. It's nothing but Omega on this boat.

—Well, yeah, the captain says, eyeing the distant ridge of cloud uncomfortably.

—Ed, you okay?

—Give me a minute.

—What a mess. I got to start the auxiliary generator. Look at them lines. No, be careful. I don't think it's any power in 'em, but why don't you sit down over by the console and catch your breath till I need you on the valves.

Silence them. Only the low crackling of static, electromagnetic noise increasing with the rising sun. Then, as the sea begins to build, tossing the crew boat about, they hear the sound of someone moving about, mumbling numbers, disconnected words to himself. Then they can make out Shad's voice. Sonny, Missy, and Marie-Claire—even Henry—move as close to the radio as they can. Boudreaux turns up the gain so they can hear over the wind, the thudding sea, the primordial howl of Okeanos.

—All right, it's two and three, Lou. You hear?

—Ten-four, Boudreaux talks back using a hand mike. —What about the linkages?

—Stiff as hell. One and four are loose. I don't know about five and six. There's junk and debris and part of the bulkhead laying on the rest of 'em. Gonna need a torch. Shit, I ain't even sure about one and four. Wait . . . I'm trying two . . . It's loose. So damn loose the linkage could be gone all the way down.

—I told Mr E.M. that damn platform is off.

—You got that right. My level says six degrees.

—Lord . . . How about the console?

—Shut down. I just got the little generator rolling. Listen, the boys did a nice job before they left . . . Did everything but sweep up.

E.M.'s voice replaces Shad's. It is distant, echoing, like a voice from a far mountain at the edge of sight. There is sleet in it, and snow.

—The old man used to say . . . we're all corpses . . . waiting to lie down . . . Dead men on furlough.

—Yeah, he did, Shad retorts in an irritated tone. —He sure did used to say that. The old man was full of shit, wasn't he?

—I thought so . . . till the night he died.

—Don't start up on that stuff, Ed. I'm working.

—You got power for pressure readings yet? Boudreaux asks.

—Will have in a . . . Lemme . . . damn . . .

—What?

—Board main patch is fused and shorted. Lemme find the backup.

—Here, E.M.'s voice says quietly.

—Yeah, you're right. What do you know?

—All I need to know. I could run this console . . . dead.

343

—Yeah? Well, short of that, read off to Boudreaux what you got when I go to turning this here valve.
—Thirty-seven hundred.
—That's fine . . . Ed, what are you messing with that for? Don't go opening that. It's the antiblowout control . . . Let it be . . . Hey, Boudreaux, that thirty-seven hundred is for number one. It's all right. And moving right along to number two . . .
—Zero.
—Oh, shit . . . Use that little pressure check, E.M.
—I know . . . the gauge is working.
—All right. It's gone. I got to get an eyeball view of two, Boudreaux. I'm gonna start closing it down. Anything?
—Nothing yet . . . Hard to see. It's getting kind of rough out here, pardner.
—Rough ain't even been seen yet, the crew boat captain mutters.
—These tight ones ain't closed. I think the blast broke up the linkages . . . or maybe they busted half open.
—There looks to be cracks out here, Boudreaux says, squinting up into the inferno, then quickly going through a thick wad of photos he holds balanced precariously on the binnacle.
—I knew what he said was true . . . when I was down in the grave with him. He whispered to me . . . You remember. When you wanted to bury me, put me underground . . .
—Goddammit, will you just . . . This here is a open line.
—I never got out of that grave, brother. You kept me down there. You took my life away . . . then you didn't even use it.
—E.M., I know you're sick, and I know you're full of dope, but I'm fixing to kick the shit out of you.
—You had my wife . . . You got your bastard on her.
Marie-Claire feels the blood rising to her face. She feels faint. It is the sum and substance of her worst nightmare being acted out in the dim gray light of clouded dawn. Missy frowns, tries to move closer to the radio. Sonny listens, able to make out the words but unable to imagine their meaning.
—You took my woman, fouled her . . . The boy should have been mine. He has my name but . . . Nothing . . . Dead, you sonofabitch. Dead twenty years. Now you're coming down . . . with me and the old man.
A thousand years, Marie Claire thinks, her face and hands suddenly chill rather than hot, her emotions churning from

humiliation to terror as she listens to the disembodied voice. He said he'd be even . . . if it took a thousand years. But . . . that was talk, words. Part of the little dream we lived in. Nothing in the world is worth waiting for so long. Is it?

There is a scuttling sound above the hiss and crackle of the radio, as if, high up there, a struggle were going on. Henry leans close to the radio, his eyes shining. Sonny turns to his mother, eyes wide.

—He . . . my . . . I think he tried to say . . . that night at Antoine's . . . he was . . . my uncle . . . Does he mean . . . ?

—Sonny, Marie-Claire starts to say, —darling . . . But the expression on her face is more than confession, confirmation, and before she can say more there emerges from Sonny a sound, a cry of anguish and realization and certainty that rises in pitch to the level of the pressured gas screaming above which they have been hearing for so long now that it is hardly even noticeable. He drops from the elevated bridge of the crew boat, jumps to the gunwale, and with a headlong perilous leap lands arms and legs askew on the bobbing platform and starts up the ladder before Marie-Claire or Missy can even call to him.

—You crazy, sick bastard, Boudreaux hears Shad yell as the women run to the side of the boat, Missy almost going into the water before Marie-Claire and Henry can reach her and drag her back.

—I done told you, goddammit, if you open that . . . There's cracks. It can't take the . . .

Marie-Claire and Missy look upward through what is now a steady driving rain. Sonny has almost reached the stairs and is still moving at incredible speed. Marie-Claire finds herself on the gunwale seeking an instant when she can leap to the platform, but even as she is about to chance the rising, tossing sea, Henry pulls her back.

—Henry, please . . . let me go . . . Sonny is . . .

—A Sentell, Henry shouts back at her, his eyes wild, his face streaming water. —He's never seen his father . . . You can't . . .

Marie-Claire turns back to him, her face ravaged, her voice breaking. —What kind of nonsense is that? He's seen him a thousand times.

—Not . . . his father.

Sonny grows small now, almost lost against the maze of broken and twisted metal up there. It is daylight, and the structure of the platform is fully visible, bent, blackened, corroded, girders splayed, beams fractured, all of it more frightening, more awesome than in the darkness before. Boudreaux sees one of the steel casings swell, contract as if it were made of rubber or of flesh. It pulses again, and they all feel beneath the boat, below the crashing waves, a profound vibration as if there were something down there awakening from long slumber, stirring at last, backward-flowing, seeking the light, the rim of the sky, and the very ramparts of infinity itself.

—Boudreaux, get out . . . go . . . You hear? This crazy bastard has done . . .

The captain awaits no further order. He hits the throttle so hard that the front of the powerful boat actually clears the waves, and, landing already at speed, sends a surge of spray upward to rival the driving rain. The heavy lines snap like threads, and the passengers behind fall into the bottom of the boat as it courses desperately away from the platform.

But Boudreaux, doggedly holding onto the rail of the bridge, still looking backward in some hopeless mode of piety, sees simultaneously the casing as it ruptures, titanic chunks of metal breaking away, not falling but rising, tearing into other weakened, brittle casings nearby, and the whole platform, its immense supports shaking, quivering, twisting as if it were some object from the freezing climes of outer space determined to break free of the confinement of earth, of the deep Gulf, lifting to find its path back into the maze of stars and suns, the very heart of the Milky Way from which it has come. That, and at the very last instant a tiny improbable figure still climbing.

The others manage to turn as the boat slices across the water, turn in time to see the ruptured casings feed their own fuel into the already shrieking inferno at the same instant, so that, when ignition takes place, it is almost identical in appearance to a rocket rising out of the water on a plume of fire and smoke and water and steam.

Except that, in the very moment of its elevation, it begins to disintegrate, to fall apart slowly, rapturously, its constituents turning gracefully in the air, arching across the enormous rising sun in the east, high against the thunderheads moving in from the southwest, to tumble back through the smoke and steam into the claiming fire and downward into the Gulf.

Epilogue

3 March 1960

> Now after our ship had left the stream of the river Okeanos... There we beached our ship on the sands... there we fell asleep and waited for bright Dawn...
> *Odyssey*, xii, 1–6

She is in the Orleans Parish Morgue, where they have been bringing the victims claimed by Okeanos for almost a week. One more has been found floating near the mouth of the Mississippi. The medical examiner had called Hotel Dieu, where she and Missy have been keeping anxious vigil over Sonny, who remains unconscious, his very living a miracle to those who know what he has passed through. The medical examiner needs someone from Omega Oil to identify another body.

The corridor down which an orderly leads her is deep blue-green, the concrete floor below almost the same color. The odor of disinfectant is overpowering. She feels herself growing giddy. The lights above are recessed in receptacles, their illumination indirect, soft, almost romantic against the colors of the distant sea below.

Marie-Claire is thinking, thinking of anything. So that she will not have to think about anything. She imagines that she hears the strains of the *Eroica* over the clatter of some typewriter in an office by which they pass. The colors of the corridor appall her. There is some memory connected with them. She cannot call it to consciousness. She does not want to. Whatever it is, it will break her heart. She pauses for a moment. She is not going to faint, and no matter what lies at the end of this oceanic corridor, she is going to face it. A dozen clucking, somber-faced Omega International officers had begged her to let them take this cup from her. They have set up a watch at the hospital like courtiers near the bed of an ailing prince, ostensibly to see to anything that she might need. In fact, all anxious to know as soon as possible the terms of the succession. Will a regent be named to rule for the grieving Queen Mother and the dreaming Prince? What will this odd and sudden marriage portend? Will there be promotions, reshufflings, even corporate restructuring?

Why would they recess the light bulbs that way? she is thinking, so as not to think. Who is going to steal the light bulbs here? Are some of the inmates unruly? Are there mysteries of pathology that no one knows except the elect? Is this aquamarine corridor, shadow of an inlet from the sea, the path only to those who have drowned? Who have gone down in the Gulf? Who have lain some time full fathom five. Like his father. His uncle.

The orderly walking ahead of her is small and dark, wearing a lab coat of blue-green. His voice is soft and mellow, its accents those of some island off to the south. Across the water where English sailors came to port for fresh water, fruit, vegetables long ago, leaving behind their language to be touched, transmuted. His shoulders are hunched, his neck drawn down between them as if he expects a blow. Is it the ubiquitous presence of death that draws him down within himself? The background music in her mind's ear has changed. Now it is the *Egmont*, slow, funereal, and grand. The anthem of life and death as the Sentells have always chosen to grasp them. Sonny would know *Egmont*.

They pass by doors with panes of glass in them. Harsh light pours out from the rooms beyond. The rooms look like operating rooms, but they are not. Those are not operating tables. Slabs of some stone or ceramic drains running down to the concrete floor. Instrument cabinets. Large pieces of equipment. Nothing there to save, only to explore.

They enter what seems at first to be a bank vault. The room is chill, and there is some odor permanently resident in it that no amount of disinfectant can cloak. There are dozens of compartments on either side. Like very large safety deposit boxes, she thinks. Each smaller chamber has its own door, its own number. The attendant has a clipboard. He looks for a number, satisfies himself, and opens a door. From the cavity within there seems to come a rush of even cooler air—and a reinforcement of that odor that is bland and sharp, earthy and acrid all at once.

Why, it's the odor of mortality, Marie-Claire thinks. It's the smell of . . . what we come to. That's why the ice boxes. Like fish. We don't hold up well. Character does no good at all.

The attendant has placed himself between her and the burden of the sliding shelf. He draws back a plastic sheet, looks, exclaims.

—Madame . . .

She does not want to do this. Now she feels panic rising within. If she faints, she will never forgive herself. The dream is over. What lies there demands her concentration. She should have left this to one of those damned obsequious idiots camped at the hospital to see if Sonny is ever going to come to. No. This is not business. This is family. All the others lost have been claimed. Whatever . . . whoever lies there is not Omega. It—no, he—is Sentell. It occurs to her that over the last several days that name has ceased to denote a family or even a clan. It is an abstraction now. An adjective? But whatever, carrying with it a destiny, a meaning all its own. Mysterious, obscure, horrendous, but its own.

—Madame, the attendant says to her again quietly in his island accent. He must have seen many drownings, she thinks, living there at the brink of the sea.

She moves past him quickly, her face revealing nothing. She is beautifully dressed in black. Even black gloves. This is going to be done right. She has paid almost the whole price. For twenty-five years. She will not stop paying now. Because in some sense she cannot possibly understand but knows for certain, the price is right. She is Sentell.

He lies in the harsh morgue light, naked, solitary, indifferent, at ease. His lips are parted in something between a smile and a sneer. As if leaving this realm of light were no loss at all. As if he has learned that Sentell is a destiny at last left unresolved in this chaos of life. Even now, he is not a corpse. He is a dead man.

His eyes are partly open, frosty, distant, unimpassioned. Her hand moves almost involuntarily to close them. There is nothing here that he would wish to see. She touches his silver hair that she has never known to be any other color. She cannot restrain a sob.

—Oh, Eddie . . .

—Is this . . . ? the attendant asks softly, diffidently, clipboard poised.

—This is Edward Malcolm Sentell the Third, she says huskily, precisely, —My . . . husband.

She looks again. It is astonishing, almost preternatural. His complexion is flushed, and the time he has lain in the waters of the Gulf has not deteriorated him. It has rather filled out his flesh, making him look young, healthy. As if he had died at the zenith of his life.

—. . . Do you want . . .

—We'll be taking him . . . home, she says quietly.

She finds she cannot move, cannot draw her gaze away from that calm, untroubled face she has known so well. Has she brought him to this end? Had she, more terrible, destroyed long before the only love, the only trust he ever had? What he felt for Shad?

The blue-green walls of the chamber begin to shudder, to move as if they are currents of the sea. She feels light-headed. She sees E.M. moving away from her one final time as the attendant pushes the metal shelf back into the darkness and the cold. She reaches out to stop him, about to beg for one last moment to achieve what she is quite sure she will never reach—some final understanding, some last peace with his silence, his departure, and his pain. But she feels herself losing control, and she realizes that she is fainting at last, and what she has seen may be all the peace there is. Then, as she is about to fall, a hand, an arm catches her from behind.

—Hold up with that, a familiar voice says. —I don't believe the lady is done.

He lies very still on the hospital bed, a small light just above playing down upon his face. He bears an expression of unutterable sadness as if, sleeping or still unconscious, he is yet in pain. Or dreaming that something priceless, irreplaceable has been lost.

Missy nods beside him. She does not want to fall asleep. She is trying to stay awake. It seems to her somehow that it would be faithless falling asleep while Sonny is not yet out of danger. Could'st thou not watch with me one hour? But it has been many hours. Perhaps she will sleep when Mrs Sentell returns. If she can.

What is most amazing about all this to Missy is that it does not seem amazing at all. If she had not had Shad's word on it, she would believe that she was indeed born a Sentell. She muses at the changes in her own interior landscape. It is as if this is how it has always been, and Greenwood and Cecil and Elvira figures from a fantasy, some film she saw and laughed at and enjoyed when she was a child long ago.

She has tried to stay awake by walking in the halls of the hospital earlier. No more. Out there are reporters, officials of one sort or another from state and federal agencies—all swearing they have some right to interview Sonny as soon as he regains consciousness. If he regains consciousness. Worst of all are the Omega Oil people. The suite is choked with flowers as the halls are choked with people from Baton Rouge, Dallas, Tulsa, Houston, New York, Los Angeles, Midland, Shreveport, and places overseas with names which never appeared in the geography book employed by the Greenwood Consolidated High School. They will not stop sending flowers, nor will those skulking in the corridors cease pressing their condolences on Missy—or anyone who emerges from the rooms and might be family.

Sonny moans, tries to turn his head, move his hands. Missy snaps to wakefulness and stands beside him. She is determined that he see her first, that she be there when he awakens and remembers everything, that he see the future before he recalls the past. She could cry inside for what he must face. If she cannot make him whole, at least she can dull the pain, make him weigh what he has gained. As well as what he has lost.

But he is not awakening. His breathing becomes regular again. The doctors say they are not sure if he is sleeping now or in a coma. A massive concussion, cracked ribs, burns, contusions. At that, a miracle. Men, even young men, do not as a rule survive being blown off an oil platform in the Gulf. There are funerals taking place even now because of Okeanos. There will be more when the Gulf yields up again what it has claimed.

Still, not altogether a miracle. Unless the character of Louis Boudreaux is taken as a wonder. Who had pushed the crew boat captain aside and spun the craft around after the final explosion, heading it back toward the water which still burned as raw methane boiled up from the depths. The captain had yelled almost hysterically.

—Goddammit, there's nothing alive in there . . . You're gonna kill us all.

—I'm gonna see, you hear? I'm gonna see . . . Don't try to mess with me.

The captain and one crewman did try to mess with him. One with a wrench, the other with a large vise grip. But Boudreaux had dipped down into Shad's rutsack and come up with the .38 Special Sonny had returned to him.

—I'm going through, Boudreaux screamed, —'cause if there's any of 'em alive, they'll be in the center of the fire.

They had found Sonny just outside the ring of flame, floating helpless, almost drowned. Marie-Claire and Henry said they had seen something white floating a little distance away, but when Boudreaux had wrestled the boat over there against the waves and wind, they had found nothing.

By then the storm was over them, and even Boudreaux had given up, handed the boat back to its crew. He had joined Henry, Marie-Claire, and Missy around Sonny's silent unmoving form.

Missy shivers. This is going to be the pattern of her life. Wittingly or otherwise, she has chosen the center of the fire. Lord, she thinks, beginning to doze off again, it's like some play. It's just not like other folks live.

Henry supports Marie-Claire as they walk back down the blue-green corridor toward the living world.

—The arrangements are all right, Henry says as they step out into the cool New Orleans spring air. —Company plane is gonna carry him to Shreveport. Wellmans is gonna take him out home. I got clothes with me. I'm gonna lay him out.

—But the details . . . I have to . . .

—Not any details, Henry replies as they climb into the Omega limo and start back toward Hotel Dieu. —No damn mourners, neither . . . I mean no company people. We had time to talk about it. He told me what he wanted. To the last detail.

—Oh . . .

—'Course I shouldn't take it on myself . . . Now, I expect you got to approve, Henry says mildly, managing nicely to allow some edge of fierceness in his voice.

Marie-Claire catches his eyes, holds them.

—No, she says. —I don't have to approve anything. I want you to do exactly what he asked. To the last detail.

—Ummm . . .

Henry is satisfied. Marie-Claire is curious.

—Was there . . . anything unusual?

Henry smiles distantly, shrugs his thin shoulders. —Plain

pine coffin. No silk, no satin. No metal but the nails. Black suit.
—Black? But . . .
—What he said. Didn't say why. I guess I know. Buried between his daddy and the Major.
—Oh . . .
—. . . Confederate flag on the coffin, to be put in with him.
—My God, I never heard him so much as say . . .
—I believe he kept hisself to hisself more than most.
—Still . . .
Henry looks away. —He said . . .
—What? Is it something he wanted me to . . .
Henry's expression is as wintry, as distant as E.M.'s had seemed as he lay on the morgue shelf.
—He said he'd like Mr Shad buried close by . . . maybe next to his momma.
—Yes . . .
—And if it could be, at the same time.
Marie-Claire nods before the implication of Henry's words strikes her. She turns in horror to face him. His own expression is pleasant now, contained. All passion spent.
—Then . . . you knew. He told you.
—Don't ask. You know what you know. I don't believe we should be having this conversation.
—No, Marie-Claire says, her voice flat, some touch of North Louisiana, East Texas, beginning to blur the precision of her accent so hard fought for, so long ago achieved. —No, I don't reckon we should.
—You want Mr E.M. held up to the funeral home in Shreveport till they come on Mr Shad?
—No, dammit, Marie-Claire says venomously. —Hell, no. You can do the rest of it, all of it. I'll be there. Sonny will be there if he can crawl. But Eddie's not going to order Shad's burying from out of the grave. Goddamn him, I've tried to see this through decently, but that murderous . . . I won't let him. No, *we'll* see to Shad, Sonny and I will do that. On his own, the way he lived. Not with the brother who killed him, who hated him.
Henry looks genuinely shocked, confused. Then almost at once his expression turns to something approaching pity.
—He didn't hate Mr Shad, Henry says softly, reproachfully, as if to one who should know better. —He loved him.

The reporter is not sober. He has not been sober in several days. Each year at Mardi Gras he chooses to get himself tanked to the point of oblivion. He deems it necessary in order that he be able to make some kind of sense of the lunacy that prevails then. Now he sits in the hospital waiting room down the hall from the Sentell suite, looking for his chance at somebody, anybody, everybody. He is, for this event at any rate, stringer for a national news magazine. There are rumors of a tremendous story of blood and money in this Sentell–Omega Oil business. Someone has said that the surviving son of one of them will be indicted for the murder of his father and uncle. The rumors go further: they claim that the murders on board Okeanos culminated earlier attempts in the Quarter before the fatal trip out to the burning platform in the Gulf.

The reporter takes a hit from a Dr Pepper bottle. There is, thank God, no Dr Pepper in it. He uses the bottle because it is dark glass and others must surmise what *is* in it. Surmise aside, it is Old Forester. Neat. If he should be driven to the need for water, there is a fountain nearby. He has been in the waiting room for hours. He has not used it. What is wrong with water? W. C. Fields has stated it succinctly: fish fuck in it.

The reporter is trying to talk to his one-eyed cabbie, who waits with him to take him back to the paper when he has something. Or down to Venice or Golden Meadow—anywhere the story requires. But his cabbie keeps falling asleep.

—For the kind of money you're getting, you could stay awake. What if I got to go to Lafayette in a hurry? Or Baton Rouge?

—You got it, the cabbie says. —But no fucking Shreveport . . . no Caddo Parish . . .

—What's wrong with Shreveport?

—Just that it's there. Oh, man, you never seen such a place. See, on the way back, I stopped off in this bar. Those guys . . . they stare at you. They all want to fight. All the time. You can see it in their eyes. They're crazy . . . the whole northwest end of this state is out of its mind.

—Yeah? The Sentells are from Shreveport . . . somewhere around there.

—Hey, I know that name. I *seen* that name. See, this old nut couldn't pay me when we got up there yesterday morning . . . I was gonna smash him. I was gonna break him across the hood of the hack, see. Then he showed me this check. Just wait till the

Pioneer Bank opens, he says. Check signed by some guy named Sentell . . . for two hundred and sixty grand.

The reporter's eyes open wide. He almost drops his Dr Pepper. —Sentell? Two hundred and sixty . . . Christ . . .

Marie-Claire and Henry sit silently in the limousine as they approach the entrance of Hotel Dieu. They have been reviewing, separately but equally, lives lived at angles to one another. It seems probable that they are prepared by now to forgive themselves and each other. Marie-Claire breaks the silence at last.

—They're not gonna find him. You know that, don't you, she says in a rich East Texas accent that is her own, burrowing out from under almost a quarter-century of fanciful veneer.

Henry smiles. —You know, I was thinking that very thing when they told me you was at the morgue. I said to myself, it's either one of them boys got blowed up last Saturday, or my Sentell. It's not that sorry sonofabitch . . . He'll never come up. Probably found hisself some kind of pussy down there.

Marie-Claire's face is mottled with rage. —You dirty . . .

—Nigger, Henry finishes for her without concern.

— . . . bastard, she finishes for herself. Then they are at the entrance of the hospital and to her astonishment, she finds that she is laughing and crying at the same time.

—You are a wretched black bastard, she tells Henry, who smiles back at her. —I see why Eddie loved you.

Henry squeezes her arm as they climb out of the limo into a storm of flashbulbs, microphones, shouted questions. Out there are ranks of reporters and cameramen blocking the entrance. Beyond are more people, some in Coast Guard uniforms, rank after rank of Omega people behind, all bearing down on her. Henry hears the sharp intake of her breath, feels her move close to him. He takes her hand, places it on his arm.

—Yes, well, Mr E.M. asked I should see you through this.

Marie-Claire enters the hospital suite. She is exhausted, close to tears. If there are emotions left over that have not passed through her like electrical current in the past few days, she would as soon not experience them. She has told Henry goodbye downstairs. They will see each other again at the Old Place. They are not done with one another.

Missy is on the phone. She looks up, fearful, expectant, as Marie-Claire enters.

—It's Momma . . . I told her you'd gone to the . . .

Marie-Claire nods. —It was Eddie.

Soon it will be on the front page of the *Times-Picayune*, the *Shreveport Times*, the *Shreveport Journal*, the *Dallas Morning News*, the *Houston Post*, the *Houston Chronicle* . . . The newsmen downstairs, the officials, all of them are mad to know more. There are rumors, incredible stories going around. No, she thinks. There are no rumors. Every single one of them is true. My husband killed his brother, the father of my son, his nephew. And himself. Laid waste to half the world around.

—Momma says she knows how you feel, Missy almost whispers.

Marie-Claire smiles. Yes. Elvira knows. She is way ahead of me in knowing. She had already turned away, already known she had lost Shad before I even knew I wanted him, had wanted him all my life.

She remembers sitting in the small office at the morgue while the dark attendant filled out something before he took her down the long sea-blue-green corridor to do her last duty by him to whom she had not been dutiful. Please, she had thought in some form approaching prayer, please, Lord, don't let it be him. I've lost him, and if it is him, it has to be me who says it's him. But don't let it be. Because if it isn't, if they never find him, I can pretend that he's only somewhere else, up to his ass in trouble or danger, laughing, enjoying every minute of it, and one fine morning when I'm very young again and much braver than before, I'll hear him coming for me. I'll hear his voice cursing an East Texas blue streak, and he'll be coming down the road to our trailer outside Kilgore, and we'll be working ourselves to death, and Peterson Number One will be ours, and he'll be the only man I've ever known, and nothing will ever part us, and there'll be Sonny and another and another . . . and no Okeanos ever . . . We won't go out that far . . .

It had trailed off then, the thought, the prayer or whatever it was, dissipating like morning mist over a bayou, an inlet of the Gulf, as the attendant's island accent roused her, asked that she follow him.

Her eyes are closed now. Her threadbare prayer or whatever it was has been answered. Shad remains the stuff of a daydream she expects to repeat every day for the rest of her life.

—No, she hears Missy reply irately. —I'm not gonna ask her any such thing, and you ought to be ashamed.

—What? Marie-Claire asks, rousing from her reverie. —What is it, honey?

Missy is blushing. —Nothing, she says. —It's just nothing.

—No, it isn't nothing. Is there something your momma . . .

—No, Missy says. —It's not Momma. It's that damned Cecil.

—What?

—I don't want to say . . . Lord, I almost wish Mr Sentell *had* been my daddy, because this one . . .

—Just spit it out, Melissa, you hear?

—Yes, ma'am. Missy looks humiliated. —The nasty thing wants to know what with both of 'em dead, if his check is still good? Can you believe that?

Marie-Claire laughs softly. —Sure, I can. There is something wonderful about being able to allay others' fears when the very worst you have ever feared has come to pass. —You tell your daddy that check is as good as gold, hear?

Missy whispers something into the phone waspishly, then hangs up. She comes over to join Marie-Claire, who is opening a bottle of Remy Martin she has spirited in from outside.

—No change? Marie-Claire asks.

—Nope. But he sure looks to be sleeping. I believe he's gonna be just fine. I really do.

—'Course he is, baby. Marie-Claire smiles, pouring Missy a tot of brandy in a hospital water glass.

Missy sips her first brandy experimentally. She nods. It beats bourbon whiskey, she thinks. —Truth is, I'm almost afraid for him *to* wake up . . . I mean, Lord, to have to tell him about . . .

Marie-Claire throws down her brandy, glances toward the door of the room where Sonny lies. She sighs and pours the glass full.

—I know what you mean. He's going to have some questions for me.

Missy studies Marie-Claire, a look of awe in her eyes. They have hit it off well. She means to learn a lot. Music and literature and lot of other stuff. —What a life you've lived, she says.

Marie-Claire laughs sardonically. —What a life I might have lived.

Missy frowns. —Two things. I can't figure *how* you did it, and I sure can't figure *why* you did it.

Marie-Claire shakes her head. —You nor me, she says. —I had a dream, and anything that didn't fit . . . got lost.

Missy's expression turns serious. —What are you gonna tell Sonny?

—This far down the line? I've been considering . . . the truth.

Missy reaches out, takes Marie-Claire's hand impulsively. —Don't you worry. I'm gonna be right there with you. He's *gonna* understand, you hear?

—It may take a long time, Marie-Claire says wearily. —You see, somehow I thought the truth could just get buried . . . I mean, if nobody ever even whispered the truth, then it's *not* the truth.

—Huh?

—Right. Because it won't stay buried. It just keeps . . . being there . . .

Marie-Claire's voice trails off as she and Missy hear a sudden uproar from the next room. —Sonofabitch . . .

They run together into Sonny's room, where he is supposed to be lying. He is not. He is sitting up, legs over the side of the bed, trying to stand.

—No, honey, don't try it, Missy says, pushing him back down.

Sonny looks confused, disoriented. —Did I . . . ? What was I trying to do?

Marie-Claire closes her eyes. She remembers Okeanos blowing skyward, dissolving, breaking apart as she watched. —You were trying . . . to do what was right, she answers lamely.

Sonny looks at her strangely. —You sound funny. It doesn't even sound like your voice.

—Yes, it is, Marie Claire says quietly. —You just . . . never heard it before.

—Maybe I ought to call the doctor, Missy says.

—No, Sonny tells her. —Wait . . . What happened? I was climbing up as fast as I could . . . I was almost there, and we lifted off like . . .

—Lord, Missy says, —you never saw nothing like it. I thought, I'm a widow before I was even done being a bride. I thought, if it's come to this, I wisht we'd made it first.

Sonny looks at Marie Claire. —I'm . . . the only one?

She nods, her voice moving out of her automatically, the

words parading one after the other as she has rehearsed them in her mind since they reached the hospital and she realized that it was not over, that he would awaken, and then it would begin once more.

—... we went back then and found you, and went on looking till the wind and waves started swamping the boat. Then Boudreaux put up the pistol and let them bring us back in.

—Nothing...?

—Today they found your... They brought E.M. in... Henry's taking him back up home.

—Shad?

—Oh, honey, what am I supposed to tell you? Once we saw a white suit, but I don't know which it was. It turned and turned in the water, and then it went down.

Sonny lies silent. He has turned his eyes from his mother as his memory clears. —What... what they were saying. Is it...

She starts to speak only to find that the words will not come out. The parade of syllables has ceased. She tries again.

—You see...

Sonny turns toward her, his eyes green, cold, encompassing. Marie-Claire shivers as she returns his stare. He does not even look like the same person. It is as if he has been possessed. Those eyes are not his eyes. They are the eyes of his father.

—I almost made it, he says distantly, almost clinically. —I came close. I remember. Another minute, even thirty seconds and we'd have...

He falls silent again. Then: —If you lie to me, I'll know, he says slowly. —And I'll even the score... if it takes ...

—Don't, Marie-Claire shouts at him. —Don't say that, for God's sake. All right, I'll tell you. Because no one else can. Because now I guess you've got to know...

Her voice trails off, and she finds herself for a singular moment in that grotto once more, turning in blue-green shadows, turning in his arms, never supposing what fateful currents are rising, finding generation there. Knowing only that if never before, never again, now, enclosed in this wafer of time and space and dream, she is happy, satisfied, fulfilled.

—Yes, she says, and even as the word passes her lips, she feels released, thrown free from that dark river-ocean of denial that has swept her away, imprisoned her so long. —Yes, he was your father... Yes, he was...

Marie-Claire bursts into tears, turning away from Sonny.

—Oh, boy, Missy says somberly, reaching to comfort Marie-Claire. —Cousins nothing . . . We almost made brother and sister, Sonny.

Sonny sits shaking his head for a moment as if the confirmation of what he has already known is itself a new revelation. —You . . . and Shad? You . . . loved him? Or was it just . . .

Marie-Claire looks up, her face stained with tears. —It wasn't. You weren't a mistake, an accident . . . You were . . . going to happen since the first time I turned around in that damned café and he was looking at me and . . . Yes, all right, you want to hear me say it? I will. I've never said it even to myself. I loved him every day after that, every day of my life. I may even have loved him more than I hated him.

She rises, walks to the window. The sun is setting. It has been a long day. The first, she thinks, of a lifetime of long days. But not one long enough, and none presaging that fine morning she has been thinking of since the doom of Okeanos blew her world into fractured atoms.

—You've got the life we gave you, she tells Sonny. —Only . . . somehow I threw my own away . . . Lost, strayed, stolen . . .

—But, Sonny begins, stops, begins again. —If you loved him, why not . . . why didn't you . . .

She does not turn. The sun is almost down now. The days are growing longer. Somehow she knows that she will come to dread the summer, the hot summer. When she speaks, her voice grows harsh, self-accusing.

—Because Samuel Shadrach Sentell was a coarse, wicked, violent man, a boozer and a chaser. He had a mouth like the sewers of San Antone, and he ran roughshod over anybody and anything unfortunate enough to just happen to be in front of him on purpose or otherwise. And because Mary Clare Fontenot was not the sort of person to get mixed up with . . . that sort of person. Don't you see? I hadn't had anything. I thought there was something to have. I thought there were places and things and conditions, and if you could just manage to make them belong to you . . .

Her voice chokes off, and she leans against the window frame, staring out into the gathering dusk of the old city. Her shoulders sag with exhaustion and loss.

—Oh, hell, what's the difference? Why should youall care?

I'm going to have plenty of time to think about it now. I can take five years to think about loving him, five more to remember how I hated him. Lord, do you know how long a forty-five-year-old woman can live? I can take ten years to think about what we could have had . . . sons, daughters, hours, days . . . I can sit in that damned palace on Line Avenue that I thought I wanted so much and watch the seasons change and the years fall away and think how I'd burn it all, destroy it all for just one night down there . . . under the sea . . . And I'll still have twenty years of leftover life to get rid of day by day . . . And none of it matters, does it?

The man who has quietly opened the door a moment before is not a doctor. Dressed in a yellow slicker which drains water down onto the carpet, he most nearly resembles some coarse wicked parody of the Ancient Mariner. He is lacking eyebrows and eyelashes altogether, and his hair seems to have been trimmed into a crewcut. By a blowtorch.

—The hell it don't, he says, grinning hugely, throwing off the slicker.

—Uncle . . . Sonny starts to say out of a lifetime's habit. Then he leaps from the hospital bed, legs tangled in the sheets, and dives into his father's arms, almost knocking Shad down with the force of his embrace.

—Oh boy, Missy says in an awed voice.

Marie-Claire has not turned from the window. Her eyes are closed tightly. She may never touch Remy Martin again. —I don't believe this, she says in a tiny voice, its accent much like Missy's —I don't believe it, I can't believe it, and I'm not going to believe it. Even a damned Sentell can't come back from the . . .

Shad still has Sonny caught around his neck in a terminal bearhug.

—You take your time getting used to it, girl, Shad says gleefully. —But you don't get no five years.

—You . . . heard all that. All that carrying on I was . . .

—I been waiting twenty-five years to hear it . . . Reckon how come I'm not stone-deaf waiting.

—But how . . . ? Missy starts to ask, then shrugs, gives up. Maybe Sentells do this all the time. She is going to be hard to surprise pretty soon.

—I went out that bulkhead like a shot off a shovel when E.M.

done what he done. Fire sale. Everything must go. A thousand feet right up into the fire, a thousand and one back down ... Lights out, folks. Pitch black when I come around, and the sea was down, and the oxygen was gone, and the damned suit was getting waterlogged, but it kind of shined in the dark. Stood out like a gold stud in a goat's ass. This damn shrimp boat come by, and a fella leaned over the side and says to me, Mister, if you're doing some government test or something, I don't want to bother you, but if you need a lift ...

—I don't believe any of this, Marie-Claire says, finally turning toward Shad, her eyes open now, seeing him there. For the very first time.

— ... so I told him the testing was over ... I told him I had me a woman and a son ... I told him I had been in far places for a long time, and I wanted to come home.

This time Shad is ready, and he catches Marie-Claire in his arms as she runs to him, lifts her almost to the ceiling of the room, his eyes and hers locked, their faces transfigured.

Shad and Marie-Claire kiss. Missy grabs hold of Sonny, pulling him back to his bed. —You ain't out of the woods yet. You got a serious concussion and confusions.

—Contusions ...

—I don't know how much more of this I can stand, Missy chortles and then feels a hand traveling up her leg. —Sonny, I told you, you're sick ...

—The hell I am ... Blue heaven and you and I ... sand kissing a moonlit sky ...

—Oh, stop it. You and your damn oasis.

Shad looks around the room curiously. —This here is a suite, ain't it? he asks.

—It sure is, Missy answers.

—And this over here, this door ...

—I've been staying there, Marie-Claire tells him. —To be near ...

—Uh-huh ...

—Shad ...

Shad has opened the door. Now he scoops her up as if she were weightless.

—Stop it ... We have to talk ... You don't know ...

—Yeah, I do ... You got no idea.

—But we can't ...

—The hell you can't, Sonny and Missy shout almost in unison.
   —Please, honey... tomorrow...
   —Ah, right... Then, too, Shad says, carrying her through the doorway. —But a piece you miss...
   —Don't say it. Just don't, Mary Clare whispers, pulling the door closed behind them.